All the Men Are Gone

a novel

K.A. CLAYTOR

COVENWOOD PRESS

Cover Design by Laura Duffy Design

First edition. March 2, 2024

For more information, visit: www.kaclaytor.com

ISBN: 979-8-9899312-0-0 (ePUB)
ISBN: 979-8-9899312-2-4 (trade pbk.)

Covenwood Press www.covenwoodpress.com

Contents

For my husband, because he told me not to
dedicate a book to him called *All the Men Are Gone,*
and I rarely do what I'm told.

1

A Savior

Fifty-seven years after The Waning

"Storm's comin', Mama."

"How bad's it gonna be, Mika? Go on and bring Vesper in if it looks like it'll thunder," Kate said. The dog had been known to turn himself inside out at the first rumble, in the sort of canine fit that would scatter the chickens all the way to the neighbor's place and back again if he wasn't brought inside beforehand. "If there's going to be some weather, then I think we should probably bring in the hay from the back field, too."

Mika looked at her mother as though peering over reading glasses, even though she didn't wear any. "Not that kind of storm, Mama. Better to have Vesper stay outside."

Kate chopped the last of the parsnips, then put the knife down and glanced out the window. It was a clear blue sky, with not a wisp of cloud to be seen. "May as well bring the hay in anyway. How about you see what your sisters are—"

A car door slammed. Then another. Kate was running for the door even before her mind told her feet to move, lunging for the dead bolt.

"Mika—"

"I'll get it," her daughter said calmly.

Peering out the peephole, Kate could see four of them. They were dirt-covered and gaunt, their thinning gray hair matted and filthy. They seemed in no hurry. But they should have been.

Small, delicate fingers tapped gently on Kate's back. She turned to see Mika, an errant brown curl tucked behind her ear and a shotgun cradled in her skinny arms. Kate took it, opening the breech and checking to make sure it was still loaded. It was. Her mind raced, wondering where the spare ammunition was, while the maternal part of her brain mentally gathered up her children.

"Where are your sisters?"

"By the creek, I think. Should I tell them to go to the hiding place?"

Peering outside again, now Kate could only see three. "Yes," she whispered. "And hurry."

"You'll need these." Mika emptied the contents of her overalls pockets into her mother's hands, some of the red-plastic-and-brass casings tumbling to the floor in a sharp clatter. Kate picked up the shotgun rounds and tucked as many as she could into her bra.

"Shoulda sewed pockets into your skirt, Mama."

"Never mind, Mika. Go!"

The soft pad of bare feet faded as her youngest ran off. Kate cast her eyes upwards, whispering a plea for Mika to be kept safe, followed by a string of quiet profanities.

By now, they'll be scouting out the house, Kate thought, *checking the windows for the telltale giveaway of shifting lace curtains in the white-knuckled clutch of a terrified woman.* Her memories were keen to remind her of how the story went.

Shouldering up to the wall, Kate knelt low, sliding the view port to the side and inserting the shotgun barrel into the slot drilled through the paneling. It was camouflaged outside under the shadowed eaves of the house, near a multitude of thistle weeds she'd meant to pull weeks ago. They'd just begun to bloom, fat and prickly—a kindred flower, if she had one.

Kneecaps were too small to aim for, but no matter. First shot to warn them. Second shot to wound them. Third shot to end them. Those were the rules. Kate aimed at a stone near one's boots, figuring there wasn't much aiming to be done with a shotgun, and pulled the trigger.

Not much aiming at all; she'd shot one's foot. Kate aimed and shot at another. Reloading, she fired again. She'd never been one for rules.

As she opened the shotgun, the glint of brass showed plain as day, the other casing on the floor. Kate pulled out another round and dropped it into the chamber, racking the twelve-gauge to the ready.

The screams were resonant, but she'd heard them before. His face twisted into something familiar, a carnal version of ecstasy, only this time without the pleasure. Another was writhing on the ground, screaming and kicking up so much dirt that Kate couldn't see dust for barley. Vesper had knocked one down and was shaking an arm like he'd just caught a rattlesnake, relentless, as though it were a neck to snap. The fourth one suddenly returned, running from around the back of the house, so close the thistle shuddered in the breeze of them passing, and then kicked the dog squarely in the head. Vesper did not even flinch. Kate shot anyway. No one kicks her dog.

Another shot rang out, but it wasn't Kate who'd fired. There were still six rounds of buckshot stuffed in her bra. Lucy walked into view, buck knife on her hip and a rifle tucked hard against her shoulder. Mika trailed behind, carrying a big stick.

Kate's hands shook as she unlatched the dead bolt before stepping outside. It had been a long time since she'd seen a man—and a long time since she'd shot one.

Lucy exchanged a glance, tipping her head towards Kate's daughter. Mika was standing defiantly with the stick held tightly in her fist. Kate wanted to wrap Mika up whole, to hold her and kiss her cheek and stroke her hair. Instead, she put an arm around her daughter's narrow shoulders, giving her a gentle squeeze.

"You were supposed to hide."

"You said to tell my sisters to hide," Mika said flatly.

Kate couldn't help it; she kissed the top of Mika's head anyway. "Go tell them to keep on hiding."

"Mama! I ain't a baby!" Mika's exasperation came out in a little huff, and Kate would have laughed if not for the circumstances.

"I know, sweetheart. That's just a thank you kiss, 'cause I love you. Mamas always get to have those, even when a girl's as old as you." She gave Mika a turn and a gentle push to send the girl away. "This time, you stay hid, too."

Her daughter lingered, eyes drifting to the men.

"Go on," Kate said again, the urging no longer a suggestion. "And Mika ... keep hold of your stick. *Just in case*, she whispered.

Kate held her breath, peering back around the corner of the house where Mika had gone. This time, the girl had listened; she had already run to the back pasture and was halfway up the trunk of the favorite tree, the little monkey. The canopy consumed Mika in short order, just the barest rustling of leaves offering a hint it had taken in an occupant. A chorus of welcomes were carried on the wind like a song to a mother's ears. Mika had found her sisters.

"Mika's a good girl, Kate. Clever, too," Lucy said.

"I know. Better if you don't let her hear you say it though."

"I tell her all the time." Lucy's face stretched wide with a sardonic grin before collapsing into grim appraisal. "So, what's to do about these fellas?"

Kate's guts were somersaulting, relieved by Lucy's presence as much as she was discomfited by the circumstance that had brought her, and the memory of what had happened the first time the men came. The one Kate had shot was quite dead. His face looked different than she remembered, his cheeks sunken in. Or maybe it was just the creep of death taking him.

The one Lucy had shot was quite dead, too. They hadn't lost their touch. The man Vesper had gnawed on would be dead soon as well, an artery having been opened, the sinew laid bare to the sun, already attracting flies. The last man was silent. He'd gone pale from shock, boney knuckles clutching his foot, breath hissing through gritted teeth.

"Seems it's just the one fella," Kate said, voice barely above a whisper.

A sense of fierceness defined Lucy's appearance, wind-tossed hair curling around her neck, covering and revealing a faded tattoo—phases of the moon, the ink faded to a deep blue. One work-worn hand still gripped the rifle, while the other unsnapped the buck knife from the sheath adorning her hip.

"Where'd you come from?" Lucy said sharply, looking ready to carve him up.

The man didn't answer. Vesper began gently licking his dead friend's ears—disconcerting to the innocent observer, and more so for anyone who knew what the dog had done the last time there'd been an encounter with men.

Lucy poked the man with the barrel of her gun. "Where'd you come from?"

He pointed distractedly, finger trembling. "Your ... your dog?"

"Leave it," Kate said.

Vesper's ears flattened, eyes narrowed, as though someone had threatened to take away his toy. But he kept at it anyway, tongue going like a metronome.

"Leave. It!"

Vesper reluctantly left his prize, skulking over to Kate's side. He went around her clockwise, plopping down on his haunches beside her and surveying the scene like a sentinel.

She scratched the top of his head. "Who's a good dog?"

Vesper thumped his tail three times. He was.

Kate could feel Lucy's eyes roll rather than see them. Lucy had always been fond of cats. Kate almost couldn't forgive her for it, but absolved her of this one transgression of character. Everyone had their flaws.

The man was one of the escapees from the Battle of Abscond three years prior. His collarbones protruded from his threadbare shirt, which was at least three sizes too big. The depression of skin stretched over his exposed clavicle was filled with dirt. Sticklike ankles stuck out from frayed trousers held up with a cracking leather belt that would likely give up within six days of Sunday. He'd obviously been living rough for a while. He wasn't quite as old as his dead acquaintances though.

"What do you think the likelihood is of him being a savior?"

"No doubt some would welcome the chance to find out," Kate replied.

The man's eyes brightened at the suggestion. Lucy took the butt of her rifle and popped him in the forehead. He collapsed in a heap, knocked out cold.

"That seemed unnecessary." Kate took a tentative step closer.

"If he was a savior, they'd have built him a gilded throne and lined us up for our turn until the damn thing fell off," Lucy said. But they both eyed him up like livestock at auction anyway, their conversation abruptly halting as they both pondered the possibility.

The man was ill-kempt. His nose was too big for his face, which was adorned with eyebrows that had gone rogue, as if they were escaping upwards to rally at his widow's peak. His hair had faded to silver, adorning a disproportionately sized head for such a wraithlike body. With his ears big enough to give him a head start in a stiff breeze, all told, Kate found him quite homely.

"Seems safe enough," Lucy suggested.

Kate stared at him long and hard, a shiver coursing through her like a horse shaking off a fly. As she cocked her head towards the man she'd shot, Kate's voiced cracked. "They don't make 'em safe."

"No, I suppose they don't." The rough callous of Lucy's thumb traced Kate's cheek.

Kate leaned in, closing her eyes. Lucy smelled of honey and bee balm. They'd been companions once, and for a fleeting moment, Kate wished they were again.

Lucy withdrew her hand just as quick. She knew Kate too well.

"This one's got to be turned in," Kate went on, discarding the moment between them like it was nothing at all. "Suppose they'll want to see if there's still some use in him."

Vesper nosed at the man's ear with a flick of his tongue to taste it, before grabbing it with his teeth and giving a little tug. The man let out a weak groan, but remained otherwise inert.

"Best take him back to your place, 'til they can get out here and get him," Kate said. "I won't keep him here. Not after last time."

"What do you want to do with the other ones? We can bury them in the clearing, by the chestnut," Lucy said. "The tree needs feeding, doesn't it?"

The chestnut tree cast a wide, heavy shadow, with branches so large they curved down nearly to the ground. It was a favorite place. Kate didn't want it haunted by dead men.

"I don't want to think about them every time I pass by. Better to take them into the woods."

"Best see about your girls first," Lucy said, gesturing over Kate's shoulder.

Kate's four daughters were peering out from behind the barn, their eyes wide, like a nest of owlets. A man was a curiosity, as near to mythical as a unicorn. Mika and Birdie had been smaller the last time they saw one, and they couldn't help but crane their necks trying to catch a glimpse. Hopefully, they didn't remember much.

Kate went to them with her arms open wide, as though to obscure the view. Mika broke loose, running towards her mother at a full sprint, like a hellion during a game of red rover.

"Oh, no you don't!" Kate said, catching her daughter before she could pass by, the exaggerated bounce of Mika's curly brown hair almost comical.

"But Mama, I really wanna see them!" Mika cried.

"I know, sweetheart, I'm sure you do." Kate put a firm hand on the back of Mika's small neck, guiding the child back towards her sisters. Interested as the older girls might be, not one of them had moved. They were old enough to know danger without being told.

"Why can't I—" Mika wailed.

"Because Mama doesn't want them to see you, silly goose," Jenna, the oldest, interrupted. At sixteen, she was a pragmatic sort, head squarely set on broad shoulders, and she could be relied upon to be the voice of reason when her sisters weren't keen on listening otherwise. She'd grown tall, sprouting up so much in the last season Jenna had begun to appear more woman than girl by the day.

"Why not?"

"'Cause they'll take one look at you and try to eat you up. You look delicious." Mandy grinned, a smattering of freckles wrinkling across her nose. She, on the other hand, was not Kate's sensible one. Fourteen-year-olds never were.

"Really, Mama?" Mika asked.

"Can't you see how skinny he is, Mika-bean? He'd eat you whole and pick his teeth with your finger bones," Mandy said.

"Enough, Amanda," her mother shot back. Crouching down, Kate held Mika's arms gently, making her youngest look at her instead of the gruesome display beyond. "Jenna's right. I don't want them to see you. I don't want them to see any of you. Best they don't even know you're here. Go on, now. All of you get inside, see to your chores."

Birdie stepped forward, taking her mother's hand gently, brows knit into creases. "You alright, Ma?"

"Yes, sweetheart." Kate absently smoothed a whorl of her daughter's short hair to the side and smiled. Birdie still held the sweetness of a girl on the cusp of their teenage years, and Kate hoped it would last a while longer. "I'm fine. Go on, now, all of you, into the house."

Jenna took her little sister's arm, giving it a pull when Mika lagged behind, her small voice lilting as she asked, "We got chickens. Don't men eat chickens?"

Jenna confidently replied, "Don't matter what they eat. They don't belong here."

Lucy had been tidying up the scene while Kate was managing the girls. The captive was dazed and barely awake. His wrists were now tightly bound, and there was a piece of duct tape secured across his bewhiskered mouth.

"I'm taking their truck." Lucy was sitting in the men's vehicle, fishing around for the keys. "He can't walk, and I'm sure as hell not carting his ass back on foot."

"It's an antique. Look, it has seats for more than one! Where do you think they stole it from?"

"Doesn't matter. Spoils of war," Lucy answered, then seeing Kate's disapproval, she rolled her eyes. "Yeah, okay. I'll ask around. Doubt anyone will claim it though."

Their captive was curiously still, watching them intently. Kate decided they needed to get rid of him sooner than not. "You want to call to have him picked up? Or should I, since it's my property they came to?"

"Don't worry about it," Lucy said. "I'll do it. Since he's not stayin' here, they'll have to come out to my place to get him anyhow. And like you said, the girls don't need all the fuss that'd come with them poking around here." She leaned over the passenger seat and began fishing around the floor of the cab. The only thing visible of Lucy was the raucous wildness of her long, dark hair, and one long, smooth leg stuck straight out the door.

"Ha! Here they are." She popped up with a grin, dangling a key, pleased with the winnings of her scavenger hunt. Lucy's smile quickly faded. "What is it, Kate?"

"So... How many more... How many men do you think might be... Do you think more are coming?" Kate began pacing in a small, aimless circle, hands pressing hard into her hips. It was an old habit, the physical pain a means to distract from the emotional kind. The knuckles of her fists pushed deeper. "It's been three goddamned years."

"You're alright," Lucy said, stopping the circuit by wrapping Kate up in her arms. "He ain't doin' a damn thing, I promise."

"Most days I think I'm fine, and then some little thing, some scent or vague memory brings it all back, and it's ... it's like rot, creeping into everything." Kate intertwined her fingers in Lucy's, focusing on the sensation of touch, caught for a moment in the memory of their connection before.

"You want me to stay? I'll stay—"

Oh god, yes, please stay, Kate thought, before letting go and running her hands across her face to reset her composure. "No. Never mind, I'm alright. Have to bring in the hay from the back field." She turned to leave, but Lucy grabbed her arm.

"Kate, don't."

Kate bit down hard on the corner of her lip, taking respite in the distraction, still staring at the man sitting silently on the ground—a man watching a woman lose her wits.

Lucy marched over to him, tearing the tape off his face without hesitation. "How many more of you are there?"

His eyes shut tight, wincing in pain, more beard on the tape now than on his face. "I don't know," he croaked.

"You have a camp somewhere? More men in your crew? How's it work?" Lucy kicked him when he didn't answer. "Damn the lot of you, just going around taking whatever you please!"

"These guys are the only ones I know," he muttered. "I only come across them maybe a week ago. I haven't seen any others—haven't for near three years now. Been on my own."

"Then why'd you come here with them?"

"Long time to be with just yourself," he said quietly, looking at Lucy as though she had three eyes and horns.

Lucy picked up the duct tape, peeling off another length and tearing it with her teeth, pushing the roll over her wrist as she bent down to cover his mouth.

"I haven't seen one of you," he said in a rush.

"What do you mean, you haven't seen me?" Lucy asked.

"Never seen ... never seen a woman before."

2

Long Time for a Secret

Fifty-three years after The Waning: Four years earlier

There was nothing a mother would not do for her child. No matter if they were grown, no matter anything they might be. That's what Odelia believed. It was why she told herself she did it. Every day, they'd made her scrub floors until her fingers were burned raw. Every day, she'd eat the gruel they'd slopped on her tray. Every time they'd bound her in chains just to walk outside for an hour of reprieve from the gray walls, gray floors, gray food.

It was all for her son. For Abe.

Her sweet boy. She'd been the envy of the whole neighborhood when Abe came. It'd been nine years since a boy had been born. Lord, she was so proud. Odelia closed her eyes. She could see him so clearly, remembering the day she'd paraded him up and down the street in a little blue suit and yellow bow tie on his first morning of kindergarten. While the rest of the schoolbook photos were nothing but girls in a medley of dresses and dainty things with their hair pinned up in curls, Abe stood out with his cropped black hair and startling hazel eyes. She'd made sure he wore a bow tie for his pictures every year after, too. One day, she'd meant to put them all in an album together, so she could watch his face grow into a man's year by year.

Odelia beamed at the memory, clucking cheerily under her breath—only to be consumed by the same chest-rattling cough that pained her down to her bones. The rasp of her breathing was like a fire of needles in her lungs. She pressed her thumb hard on the button, just once. The Dilaudid went coursing through her veins like a warm summer breeze. More would have been nice, but she needed her wits.

The nurse's trim frame lined the doorway, body fuzzy, like someone had smeared her edges. Odelia peered back at her. "Morning, Nurse Ratchet."

"That's not my name, Odelia," Noemi said as she whipped the stethoscope off her neck, pressing the cold bell to Odelia's chest. "Let's have a listen, okay?"

A small scowl crept onto the nurse's normally benign face, a strand of fine wheaten hair escaping its bobby pin. Pushing the restraints out of the way, Noemi pressed her fingers against Odelia's wrist, watching the clock. "On a scale of one to ten, what's your pain—"

"What d'you think?" Odelia pulled her arms up to the limits of her fetters, the straps pressing into her skin. "I'm dyin' and chained to a bed, so it don't matter now, does it? Pain just reminds me I'm still alive. It's alright. I still got some things to do."

"Your doctor is on rounds right now. She'll come in to see you soon, maybe up the narcotics a bit. If you promise you'll try and behave, we can see about having those removed," Noemi said, nodding towards the restraints.

"Never mind the doctor. Send the pastor," Odelia said. "And give me a pen and paper. I've got to write my daughter afore I go."

"Got it." Noemi tapped her finger against her forehead as though planting a seed. "Need anything else?"

"Don't forget," Odelia said.

Noemi scribbled a note and stuck it to the electronic charting pad tucked into the front pocket of her royal-blue scrubs. "I won't forget. I'll send someone back after shift change."

"If I don't see you..." Odelia's voice trailed off. "Goodbye, Nurse Ratchet. You weren't half bad."

Noemi hesitated at the threshold as her patient's scratchy voice rose tentatively behind her. "Never mind that now, Odelia. I'm sure I'll be seeing you next time." Their eyes met briefly, both knowing the lie for what it was, but leaving it between them, nonetheless.

Noemi didn't like Odelia, no matter the vulnerability the cancer had forced the woman to endure. She had an obstinance rivaling a mule in a mud flat. Odelia tried every shred of Noemi's patience with the old, tired nickname she'd heard a thousand times. It wasn't as if the woman was ever going to get out. She was a lifer. Death would be a kindness.

Noemi hadn't seen Odelia's sentencing paperwork, but she'd heard the stories: mother of the last boy; fought the authorities so fiercely, she'd blinded one and nearly killed another. Then threatened to hunt down and kill their daughters, before they finally got her down on the ground and zip-tied her limbs. That didn't stop Odelia from kicking one in the teeth though. Broke someone's jaw, too. With a woman as violent as Odelia, it was hard to imagine she'd been an academic before. Sometimes Noemi wondered if it was just another story to add to the legend Odelia had become.

And in all these years, Odelia had never settled, spending more time separated from the others—women society deemed too dangerous to put to use—than anyone else housed here. The other incarcerated women respected her for fighting back, but more likely because Odelia had been mother to a boy. The idolization had only served to make the woman more of a problem. She had an army of dissidents backing her. Even the ones who fought each other would unite behind Odelia, until security learned not to provoke her for fear of an uprising. There were plenty among the staff who would be glad to have the woman gone.

Working as a nurse in the penitentiary wasn't much different than working at a hospital on the outside. But it was easier for Noemi not to get attached to the patients—easier to go home at night and forget they existed at all. There were fewer nights she had to find relief at the bottom of a bottle, and fewer days she had to show up at work unable to see straight. And she was less likely to lose a job after accidentally injecting a patient with Vecuronium instead of Versed and watching them die, no matter the efforts to revive them. Noemi was relieved the facility was little more than a Band-Aid dispensary most of the time, and offered nothing more than palliative care for the rest.

Noemi stared at the note stuck to the electronic chart, then plucked it off and put it on the desk so the night nurse wouldn't miss it: *Odelia needs last rites. Pastor, paper, pen.*

Pulling up Odelia's medical record, Noemi made the necessary entries: *patient jaundiced, respiration shallow, bradycardic, blood pressure thready.* She recalled the blue of Odelia's nail beds and added, *cyanotic.* It wasn't going to be long now. The woman had about a week, tops. It was a wonder she was even coherent, considering. But that was Odelia—obstinate to the end.

Mother of the last son. For a moment, it struck Noemi hard in the gut, with no notion of why it suddenly bothered her. But she wasn't willing to dwell on the matter long enough to figure it out. Shoving the stethoscope in the desk drawer, Noemi threw on a jacket, pausing briefly outside Odelia's room. Her eyes started to burn, throat tightening with the familiar sensation of anguish that could so easily overcome. She flashed her ID badge at the wall scanner, pressing her fingertips onto the authentication panel, waiting for the sound of the ping opening the unit doors and rushing past the old mint-green walls of the exit corridor, swallowing any emotions threatening to escape. Her phone vibrated as soon as she was outside the concrete block.

"Hiya, darling. How was school? ... Yes, I'm on my way now. Sorry, running a bit late. Jayne's not home yet? ... Alright, how 'bout you get dinner started, and I'll see you in a little while."

Odelia's hands shook, the envelope shifting when the pen pressed onto the paper. She sealed it shut, setting it aside, intent on writing the second letter. They'd left her in a restraint vest, legs still tied down, but one hand was adequately free. She didn't have the energy to protest. Besides, what did it matter? By the time anyone did anything about it, she'd be dead.

Her daughter, Etta, had been born in prison. Odelia had barely been pregnant when the Governing Council took her, still so new with child, even she hadn't known yet. Maybe knowing would have changed things. They let Odelia keep her daughter for a year. Then they only ever let Etta visit on Odelia's birthday. It was never enough, but not once did she complain, for fear of losing that child, too.

Etta had always been good, if a bit defiant. Odelia smirked. *That's* my *girl*. It was always a surprise whenever Etta visited, to see a raven-haired sloe-eyed girl staring back at her. Nothing about Etta's appearance came from her—but her daughter was all attitude, and that part Odelia was proud to call her own. It had been hard watching her daughter grow up in annual incre-ments. A child lived a lot in a year. First words. First steps. First girlfriend. First heartbreak. University. Graduation. Marriage. Divorce. Odelia had been witness to only single portions of her daughter's life.

It had been seven months since they'd last seen each other. Odelia had told her then about the cancer. She wanted to be the one to say it, not wanting Etta to find out when some stranger called and said her mama had died, and to come collect her things if'n you please.

Odelia didn't know why she hadn't told her daughter about Abe before. Maybe Etta already knew; maybe she'd heard it along the way after all those years gone. *"Should have said so myself,"* she whispered with regret.

Etta love,

It's time. There's something you should know, before it's too late to tell you myself. Before it's too late, and no one's left to tell anyone at all. It's been a long time for a secret I never should have kept from you. Lord knows why I did. I just didn't want you to lose everything. I didn't want you to be like me.

You've got a brother. His name is Abe. He's got to be about fifty-some years old by now. They took him when he was just a little boy, like they took all of them. Do you know that's why I'm in here? It's wrong, what they did. And I wasn't having them take my son. So, here I went, and here I stay, 'til the day I die.

That day is coming soon, Etta. I'm sorry I won't see you again. I'm sorry for not telling you sooner about your brother. You grew up without a mama because I wanted to keep my boy. Try and forgive me for it, would you?

Etta, I want you to find him. Bring Abe home. Bring him home for me. Give him my letter. Show him my grave, if I get one. I don't know where he is, love. No idea at all. But I feel him. A mother knows. My boy is still out there. And he's all you've got left. No child deserves to not know his kin, to believe his whole life that we left him behind.

Go find him for me, Etta. It's my last wish.

Your mama loves you. No matter what. Always. Forever.

18

3

THE BIG SISTER

"MOM, HAVE YOU EVER seen one? In real life?"

The topic of men had consumed almost every single conversation in Noemi's household since Odelia's death a month earlier. Noemi was, quite frankly, sick of it—particularly now it was only going to get worse. She stopped chopping onions for dinner just long enough to shove another piece of bread into her mouth to keep her eyes from tearing up, setting the knife down with a sigh.

"No, Rosena, I haven't. They all died before I was born. They still showing the same movies about them at school?"

Her elder daughter nodded, running a hand through her bangs with a well-practiced flip to get them out of her eyes and look all the cooler for it. "The ones they show are so ancient, they have to bring in some old video machine. It isn't even dimensional. It's so boring."

"Were men-people made with color in real life, or were they all gray, like in the movies?" Where her sister was lanky and fit, Noemi's younger daughter, Stella, had yet to outgrow the softness of childhood. Pixie hair and big eyes made her look like a living cupid. Stella didn't wait for an answer, pushing forward with more pressing matters. "Mommy, is Auntie Jayne ever coming back?"

"I don't know, honey." Noemi chucked her younger daughter under the chin and smiled. "Probably not. Does it bother you?"

"No." Stella grinned, then promptly ran off, skating across the tile floor in socks, tumbling around the corner, and dashing upstairs.

"Dinner's in twenty minutes!" Noemi yelled before eyeing up Rosena, who was studying her turquoise-painted nails with significantly more interest than they warranted. She leveled a commanding look at her daughter. "Set the table."

"Why is it always me?" Rosena protested, suddenly sullen, arms crossing defensively.

"Would you rather clean up after?" Noemi asked, waving the knife for emphasis.

Rosena's hands flew up in mock surrender before she cocked her head to the side, bangs hanging just so. "If I set the table, does Stella have to clean up?"

"Yes," Noemi said.

Rosena flung open the cabinets and pulled out four bowls, hesitated, then sheepishly put one back. She began rearranging the soup spoons, pleating the napkins, smoothing the tablecloth, all while casting furtive looks at her mother. But teenage melodrama was keeping some notion securely hostage.

Noemi had reluctantly learned to keep her mouth shut and leave Rosena to her stewing. As many times as she'd tried to pry, provoke, persuade, and eventually beg for information out of her daughter, it invariably ended up with shouting, crying, and slamming doors—and wine, when it was all said and done. There was something to be said for the silent treatment, and that was a quiet house without interruptions.

Today was no different. Noemi eyed the time and the wine bottle, knowing Rosena would wait until the last possible minute to pose whatever quandary she had, leaving her mother no time to offer a long, thought-provoking, emotionally available response.

Instead, Noemi would only be left with enough time for a rushed explanation and a promise of "We'll talk about this more later," which would never come to fruition.

She had begun to doubt her certainty about this pattern and was almost ready to tell her daughters to wash up for dinner when Rosena finally caved.

"Why'd she go?"

Noemi looked at the timer on the cooker. Three minutes.

"Because Auntie Jayne felt strongly. About a cause. And needed to be a part of it. And wanted her voice heard." Noemi spoke more loudly than she'd meant to, clipped speech barely suppressing the desire to complain loudly and at length about what a lifelong nuisance Jayne had been. She cast her eyes to the ceiling, inhaling through her nose and holding her breath, before turning her gaze toward Rosena with an attempted smile and forced calm. "I suppose some would say it's noble and worthy. Would you?"

Rosena was at a highly impressionable age, when the romanticism of a revolution could still catch a girl's imagination, and—if she wasn't careful—the next thing Noemi would see is Rosena walking out the door with a backpack slung over her shoulder, off to join Jayne in whatever nonsense had been conjured up. Everyone always wanted to be part of something. They wanted to matter. They needed to feel important. And they always thought they were right—well beyond the point where they actually were.

"Not for that. Not for *them*!" Rosena's hands pushed into the front pockets of the olive-green cargo pants she always wore—the ones Jayne had gifted her on her last birthday. The toe of her boot was adding black rubber scuff marks to the kitchen floor, bit by bit.

Two minutes.

"What do you think about Jayne leaving us?" *And are you thinking you might want to go after her?* Noemi's mind silently offered up the real question. Maybe Rosena didn't want to follow the cause, but she might want to follow Jayne. She idolized her aunt, always the rule-breaker, the defiant one. Jayne had electric-blue hair. Artfully torn clothes. An array of ever-revolving girlfriends. But the last thing Noemi could bear was to lose a sister and a daughter in the same week. Noemi wouldn't have it. She'd lock Rosena in her room. Her daughter wasn't leaving, and that was that.

One minute.

"How about we talk more about this after dinner, hmm?"

"Auntie Jayne was supposed to help me with my lab homework," Rosena finally said.

Homework? She only cared Jayne was gone because she couldn't do her chemistry?

The timer went off. Noemi sighed, reaching for a wine glass.

"Ro, I'll get you a tutor, okay? It's no big deal."

"Mom, it is, too! You just don't understand."

"Then make me understand!" Noemi slammed the ladle on the table to satisfying effect. "Jayne left. Us and grandma are all she has, but it wasn't enough for her to stay. And all you care about is your chem grade? Really, Ro?" It was all Noemi could do to keep from grabbing her daughter by the shoulders and shaking her until some common sense rattled loose and finally fell into place. Instead, she started slopping dinner into the bowls with so much force it splattered on to the table, leaving trails of potato chowder running down the sides as though the place settings wept potato tears.

"She was helping me get through chemistry, so I could qualify for nursing school—to be like you, Mom! So I could be like you! But Auntie Jayne left, like I don't even matter at all!" Rosena kicked the wall with her boot, leaving a black smudge angled sharply across the ecru paint. Then she stomped up the stairs. The bedroom door slammed hard enough the whole house shook.

Noemi poured the wine so close to the rim, she had to lean over the table to sip the top down before she could pick it up to drink it. She was managing her one-glass rule just fine.

Odelia had held on longer than anyone thought she would. She'd lasted nearly a month, although the old woman was too far gone to notice anyone coming or going by the time she was on Noemi's rotation again.

Noemi had read Odelia's letters. She knew she shouldn't have. But she did it anyway. She'd taken them before they were discovered and confiscated, then slipped the one addressed to the daughter back in amongst the stack of legal papers just before Odelia's prison belongings got sealed and shipped off. Noemi didn't know why she hadn't just put them both in the shredder. Would have saved a lot of trouble.

It had been a mistake, telling Jayne. When Noemi had come home, her sister took one look at her and immediately took the girls out for a hike in the restored woods, knowing it had been a rough day without even asking. Jayne was eight years younger, and though she sometimes acted like a third child, occasionally she acted like the sister Noemi needed her to be. Jayne didn't believe it, hearing about Odelia's letter to her daughter. Then Noemi handed over the letter she'd kept—the one Odelia had written to her son, Abe. The one that really should have been shredded.

It was surreal to Noemi, the notion there was a man—god, maybe more than one—still living. They could be out there, and no one knew a thing about it. Jayne said she cared less about one man than she did about the Governing Council hiding him—the obvious cover-up, the secrets they were keeping, why, and what were they going to do about it. Jayne was on a mission, and no one was going to stop her. She was going to tell everyone.

Noemi tried to throw the letter in the incinerator, twice, before Jayne finally took it and hid it. She'd lose another nursing job if they found out she'd perused a patient's things, much less taken a contraband letter that, evidently, was going to incite a rebellion.

Jayne had left the week prior with all her belongings, spouting something about being part of an uprising, a revolution for the ages, and a return to the old ways. Nonsense. There were no "old ways." Their generation had never lived among men; it was the stuff of her great-grandmother's time. Jayne had no idea what she was talking about, and no idea what she was getting herself into.

Noemi opened a new bottle of Syrah, pouring some into a wine glass and sipping enough so it wouldn't spill on the snot-green couch, drinking a little more before setting it down. The girls had gone quiet, maybe plugged into games with friends. Or more optimistically, maybe they were doing homework. Or plotting revenge. All fair possibilities. Noemi eyed the half-full wine bottle on the counter, sitting forlornly amongst the other empty ones. It had been a tough day, and she'd worked hard, and she had a teenage daughter. Damn right she deserved another glass.

She was toward the bottom of the glass before Stella appeared quietly in front of her, staring.

"What'sit, honey?"

"Any dinner, Mommy? I'm hungry."

Noemi looked at the clock. The numbers blurred. She was sure it said eight thirty, but that couldn't be right. "Sure, honey. On the counter. Give it a zap to warms it up, okay? You were so busy in your room, I didn't wanna inner-rupt."

"Can you do it? You do it better, Mommy. Dinner always tastes better when you make it." Stella regarded her with big, sad eyes and a hand rubbing her stomach, a sure sign she was set to wither to bits and blow away in the wind.

Noemi eyed Stella skeptically but couldn't resist such a sweet face. Maybe her daughter was up to something, or maybe there was still some childhood innocence left. Soon, any remaining sweetness would evaporate like fog off a lake on a summer morning, turning into the irrevocable storms of the tween years.

"Of course, honey. How abouts you pour yourself some apple juice while you're at it?" Noemi stood up, then promptly sat back down, waiting for the room to settle. "Be right there, okay?"

"Play music!" Stella yelled with a grin.

The house speakers came to life instantly, the latest music popping with sound in a stream of synthetic voices. "Come on, Mommy, dance with me!"

They were on their feet, Noemi with a wine glass still in hand, swaying and knocking into the corner of the kitchen table, spilling wine across her shirt. She drank to the bottom, until there was no more worry of that. Stella was giggling, both of them dancing and singing at the top of their lungs, until they sat down on the couch in an exhausted heap.

"You go on and eat your dinner, Stell. I'ma just gonna sits right here, okay?"

"I got it, Mommy."

Noemi curled up on the couch, but kept one foot solidly on the floor, the room pulsing as though it had a heartbeat. Stella sat cross-legged nearby, watching her with an odd intensity while blowing steam off the soup.

"What do you... Why are you... Stell, stop. Whatch you want?"

"Tell me how you picked me."

"I made you," Noemi said. "Had you put in my own belly. You know that."

"I know, but where'd you make me from?"

"Whatsit about, honey?" Noemi tried to sit up, then thought better of it and plunked her head back down on the throw pillow, determinedly focusing squarely on her daughter's noses. "I've told you before. You know the story."

"Tell me again."

There was a time when it had been Stella's preferred bedtime story, but it had been years since she asked to hear it. Noemi sighed as she began, the words falling out of her mouth nearly by rote.

"It was my turn to try and make a boy. So, I went to the baby-making factory, and I looked at all the stories of all the men that were—thousands and thousands of them—until I found just the right one. And in you went. And I waited, and I waited, and I waited. You grew so big inside my belly, I couldn't even see my toes. Then one day, there was so much clamoring in there, I knew it was time for you to come out. And when you finally did, you were the most beautiful little girl in the world."

In truth, Noemi had been in labor with Stella for three days and thought she was going to die. She'd vomited with every contraction, dry-heaving so badly by the end that she couldn't push, and the midwives resorted to mechanical means to get her baby out. Noemi had thought Stella was stillborn, like the prior one had been, so quiet and motionless ... until finally, Stella had opened her tiny, perfect mouth and announced to the world she'd arrived.

"Can I have a new sister?"

"What's wrong with your old sister? She no good now?"

"I just think I'm going to need a new one, that's all. It's my turn to be the oldest."

"That's nice, honey. Pass ... pass me the bottle, wouldya?"

"Good morning. It is six thirty. Good morning. It is six thirty. Good morn—"

"Shut. Up!" Noemi croaked. The lights had gone from slumber dim to morning bright, and the coffee maker was sputtering and steaming with a persistent drip. She cracked open an eye, one arm slung protectively over her forehead.

The living room. On the couch. Warm. Noemi opened the other eye, wary, finding wakefulness to be unfortunate, but not as bad as it ought to have been. It was a sure sign she was further down the road with the drinking again than she would have preferred to admit.

Good god, why couldn't she move? Noemi pulled her chin to her chest, eyes skimming her prostrate body. There was a scent of patchouli and something else botanical lingering on Rosena's quilt, which was pulled tightly around her. Noemi couldn't move, could barely turn at all. It was somewhat comforting, realizing Rosena had tucked her in— until she noted the coffee table was pressed up against the couch, too. Noemi had fallen the last time—whacked her head so hard she nearly passed out.

Well, it was strangely considerate, nonetheless. After all the drama, Rosena could still be so sweet. Noemi smiled again, even though it hurt her head a little. Shimmying out of the cocoon, her body moved slowly, not wanting a repeat of the last time, and pushed the table back where it belonged, its iron feet dropping into the little depressions in the bamboo carpet.

The kitchen was clean. Spotless, in fact. Wine bottle—bottles—gone. Dishes put away. Even the sink was empty. The boot scuffs that had been haphazardly painted across the floors were faded from someone trying to buff them out. Noemi grinned. She'd won; the kid obviously felt bad. She poured herself a cup of coffee happily, the rest going into the tumbler for Rosena to take to school. Noemi didn't usually let her have caffeine. It wasn't good for a girl's skin, or attention span in class. But it would be an obvious peace offering, and Noemi knew a little bribery would go a long way.

There was a thunder of footsteps across the upstairs hall, then tumbling down the stairs, Stella skidding sideways into a chair before stopping.

"Hi, Mommy! Is there breakfast?"

Noemi gripped the coffee mug, realizing she had forgotten Stella entirely.

"Give Mom a hug, honey," she said and thrust out her arms.

Stella dove in, giggling, then popped back up. "Breakfast?"

"Better." Noemi dug into her bag, rummaging through handkerchiefs and electronics and sunglasses before finding her wallet. "Here's my exchange card. You can have anything you want to eat today. I hear school has the best breakfast—better than anything your old mom can make."

Stella's face fell, sad eyes regarding her calmly, and reached out to take the card. "Okay, Mommy."

"What's keeping your sister? She'll walk you to school today."

Stella shook her head. "No, it's okay. I can walk myself now."

Noemi tilted an ear toward the ceiling, realizing there was no activity, no hair dryer, no complaining. "Ro! Get your butt outta bed! You're going to be late for school!"

"She's gone with Aunt Jayne, Mommy. She said to make sure you and me were dancing real loud, and then she left. Don't worry, I know how to take care of you. Ro said I'll be the big sister now."

4

NOTHING BUT TROUBLE

THE BOX OF HER mother's things sat forlornly in the corner of Etta's kitchen like a trampled stuffed animal left behind at the county fair. It had been there for three months, and on occasion had been festooned with its own array of ornament: discarded mail, coats, groceries, and the cat, Eeyore, who had earned his name with his emotional state and physical description alike.

When it had been delivered by the courier, Etta had thought to open the box that night, curled up with a stiff drink. But she just couldn't bring herself to do it—though she had four fingers of whiskey anyway. Liquid courage be damned.

Etta stared at the box this morning, Eeyore atop it with one hind leg straight up in the air, cleaning his parts with no shame. Memories of her mother had been flooding her thoughts. When Etta was little, she'd said Odelia was an opera singer, traveling the world, performing for dignitaries, and had told her classmates her foster mothers were the hired help. Odelia had actually been a university professor. But professors were stationary, and Etta couldn't contrive any excuse as to why a mother who was a teacher wouldn't show up for her daughter's talent show or concerts or competitions. When she was thirteen, Etta updated the story, making Odelia a dignitary working internationally for the Governing Council. By the time Etta reached university, she simply told people her mother was dead.

And now she was.

Since she was one year old, Etta had seen her mother precisely forty-one times. Forty-one hours. Etta had known her mother a grand total of a week.

Etta pushed the box with her toe, as though her mother were inside it.

Oh, Christ, is she? Etta thought.

"You're going to open it. Right now." Her wife, Kieva, had quietly appeared, sliding an old kitchen knife across the counter.

"How long you been standing there?" Etta asked.

"Long enough." Kieva's hand rested neatly on her hip, the other clutching coffee, giving Etta the exaggerated once-over she was often inclined to do when Etta was being irrational. "Open it. There're dust bunnies collectin' in the corner because the vacuum has bumped into the damn thing for so long its program code recognizes it as furniture now."

Etta slipped her hand inside the gap of Kieva's old, fuzzy orange plaid bathrobe—an abomination of fashion—feeling the damp skin fresh from a shower. Etta wrapped an arm around her wife's waist, pulling her close.

Kieva leaned toward her, soft lips to Etta's ear, voice low and sultry like a sleepy morning. "Open the goddamn box."

"Fine," Etta sighed, retreating from the hopeful distraction of her wife's body. "Bring it here."

"Oh, hell, no. I'm not touching that thing. Your mama might be in there." She skittered off with a high-stepping tiptoeing march, like a coffee-wielding drum major at the front of a parade. "If there's money, we're goin' shopping. If it's no more than a bag o' ashes and a shiv, you can go on and keep it for yourself. I don't mind." Her cackling was both wicked and infectious, and Etta couldn't help but laugh; never mind the tears that had escaped.

Her mother was not in the box—at least, not physically. But it felt like her mother's soul had crept in under Etta's skin and made a home there. She pulled out Odelia's old mauve cardigan, shoving her arms through the sleeves and wrapping it around her body like a hug. That was better.

"I knew the woman for forty-one hours, Kieva. Forty-one. I don't even know if I hated her or loved her."

Kieva put a hand on Etta's back, stroking in a soft circle to comfort. "You loved her. She was your mother. Doesn't matter if you didn't know her." Kieva sat down and began rummaging through the array of papers—sketches and drawings and little poems. "You never said your mother was artistic."

"Didn't know she was." Etta picked up a tidy stack of paper, handing it to Kieva. "She drew me—from memory. There's one from every year. Every year but this one."

"Well, that's a shame, 'cause you're looking rather fine this year, too," Kieva said, taking Etta's hand and giving it a squeeze.

They laid each sketch out before them. Forty drawings, like small, square postcards. The early ones were rough, the lines simple but expressive. The later ones were more nuanced and refined. It was the evolution of Etta through her mother's eyes—and the evolution of Odelia.

"Honestly, I'd have been better off if she'd just died and let me be. Never wanted to know any of this," Etta said, glancing up at her wife. "And don't look at me like that. Judgment doesn't suit you."

"Knowing your mother loved you so much is more important than your inability to cope with it," Kieva said. Ignoring Etta's dagger-eyed protest, Kieva continued pulling things out of the box, organizing everything into little piles: drawings, Etta's letters to Odelia, envelopes from the lawyer, an odd assortment of small rocks and pressed flowers, and clothes from another era some forty years gone.

"These are spectacular," Kieva said, holding up a lavender velour track suit and shin-high camel-colored suede boots with faux wool lining. "These must have been what she was wearing the day she got arrested." She held up large gold hoop earrings and rimmed aviator sunglasses. "I bet your mama was fly as hell in her day."

"Fly enough to go on and get herself locked up, yeah," Etta said. There'd been some stories about Odelia before prison, but not many. Etta's foster family was from the rural zone, and she'd been placed with them as a baby. By the time Etta was old enough to hear the stories, they'd been forgotten, the currency of gossip already spent. Whenever she'd visited growing up, and Etta brought up the topic of her mother's incarceration, Odelia would wave her hand dismissively and say, "Aww, hush, baby girl, it's bygones now." And then she would change the subject, whether Etta wanted to or not.

Etta's imagined stories about what had gotten her mother incarcerated were just about as vivid as her childhood stories of what her mother did for a living. Eventually, those stories succumbed like the others to a slow and quiet end, until Etta had stopped wondering altogether.

Etta stared at the pile of her mother's belongings neatly laid out before her—the summation of a woman's life reduced to a box.

"I'm the only one who will remember her," Etta said. "And I didn't even know her. Who's gonna remember me?"

"I'll remember you." Kieva grinned. "You're older. You'll definitely die first."

Etta pushed her away playfully, then grabbed a fistful of Kieva's shirt, pulling her close. She kissed her hard, before giving up and crying into Kieva's shoulder like a child who'd lost her mother. Kieva held her, rocking slowly and stroking her back until the desperate sobbing had subsided into the gasping sort, as though Etta was a fish who'd flung itself out of the sea.

"You always been an ugly crier," Kieva crooned.

Etta sucked in a long breath, followed by a few more shudders of tears. "Don't know what you're even talking about. I never cry."

"Oh, right. I forgot," Kieva said, wiping her thumbs across Etta's damp cheeks. "Go on and stuff those emotions down, and keep on stuffing, you ornery old bat," Kieva said, motioning with her hands as though tucking imaginary feelings down around the kidneys and shoving them to the side to make space for more. "You like to stuff it for a real long time, 'til there's no more space, and then you go on and get rid of it all at once. Don't matter if it's 'cause your mama died, or 'cause someone go on and tell you to eat some eggplant—"

"You know I hate eggplant."

"Oh, love, I know you do." Kieva laughed.

"Why you poking at me? My mama died."

"Because you been holding it in there for months, Etta. I'm saying you gotta give over some of them feelings of yours more easy like, instead of holdin' onto them for yourself, thinking somehow letting them fester is gonna make it better. It don't." Kieva wrapped a warm hand around Etta's neck, pulling them towards each other until their noses touched. "It's alright, Etta. You're mine now. And I don't scare."

They'd been married for five months. It had been a fling born out of a series of bad circumstances: Etta's former wife had left her, shortly after Etta's mother told her about the cancer. Thus followed a logical desire to drown her sorrows first in in beer, then in mai tais, tequila, and wine, in no particular order. Not an advisable combination, but alcohol worked its charms, and Etta had invited a rebound—a curvy, vivacious, sarcastic woman named Kieva—back to the apartment, where the remainder of the evening had been spent with Kieva holding Etta's head out of the toilet while the microbrews and umbrella drinks made a hasty and prolonged departure. They'd been together ever since.

"I love you," Etta said, taking Kieva's hand. "More today than yesterday. More than I've ever loved anyone."

"Hope so," Kieva said. "Love you back."

Etta resumed her earlier invitation, caressing the smooth skin of her wife's hips in an invitation to distraction.

Kieva let Etta's hands stay a moment before putting a long, elegant finger against Etta's mouth to stop any objection. "You gotta go on and finish with your mama first. You just got done letting yourself spill out. No sense having to start all over and do it again later, right?" She picked up the empty box and turned it over, shaking it to see if anything else fell out, but it was empty.

"I take it back. I don't actually like you at all," Etta said.

"Uh-huh. Here, I'll get all this stuff over on the table. You just sit on the couch and cozy up with Eeyore. I'll bring you some tea. Then you go on and spend some time remembering your mama, alright? I'm going for a run. After I come back, you tell me what you recollect about ol' Odelia, and I'll make you something to eat before you go to work." Kieva stacked the folders and letters and drawings on the table next to Etta.

"How long do I have before you come back for the inquisition?"

"Couple hours, maybe?" Kieva went to the door, lacing up new shoes before fighting her way through an orange pullover, hair springing out of the top of it. She returned to Etta, kissing her briefly. "You'll tell me everything when I get back, alright?"

Etta stared at the words on the page for a long while. She'd read her mother's letter three times, and yet the words stayed the same, no matter how many times she looked. The creep of numbness that had first overtaken her had subsided into something entirely more visceral: an all-consuming miserable rage twisting into sobbing, yelling destruction, punctuated by a fit of throwing things.

"God, I'm pathetic. Where the hell are you, Kieva?!" Etta lay curled up on the floor, wiping her nose with a sleeve.

She finally heard Kieva's footsteps coming up the stairs and leapt to her feet. By the time Kieva had come in, kicked off her shoes, and hung up her hoodie, Etta had rearranged all the papers into one neat stack and was sitting silently on the couch like a statue.

Kieva dropped a mesh knit takeout bag on the counter, filled to the brim with square glass boxes. "Got lunch. Thai from Seven Sisters." The contents were emptied onto two plates, the aroma of yellow coconut tempeh curry wafting across the room. Kieva finally looked at Etta, and her face scrunched up with recognition of a woman locked in an inner battle with familial demons.

"You okay?"

"Fine," Etta muttered.

"The hell you are." Kieva leaned over, kissing Etta on the forehead before handing over a plate and sitting down on the couch, leg tucked up underneath her. She shoved her hand in her pocket, outstretched fist opening to reveal a crumbled wax parcel. "Forgot. Here. Fortune cookies. Open 'em."

Etta always ate the cookies first, indulging Kieva by reading it out loud. "'The person next to you will be a significant factor in your life in two years.'"

"... 'in bed.'" Kieva smirked. "But that doesn't actually work." She blew the steam off the potatoes, the threatening little hot pockets guaranteed to burn a tongue. Kieva always ate too quick, open mouth blowing out "hot-hot-hot!" while her eyes teared up. Kieva went to the kitchen for a glass of water, waving a hand by her mouth as though it would make a difference. "So. What's got you fussing'?"

"Nothing. It's nothing." Etta set the plate aside, getting up abruptly, then picking up the drawings and letters and clothing in one motion and dumping it all back into the box.

"How long we gonna do this for? 'Cause you know I can wait you out, but I got things to do today, so it'd be just as well if we could get to the part where you tell me everything, so I don't have to keep pestering 'til you do."

"I don't want to talk about it, Kieva. The damn woman's been nothing but trouble my whole life. No sense digging up drama, now she's dead. I'm just going to get on with it, like I never knew Odelia, because I never really did anyway."

"It's fine, Etta, if that's how you wanna do it. But you're still telling me why." Kieva crossed her arms, looking as though she were prepared to be hit by a truck and intending to be on the winning side of the encounter.

"Why you have to push me? Why can't you just leave it alone?" Etta was trying to stay defiant. But she didn't have the resolve, and collapsed in a dejected heap on the couch. She sighed heavily, eyes on the floor.

"I have a brother."

"You have a broth... You have a *what*?!" Kieva took two bounding steps, sitting down again next to Etta, grabbing her arms. "What'd you just say?"

Etta dug through the box, plucked out the absurd letter, and thrust it into Kieva's hands. "A brother."

Kieva read it, soft lips moving as she did, eyes getting bigger as she went, until they nearly popped out of her head at the end of it. She read aloud with emphasis, "'Go find him, Etta. It's my last wish.'" Her hands dropped to her lap along with the letter. She kept staring at it, then at Etta, then at the letter, and back again.

"What are you going to do?" Kieva finally asked.

"Not a goddamned thing."

5

DISCRETION

ETTA FOLLOWED THE GRAVEL path through a woodland of skinny trees, the oaks and maples all lined up in neat rows. The moss-covered forest floor was dotted with swaths of ferns and trillium offering the first blush of returning wildness. The squirrels chattered at her when she passed, the occasional acorn shattering down through the leaves with a resounding thump. The low, rambling building at the end of the trail sat quiet, its stone walls and wooden trusses camouflaged by forest leaves. The morning workers were just beginning to trickle out like a stream of ants. Etta hurried along. She hated to be late.

Her morning counterpart sidled up beside her in the relay pavilion as Etta drank the last of her tea. Etta job-shared with Jill—a woman she secretly referred to as Minnie Mouse, thanks to her squeaky voice and unfailingly bright-eyed, chipper demeanor. She was staggeringly enthusiastic about everything, always. It was as infectious as it was nauseating, and Etta couldn't help but grin and sigh heavily as Jill began with the usual barrage of cheer.

"Good morning! How are you today? What's new? Lovely afternoon, isn't it? Oh, look! I brought you something." Jill rifled around in her bag, finding her prize and offering it to Etta. "This one's for you. I've got more zucchini than I know what to do with.

They're stealth growers, you know. I'd have sworn I checked under every leaf, but there it was this morning, hiding the whole time." It was enormous. She thrust it at Etta as if she were wielding a weapon.

"Jill, I thought we were friends. What am I supposed to do with a three-kilo vegetable?"

"Oh! Well ... I betcha you can make a lot of bread with it. Or slice it up and make chips, or mash it down and make a guacamole. Or maybe a casserole? Really, you can do anything with zucchini!" she said, voice rising to her trademark squeaky pitch. The shift transition sounds played overhead in a soothing *pong-pong-pong* of low tones meant to initiate the hand-off between staff. Etta took the offending vegetable monstrosity, grimacing at the thought of the added weight in the bag during her walk home in the evening.

"Well, thank you. I think. So, what's on the docket for me to-day?"

"Your first appointment is in twenty minutes. Newly married. They need their initial interview and orientation. They think they both want to be implanted at the same time, with the same source, because they want siblings," Jill said, shaking her head with a tiny frown. "Probably ought to counsel to differentiate the source and separate their implantation cycles. They shouldn't both go through it at the same time."

"They'll insist. They always do," Etta said. She never intervened. No one listened anyway. But she always told Jill she had tried, with a shrug and a shake of her head for emphasis.

"After them, you've got a few couples on their second and third round, then an unattached single, from..." Jill scrolled through the screen, the smiling faces of the day's appointments flipping past until she landed on the last one. "Oh, she's from nearby."

"Assign the last one to someone else," Etta said, casually adding, "My first appointment is bound to run late. Whenever they say they both want the same thing, they rarely actually do."

"Can't. You're it for today. No one else is doing orientations until next week. There's some big closed-door meeting or something taking up capacity," Jill said.

Etta looked at the last appointment on the screen—and saw the face of her ex-wife staring back at her. Smug, like she always was. *Now* she wanted a baby? Of course she did.

"Alright. Thanks, Min— Jill," Etta stuttered. "Thanks."

"Etta, you know I don't like that name."

"I say it with fondness, Jill. I don't mean anything by it." Etta had slipped up once before, calling her Minnie Mouse, believing she wouldn't mind the moniker. She'd been very wrong.

"All the same, I'd rather you didn't." Jill took a pullover out of her bag for the walk home, the afternoon chill coming as the sun dipped below the trees.

"Have a good day, then," Etta said, slipping the zucchini back into Minnie Mouse's bag while her head was caught inside her sweater. "Gotta run. The clients are on their way in, and I'm gonna need more tea to get through the newlyweds."

Etta dashed inside, smirking to herself as she imagined Minnie Mouse getting home and discovering the gargantuan vegetable, like a garden ninja, tucked in amongst her things. Of course, it wouldn't be a surprise to find the damned zucchini on her desk come Monday. Minnie Mouse might be adorable, but it didn't mean she wasn't apt to get even, if she was so inclined. Etta imagined there'd be an ensuing vegetable war, each of them leaving larger and more abundant crops on the other's desk for them to find, until the advent of winter finally called a truce. Her own garden was woefully neglected and bound to have a few vegetables of unusually large size hidden amongst the detritus.

Etta sipped at her tea, irritated to find the tumbler empty. She needed to pull the documentation for her first appointment, but couldn't help dwelling on what her ex-wife was up to, and what it would be like to interview her. They hadn't spoken since Carol left her house key and wedding ring on the kitchen counter, sitting atop a note that simply said, *I'm done.* Etta had called her at work in a fit, demonstrating a loss of all virtue and an abundance of vice by reducing Carol to baleful sobbing while she was in the middle of an all-department meeting—on speaker. It had not been one of Etta's finer moments. Or maybe it had been her best one. It depended on who she told the story to.

A quiet *ping* interrupted her daydreaming, announcing the arrival of the first appointment. Etta scanned their profiles, reprimanding herself for not having briefed herself on their case before they showed up.

"Abby and Diane, married eight months. Dual pregnancy, same seed source. Both are teachers. Abby is in her late twenties, and Diane... Ah, thirtieth birthday last week. Gets them every time," Etta murmured. Gathering her fortitude, Etta smoothed her hair, pressing down on the desk and standing up, wearing a big smile as the young couple walked into the office.

"Welcome! I'm Etta, the case coordinator for the duration of your experience here at The Midwest Center. I'm going to orient you to the whole process, I'll be here to advise you both along the way. Please, have a seat. Can I offer you some tea, or would you like coffee? Scone?"

They nervously clutched each other's hands, grinning wildly and bumping into each other when they tried to sit down, erupting in a fit of laughter as they made their own introductions. Etta sat patiently, waiting for the usual cycle from excitement to nervousness to fear, and then down to business, to run its course.

"You'll have to excuse us. We just can't help it. We're so dang excited to be mothers, and honestly, we can't wait! We wish we were nine months along already," Abby said.

"Well, if you were nine months pregnant right now, you'd be wishing for it to be over with," Etta said, realizing too late, she shouldn't have said it out loud. "That is to say, you'd be so much closer to having your first baby in your arms. How exciting!"

"Oh? Oh! Yes, right!" Abby exclaimed.

Diane was wise to Etta's cynicism, but was measured enough to play along. "Can you imagine, Abby?"

"Let's start with a little overview, okay? Everyone is provided the option of choosing their pater-seed source via interactive digital video archives, so you can view the specimen providing you with your child. Or you can opt to have us review your genetics, medical history, and characteristic preferences, then we'll choose the donor for you who is most likely to suit your genome profile, thus increasing your odds of potentially having a male offspring."

"We'd like to pick—"

"We'd like to be surprised—"

"Are you sure I can't get you some coffee? Tea? Honestly, the scones are lovely." Etta was halfway out the door before they called her back, apologizing, swearing they'd discussed it before they arrived, but...

"I just don't know," Abby said, face drawn down into a brow-furrowed, pinched-lip pouting expression Etta suspected won many arguments in her relationships.

"Darling..." Diane tugged ever so slightly at her wife's tightly clasped hands. "We talked about this."

"I don't know why you've got to make such a big deal out of it. It's just like picking something out of a catalog, or choosing a movie or something." Abby's pouty appeal was drawn out, a trait she'd no doubt learned when she was nine. Diane didn't stand a chance.

"Well, if you want to watch dead men in home movies, and, I don't know, maybe end up picking your grandpa or something—"

"We screen for that," Etta interjected.

"—then you absolutely can. I find it kinda creepy, but I mean, sure. That's your prerogative. If you think your heart can pick better than science can, go with that," Diane said.

"We've got cookies. Would you like cookies?" Etta stood up again, inching towards the door.

"You're right." Abby offered a wan smile and squeezed Diane's hand, giving it a little pat. One single tear ran down her cheek, and she added with a whimper, "I don't know what I was thinking."

"Guess we're watching old dead guys," Diane said, sighing. "Tell me you have cocktails."

"Quite a variety, in fact," Etta said. "You need any more time to discuss—oh, no? So, we're all set? On to business, then?"

The wives looked at each other. Abby was eager and close to tears—the happy sort now—and she reclaimed Diane's hand in earnest. She was nodding enthusiastically, grinning like the Cheshire Cat, a tiny bounce to her body, as if it were no longer possible to contain her energy. Diane returned the smile, thumb methodically tracing the gold wedding band spinning loose on her finger. Her eyes raised to Etta's, blinking slowly, resigned. "On to business, then. Can we select a specific year?"

"Well, I suppose you can, yes, of course. We can narrow it down any number of ways," Etta said. "All the product is numerically coded, so we can focus on things like the collection year, or if you have a region, ethnicity, or other preference, we can accommodate those types of requests. Our source product is guaranteed viable and was collected and cryo-frozen within minutes of receipt. While there's been some, shall we say, 'folklore' regarding earlier collections having a higher likelihood of producing a viable male, well, as we all know, there's been no truth to the rumor."

"I'd like to select from the last year available. Newest is best. And then Abby can pick from those, from whichever ones are our best genomic matches." Diane squeezed her wife's hand with a reassuring smile. "You can watch as many movies as you like, honey. Fair?"

"Oh, yes!" Abby was nearly bursting with excitement by now, wiggling in her chair like a little girl being offered to pick any toy in the store. "What year? Oh, and how many will it leave us with to choose from?"

"Can't say I've ever had anyone ask for the newest before, but offhand, I think the most recent is from about five decades or so ago," Etta said, then paused. The numbers struck a chord. *"You've got a brother. His name is Abe. He's got to be about fifty-some years old by now..."*

"Not sure I'm right about that. Anyhow, we can pull whatever the year is and run your chemistry panels for the remaining collection. If the number is too small, we can expand the criteria from there." Etta ran her finger down the screen, looking for any other salient points she may have glossed over. "Have you already gone to clinical to have your profiles generated? ... Ah, I see here you have. And you're certain you both want to be implanted together? It's quite a lot—to both have infants and be convalescing at the same time," Etta added.

"Oh, yes!" Abby exclaimed. "Same time. We want to experience everything together. We'll have the nanny, too, of course."

"That's what sets The Midwest Center apart," Etta said with a forced smile. "Your nanny will arrive on the first day of your ninth month of pregnancy and will help make certain you and your partner are prepared for the arrival of your children. They'll move with you into the birthing center, and remain there for the duration of your admittance, assisting you and the clinical staff with all your needs. Then they'll stay with you for the first three months at home, and you may opt in on a monthly basis afterwards for up to a full calendar year at no additional cost." Etta recited this by rote. The addition of bespoke nanny services caused Etta to speculate some women opted to continue having children for the federally subsidized in-home nanny services alone.

"When do we start?"

"How about now?" Etta said with her best customer service smile.

She escorted them out of her office and down the hall, past the central atrium with its old, gnarled tree set into a moss-covered floor, evoking the spirit of the Tree of Life, Goddess of the forest and fertility. Its image was used in every one of their marketing brochures.

"We have an experiential demonstration room to orient you to The Midwest Center, as well as what to expect each step of the way throughout the entire process—from today's visit, to implantation, to arrival and delivery," Etta said, guiding them into a darkened room lit only by an array of dimensional media walls synced with vibrant pictures and soothing music. "You can select from a list of available nannies, although we do ask you to choose at least three. The nannies always have a voice in their placements, but we've never had any decline, so really, it's just a formality. The orientation experience is about an hour. By the time it's done, I'll have your options ready, and then we'll send you on your way with your selected donor profiles, so you can take some time to decide."

"And you said there'd be cocktails," Diane added sarcastically.

"Tap the screen on the left," Etta replied.

Seeing Abby was already crying as soon as the music started, and now Diane had a tall, colorful drink in hand, Etta returned to her office, relieved by the quiet prelude before the appointment's end.

In her six years of working as a fertility counselor, not one client had asked for the most recent pater source, the conventional wisdom being, while older specimens could degrade over time, they were thought to be more virile, due to being collected closer to the time when men were still being born, and therefore they raised the probability a male zygote would implant. They never did, but that part was left out of the brochures.

The couple's clinicals and remaining broad spectrum samples populated Etta's fertility dashboard, resulting in thousands of initial potential matches. The sample by year should take the form of a cosine graph, collections being limited in the early years, before taking off in earnest when realization hit across the nations boys were no longer being born. The only way to save humanity was seed propagation. Men took up the banner and did so in earnest—for payment and a quick artificial screw—all in the name of saving the species. It hadn't been a difficult campaign.

The decline in product came as the number of men dwindled, the sources drying up, as it were. Accordingly, there couldn't have been additions to the stores in more than fifty years. This was known. It was taught in school and written in the history books. It was in the brochure.

Etta stared at the screen for a long time. There were 1,776 resulting matching samples. There should have been, at most, a dozen.

"I've got the top ten profiles for you to view," Etta said as the couple settled into their seats. They were thoroughly smitten, holding hands and glowing. Even Diane seemed pleased, her earlier skepticism having been won over by slick marketing and ethereal mood music—and, judging by the slight glassiness of her expression, by cocktails.

"We can't wait for baaaaabies," she said with a momentary sway. Diane clutched her wife's hand in her fist, thumping it down on the desk for emphasis.

Etta leaned forward, whispering conspiratorially, "Margarita?"

"Three," Abby said.

"Well, there's plenty of time to decide on the details, never you mind about it," Etta reassured them. "I'm sending you home with video links to watch—and your baby bundle, of course."

"Baaaaaby ... bundle?" Diane tipped alarmingly to the side. Abby slipped an arm around her shoulder as though putting the moves on a first date in a movie theater.

"It's a starter kit. Prenatal vitamins, some onesies and diapers, and reading material—books on motherhood and body changes. And the bundle is your bassinet for the first weeks."

"Oh! How lovely! Do you see, honey, our first things for the babies?"

Diane leaned over, flat hand clumsily brushing hair from Abby's ear.

"Baaaaay-bies," she whispered.

"We should ... we should probably go." Abby stood up, one arm under Diane's shoulder, the other hand reaching for the baby bundle and tucking it under her other arm.

"Your next appointment is in one week, for you to provide your selection, and then we'll square you up for timing your cycles, okay? And you can take the second bundle then, too."

"Yes, of course. You've been a delight, truly! Looking forward to seeing you again, can't wait, thanks so much, bye bye now!" They quickly shuffled out of Etta's office, Diane bumping into the doorjamb, loudly exclaiming, "Watch out! Baaaaay-bies!"

The other appointments were procedural, as Etta knew they would be—couples who had been through the process before and didn't require much more than a seed source and an implantation date. Etta was fidgety, half wanting them to hurry it along, as much as she wanted to stretch out their time, so there was no choice but to push Carol off to another day and another counselor.

She anticipated the coming encounter: Carol arriving at the door, eager and vulnerable, desperate for a baby—a baby Etta had never wanted—and Etta telling her ... what, exactly? *"Here's your match, now be on your way, I'll be here throughout your experience, and don't forget your baby bundle on your way out"*? Or telling Carol how much it had hurt when she left, that she still wasn't over it, how much she hated Carol for how it felt to be so easily discarded, before stating Carol would never be a good mother, and she felt sorry for any child suffering the fate of being burdened with half her genetics?

Maybe the last one had merit. Etta scrolled through Carol's profile, wondering what her life had been like after, and how Carol would feel finding out Etta had remarried. She switched on the workspace personalization—there hadn't been time earlier—letting woodland sounds and birds and waterfalls accompany the photos from the honeymoon with Kieva, in all her youthful glory. Etta set the photo on the shelf behind the desk, eyeing up the sight line between it and the client's chair.

As she flipped through Carol's information, Etta fixated on the personal details: single *(good)*, aged thirty-eight *(hag)*, two sisters *(trolls)*, income of twenty marks above base wages *(of course, now you're the moneybags)*, working for—

"What the hell, Carol? Why are you working for them and coming here?" Etta muttered out loud.

"Discretion," Carol replied from the doorway, looking over her shoulder and glancing around the waiting area before stepping into Etta's office and closing the door. "And because I've missed you."

6

STIR UP TROUBLE

CAROL WALKED TOWARDS ETTA, stopping abruptly when her eyes settled on one of the honeymoon photos: Kieva in a wet sundress, standing under a waterfall, with Etta's hands resting familiarly on her hips, beaming at each other in a mixture of love and lust. The image faded into a pale pink lotus flower, drawing Carol's attention back to Etta once more.

"I see you didn't waste any time." Carol cocked her head to the side, taking in Etta's blushing face and sly grin. "You always did have a certain charm about you. So, what's the little tart's name?"

Suppressing the need to answer, Etta stood up, reaching across the desk to shake Carol's hand. "I'll be your counselor throughout your experience here at The Midwest Center. Would you like coffee, or tea, perhaps?" *No scones for you*, she thought. Upon being met with no reciprocal response, she gestured for Carol to take a seat.

Etta went through her entire spiel with no more than stony silence from her ex-wife, who was hypnotized by the photos being broadcast over Etta's shoulder.

"... thus increasing your odds of potentially having a male offspring."

"How long's it been?" Carol asked.

"How long has what... Good god, Carol, nearly eight months!"

"I meant, how long has it been since a 'male offspring' has been born?" she said, pantomiming air quotes for emphasis.

"What does it matter? Your supply running out over there? You worried you'll be out of business soon? I suppose a few of your folks will come looking for jobs over here, eh?" Etta said sarcastically. But there was a voice in her thoughts pushing forward, first nagging, then insistent, as though tapping a finger on her forehead to get her to pay attention. The available options for Abby and Diane's source shouldn't have been possible, and yet they were.

"See, now, that's the thing. We're not running out at all. Our numbers are steady. Always have been. Doesn't it make you a little bit curious?"

Curious or not, Etta wasn't about to concede anything— not to Carol. "Governing Council doles out of the central stores to you, just the same as us. There's no conspiracy. You gone soft-headed without me around? Besides, isn't your sister some important—"

"There are rumors, Etta, some coming all the way down from the top. And people are starting to do more than just talk about it."

"There have always been rumors. Don't go on telling me now that you've been suckered into believing them."

Carol looked at Etta long and hard, her hands clasped, thumb tapping away like she always did when she was agitated. Etta knew all her signs, and all her buttons.

"Well, I suppose you always have been prone to believe those kinds of things," Etta said, voice remarkably controlled, despite the thrum of blood coursing through her veins so hard it made her heart stutter. "Understandable, without anyone around to talk sense into you. Easy for your imagination to have gone running off, wild with nonsense—so much so, you thought you could just show up here and stir up trouble. You may as well go on home. I won't help you drive down that road. You can do that just fine all by yourself. Alone. Like you wanted."

Etta got up from behind the desk, angling toward the door to send Carol on her way. Carol grabbed her arm, roughly pulling Etta toward her. Her hands were around Etta's waist, in her hair, her scent familiar. Mouth warm, searching. They were pressed against the wall, anxious and angry, and Etta could not stand it as much as she could not bear to resist. And then they were apart, just as soon as they'd started, breathing hard, studying the floor.

"Those boots new?" Carol asked, breath coming in rasps.

"On sale," Etta said.

Their eyes ventured to look at each other's, and just as quickly returned to the floor, the chair, the walls. The photos. Kieva smiling from beneath her sunhat.

"You should go."

"It's obvious you've missed me, too," Carol said.

"You really should go."

"I need your help." Carol touched Etta's hand, twining their fingers together. "You're better at this than I am. You always were smarter. Just help me find out a few things. That's all I'm asking."

"That's not all you're asking, and you damn well know it. Fucking hell, Carol! Why'd you think you could just show up like this? Go on, get out."

"There's talk of men being hidden down valley. We just need more information, to compare what we know with what you do. You don't have to be any more part of it, if you don't want to. Just help us get a little more data. It's all I'm asking." She squeezed Etta's hand, then inched closer, until their bodies were touching. Carol ran a hand down Etta's cheek, cupping her chin and drawing her lips close. "Please help me," she whispered.

Etta closed her eyes, sighing as her back pushed against the wall, shaking her head. "Goddamn you, Carol."

The door clicked quietly shut as Etta walked into her apartment, sliding off her shoes in the vestibule and shoving them under the bench. The glow of the living room lamp illuminated her wife, knees tucked up beneath her on the couch with an old chenille blanket draped across her legs. Their rotund gray cat was snoring. Kieva barely looked up from her book when Etta walked in.

"Long day?"

"Sorry. Yeah. Last appointment was more ... more than I expected," Etta said.

"Dinner's in the fridge. Zucchini casserole," Kieva said, absently stroking the cat, the thrumming of his contentment plain.

"Please tell me you're kidding."

"I never kid about zucchini."

Etta grabbed a plate, then slammed the cabinet shut, regretting it as soon as the noise ricocheted across the living room.

Kieva looked up from her book, letting it fall into her lap, much to the displeasure of Eeyore. "Didn't realize you hated casserole enough to go around slamming things. I'd have told Jill to keep her garden fixin's if I'd known."

"The zucchini is fine. Never mind. I'm fine. Just a bit out of sorts," Etta said, pulling silverware out of the kitchen island drawer and laying it quietly on the counter. "And don't go on worrying and asking me questions. It's fine."

"Well ,obviously it ain't, or else you wouldn't be goin' on saying you're so fine. You can keep it to yourself this time. I won't pry." Kieva picked her book tablet up, apologizing to the cat, who had dejectedly wandered off.

"Wait... Minnie Mouse came here?"

"The one and only, yes," Kieva replied. "Said you'd forgotten something important, and she wanted to make sure you didn't go without. She was quite adamant about it, too. I wasn't asking particulars, so I took it from her, and off she went, happy as a peach."

"Goddammit," Etta muttered.

Kieva plunked down her book again and sighed, long and loud. "So, what is it: work, Jill, or zucchini?"

"Yes. All of it. But at least I didn't have to carry the damn thing home. No, it's just—"

"An all-out vegetable war? Got it. Well, we got about a thousand cherry tomatoes in the roof garden. Can't eat them all, and I ain't peeling them bitty things just for sauce. Bet you could line up an entire tomato army on y'all's desk, if you're planning on being vengeful about it."

"Maybe."

"What? Is that not ... ap-*peel*-ing to you?"

"No, Kieva, don't start—"

"Hold on a minute and let me think about it, so I can *ketch-up*."

"Oh my god, Kieva, please stop..."

"I know. I shouldn't get *saucy* with you. In *Heinz* sight, I'm guessing I shouldn't have brought it up. Just always remember, I love you, from my head ... *to-ma-toes*."

Etta stood there in the kitchen, head hanging in resignation. Kieva erupted into a fit of laughter, unable to go on, body shaking so hard tea spilled onto the chenille.

Forgoing the casserole dish heaping with cheese and vegetables, Etta poured herself a dose of whiskey instead. She sat down near Kieva, clutching the glass with both hands, staring into it as though the answers to all of life's mysteries were contained within its soothing amber-hued depths. Taking a long drink, Etta dove straight in without a word of warning. "When you were growing up, still in school, what did they tell you about the last generation of men? I mean, what do you remember, really?"

Kieva nearly dropped her tea this time, jaw gaping open, making it much easier for the string of quiet curses to tumble out of her mouth. The chenille was soaked by now, and she tossed it on the floor before regarding Etta with a fixed stare.

"What do I rem... What do I remember? About what? This about your mama's letter, about some brother she says you have?"

"Maybe. Not really. Oh, hell, I don't know, Kieva! It's just, things don't make sense. There was a couple in today, asking for the last year of collections, and when I pulled the data—the numbers, they just don't add up. And then my last appointment, when..." Etta's face flushed hot, and she quickly took another drink of whiskey, the scent of it like consuming smoky earth, warming her throat.

"Men ain't real," Kieva said. "Never saw one. They're just stories in the history books. It ain't real life. As far as I know, all that stuff in the seed vault y'all sell is just something they make in the lab. Whatever it is, Etta, it don't matter to me, and I don't think much about it—and neither should you. So, you gonna tell me—for real—what's got you all riled up?"

"They didn't teach you about men at that fancy forestry school you went to?" Etta asked sarcastically. "Well, I've seen the profiles of thousands of men. Seen their faces, the damn movies, heard their voices. And I know they died out, and we all know why. But I'm telling you, Kieva, something doesn't make sense to me. And then when the ... when the last appointment came in today, saying there were rumors of men down the valley, well..."

"You have got to be kidding me." Kieva reached over and grabbed Etta's whiskey glass, throwing back the rest of it, eyes watering as she coughed and wheezed. "Fucking peat. The hell—how can anyone drink that?"

"Never mind the whiskey, Kieva. I have to go find my brother."

7

WHAT ABOUT YOUR GODDAMN EGGS?

THE FREEDOM WOMEN, AS they styled themselves, had been gathering near the middle valley for weeks. A camp had formed off the riverbanks, eventually stretching all the way to the edge of the timberlands, with a few more sites scattered beneath the trees.

Noemi had arrived the night prior on the midnight monorail, walking the last three kilometers along a road illuminated by the night sky and a waxing moon. She wasn't alone. There were others, following a horde of beleaguered women toward the same destination. Some were there to join in whatever imaginary rebellion was brewing. But a few, like Noemi, had come in search of their wives, sisters, or daughters, there to beg them to see reason and compel them to come home—or drag them, if need be.

It had been too dark to search for Rosena when she arrived. Noemi had tried, walking along the disordered pathways of the camp, but she'd tripped over one too many legs, kicked too many pots, and been sworn at when she'd toppled a poorly erected tent. Noemi was surprised the inhabitant hadn't attacked her. She finally settled on a bed of pine needles against a tree at the edge of the clearing, stuffing herself into an old raggedy sleeping bag Stella had used for slumber parties. The bag was entirely inadequate for anything more than sleeping on a thermal floor. But she was too exhausted to bother and had fallen asleep with no more than a lingering thought, wondering if Stella would survive the oppressive coddling of her overbearing grandmother. Noemi's mother never missed an opportunity to remind them that they didn't visit enough, and she was likely to take it out on her granddaughter by means of ice cream and bread pudding.

The scent of pellet fires and solar cookstoves wafted across the meadows, and Noemi's stomach growled in complaint before she'd even opened her eyes. She groaned as she sat up, her body protesting after having spent a fitful night shivering. Everything hurt, and she was queasy, tremors coursing through her body as she sat propped against the tree. Orange, green, and blue tents dotted the ground under the neat rows of tall pines behind her, while an array of canvas and nylon spread out across the meadow below for a quarter mile. Noemi couldn't have imagined so many would come—and more were still coming.

And it was all her fault. She'd started it with that damnable letter.

Noemi rifled through her pack, shaking, casting aside smashed protein bars and a half-empty water bottle. A hoodie, mittens, and a toothbrush were flung out on the ground before she found it, shoved to the bottom of her things and wrapped in one of Rosena's shirts.

Not even a day, Noemi thought, while unscrewing the cap on her flask and taking a long, soothing drink, then one more for good luck. Shoving it back into her pack, she briefly considered pouring the rest of it out, then thought better of it. Though she was not partial to rum, wine in a flask seemed like a sacrilege, and rum would—*should*—last longer.

The sleeping bag was damp from the morning, but Noemi rolled it up anyhow, dumping the rest of the stuff in her bag and hoisting it onto her back with a grunt. She'd managed four days off work, trading shifts and backloading her schedule to work a few twelves in a row when she returned. It was enough time for a day to get there, one day to find her daughter, one day to get home, and one extra day, just in case. She needed to find Rosena and get the hell out of here. She needed to go home in time to spare Stella from her grandmother enticing her to spend entire days in pajamas, eating cake for dinner while watching cartoons on a loop.

Noemi was sure her sister, Jayne, would be in the thick of things. After all, she was the holder of evidence. The letter was her key to prominence. Noemi would throttle her sister when she found her, but would leave enough air in her lungs for her to apologize for being an idiot, so Jayne could tell Noemi where Rosena was. And then Noemi would find her daughter and throttle her, too.

The epicenter of the camp was likely somewhere along the midline. The first arrivals would have wanted to be nearest the action, the later arrivals expanding concentrically from there. Find the hub, and Jayne would be nearby. Noemi traversed the forest edge, trampling pinecones along the way, their crushed scales smelling pleasantly of turpentine, clearing her mind as much as her sinuses. She began weaving a path through the melee of a waking camp, bodies emerging from tents bleary-eyed and stretching, others still strewn on the ground, curled up in blankets and sleeping bags.

A few resilient women were already sipping coffee from the relative comfort of their camp chairs, hands gripping the ceramic mugs reverently, sleepy faces hovering over the steam. Most of them were young, barely in their twenties. They seemed like disaffected youth looking for purpose and notoriety and were willing to latch onto any agenda offering it. All that mattered to Noemi was finding her daughter before the shift of youthful motivation turned in on itself, or was redirected towards the capital when no better distraction could be found. Energy always needed to be expended somewhere. Their course was bound to veer into the unexpected. Large gatherings without purpose would soon find one, whether real or imagined.

"Have you seen her?" Noemi asked, holding out Rosena's image to a girl who appeared to be close in age. "She's about your height?"

"No, ma'am." The girl shook her head, pointing south along the river. "But if you go to headquarters, someone's bound to. They know everyone."

"Thanks," Noemi mumbled. They had *headquarters*? So, they were *organized* disaffected youth.

While she kept half an eye out for her daughter, it was unlikely to see Rosena up and about before noon. That child could sleep until supper and still wake up fit to fight about it. There was more activity the further in Noemi went, progress slowing due to the sheer volume of riffraff dotting the ground, with people ducking in and out of their tents, causing her to collide with one woman hip bone to forehead.

"Oh! God almighty, that hurt!" Noemi said, rubbing her hip while the other woman stayed bent over, hand to her head and eyes shut tight as a string of profanities greeted her.

"Are you alright? Stand up, let me look at it. My name's Noemi. I'm a nurse."

"You got some damn pointy bones," the woman said, face scrunched up tight. She stuck out her hand. "I'm Kieva."

Noemi steadied the woman upright. There was already a lump forming on her head, the skin discolored and raised, but she was otherwise fine. She was a pretty thing, with the sort of sweet expression that could make a person smile without meaning to.

"Well, Kieva, it's a bit of a knock, and you won't like it much later, but some butterbur ought to settle it some," Noemi suggested.

"To be honest, I don't much like how it feels now," Kieva said, pressing the palm of her hand to her forehead. "And I hadn't a mind to pack herbals. But headquarters ought to have something for it."

"Are you heading over there now? Can I tag along? See, I just arrived last night, and I haven't quite gotten my bearings."

"Long as you promise not to hip-check me again, I don't mind. Best we get going anyway, afore this rabble wakes up. Get there early enough, and we might still get some pancakes," Kieva said.

"They feed this whole lot?"

"Maybe not all, but a fair number, yeah," Kieva replied. "Some of them's no more than kids. They couldn't pack enough food in themselves if they were staying a while, you know? Besides, it's hard to get them to do what they're supposed to if they're always hungry. Gotta feed them if you want 'em to follow orders."

It was beginning to sound like more than just a protest. Noemi wanted no part of it. But she figured if they all went there to eat, then it would be much easier to find Rosena—so long as the kid got out of bed for breakfast.

Noemi fell in step behind Kieva, and they quickly found themselves at a large open-air mess, with makeshift tables made of boards propped on buckets, lined up row after row. There were already several people there, sitting on the ground cross-legged as they scooped up eggs and pancakes being doled out by a woman who looked none too pleased about it. Kieva waved to her, and for a moment, the woman's face lit up, until someone stuck out their plate for more.

"You say you're a nurse?" Kieva asked. "We got a clinic, just no one decent to know what to do with it. One of them's even a veterinarian."

"All these people, and no doctor?"

"Aww, well. Yeah, we got one. But she's old. Like, *old*-old. I don't even know if she's sure of where she's at. Her hands shake real bad, too. Most of them..." Kieva said, gesturing with a sweeping hand. "Well, they just kids."

"Why not send them all home? I mean, what on earth do you think is going to happen here, anyway?"

"The ones that ain't kids, and the ones that ain't us—that's my wife." She nodded to the woman doling out eggs. "Well, truth be told, they be a bit fanatical. Saying there's saviors in this valley needing to be freed, others holding vigils and the like, where they all be prayin' and swayin' like they mean to call the Rapture. We can keep the rest safe enough, have things orderly, you know? Keep it all from going off the rails, and keep those girls from getting into too much trouble. You hungry?"

"Haven't eaten since yesterday afternoon, and all I've got in my bag is a crushed chia seed bar and some rum," Noemi said.

Kieva looked like a turtle who had just eaten a lemon, scrunching up her face and shaking her head, lips drawn into a puckered grimace.

"They say rum goes with everything." Noemi shrugged.

They sat down on the ground in front of a makeshift table, and coffee appeared as if by magic, handed down by the ornery woman Kieva had declared was her wife.

"There's no tea," the woman stated flatly, setting the carafe down and crossing her arms defensively. "So don't ask."

"You're chipper this morning," Kieva said cheerily, not put off by the woman's impressive glare. "Etta, meet Noemi. All she's got to eat is some bitty seeds and rum. We're hoping you might do better."

"Best keep the alcohol, you'll need it," Etta said, nodding at the earthenware mugs as though they needed it *now*. Noemi thought she might be right.

"And waitress," Kieva said in a high-society voice, grinning wildly, "we'd like a mushroom quiche—Noemi, do you like mushrooms? And fresh-squeezed orange juice—oh, make it grapefruit, and maybe a muffin if you don't mind, but only if they're cinnamon and still warm." Then she gave the coffee mug a little push.

"And some Earl Grey." She pressed her hands together as though in prayer. "Please."

"Does this look like a café to you? You know as well as I do, we ran out of tea two weeks ago. And if we stay here much longer, we'll all be stuck with nothing more than chicory. Now quit fussing, and I'll bring you some damn eggs."

Kieva opened her mouth in ready protest, but it was quickly clamped shut when Etta held up her index finger and shook it, just once, before turning around and walking away.

"She seems nice," Noemi said with a speculative glance.

"Ah, well. She is, actually," Kieva said, adding, "I mean, not really. But I love her anyway."

"How'd you two get mixed up in all this? I mean, no offense, but you don't seem the type, and your wife, Etta... Well, she doesn't seem so happy being here, you know?"

There was a sudden shift between them, Kieva's body becoming subtly rigid, her eyes diverting to scan the crowd, as if wary of eavesdroppers. Noemi leaned in to hear whatever sordid story was about to be presented, their shoulders nearly touching. She could almost feel Kieva shudder, as though shaking off whatever was diverting her thoughts.

"Long story," she said softly, adding with a shallow smile, "but we're in it now. No going back. How 'bout you?"

Noemi took a deep breath, refraining from blurting out, *It's all my fault. I'm the reason all of this is happening, the reason all of you are here.* Instead, she offered a simple but honest reply. "My daughter, Rosena. She's sixteen." She dug into her pocket, pulling out the image card and passing it over to Kieva. "I don't suppose you've seen her, have you? I'd hoped she be here, at breakfast. But see, that kid, she never gets up before noon, so I figure I'll wait here a while and just—"

"I know her." Kieva shot up from the ground, whirling around, glancing over the growing crowd of arrivals, and started walking quickly towards a large tent near the river. "Come with me," she shouted back over her shoulder.

The invitation was unnecessary; Noemi was on her feet the second "I know her" reached her ears. She was nearly stepping on Kieva's heels, with Etta's shouts in the background falling on deaf ears.

"What about your goddamn eggs?!"

The tent was obviously the clinic, if not judging by the disorder, then by the stench. There were mounds of used linens, pails filled to the brim with a stew of questionable fluids, and a doddering old woman in the middle of it all, holding an injection pump and seeming surprised to see it in her hands.

"Your daughter comes here, to help out," Kieva said as they surveyed the scene. "Every morning, right at sunup. Sometimes before... Are you alright?"

"Our children are never who they truly are when they're at home with us, you know?" Noemi's arms flailed about, waving around her head as though electrified. "It's our fault they aren't who they're meant to be, because we smother them with our own doubts." Noemi spun around like a top. "Where is she? I don't see her."

They wound their way down the center aisle, around the stout pole holding the tent up, until they were squared up in front of the physician. She was a round woman with a shock of white hair and a face that bore a history of sadness within its deep-set wrinkles and down-turned mouth. She peered at them over glasses that had slipped halfway down her nose.

"There you are, my dear! Wasn't expecting you. Things are piling up. Come now, get to it," the woman said, with a brusque cluck of her tongue at them both.

"Marta, it's me, Kieva. And this is Noemi. She's looking for her daughter. You know her." She pushed Rosena's picture in front of the old woman, who reached out with gnarled fingers, trembling just a little as she held the image a few inches from the tip of her chin.

"Oh, Rosie? Sweet girl. Hard worker. Carol took her. A shame—I needed her today, too," she said, and turned to leave.

"Took her where?" Noemi grabbed the woman's arm, hard.

"Scouting," Marta said, pulling away with a frown.

Noemi's stomach turned, and she instantly broke out in a cold sweat. She looked at both women expectantly, voice wavering. "Scouting for what?"

"For where the men are hidden. Scouting parties have been going out daily since we arrived," Kieva said, then turned to the doctor. "You shouldn't have let her go, Marta. Why'd you let Carol take that girl?"

"You know how the woman is, Kieva. Won't listen. Won't take no from no one. Carol waltzed through headquarters, calling for volunteers—saying it was for the vanguard—yelling she was recruiting only the best, and being part of it was an honor. Me telling Rosie to stay wasn't going to make her stay when all I got to offer is this." Marta gestured to their surroundings with a sweeping motion of her arm, triceps wobbling like a turkey wattle. "Now, unless you plan on making yourselves useful—get out. You can see plain as day I got things to do."

"Calling for a vanguard isn't a scouting mission," Kieva said. "Etta know about this?"

"Suppose she does by now. Etta was on resupply when it all went down. They'd gone by the time she came back. Nothin' she could do about it either. Can't talk sense into someone who ain't here. Gone is gone."

"Where did they go?" Noemi grabbed hold of the old woman's shoulder, pleading. "Tell me which way?"

Marta looked at her a long while, then reached out and pulled Noemi's chin forward with a thumb and forefinger, staring for a moment and frowning before letting go.

"Best you stay here," she said. "We don't have any liquor in the camp. You won't last long traipsing through the woods."

The woods. There was the river to the west, Noemi had come through grasslands to the south, and she'd slept in the timberland to the east. If they were going through woodlands, they would have to have gone north. "Never you mind. I'm fine. I'm a nurse, and she's my daughter. I have to find her."

"If you're a nurse, you'd be more use here—"

"I don't care about anyone here!" Noemi shouted, stamping a foot with clenched fists as she stepped back, turning to go.

An all-too-familiar voice chimed in from behind her. "Not even your sister?"

It had always been the smirk Jayne wore. Noemi could hear it blind, no matter the addition of her sister's provocative tone, that pure confidence bolstering whatever contrary position she had taken. Because even if they both saw the same blue sky, Jayne would always, *always* argue it was something else, just for the joy of the torment.

And Noemi was not having it. Not today. For fuck's sake, not *any* day.

Noemi leapt straight for her, hands around Jayne's neck without hesitation. They tumbled to the plywood floor in a heap, kicking over buckets of effluent and medical waste, thrashing around, falling over each other. Noemi gasped as a knee went into her stomach, once, twice, and again. Her sister was never one to go down easy. There was a loud smash, then the sound of reverberating metal, Noemi's eyes fuzzy and burning. Jayne was pulling her hair. Noemi's knee went into her chest, pushing her sister's face into the ground. She was dragged off her spitting and screaming, Noemi's arms held firmly behind her back.

Her head was throbbing, and she couldn't see, but Noemi could hear her sister laughing. She lashed out at the sound, trying to wipe her eyes of the sweat, but blinding pain stopped her as she was set down on the ground, Marta's voice hovering over her.

"Sit still and let me look."

Gauze was pushed against her brow, then Marta took Noemi's hand and pressed it over her eye. "Hold it while I get my suture kit. And don't you move."

Noemi was shaking all over. Her adrenaline was pumping like a freight train, her body surely thinking it was time to slay a locomotive beast. Or her sister.

"Tell me you didn't bring Stella with you," Jayne said sharply.

"Of course I didn't bring her! She's with Mother, being spoiled to pieces. Stella will be fine there for a few days—"

"A few days? Did you really think you could just waltz in here and take over it all? That we'd both just stop what we were doing, walk away from what we've committed to, and follow you home like dogs?"

"For god's sake, Jayne, she's *sixteen*! Sixteen. What were you thinking?" Noemi let go of the gauze, startled to see the square was crimson from corner to corner. Other people's blood didn't bother Noemi, but her own blood did. She toddled to her feet, grasping for purchase on the footboard Jayne was leaning against, her vision going black at the corners. Then she was down on the ground again without meaning to be, next to Jayne, grabbing hold as she began to tip over.

"You don't listen, do you?" Marta said brusquely, crouching slowly down on her knees in front of Noemi. "Nurses never do. Stop it. You're not invincible." She set down a medical caddy, plucking out another wad of gauze to stem the bleeding, which had begun dripping onto Noemi's clothes.

"Our mother always said I was the good one," Jayne said, taking her sister's free hand and holding tight. "Don't die on me. I don't want to lose my status as the favorite to a martyr. Although, I suppose if I was her *only* daughter, I'd win by default. But don't die anyway."

"Shut up. I'm not dying. It's just a cut. You're always so melodramatic. You'd probably show up at my funeral decked out in black, veil and all, the murderess," Noemi said, voice going hoarse. Eyes closed, she leaned against Jayne. It was all going to be fine, just as soon as she could get out of this godforsaken tent and find Rosena.

Marta's hand pushed against her forehead. "This will hurt."

The old woman sprayed alcohol wash directly into the wound, flushing out the grit with a vigor that seemed a bit unnecessarily enthusiastic. Noemi hissed through clenched teeth as the sutures went in, each perforation tugging at the skin as though it were being stretched and plucked, like a drunken quilter had gotten hold of her. Marta was leaning inches away from Noemi, eyes squinting behind thick clinical bifocals.

That's what it is. Noemi sniffed. *Marta's a drinker, too.*

"Folks don't usually grin when I'm poking holes in them," Marta said, pausing mid-stitch. "You going to pass out on me?"

"Takes one to know one." Noemi opened one eye, fixing her gaze on the magnified eyeball staring back at her. "You drinking wound wash, or you got something better?"

Marta's hand paused in midair, the needle trembling slightly as the silk went taut. Looking down her nose, she clucked quietly and tied the last one. "Aquavit. Looks like water, so most don't think anything of it," she said under her breath, adding, "Twenty-three. That's how many stitches to sew you up. In case you're wondering."

"It doesn't matter. Thanks though." Noemi turned toward her sister, whose expression offered a degree of remorse. "You can look sad and pathetic all you like. I'm staying mad at you. Might smother you in your sleep. But if you help me find Ro, I won't tell Mother what you made me do."

Her sister shuddered. They were full-grown adults—old enough to have stopped telling on each other. But while their mother took grandma duties to a preposterous level, such kindnesses didn't extend to her own daughters. When they were children, she'd smack them with wooden kitchen spoons when they misbehaved. One time, Noemi had taken all the wooden spoons and buried them in the yard. Their mother didn't waver; she used a metal spatula instead. They'd always been afraid of their mother, and would be until she was ash on the wind—and probably even then. Some things didn't change with time or death.

"Come on, then, ya snitch." Jayne stood up, extending a hand. "I'm a heavy sleeper. It'd be too easy for you."

They gave their apologies and farewells to Marta, offering false promises to return and help clean up, their boots sticking to the plywood floor as they walked outside. Kieva had disappeared sometime during the melee, but neither had noticed. They found her outside, going at it with her wife, fists clenched at her sides. Even from where Noemi was standing, it was obvious whatever was going on between the two women wasn't nothing. It didn't matter though, for the mood of the gathering crowd of curious onlookers was drawn to what was coming down the hill.

It was a gang of girls, whooping and hollering like banshees, the lot of them screaming at the top of their lungs.

"Men! There're men! We found them!"

8

The Promise of Violence

"We will return to the righteous ways! We will find these men and consecrate our unions as nature desires, and sons will be born again, and we will all be saved! The Governing Council has kept this secret for fifty years—kept fathers and brothers from us. We will find them! We will free them! And we will take them back!"

The woman's voice rang out from her makeshift pulpit across the crowd of women who had joined up, some two thousand strong and growing. Word had been spreading, and more were coming every day, the encampment overflowing until it was determined there was need for another, and work had begun across the river. Timberers had erected a crude bridge to link them, and a rainbow of prayer flags had been tied to the railings, spiritual pleas to return the men they'd never known.

Etta didn't know how they were going to feed them all. She'd been stirring a pot of porridge for the better part of a quarter hour when Kieva walked up, peering into the oat stew with a raised brow and a grimace.

"Makin' oat paste? Looks like you could mortar brick with that schlop," Kieva said.

There was an odd calm about her, and Etta's hands immediately went clammy. "Never you mind, and keep your voice down, 'cause this schlop is getting served to whatever poor souls slept in and missed breakfast," Etta muttered. She turned to go, the barrel of porridge held in the crook of her arm, when Kieva's voice stopped her cold.

"What is it between Carol and you? What's she got over you that you just let her do whatever the hell she wants?"

"Nothing. There's nothing, Kieva." But Etta's reply was so rushed, she didn't even believe herself.

"I'm only giving you the once," Kieva whispered. "I'm your wife. Not Carol."

The metal ladle clamored against the side of the pot when Etta dropped it onto the grill, the sound of it unsettling her nerves more than they already were. "Kieva, I don't know what you—"

"Don't you say it, Etta. If you do, you'd be lying to me—and you'd best never be lying to me, understand? She *was* your wife." Kieva stood close, hands on her hips, a spring of hair escaping from its tie and wisping across the bridge of her nose. "I'll give you a pass on whatever the hell's been going on between you, just this once. But that's it. No more. You're with me now. I don't want to see anything. I don't want to hear anything. Not one single damn thing. You got me? We're seeing all these girls safe, and then we're goin' home. I said what I gotta say, and now I'm done with it. It's yours now. Sort it out."

"Kieva, doll, it's nothing, really," Etta said. "It's just weird with Carol is all, having her be here and whatnot. You're going on about it for nothing."

"Don't call me 'doll.' And you know plain I don't hold grudges. Once I tell you I'm mad, I'm done bein' mad, 'cause I gave all the mad to you. But if I have to come back and be mad again, then that's all you're getting from me, and the last you'll know of it, too. Nothing good comes after that." Kieva's hands had closed into fists, her stance wide, daring Etta to say another word.

The chatter around them had subsided to murmurs. They'd become a spectacle.

Or not. There was a collective shift as everyone's faces turned towards the forest to the north as twenty girls emerged from the trees, running and shouting, looking like a herd of fillies galloping across a hilltop in springtime. Everyone started moving towards them, tentatively at first, unsure whether the returning girls were running away from something, until they heard gleeful shouts and saw the looks of victory as the vanguard returned.

They'd found them.

Etta raced through the crowd, pushing past until she was in the open. She had to know, had to hear it first. Was it true? Had they found them? Were they alive? Was her brother there? She locked eyes on Carol, who'd spotted her, too. They nearly ran smack into each other, Carol hugging her tight just long enough to catch a breath.

"We found them! They're right where she said they'd be," Carol said, nearly bursting with excitement.

"Right where who said—"

"Your brother is there, Etta, I'm sure of it!" Carol said in a rush, holding Etta's face between her hands and kissing her.

It was so familiar, and Etta was drawn in, the rush of excitement and fear rolled up into a ball of hope and desire, only too late realizing her mistake. She knew before she even turned around that Kieva would be there. She put her hands against Carol's chest, pushing hard and shouting, "Stop!" Etta didn't turn around—couldn't turn around to see Kieva's face, filled with hate or despair or something in between. Instead, Etta took a step back and walked away, hoping that would be enough.

Etta walked the camp for almost an hour. Thoughts of men, her brother, Carol... Who had she been referring to—*who* knew they'd be there? That and the image of Kieva were all swirling around in her head, clamoring for attention. As much as she wanted to ask Carol every little thing—to find out where they were, what they looked like, and what on earth they were going to do about it—Etta determined the men could bide a minute or ten more, because Kieva wouldn't bide at all.

It really wasn't a big deal. It was all just a misunderstanding. These thoughts rattled around Etta's mind, and she wondered who she was trying to convince. Kieva just needed a little time to cool off, to not get caught up in an emotional moment.

The valley was beautiful, bordered by forested hills, the trees gilded with the first touches of autumn. Parts of the basin were covered in swaths of goldenrod in full bloom, and the birds were in constant chatter, fattening themselves for winter. Etta wanted to do the same, to gorge on cheese and bread and chocolate until she was too fat to think straight, and happier for it. She had been living on poor culinary offerings at the camp long enough; her thighs could stand a bit of indulgence. She ached for home and Thai food. She missed Eeyore. She could hear his pleas for help in her head. He'd never managed a proper meow, just a plaintive "mwat." The poor thing had been left with the neighbors and their rapscallion children. They were probably dressing him in doll's clothes by now. She never should have left Eeyore there. She never should have left at all.

Etta stopped at the creek, sitting down on a boulder and listening to the water babbling beneath her feet, letting the guilt of everyone she'd ever disappointed wash over her. Kieva had become her soul partner. She tolerated Etta's foibles and quirks, seeing past them if they didn't matter, but holding her to account if they did. Kieva made her try harder—at everything—not because she wasn't good enough, but because Kieva would beam with pride whenever Etta accomplished something of merit.

When she'd been with Carol, it was a battle of never living up to her expectations, no matter how hard she tried. They'd been married for three years the first time Carol had tried to leave. She rolled over in bed one morning and simply said she wanted a divorce. No reason. No warning. Not even a preemptive "Honey, we have to talk." But Etta had convinced her to stay, first by saying it was unfair, then by crying—a lot. The second time came a few years later, when Carol had bought a one-way ticket on the monorail and disappeared for three months. She hadn't called Etta the entire time she was gone—not once. Etta had never been enough for her.

"And never could be," Etta muttered. She stared at the sky, clouds huge and puffy beyond the ridge. Her mind went still, absorbed by the view, the berating voices quieting until there was only silence. Then it vanished in an instant, a sudden unease leaping into her thoughts: if she did not return to her tent, at this very instant, Kieva would be gone, too. She hesitated, dismissing the notion as though she'd been taken by a moment of madness. But her mind wouldn't settle. Etta tried to focus on the boulders in the stream, the eddies spiraling around them, leaves careening atop the clear water like verdant catamarans. She waited no more than a minute before sliding off her sarsen perch and purposefully walking back into the madness.

Etta did not see the collections of tin cans and wiring accumulating in corners, or smell the acrid scent of old explosives on offer, or hear the rising cacophony of women shouting, "Bring me the..." It faded to a buzz, her focus solely on threading her way through it. She rounded the corner, the chartreuse tent she and Kieva had been calling home coming into view. The zipper was undone, the flaps limp. She reached out to push them aside, holding her breath, expecting to find it empty. The door fluttered once, twice before Kieva's head popped out, looking behind her as she dragged her duffel bag over the nylon threshold. She put the bag down and carefully zipped the door shut, turning around just in time to keep from running into Etta.

"Wait—are you... Are you really leaving?"

Kieva offered nothing more than a steely-eyed glance, then picked up the bag and left.

Etta's mouth hung open on a hinge, throat already starting to tighten with the onset of every emotion on offer. She stared after Kieva's retreating form as it disappeared down the next row of tents. She stood there, unsure of what to do, knowing full well she was about to completely lose it. Etta opened the tent and ducked into the diffuse light.

It was a silent, rib-wracking crying—the kind that hurt so much she couldn't breathe. Her hands pushed into her hair, fingers grabbing hold at the roots, body doubling over before she collapsed on the cot, whispering Kieva's name. Their promises to each other had meant nothing.

Etta stayed that way for what seemed like an eternity, erupting into small fits, until she found herself on her knees, forehead to the lumpy floor, unable to catch her breath. Her whole body hurt. She wrestled herself back up onto the cot, staring at the empty space next to her—empty but for a tiny strip of paper, set neatly on the pillow. It was too small to be a note. She picked up the fortune cookie strip with trembling fingers.

The person next to you will be a significant factor in your life in two years.

Without thinking, she grabbed her camp lighter, the flame flickering bright as it singed the words black before setting the note on fire. This brief gratification was immediately replaced by panic as she realized she was in a nylon tent that could be set alight and become a melting deathtrap. Etta shot out the door like a cannonball, dropping the burning bits on the ground just as the flame reached her fingertips. There was probably a message of symbolic fate in there somewhere, but there wasn't time to contemplate it. She was running, head on a swivel, pushing past the women lingering in the aisles, past the latrines, past the clinic, past the kitchen.

Soon, Etta spotted the telltale wild curly hair and orange hoodie of her wife. Kieva's back was to her as she stood outside the large canopy designated as the headquarters. A line of women snaked around the tent, some just on their way in, others leaving with backpacks weighted down, hanging heavy on their shoulders. Kieva shifted—and Carol's face came into view. They were standing there together, talking. Carol wrapped an arm around Kieva like they were old friends, guiding her into the shadowed entrance.

The edges of Etta's vision darkened to red, and her heart began pounding with the promise of violence, intent on meaningful destruction. Hers was a temper buried, created layer upon layer over time, until there was no more room and the stasis erupted and overflowed well beyond the occasion calling it to task.

Only this time ... this time it was right.

"Save it for the field, Etta. We'll need strong women like you. We're leaving in fifteen minutes. Come with us," Carol said, her eyes never leaving Etta's as she reached for the hammer on the table beside her.

Etta was dizzy with adrenaline and indecision. She could only hurl herself at one of them: Carol or Kieva. Her weight shifted between her feet, hands gone clammy, fingertips numb. She took a step.

Carol tipped her head, and three women darted out from the edge of the tent, grabbing hold of Etta's arms, twisting them when she resisted.

"You're a coward." Etta was on her knees. "Both of you are cowards!"

Kieva had begun industriously filling a daypack with supplies. She paused when Etta spoke, then kept on filling it as though not listening. Kieva buckled the canvas lid, slung the bag over her shoulder, and walked out. Again.

There was nothing more maddening than being ignored. Etta strained to gain her feet, arms still held tightly behind her—enough to keep her restrained, but not enough to keep from tipping over. She flailed, feet scraping in the dirt, trying to shake off the women holding her tight, to no avail. Etta's forehead was inches from the ground, one knee beneath her, the other leg shoved out to the side.

Carol's boots appeared beneath her nose. "I won't tolerate squabbling, Etta. Pull yourself together. Remember why we're here. Will you finish what your dying mother asked of you? Or have you forgotten about your brother?"

"Let go of me!"

"Come with us, and do what you're meant to do." Carol held out the hammer as though it were an olive branch for peace. "Free these men, Etta. Free Abe. The Governing Council has no right to keep him from you."

"I'm not going anywhere with you," Etta hissed." Let me go. Now."

"Well, ain't that just a shame. I don't think I could live with myself, knowing I broke a promise to my dead mother and let my brother rot. Or sat here and watched my wife go off to fight battles for me. I'd have to ask myself who's really the coward," Carol clucked with a shake of her head. She bent low, mouth to Etta's ear. "I need to hear you say it, Etta. I need you to tell me you're not going to cause problems."

Etta stared at the neatly laced boots and olive-green pants in front of her. She thought of her mother. She closed her eyes tight and tucked in her chin, then shoved her head hard into Carol's face. There was a white flash of pain behind her eyes and a ringing in her ears. A scuffle of feet, and the tight hold on her arms fell loose. She scrambled to her feet, wrenching free from the stunned woman still holding on. Etta snatched the hammer off the floor, surprised at how easy it felt in her hand.

She crouched down in front of Carol. Both of Carol's hands covered her forehead, one gimlet eye peering up at her.

"I'm not a coward," Etta said.

"Then prove it."

9

Where Common Sense Ought to Be

"There're ladies fighting. Best we get over to the clinic. Marta's probably gonna need help."

Rosena's cold-eyed stare lingered on the stitched-up gash above her mother's eye, but pointedly didn't ask how she'd gotten it. In fact, Rosena hadn't asked anything at all after returning with the vanguard. She'd bounded through the crowd, straight to Jayne, who wrapped her in a gleeful hug, spewing congratulations for being part of the most important discovery in a generation. It was only when the excitement had ebbed that Rosena acknowledged Noemi with a trite "Hello, Mother."

Rosena stood there now, arms crossed, equally expectant and indifferent. Her hair had been neatly braided, skin darkened by the sun, a hint of freckles across the bridge of her nose. She seemed taller than Noemi remembered. It hurt a mother's heart to have a daughter so beautiful and proud, with a hate towards her so plainly worn. It was all Noemi could do to not shake her, scream at her, tell her how stupid it all was. They were all so stupid.

"Aren't you ready to leave, Rosena?" Noemi stuck a spoon into the porridge, and it stood on end before slowly tipping over. Powdered milk and rum were a poor substitute, but Noemi had done her best to amend her breakfast to resemble something palatable, or at the very least, not solid. "As soon as things start to fall apart, folks turn on each other. You've done your share. Leave the politics to the adults." Noemi sat back in the camp chair, balancing the bowl on a knee. "We need to go home and get Stella. I've got to get back to work before I'm fired, if I haven't been already."

"Then go. Me and Auntie Jayne are staying."

"Maybe your mother's right," Jayne said, sheepishly pushing her breakfast around with the end of a spoon. "You'll always be a part of this, Ro; the vanguard who found men decades after the last one disappeared. But Carol says we can't all of us go to free them. It's too many to manage."

"I'm going where you go, Auntie Jayne. No matter what," Rosena said. "I'm not stayin' here like some little kid hoping my mother will come home."

"What the hell do you mean?!" Noemi yelled. "I never—"

"Save your excuses, Mom. I've already heard them all before."

Noemi shot out of her seat and slapped her daughter across the face. She couldn't even tell herself it wasn't intentional. It was. "And now your little sister is hoping you'll come home. Did you ever think of that? Do you think of Stella when you've got us out here in the middle of nowhere, for nothing? I'm not at work. Do you realize we could lose everything—*everything*—because I had to be out here chasing after you?"

"Don't you think you're being a bit harsh?" Jayne stood beside her niece in solidarity—or protection. Rosena's eyes had welled up with tears, stunned, hand held to her reddened cheek.

"A bit harsh? Are you kidding me? If the kid tears up at this, what the hell do you think is going to happen out there—when there's a mob of women clamoring for some ill-conceived dream of lust and glory that doesn't exist? When they're already fighting themselves and haven't even left the godforsaken camp yet? The first hint of men, and we regress to their warring ways. She's just a kid, Jayne, whether you can see it or not."

"I'm sixteen!" Rosena shouted, hands balling up into fists.

"And I'm responsible for you for two more years," Noemi said, voice raised and teetering on the edge of control. "Anything that happens to you is my fault. Any wrongs you commit, I'll be punished for. I'm here to protect you from being stupid. And you are. You are being so, so stupid. It's how I know you're still a goddamn kid. *My* goddamn kid. Now get your stuff. We're leaving."

Noemi didn't wait to watch Rosena go, rounding on Jayne with the full force of everything that had been building up inside her. "If you were smart—and you never have been—but if you decide to start today, you'll leave right now and come with us," Noemi said.

Jayne rolled her eyes mockingly. "I'm not coming with you. And you can save your high-and-mighty lecture."

"So be it. Hope you don't die. And if you're lucky enough to get out of this mess, don't come home. Rosena doesn't need you in her life. You've ruined her enough already."

Jayne laughed, shaking her head, hands on her hips and scuffing the ground with the toe of a boot. She looked up at Noemi, the twisted grin on her face meant to temper the fact she was angry. "Oh, god, Noemi. You're the one who's stupid. Don't you see what happens if we don't do this? All of us will die. Maybe you and I will be lucky enough to keel over from being old. But Ro won't, and Stella definitely won't. They'll never have children, because there won't be anything left to make them with."

"The seed stores are meant to last five hundred years. You've been sold a hoax by a bunch of zealots, Jayne. You've been indoctrinated into a cult And if you can't see it, I can't help you. Now, either go get your stuff and come with me and Rosena today on the afternoon monorail, or don't bother."

Jayne stared at her sister with a mixture of contempt and mockery. "Ro isn't going with you, Noemi. And you're even stupider than you say *I* am if you honestly think she went and got her stuff to go home with you. She's gone. The only way you'll find her is if you come with us."

Noemi ran through the rows of tents, looking for her daughter, begging women to speak up if they'd seen Rosena. Each one politely glanced at the image Noemi held out with a quivering hand, shaking their heads, no. A chill had taken up residence in Noemi's bones, and her clothes were soaked with sweat. She wanted to crawl out of her skin, if only just to make it stop. If she was going to find Rosena, she had to find Marta first.

The was a buzz of activity in the center of the camp. Women were streaming out of the main tent in hordes and starting to gather near the edges, others lining the way, cheering them on. They'd been consumed by madness and whipped into a frenzy of nonsense. Some of them were breaking into song, the grins on their faces ridiculous. Noemi wanted to hurl every one of them into a bottomless abyss, then either bask in the quietness of their sudden departure or follow them into the relief of darkness.

Evidently, Rosena was old enough to know predictability was a trap, because she wasn't among them. But Marta was. Noemi weaved her way through the crowd of remainders, jostled by their enthusiasm and shouts of "Bring our men home!"

Noemi stood next to Marta for what seemed like hours, the ringing in her ears making her dizzy, her mouth dry as cotton. "I need to find my daughter," she said, voice a garbled whisper.

Marta's giant grin quickly diminished into a hard line when she saw Noemi. She didn't hesitate a moment, reaching into the bag at her hip and holding out a water bottle. "Drink this. You need it." The old woman held the bottle to Noemi's mouth, hand cradling the back of Noemi's head as she pressed it to her lips. It tasted like drinking toasted rye bread, the scent of fennel itching her nose, but Noemi didn't care what it tasted like. She took long gulps of Marta's aquavit as though discovering an oasis in a desert.

Marta took it back, taking a swig of it, too, before screwing the cap on and shoving it into her bag. "You're in a right state there, ain'tcha?" She sized Noemi up, not even trying to hide her judgment.

"Have you seen Rosena? Is she with you?"

"Can't say I have. No doubt she'll be in the thick of it though," Marta said, nodding towards the congregating women.

"When I find her, I'm going to wring her stupid skinny neck," Noemi muttered under her breath, while wondering where Marta stashed her supply of alcohol.

"You'll be coming with us, then? Sure could use someone who's not afraid to stick a Band-Aid on a blister. I'd be glad to have you along. Go put together a kit for yourself from the clinic," Marta said. "And don't worry, I've got a spare bottle for you, too. Best hurry now, we'll be heading out soon."

Noemi's mouth opened and closed like a gasping fish. Every fiber of her being said to leave. But just as strongly, the pull every mother had—the one they felt in their womb, in their heart, in the place where common sense ought to be but wasn't—told her to get her daughter, and get her quick.

"I'll come with you, so long as you swear Rosena will be there," Noemi said, hand outstretched—this time steady. "And I'll carry my own damn bottle."

10

No Skin in the Game

THEY'D BEEN WAITING AT the edge of the field for an hour. Everyone was growing restless, but Etta knew something would happen soon. Carol wasn't one to stay idle for long. What was strange was there was no one here—no opposition, no defense systems, not even surveillance drones. There was nothing but a solar light cube next to an immense concrete platform, nearly fifty meters across, but only three meters tall at its highest point. It looked like a giantess had dropped a plate in the grass on her way to a picnic.

There was a structure beneath the dome, and there were men—evidently a lot of them—being kept there in something akin to a concrete cave. Etta wondered if her brother was among them, and whether she would know him by sight, or if he would know his sister. Would he be a monster? What did a person become when shut off from the world for decades? A trickle of sweat ran down Etta's spine.

They had no idea what they would be letting out.

Etta felt like she was in a silent bubble, all the chaos around her fading into nothing, just a fuzzy high-pitched tone in her brain, as though she were standing on a high wire without a net. Her stomach turned over threateningly, her insides congealing like the porridge she'd served at breakfast. Carol was shouting at her army of minions, rallying them forward with a voice-cracking battle cry.

They'd watched a scene together in an archival movie once—a man racing down the front line of a ragtag army, wearing a ferocious glare, daring soldiers to follow him to a certain death, seemingly desperate to meet the Reaper in a defiant and violent end. Etta wondered if that's what this would be: death in battle. She laughed out loud, quickly stifling the outburst with a cough, muttering "sorry" to the queasy-looking woman standing beside her.

The mass of women and girls, most armed with nothing more than their wits and a smattering of sledgehammers, watched Carol with anticipation, their faces transforming from fear to eagerness. They were going to smash their way in. The impact hammer Etta held felt woefully inadequate. The few who'd stated they might be able to improvise explosives had gathered at the periphery. They were weighted down with knapsacks filled with wires and tin cans, some were hauling heavy sledges, others carried buckets of mud clay and crates of old gunpowder from God knew where.

And Kieva was one of them.

They'd marched the three miles to the men's site without acknowledging each other at all. Etta was surprised Kieva had come. This wasn't her cause; Abe wasn't her brother.

"How do we know this is the right place?"

Etta startled at the voice next to her, casting a sideways glance at the long-limbed woman standing there, jittery, eyes darting around incessantly.

"We met. This morning. Name's Noemi," the woman said, introducing herself. She held out a water bottle. "It ain't water."

"You're an angel," Etta said, gladly taking the offering, letting the bite of the alcohol quiet her nerves. "According to her," she said, gesturing towards Carol, "there's a pop-up station just north of here by a service road. The road leads to a campus of secure buildings a few kilometers away. The conjecture is, since we presume the Governing Council is hiding something, and since there's a rumor something's being hidden in these parts, this must be what we're looking for."

Etta handed the bottle back. Noemi drained the rest. It had been full, and Etta had only taken a polite but respectable swig of it.

"So, we're just going to blow shit up and see what happens?"

"Seems like it," Etta said.

Noemi shook her head with a sarcastic grin, sighing as she shrugged off her backpack. It was overflowing with medical supplies, gauze and bandages and wound wash, vials and syringes neatly secured to a parcel of canvas, ready to be rolled out in seconds. "It won't be enough," she said half under her breath.

"You a doctor?"

"Better than that. I'm a nurse." Noemi's eyes skimmed the crowd, settling on a teenager who was the spitting image of her.

"Your daughter?"

"Yeah. At least she hasn't gotten conned into joining up with some rickety bomb squad," Noemi said, squaring up Etta as though sizing up a boxer for a fight. "This is ridiculous, you know. Ridiculous. You seem like a smart woman, Etta. You got no skin in this game. If I were you, when this thing starts, I'd stay at the back of the line."

As though a decision had been made and no one else was the wiser for it, Noemi shrugged her pack over her shoulder. She pulled out the bottle again, unscrewing the cap to throw it back for another drink, frowning when just a few drops fell onto her tongue. She grumbled under her breath, looked Etta fixedly in the eye. "Good luck to ya," she said and walked off.

No skin in the game? I'm the only one here with actual skin in the game, Etta thought to herself. She watched Noemi go, weaving through the melee of musky agitated bodies, arriving beside her daughter. She was a mother desperate to protect her child—but it was too late for a girl that age to listen to her mother.

All at once, the militia started to move en masse. Etta's feet followed of their own accord, shuffling robotically beneath her. She felt everything and nothing. Limbs numb. Skin on fire, prickly and sharp. Sense of focus keen, mind racing, thoughts empty. Onto the concrete, up the low rise, intent on the middle. Trudging upward with the others, unsure of where to begin.

She felt the sound in her chest before the piercing screech hit her ears with pulsating vibration. Her eyes skimmed over the trees, seeing the sound drones, painted black, hovering up among the branches of the pitch pines. So, there *were* security forces, warning them to stay back. Everyone around her crouched down, hands clapped to their heads like muffs, while others frantically pushed things into their ears and then started to run forward, only momentarily deterred.

Etta pulled off her overshirt, doubling it up, tying it around her ears three times over to dampen the sound. It wasn't enough, but it would do. She started to run. The thrum in her chest felt like an extra heart, giant, beating against her. Another barrage—more, louder, higher-pitched. Kieva was beside her, running hard. Etta followed.

The hammerers were across the rise, at the top of the slight dome. Bombers were coming up behind them. Kieva was shoving wires into a can, packets of gunpowder tucked deep inside. Hammerers furiously chipped holes out of the concrete, the bombers shoving their creations in and covering them with a thick layer of mud and a slate over top to direct the blast downward. Others beyond her were doing the same. The vibration of sledges striking concrete rattled Etta's shinbones, hips, and back, ringing through her ears. The pulse waves grew stronger, the drones coming towards them, away from the relative safety of the trees. Rocks and sticks were thrown at the rotors. Someone with a rope tried to lasso one, winging it with a defiant yell when it came crashing to the ground. A smattering of subdued cheers was followed by screams when even stronger pulses hit their bodies. The small sound drones were followed by larger push drones, waves of energy hitting them, freezing them in their tracks, unable to move, like trembling statues.

Kieva lay flat on the ground, still working, desperately trying to get the line to light. Others were doing the same, on their stomachs, with varying sizes of improvised devices in various stages of construction. Other women were on their knees, hammering with great swings of their shoulders. There were makeshift bombs around them everywhere. So many had their lines already lit. One woman had a powder bomb as large as a watermelon. Etta fleetingly wondered where she'd gotten so much ordnance. The woman lit it, running away fast, unwilling to stay and see if it remained lit. It did.

Etta was screaming, grabbing at Kieva to run, pulling her arm. But Kieva was intent on her goal. As she lit the line, the spark finally took the invitation, starting its race to the finish. The first explosions fired off. The women stood up to run, the push drones stopping them cold. Etta's had a fistful of Kieva's bright orange shirt, dragging her to the ground, crawling around the others. Tremors beneath them flowed through their hands, their skin, their body. Detonations went off everywhere.

No way to run.

Kieva was on her knees, bent over, tears spilling down her face, trembling hands over her ears, screaming. Etta wrapped her body around Kieva, holding tight, caressing her face.

"I love you. I love you. I love you..."

She wanted her to know love at the end.

"I love you, Kieva. I love you..."

The last words she would ever hear.

"I love—"

The ground opened up beneath them.
Falling.

11

THE FIRST ONES

NOEMI PUSHED HER WAY through the crowd. Everyone was vying to be on the front line, inexplicably desperate to be the first ones. *The first ones to blow off fingers,* Noemi thought cynically. It was madness—all of it. Her focus never left Rosena. Her daughter was as eager as the next woman, eyes bright, body fidgety. They had to get out of here. They couldn't be a part of this.

"You're going to get these girls hurt, or worse!" she shouted at Marta without preamble. Noemi reached for Rosena's hand, but quickly realized her error. Her daughter wasn't five years old anymore, no longer a child to be reprimanded into submission with a sharp look.

"No, Mother. Stop! I'm part of this now." Rosena crossed her arms, tucking her hands into her elbows so they couldn't be grabbed.

No matter, Noemi thought, and took hold of an arm. "You're coming with me. Right now. Where's your aunt?"

"With the bombers," Marta said.

"Bloody hell," Noemi muttered. To find her sister was to lose her daughter. Jayne was old enough to know better, whether she actually did or not.

"Noemi, we need you here. You see that, don't you? Rosie and I can't manage all of them on our own. There's too many. Stay and help us."

Noemi ignored the old woman. It was all she could do not to shake her daughter, rattle some reason into that damnable teenage brain. "Ro, we have to leave. Right now. You can't handle this."

"No, Mom, *you're* the one who can't handle it," Rosena snapped.

Sighing loudly, Noemi resorted to force, since all sense of reason had evidently been left behind. She grabbed Rosena's shirt collar like a wolf would snatch up a pup by the scruff of its neck. "We're not staying here and getting ourselves killed over some hoax. I don't care what you say or what you think, we're going home. Your sister needs—"

All at once, everyone started pushing forward. Noemi hadn't even heard a command. It was as though the mob had decided they couldn't wait any longer, their hive mind driving them to move of its own accord. Rosena almost broke loose of her mother's grip, intent on following.

"Mother, let go of me! I have to help Marta!"

Marta had already started untying a pack of medical supplies, looking intent on setting up a crude surgery right there in the thick of it all.

"Goddamn it all to hell anyway." Noemi's hand began waving wildly around her head, as if to exorcise the demons compelling her to stay. "If we're going to do this, we fall back. Set up a proper triage." Noemi spun around, looking for level clear ground. "There," she said, pointing to a space up the hill, bounded by a granite tor and a small stream of water trickling off an outcropping and into a cobbled swale. It would have to do.

Rosena was tasked with collecting water, while Noemi started a fire for sterilizing and cautery, if need be. She made a mental inventory while Marta hastily unpacked their medical provisions onto a rock slab. There were only enough supplies for maybe twenty or thirty marginally wounded at best. Her gaze drifted down across the army of women moving toward the concrete platform. The leaders had recruited anyone from the main camp with useful skills, or those too fanatical to stay behind. There were several hundred, at least.

The waiting gnawed at Noemi's nerves. She wondered where her sister was. Jayne always needed to feel important, desperate to be a part of something big. Noemi finally spotted Jayne towards the front, as expected, sporting the lime-green pants she'd "borrowed" three years ago and claimed she'd lost. Jayne was moving quickly, despite being weighed down by an enormous backpack and carrying buckets in both hands. She had enough material to make something happen; that much was obvious.

The woods beyond were empty. Noemi kept waiting for an armed guard to appear, some indication the Governing Council wasn't going to let a ragtag group of women just show up and steal their secret stash of men. But there hadn't been any indication of resistance—no guards, no fences, nothing at all. It couldn't be that easy. Maybe they were in the wrong place. Maybe the concrete thing, whatever it was, wasn't anything but a remnant of another time, some forgotten installation.

All at once, every single one of the women near the slab structure dropped to the ground. Marta was shouting at everyone to get down. Noemi was already sprawled over top of Rosena, her hands over her daughter's ears, when the sound blast reached them.

Marta appeared beside them, lips moving, but no sound came out. The woman spoke more urgently, face pinched, eyes magnified behind her thick glasses, imploring her to do something, shaking an outstretched fist at Noemi.

Ear plugs. She had ear plugs.

Noemi shifted her weight off her daughter, pulling Rosena's hair back and stuffing the pink foam into her ears.

"You're alright," she said, dusting the dirt off Rosena's clothes. "Are you okay? You're alright. Let me see you." Noemi squeezed her daughter's arms, checked her pupils, then held her wrists. Rosena's pulse was going like a hammer, strong and reassuring. "You're alright. Let's go. We're going home."

Rosena stared at her blankly, shaking her head once. "No." She jutted her chin over her mother's shoulder. *"They need us,"* she mouthed.

Women were coming towards them, some in a hurry, others barely able to walk, hands over their ears and wincing in pain. Another approached with a blackened hand, fingers charred. A bomber too eager had set herself on fire.

Noemi was instantly duty-bound to comfort and care for them. It was as though another person existed within her body, telling the other version of herself to go over there, sit down, and shut up.

The air was buzzing loudly, and Noemi shook her head to be rid of it. She guided the burned woman to sit on a boulder, making a quick assessment. "Don't worry, I'll take care of you. You're alright. My name is Noemi. What's your name?"

"Emma."

"Okay, Amy, sit tight. I'll take good care of you." Noemi's voice sounded tinny and distant inside her head, a high pitch whining incessantly in her ears. She opened her mouth as though to yawn, hoping to equalize the pressure.

"It's Emma," the girl said again. "Em—ma."

Noemi gently pulled back the girl's sleeve, the edges of the flannel like cinders crumbling to dust. "Ro! Bring me water!" she called over her shoulder, then turned back to her patient. "Here, take these, for the pain that comes later," she said, practically pushing the hydrocodone into the girl's mouth.

"Hurts plenty already," Emma said, swallowing them dry.

Noemi rifled through the vials and syringes, finding lidocaine and drawing some into a syringe, then flicking the sides of the plunger. "A bit of a pinch." She pushed the needle into Emma's wrist, withdrawing it, dipping the needle in alcohol, and injecting more into the meat of the girl's thumb, then her forearm, too, for good measure. Noemi counted to one hundred, then put the girl's hand into the water Rosena had brought, numb or not, trying to stop the arm from continuing to cook. It had taken on the appearance of a skin marshmallow, toasted and bubbling and blackened at the edges.

Emma hadn't passed out. She was tougher than she looked—and she'd looked pretty tough to begin with. Either the lidocaine was working its magic, or shock was.

"Best not to look," Noemi said. The girl turned away obligingly. Noemi took a hooked probe, delicately sticking it into the barbecued flesh.

"Feel that?"

"More than I'd like, yeah," Emma said.

Hearing no reply, Noemi held on tight, wadded up a roll of gauze, and began pushing the blackened skin off slowly. "Try and sit still," she muttered, intent on debriding the wound and sloughing off the char.

Rosena's face was suddenly in view, with a voice so faint it sounded as if someone were speaking into a tin can at the end of a string. "Mother! Stop! You're hurting her!"

"Ro, you're in my light." Unwavering, Noemi began removing the necrotic overlay, revealing pink layers beneath. Satisfied, she wrapped the hand in a layer of adaptic gauze, then another layer of fluffed dry bandage, and an outer layer of elastic. She took a bit of the remnant and inserted rolled cones of it into the girl's ears.

"Go home," Noemi said, "and see a doctor. They'll grow you new skin. I mean it. Get out of here."

The girl stood up, wobbling a bit. She looked down toward the battle, then cast a forlorn glance at the trail toward home, before turning on her heel and walking back into the fray.

Noemi mouthed the word *"No,"* the sound unable to escape her slack-jawed mouth.

The women on the dome were standing still, seemingly ignoring the small explosions beginning to erupt around all of them. None were running away. Some had caught fire, the flames setting their clothes alight.

Someone grabbed Noemi's arm, and she spun around, ready to fight. Marta was beside her, mouth moving. A jumble of words. What was wrong with everyone? The old woman dug into a pocket, scribbling on a small notepad and holding it up in front of Noemi's face: *You're deaf.*

Noemi began shouting. And then she stopped, as still and quiet as the women frozen in battle. *It'll come back,* she thought. *Temporary. Not a problem at all.*

"What's happening? Why have they stopped moving?" Her mouth made the words, she was sure of it.

Marta scrawled an answer: *Push drones.*

The drones had circled, focused on the vanguard of fighters on the platform, pushing fields of energy towards the women until they couldn't move. Some of the bombers were burning from detonating devices, forced to suffer every inch of fire creeping across their skin, unable to move to escape. Some had been able to evade them, flattening themselves on the ground, still lighting trip lines or hammering at the surface as though their lives depended on it.

And then suddenly, they were all gone, like vapor on a stiff wind.

Dust from the rubble glittered in the sunlight, a gentle breeze spreading it across everything. Concrete blocks as big as buses lay below, an errant arm sitting atop a slab as though someone had taken it off and left it there. There were still slides of debris occurring, women vanishing abruptly as the walls collapsed, their dust-covered faces frozen in silent screams.

Noemi hid behind a boulder, huddled with Rosena. There were a few others gathered with Marta, crouched behind trees, afraid to move, staring. They had all run toward the disaster at first, desperate to save any of the hundreds who had fallen into the bunker fifty feet below when its roof caved in.

Then the first ones had emerged from the wreckage.

The whole structure was unstable, but that hadn't stopped the men from clambering up the sides as though hell beckoned them from below. When they summited, some stood at the precipice, looking back at the place from which they'd emerged, born from the ground. Others stood quietly blinking against the sun, shock plain on their wrinkled faces. More than a dozen dashed straight into the woods without so much as a glance over their shoulder.

The only men Noemi had ever seen were in museum displays or in school history books, or when selecting a donor from the short movies at the fertility clinic. And now there were some, alive, and standing right in front of her, careening out into the world after they'd supposedly been extinct for fifty years.

Men had declined over the span of generations, fading from memory to myth. The old women who'd been around when men were alive told stories of their youth: vying for a man, sharing them if they had to because there were so few left. Only the wealthy could afford to keep private company. Each woman who bore a son revered him, hoping their offspring would be the savior of the species. Inevitable disappointment came when none of them were. Eventually, there were no men left at all. At least, that's what they'd always been told.

Noemi would forever associate the stench of burning flesh with men, for the smell had permeated her nose, and she could not distinguish the foulness of one from the other. The men were beastly pale creatures, with hair all over their wrinkled bodies and faces. Some were clothed, others barely so. Each wore a metal collar.

"Someone controls them," Noemi muttered under her breath.

Rosena's hand clapped over her mother's mouth, eyes round like twin moons, forefinger to her lips to quiet her.

Noemi retreated to the makeshift triage they'd set up and began ransacking the supply stash. Marta followed, furiously scribbling on the notepad, shoving it in front of Noemi's face. *What are you looking for?*

"A device. Anything that looks unfamiliar and electronic," Noemi said. The hum of her voice was like bees in her head, her ears unwilling to acknowledge the sound.

Marta's face bore the expression of a skeptic, head cocked to the side, mouth forming the word *"Why?"*

"Just help me," Noemi pushed bandage packaging and bottles of antiseptic wash aside, keen for anything with a cord or a display screen.

A vitals scanner appeared in Marta's outstretched hand. The old woman's penciled-in eyebrows arched, as though to ask if it would do.

"Yeah, that works." Noemi shouldered into a backpack, tightening the straps before pulling back her hair into a tight ponytail and dusting off her clothes. Taking the device, she turned on her heel, marching straight down the hill towards the collapse—toward the men.

"You will comply!" she shouted, raising the scanner over her head and shaking it. "You will comply!"

The men's hands went reflexively towards their necks, others raising their hands over their heads in surrender.

Approaching the rim opposite them, Noemi could see them for what they were. Many of them were injured. All were thin, their muscles atrophied, their backs hunched, graying beards hanging in limp knots beneath wrinkled faces. Old.

She held the scanner up, ready to command them to retrieve the women who had fallen below.

Then every single one of them fell to the ground, still as corpses on a battlefield.

12

A Storm Coming

FIFTY-THREE YEARS AFTER THE WANING: TWO DAYS
AFTER LIBERATION

"SUSURRATION." KATE RAN HER fingers over the stems of grass, the seed heads whispering above her, the long stalks bent around them. The breeze touched the clouds, like white horse tails painted across an impossibly blue sky. "If ever there was a perfect word..."

Lucy rolled over, propping herself up on her elbows, her round backside glowing in the sunshine. "I swear to god, Kate, I think I've got dirt in places dirt shouldn't be. Will we ever get a chance to love each other in a proper bed?"

"Oh, I rather doubt it." Kate laughed. "But if I find my bed empty of dolls, books, one of my kids, or that vexing rabbit, by all means, let's."

Lucy leaned over, her warm soft lips brushing against Kate's. "Then come to my house."

Kate imagined the quiet of escaping to somewhere free of adolescent anarchy. But her mind drifted to the inevitability of her girls looking for her. Someone crying over a scraped elbow, a lost toy, or a hurt feeling. The goat loose in the kitchen. Something inadvertently set on fire, spilled, or shattered in their mother's absence.

"We should just stay here forever," Kate whispered. Close enough to the house to know if pandemonium ensued. She ran a finger through Lucy's hair, hands trailing down across the tattoo on her lover's long neck, thumb tracing the upturned curves of her mouth.

Lucy kissed her before rolling over and shimmying into jeans that had been urgently discarded earlier. With her hips propped up in the air, her eyes went wide as they slid up to her waist.

"You just realized you sunburned your butt, didn't you?" Kate laughed.

"Well, I don't imagine you'll much like how yours feel neither." Lucy arched a brow, nodding towards Kate's front.

Kate reflexively put a hand to her breast, the heat already apparent.

"Best you toss on some clothes, my love," Lucy said, grinning wickedly. "Because you got about thirty seconds before your brood arrives, followed by..." She craned her neck to see above the grass, quickly buttoning up her shirt. "Christ on a cracker... Followed by what appears to be an entire farmyard."

Rapidly approaching shrieks and howls drifted across the meadow. Kate fished around for her dress, tugging it on over her head and plucking the grass out of her hair, feeling decidedly like a guilty schoolgirl. Lucy regarded her with a smirk and a steady gaze.

"I haven't told them. About us," Kate confessed.

"Oh. Well, I did," Lucy said. "Last week."

She had no time to reply. Mika had broken free of her sisters and launched into her mother's arms, bowling Kate over onto the ground. The dog was of the same notion, and soon they were a tumble of arms and legs and a furiously wagging tail. Kate hoped it was Vesper who was licking her ear; Mika's five-year-old mind still thought she could become a dog too, if just she tried hard enough to act like one.

"What're you doing down there? Did ya lose something, Mama?" Birdie's eyes scanned the ground. "'Cause I don't think you're gonna find it in all this grass." She was undeterred though, and was soon bent over, hands on her kneecaps, peering into the reedy stems.

"Naw, Bird. Mama's just talking with Miss Lucy is all," Jenna said. "They're out here so as we don't interrupt 'em." Jenna was holding a chicken, its perpetually surprised beady eyes looking as though it were contemplating flight just to be a part of the mayhem. She smoothed a hand over its wings, re-situating the avian parcel into the crook of her arm to dissuade the notion.

Mandy surveyed the lot from her bareback perch aboard Fred. The old pony was thirty years old if he was three. He was as fat as a couch and about as tall as one too, with a crested neck, a mop of flaxen mane that fell to both sides, and a forelock inclined to cover his entire face if not for the polka-dot ribbon tied in the middle of it.

"Oh, they ain't just talkin'." Mandy grinned as knowingly as ten-year-olds did whenever they thought they knew something they truly knew nothing about, but desperately thought they ought to.

"Come help me look, Birdie," Lucy said with a mischievous smile. "Your mother has lost her senses. They must be around here somewhere."

They pushed into the meadow hand in hand, eyes on the ground, Birdie's soft voice saying, "What do senses look like, Miss Lucy?" and Lucy's reply, "Don't worry, we'll know 'em when we find 'em."

They were accompanied by Vesper, who had abandoned the tumble of child and mother and was blazing a path in wild canine glee. The pale inflorescences of the tall grass parted in a trail as the hodge-podge party was consumed by the field. The dog was porpoising through the meadow, his tail held up like a flag. Mandy was kicking Fred's sides, begging to follow the procession, but the greedy pony had his head down, happily munching on grass, and was thoroughly uninspired by any suggestion to move. Mandy finally slid off his rump, racing to catch up to the quest.

Jenna stood at Kate's shoulder, staring after them. "Do you love her, Mama?"

"Do you mind if I do?" Kate picked up Mika, setting her youngest on her hip. The little girl's face was covered in dirt and snot and bits of chaff. She plunked her solid head down on her mother's shoulder, too old for naps, but too tired to be awake.

"Miss Lucy has always been nice," Jenna said. "I don't mind it."

Lucy had moved into the house across the meadow on the other side of the creek the prior summer. Fred had met her first. She'd encountered the equine nighttime bandit after he discovered an abandoned hay store in her old barn. As he was never a pony to miss a meal—his or anyone else's—Fred availed himself of the offering of his newly favored neighbor, no invitation necessary. When Lucy heard the desperate cries of "Fred!" from a chorus of four sad little voices the following morning, one would have thought she'd returned to a hero's parade when she hauled the portly beast home.

Lucy had been a fixture ever since. She was good with the girls, patient and attentive, but not swindled by the sort of childish pleadings a mother's heart couldn't refuse. Lucy expected them to be respectful and kind, but never had to tell them to be.

Kate watched as Lucy walked back with the girls now, all of them consumed by fits of giggling. Somehow, they had acquired the goat, Agatha, along the way. Vesper raced ahead, wearing a shirt, while Mandy did not.

"Do I ask, or shall I assume the dog has developed a fondness for clothing?"

"Never mind, Mama! Lucy is going to build us a tree fort!" Mandy exclaimed, pointing at the giant chestnut tree on the south slope toward the creek. "With rope swings and bridges and chairs just for us, and—"

"How on earth did you get him to sit still for this?" Kate was trying to extract a paw from a sleeve with little success. Vesper had thrown himself to the ground and was doing his level best to impersonate a crocodile with a fresh catch, rolling around until finally Kate had to straddle the dog with a sharp "Stay, goddammit!" It had absolutely no effect whatsoever. She let go, shirt securely in hand, and the dog bolted, Agatha following in hot pursuit.

"Goats are demon spawn," Lucy said. "That smelly thing got me up against the fence with those nubbin horns just yesterday."

Mandy fished around in the pockets of her overalls and pulled out a handful of gingersnaps. "She likes raisins, too, but those are almost always sticky," she said, depositing the cookies in Lucy's hand. "Agatha won't stab you if you have cookies. She'll just follow you around trying to get into your pockets is all. But I ain't got bruises."

A sleepy head perked up from Kate's shoulder, grubby fingers outstretched. "I wanna cookie. Please, Manda? I'm hungry."

"Oh my gosh, you poor wretch, you're just skin and bones," Kate teased, giving a tiny poke to her daughter's belly. Looking at them all, Kate felt a rush of guilt for her afternoon gallivant. She kissed Mika's cheek and squeezed her tight. "Come on, girls. Who wants cake for lunch?"

After a luncheon of chocolate milk and chocolate cake, the girls abandoned their mother in a rampage of icing-smeared faces, screaming and leaping and running as though there were a dozen of them, not four. Lucy had sent them on a task to collect lumber for their fort, suggesting they start with the dilapidated shed on the edge of her property. Jenna had been given sole custody of a hammer and warned to not let it out of her sight after Mandy grabbed it and tested it on the kitchen table.

"Only the shed, Amanda Jean MacKatherine! You listen to your sister, or else you get manure duty for a week."

Their screeches faded into the distance as they careened down the hill towards the creek and across the small bridge joining the properties, Vesper barking his joy alongside them.

"Fairly sure that girl will be shoveling shit for the better part of her teenage years," Lucy said.

The house had fallen into a sudden eerie silence. They stared at each other just long enough to realize it, the sound of their chairs simultaneously scraping back from the table jarring them both into an excited urgency.

"Upstairs," Kate whispered.

Lucy pushed her hands into Kate's long hair, pulling her close, mouth warm and inquisitive. "Hurry."

They tumbled into Kate's room, falling onto the bed. Lucy flung a toy off the mattress, the sound of it skittering along the floorboards. Kate pulled off her dress, breasts laid bare, back arching as Lucy traveled her body intimately, tongue and fingers trailing along her skin, stroking and pressing. Urgent with lust and the absence of time combined, they moved together in desperate exploration and a tangle of limbs until Kate cried out, her body shuddering so violently, she retreated from Lucy's touch, until Lucy collapsed on top of Kate in her own crushing end, both gasping laments to God.

"What on earth is wrong with us?"

Kate felt Lucy's body shaking with quiet laughter, followed by a mumbled "I don't know."

They lay beside each other, beginning to settle into the hazy satisfaction of the realization theirs was a love only just beginning. Kate had had other lovers, some lasting for a time, others fly-by-night. But none had been like this—a need so consuming, and feeling as though time stopped when they were together. She took Lucy's hand, intertwining their fingers, thumb caressing work-hardened knuckles.

"Stay with me," Kate whispered, staring at the ceiling and holding her breath, feeling faint. She dared a sidelong glance.

Lucy was propped up on her elbows looking back at her, beaming. "Stay? As in ... *stay*, stay?"

"Yes."

"Like, move in with you and your wild children and the dog and the pony and the goat and the chickens, stay?"

"Don't forget the rabbit."

"And where is the flop-eared little monster?"

"In the corner. He saw the whole thing." Kate laughed.

Lucy sat up, spying the infiltrator peering out from beneath her discarded shirt. "Mops and I will have to have a talk about his indecent proclivities with me living here now."

"Is that a yes? You'll live here? With me and the girls?"

"Oh. Well, I rather thought the girls could live at my house, and we could be here in the quiet of our own little animal sanctuary," Lucy said teasingly.

Kate sat up abruptly, ear cocked toward the window, listening. The white lace curtains caught the breeze, billowing into the room, carrying the sweet scent of ozone in the air. "It's too quiet. And there's a storm coming." She began to get up, but Lucy stopped her.

"I'll go. It was me saying I'd build them a fort and who sent them off to scavenge. I'll keep them busy hauling everything to the tree until the rain starts, give you some quiet time to read or take a bath or whatever you like," Lucy said. She ran her fingers along Kate's cheek, kissing her with a reluctant moan.

The thought of a quiet house was too tempting, and Kate guiltily agreed. The notion of her daughters and Lucy spending time together filled her heart with every kind of joy.

Lucy dressed, wincing again when the jeans rolled up to the lovely curve of her hips, then smirking as she caught Kate's eye. "Yeah, well, it was a sunburn worth getting." She walked over to the bed, leaning down for one more kiss for good measure. "Back in a bit."

The house grew still. Kate lay across the crisp linen sheets, the warm air of the coming rain whispering across the damp of her naked body. Her mind wandered to how she could spend the time: a hot bath, or reading, or a hot bath *and* reading. She sighed with the possibility of it, abandoning the comfort of the bed, intent on realizing her mind's suggestions.

The old claw-foot tub was steaming as Kate slid in up to her chin, the aroma of the lavender oil filling the room. It was divine. She lazed there until the water began to cool, then donned exfoliating gloves and began smoothing her skin to a glow. She hadn't bothered with such things for a long while; no one to appreciate it but herself, and she was usually too tired for anything more than a cursory shower anyway. She dried off and got back into bed, curling up with a replicated book, complete with bamboo pages and soy-ink-printed words.

The yard suddenly erupted outside with a clamoring of beasts, chickens squawking and Agatha bleating in alarm. Kate dashed to the window, muttering, "What on God's green earth are those girls up to now?"

Pushing the curtain aside, she stopped dead. Her heart began pounding out of her chest, eyes scanning the grounds. The girls and Lucy were nowhere to be seen. Instead, there were pale beasts in ragged clothes, their necks collared, grabbing the chickens and flinging them aside, snatching the eggs and breaking them into their gaping mouths. One came out of the barn. It walked across the yard, hacksaw in its clutches. Kate ducked behind the curtain, back against the wall when she heard them yell.

They'd seen her.

They were coming.

They were in the house.

13

WHAT WE COME FROM

LUCY WALKED THROUGH THE meadow towards the ramshackle shed the girls were supposed to be hacking to bits. Not a single thing was moving—no sounds of hammers nor bickering of sisters, as one might expect when leaving children to their own devices. She crossed the tiny bridge over the stream and made her way up the rise, listening for any signs of mishap or discontent. There was none. She quickened her pace.

There in the shadows inside the shack, sunlight beamed through the gaps of the wood siding, illuminating the four girls sitting quiet as church mice. Each one had a bright, smiling face, holding tiny kittens in their laps. Jenna had set her attentions on the black-and-white-spotted mother cat, which was purring with furious abandon.

"We found kittens!" Mika whispered excitedly.

"I see that," Lucy said.

"How do you tell if it's a girl or not?" Birdie delicately stroked the head of a tiny calico, thoroughly smitten.

"Turn it over and look for dangly bits," Mandy said.

"They're too young for anything to be dangling," Lucy said, leaning against the threshold, "but calicos are almost always girls."

"Are they yours?" Mandy asked.

"No, but their mama and I are good friends. Her name is Mooey Gorda," Lucy said. She bent down and scratched the cat under the chin. "Hadn't seen you for a while, Moo. Been wondering where you'd gone off to. I suppose now I know."

Mika was peering at the underside of an orange kitten, which was mewling in protest at the inquisition.

"Go easy, Mika, and put the little guy down. His mama won't like her babies bein' bothered that way," Lucy said.

"Can we keep them?" Birdie could barely contain herself, as though wanting to flood all her love out at once, but was being forced to offer nothing more than a drop at a time.

"Not yet, Birdie. They've got at least another month of stayin' with their mama," Lucy said.

There was a collective whine among the girls, their hearts already set on bringing them home. Lucy was partial to them herself and was already devising a scheme to persuade Kate to allow it, her being the sort that was keen on the canine variety.

"Where is Vesper, anyway?" The dog was nowhere to be seen.

"Tied him to the tree. Didn't want him chewin' on the kittens," Mandy said.

The dog was yipping in escalating octaves outside. Thunder rolled in the distance, wind rattling the doors, the farm erupting in a cacophony of despair.

"Best we get home, girls. There's a storm comin'." Lucy retrieved each kitten, tucking them in with Mooey. There were seven in total, showing a kaleidoscope of colors, provoking speculation there had possibly been more than one father to the bunch. Lucy stroked behind Mooey's ears once more, casting an envious glance at the cat with her babies. "Shoulda named you Harlot, you fat old thing."

She walked out after the girls. The three youngest were down in the creek, while Jenna stood on the bridge, eyes cast up towards the house.

"Vesper settled right down, didn't he?" The rope hung limp, the dog hidden by the grass. Lucy laughed as the girls stomped through the water. Mika had slipped into an eddy and was soaked to her thighs.

"Seems so." Jenna was quiet, her body taut and back rod-straight, as though trying to grow taller to see better. "I don't know."

Lucy followed Jenna's gaze, past the tree and the slack rope, up to the house. A storm roiled on the horizon with spikes of white cumulous clouds against a dark indigo sky. A shiver of unease ran down her spine. "Get your sisters," she said flatly.

"Come on. You know Vesper hates thunder," Jenna called.

Her sisters scrambled up the slope, muddied and wet and grinning from ear to ear, paying no heed to the change in Jenna's demeanor. They raced up the hill toward the chestnut tree, Lucy and Jenna in close pursuit.

Birdie arrived first, coming to an abrupt stop, staring at the ground, then whirled around as though the dog had snuck up behind her. She held up the rope, empty. The end of it was wet and frayed. "Why on earth…?"

"Get down!" Lucy grabbed the girls, pulling them below the tops of the meadow grass, two girls on each side of her, arms over their backs like a hen shielding chicks from the rain. Mika started to cry. Jenna put her index finger over her lips, shaking her head to shush her.

"Where's Mama?" Birdie's head began drifting up, curiosity almost outweighing fear.

"You all stay put. I mean it. Don't fucking move. Do you understand?" Lucy looked to Jenna for assurance, old beyond her twelve years. But not old enough.

Lucy saw them in the courtyard, wild and stalking. And she knew what they were. Then the shot rang out.

There were paw prints following the smears of blood down the hall and out the door. Vesper was nowhere in sight. Lucy took a kitchen knife from the block, gripping it overhand, silently making her way through the house. She followed the trail of spattered crimson up the stairs.

She found Kate huddled in a corner of the bedroom, pointing a shotgun directly at her. Kate's tear-streaked face was swollen and vacant, the gun trembling in her hands.

"It's me," Lucy said gently, hands outstretched in submission. She tossed the knife onto the bed. "I'm here now." The sound of the words was choking her. *Too late*, she realized.

Suddenly Kate snapped to, eyes sharp. "Where are the girls?"

"Hiding ... in the grass ... in the meadow. They're ... they're by the tree," Lucy stuttered, flustered by Kate's quick change in demeanor.

"Not likely to stay there," Kate muttered, grabbing the scattered shells of bird shot off the floor.

"You need..." Lucy's voice broke, her hands started to shake. "You need to put on some clothes, Kate. Please tell me ... tell me what happened. I want to help you—"

"Just leave me be!" Kate brushed past her, free arm pushing Lucy away. But Lucy tried to pull her close, to wrap Kate in her arms and say it was okay—knowing it wasn't, but needing to hold her and tell her anyway.

"Don't. Don't touch me." Kate pushed past, snatching a work dress off the chair and hastily pulling it on. She walked out of the room without another word, shotgun in hand.

The patter of rain started to hit the roof, and a flash of lightning was followed by a quick roll of thunder. Lucy snatched the knife off the bed and raced down the stairs and out into the yard after her. Kate was running through the meadow as the chestnut tree's branches swayed in the wind. Four heads popped up from the grass. They were all soon reunited and in their mother's arms.

A series of short yips came from the other side of the barn. Lucy cautiously crept around the corner, wishing she had more than a kitchen knife. There was a heap on the ground, motionless. Vesper had part of it in his mouth, tugging and shaking it violently. The dog looked at Lucy, before grabbing the heap by the side of the head in earnest.

There were footsteps behind her. Lucy spun around, knife at the ready.

It was only Kate. "It's one of them," she whispered. "There were three. I shot one. But it was only bird shot."

"Give me the rifle. I saw them run off, but they may come back," Lucy said. "And get the girls out of here." They were peering around the barn, Jenna holding them tight, all of them unable to look away.

"Vesper!" Kate called, and the dog's head popped up. His snout was bloodied, and he looked more wolf than hound. He bounded towards her, tail wagging furiously. There was flesh between his teeth. Then the heap groaned, and Vesper stopped dead, hackles up, growling.

It struggled to stand, its body quaking on unsteady legs.

Lucy fired. One shot into its neck. Another into its chest. It was screaming, stumbling into the woods, slamming into trees, falling and scrambling to its feet. Lucy made to follow, but Kate grabbed her arm.

"What is that?" Kate asked, her voice sounding as though it were a thousand miles away.

"A man."

The videocast came through later that afternoon, warning residents of the central rural zones to contact the authorities immediately if "suspicious activity" was observed, and for everyone to be vigilant. There was no mention of what, exactly, they were to remain vigilant for, only that a high-security area had recently been disrupted by a small group of dissidents calling themselves the Freedom Women, and no quarter should be given to any of unknown acquaintance.

"Why aren't they saying what's really going on?" Lucy paced the kitchen, hands on her hips, stopping near the window to peer outside. Her eyes invariably drifted back to Kate, who was sitting at the table, hands wrapped around a cup of tea that had gone cold, shivering, despite the warmth of the day. Vesper lay protectively over Kate's feet.

The rain persisted, the storm rolling through in waves. Sporadic downpours shattered the silence, so loud they couldn't hear themselves think. Lucy had already installed bolts across all the doors and was eyeing the windows with equal misgivings. There'd never been any need to protect their home—not from other people. The old rifle lay on the kitchen table, only ever used to scare off the occasional fox, until they'd gotten Vesper.

"We're going to need more than bird shot," Kate said.

"We have to call them," Lucy said, as though Kate hadn't spoken at all. "People need to know what's out there, what might be coming. We have to tell them they were here."

Kate was staring at her hands, thumb stroking the backs of her knuckles. "But why aren't they saying that already? Where the hell did they come from? What were they doing here?"

"Kate, you're not listening to me."

"We have to tell the girls," Kate said.

"Tell them what, exactly?"

"The truth."

Lucy sat down and made a move to take Kate's hands, but they balled into fists. Lucy clasped her own hands tightly on her lap. "Please. Just tell me what happened."

Kate pulled her knees up to her chin. "Nothing."

Birdie's lyrical voice carried across the room from where she stood at the threshold, half hidden behind the doorjamb. "Mama?"

Kate transformed. Her face lit up with a bright smile, and she stood up with arms wide. "Come here, sweetheart." She enveloped Birdie in a hug, squeezing tight. They sat back down at the table, Birdie curling up in her mother's lap as though smaller than her eight years.

"What was it, what we saw today, Mama? 'Cause Jenna says she knows, but she won't say, and Mandy's saying its monsters and making Mika cry. I don't wanna be scared, Mama. But what if it comes back?"

The air blew out of Kate's bluster in an instant, the façade from a moment ago fading. She began rocking Birdie in a reassuring sway, chin resting atop her daughter's head.

"It ain't coming back. Miss Lucy and Vesper scared it off. Don't you worry."

The wind rattled the shutters. A loose bucket tumbled across the yard, and Agatha could be heard bleating in complaint. But conversation around the kitchen table had ceased, leaving all that was unsaid to die a quiet death in their own imaginations until it was unbearable, free to run amok to its outermost extremes.

"Go get your sisters," Kate finally said. "Better for you girls to hear it from your Mama than to hear it anywhere else."

Birdie slid off her mother's lap, looking pensive for a long moment, before turning around and walking silently out of the room.

"We'll tell them first," Kate said.

"Kate, I think we should talk about—"

The charge of bare feet on the stairs meant Lucy had no time for questions of her own—questions beyond the scope of what the girls could ever be allowed to know.

"Whatever it is you're going to say, Lucy, never mind it now. I have to talk to my girls."

The anger Lucy felt brimming just beneath the surface started to rise. She wanted to grab Kate and force her to confess everything. Or maybe it would be better to hold Kate and protect her from having to utter the words of what tormented her. Lucy wondered if she could confess her own part in it, or if she'd lose Kate either way.

The girls clustered around their mother on the couch. Mika took the youngest's rightful place on her mother's lap. Birdie stood beside them, one hand on Kate's shoulder, the other holding Mika's hand. Lucy felt a pang of envy, but quickly pushed it aside.

"I'm going to tell you what happened today," Kate began. "This is grown-up stuff. But I need you to hear it from me, so you understand. Do you think you can do that?"

"Was it a man, Mama?" Jenna asked solemnly, pulling at a loose purple thread on the perpetually half-done afghan folded up in a basket next to the couch. It seemed as though she'd aged ten years in a day.

"Yes," Kate sighed. "It was a man. Or rather, men. There were three of them."

"But Mama, our teacher told us all the men are gone. They been gone for, like, a thousand years," Mandy protested in a huff.

"Not quite a thousand. More like fifty years. They'd been dying off for a long time. The last men died a couple of decades before I was born. We learned it in school, same as you. I'd never seen one before either—well, at least not in real life. And they don't even look like they do in the pictures. I don't know where these men come from, if they've been hiding all this time or what. But somehow, they came here, and now we've got to make sure they don't think this is a good place to come back to. You understand?"

"But our home is a good place, Mama," Mika whispered. "It's the best place."

Tears sprung into Kate's eyes. Lucy held her gaze, trying to give her the strength or the rage she needed, or whatever could be taken out of Lucy's soul and given over for the borrowing.

"Is that what we come from?" Birdie asked. "A thing like that?"

Kate smoothed her daughter's hair and smiled. "You come from me, sweetheart. Their bit is just a necessary drop of science, nothing more. The pater-seed is chosen out of a catalog, sort of like how we order crop seeds every year. You flip through the genetic descriptions and choose what you like, what you think is important. For you girls, I saw an old-fashioned photograph of a man washing dishes. He had a towel thrown over his shoulder. I picked him because he seemed nice and because he was smiling."

"Did they hurt you, Mama?" Jenna's voice broke. She quickly wiped the edges of her sleeves across her eyes.

"No, sweetheart. Just … surprised me, is all," Kate said with as much reassurance in her voice as she could muster. "Wasn't expecting to see such a thing. May as well have been a unicorn, you know?"

"I want a unicorn," Mika said softly. Her head lay heavy on Kate's shoulder while she absently stroked her mother's chin.

"I promise, if a real unicorn shows up, you can keep it." She smiled briefly, before her face faded to a look of seriousness. "Now girls, there's going to be a lot of fuss, with these men coming here and all. People are going to say a lot of things. And I'm telling you right now, don't believe a word of it. You hear something that doesn't make sense, or it's got you scared, or you just don't know—you come and tell me, okay? I'll tell you the truth of it."

They all sat there with their heads hung low, worrying with the full array of childhood imagination. Lucy was sure it would be weeks and months of nightmares for everyone. She would have to distract them, give them enough to occupy their minds and tire their bodies so that no energy would be left for worrying.

"We're going to build the most magnificent tree fort ever," Lucy said. "And I'm going to teach you to be mean and kick and hit really hard, so this is only the best place for girls, okay?"

Mandy's face brightened. "The tree house can be our hiding place."

"That's a good idea, Amanda. We'll start tomorrow," Lucy said. It was little consolation, protecting them from a thing that had already arrived, but it was all she had to hold onto at the moment. And that would have to do.

"Now, up you go, girls," Kate said. "You've got school to get ready for. It's biosciences this month, and I know you all haven't sorted out your projects yet. Jenna, make sure Mika has her botany samples ready, okay?"

They bounded upstairs with a clamor of "Yes, Mama!"

Their sudden absence made the room feel emptier than was warranted, and an uncomfortable stillness settled between Lucy and Kate. Lucy took up the afghan, plucking at the loose end, mind running through a host of notions to equip the house and train the girls.

"Last month, all Mika would talk about was bryophytes," Kate said in a high-pitched voice, a hollow smile plastered across her tear-stained face. "We still have jars of moss, the favorites she's not willing to 'set free' yet. I've been taking them outside and putting them back in the forest, one by one, hoping Mika doesn't notice. And Jenna has selected ethnobotany this month. I wouldn't be surprised if she takes up permanent residence in the tree house."

"Building it will be a good distraction," Lucy said, voice trailing off. Kate was retreating to the shelter of pretending like nothing had happened, emotional bricks being placed for an impenetrable wall. Lucy couldn't let her retreat.

"Is all that true, Kate? What you told the girls. That they didn't—"

"Enough of it's true. The part that matters. Just leave it alone." Kate walked into the kitchen, setting the kettle to boil for more tea.

Lucy followed, unwavering in her pursuit. "Is it possible, could you... Did it try... Could there be a natural implantation, Kate?"

The cupboard banged shut, and Kate slammed a spoon down on the counter next to a tin of chamomile. Then she swept both to the side, leaning hard on the edge of the sink with her arms set wide. Kate stared out the kitchen window, chin trembling and cheeks flushing pink, then spun around, arms crossed tightly over her chest.

"'Natural'? Did it try and breed with me, you mean? No—and I've seen enough farm animals going at it to be sure about that. He stood right in front of me, ogling me and grunting while his hand worked away on himself like he was milking some cow. And then he spilled his seed all ... all over the floor."

Lucy breathed a long sigh of relief, smiling a little. "So, you're alright, then."

A small cry erupted from Kate. She was shaking, her whole body trembling so hard it looked like it was about to break into a million pieces. "Go home," she whispered.

"But Kate, he didn't—"

"Leave me alone. Just leave. Get out!"

14

RULES OF ENGAGEMENT

THE MUFFIN TIN WAS beaten flat, and Kate couldn't have been more gratified. She was on her knees in the middle of the barn, the mallet held loosely in her grasp. The chickens had scattered at the sound of the first strike of metal on tin, as had Fred and Agatha. But Vesper remained, despite the piercing sound and the string of profanities screamed into the hay bales.

Tipping back on her heels, Kate let the pendulum of her backside plant onto the ground, legs splayed out in front of her. She coaxed the dog over to offer an apology. The soft *bomp* of Vesper's blocky head pushed against her chest and she began to sob. He lay down with a low groan, the front half of his body draped over her thigh. Vesper held no judgment for what she had done.

Kate stroked his ears, soft like velvet. "Who's the best dog?" His tail thumped. "You are," she whispered in their usual repartee.

The earlier scene replayed in her head on a loop with every outcome that could have been. Hide. Barricade the door. Kick him or hit him or throw things. Shoot him at first sight. Anything but just stand there, mouth agape, too stunned to make a sound, watching him, his face a twist of ecstasy, eyes fixed on her until they rolled back in his head with a grunt and a shudder.

She'd done nothing to stop it. It was as though the foulness of the act was her burden to bear. Done under her roof, in her own bedroom, where the scent of sex still lingered from the encounter with Lucy only just the hour before. She had never felt so vulnerable, naked in her own bedroom watching a beast take pleasure in front of her. Because of her. Wondering if he would come back to do it again—or what else he might do. And wondering if she would let him, mute, incapable of doing anything more than whimper in fear. The shame of it was beyond expression. She'd always thought she was stronger than that.

Vesper lifted his head, turning towards the door. The fur running the ridge of his spine stood on end. Kate's vision blurred, adrenaline coursing through her veins so fast it made her heart hurt as it pounded inside her chest. She was on her feet, mallet in hand, peering out from the shadows. Vesper was at her side, hackles up, growling like an engine.

There were a dozen one-cars, each with tinted windows, puddle mud spattering their shiny black paint to dullness as they rolled up the driveway. The insignia of the Governing Council marked the armbands of the garda getting out of their vehicles, while a woman in a dark suit with her hair pulled back in a severe chignon disembarked from the plush seat of her own.

Kate took a deep breath to calm herself, nerves and anger tumbling around like a ball in her belly. Lucy stood on the porch, wearing a grim yet satisfied expression. Kate stalked across the yard, looking sidelong at Lucy while shoving the dog inside the house. "You and I are going to have a little chat when this is done," Kate muttered under her breath.

Lucy's bluster faded for an instant, only to be replaced by crossed arms and an insolent frown. "It had to be done, Kate. For the girls. For you."

"Don't you even begin to tell me—"

"Katherine MacShannon, I presume?" The woman interrupted, wearing a crisp black pant suit ironed to a knife edge, approaching with a manicured hand outstretched. "Overseer Evelyn Emmett, primary administrator for the CRZ. We understand you had an unexpected encounter today. Is there a place we can chat while my staff investigate the area?"

"Unexpected?" Kate scoffed. "That's one way to put it." She wondered how someone as pristine and tightly wound as Evelyn Emmett of the CRZ would have fared. *Probably better than me,* she frowned. "My daughters are inside, and I won't have them involved. Besides, there's not much to tell—at least, not enough that warrants more than a minute. Three... They were ... they were men. Old and thin and looking for food. I shot one of them with bird shot. My dog got hold of another. Back there..." She pointed toward the barn. "And he ran into the woods. That's it. Nothing else to tell."

"And the other two?"

"Ran off with two of our chickens," Lucy said. "The chickens jumped out of their arms, but they kept running."

Kate spun toward Lucy. "Where were you when you saw all that?"

Lucy's eyes grew wide, and she shook her head as though consumed by a subtle twitch. "Never mind it," she whispered.

"Did you notice if they were wearing collars?" Overseer Emmett gestured with both hands, long, delicate fingers wrapping around her own throat. "On their necks?"

The image of the man sprung into Kate's mind, clear as day, his lips wet, breath coming out in a tune of desperate huffs, his eyes fixed on her body.

"Maybe. I don't recall. Could have. He ... they ... barely wore anything. Mostly rags," she said.

"Collars? Why would they be wearing collars? I think we're at least owed an explanation of what this is all about," Lucy said. "You haven't even said where these men came from! You haven't explained why there even *are* men, when there haven't been any—aren't supposed to *be* any." Her face was flushing red, and she'd begun gesturing so wildly Kate had to duck to avoid being a casualty. "You have to tell us at least that much. We're owed that. How are we supposed to be safe? Are we supposed to put locks on our doors now? What else haven't you been telling us?"

Overseer Emmett's watchful eye never left Kate, shrewd, undeterred. "And did any of you, or your daughters," she continued after a long pause, "come into direct contact with these men? Did they approach you, try to speak to you?"

"No contact," Kate blurted. She shook her head, studying the dirt, wanting to burrow into it. "One came in the house. I was the only one there. He didn't ... say, no, he didn't... No. Then my dog, Vesper, he chased him out of the house. Then I shot him. The man. Just bird shot. He ran off."

"Yes, I believe you'd already mentioned that," the woman said. "We'd like to speak to your daughters and—"

"Absolutely not. They're too young. They weren't even there. They were with Lucy."

"All the same, it's procedure to speak to all potential witnesses," Overseer Emmett said. She took a step toward the house, her hand sweeping in front of her as though opening a door. "May I?"

"I said no. You say you speak to all witnesses. Well then, you have. Unless you want to interrogate my dog. I'm your witness. My daughters were across the meadow."

"But Mama, I saw—"

Kate turned on her heel so quick it made her dizzy. Jenna was standing just inside, little sister held on her hip, swaying and humming softly in a noble effort to calm Mika, whose tear-stained cheeks tore a hole straight through Kate's heart. Birdie stood beside them, silently holding Jenna's arm but faring no better, her small trembling chin betraying the brave face she was so desperately trying to wear.

But Mandy would have none of it. She stood defiant, arms crossed, feet set, a fixed scowl daring anyone to test her. And Kate loved her all the more for it.

"Well, hello, young lady. What did you see?" The woman had taken another step closer, her long neck craning to see the hidden brood.

The overseer's sight line quickly vanished, obscured by the girl's mother. "I. Said. No." Kate's hands were clenched, arms drawn back as though ready to pounce. The garda had closed quarters, drawing nearer the more strident Kate became, but she didn't care. "They're little girls. And they're terrified. I will not have you feed their nightmares. Now you can take your people and get off my property."

The Overseer tipped her head, smiling politely. "The property isn't yours."

"Of course it isn't, but it's been allocated to me," Kate snapped back. "And I've made it productive. It's been measured as a sustainable contributory parcel, too. We both know you're not removing regency, so don't you threaten me with it. Now, I have asked you to leave my girls be. I've given you what you came here for, while you've offered no explanations in kind. Are these beasts—these men—a threat? I want to know what you're going to do about them."

"We have Vesper, Mama. We'll be fine." Mandy was standing beside her mother, small hand gripping the dog's collar, the other stroking his blocky head.

"Vesper, stay put," Kate whispered. Though it was tempting, the last thing she wanted was for her daughter to let go and have Vesper charging off the porch. She reached down to hold his collar anyway, just in case the dog held his own opinions on the matter.

"And what's your name?" Overseer Emmett knelt to eye level with the girl.

"Never you mind her name—" Kate began.

"Amanda!" Mandy shouted. "And my Mama wants you to go!" She quickly let go of the dog, who lurched forward with obvious intent.

"Vesper!" Kate held tight, bracing against the weight of him, leather digging into the backs of her fingers and shoes skidding forward on the slate stoop.

"Well, Miss Amanda MacKatherine, it's lovely to meet you. And you're right, we should be going along now. Wouldn't want to outstay our welcome." The woman had made her way within arm's reach of where Kate stood, boldly and unabashedly sizing her up. "The CRZ is sending out information on the intermodal. You'll have it shortly. It will include rules of engagement, in the event you come across the saviors again."

"The what?" Lucy asked incredulously. "Did you say 'saviors'?"

"Is that what they're calling them? Because if you think those scraggly creatures are the answer, we're all doomed," Kate added.

"The message will be available shortly. Proof of viewing is required for all inhabitants of the Central Rural Zone within forty-eight hours. I trust your curiosity will not delay you one moment. And should any of you wish to expand upon the events of the day, please contact us." The overseer winked at Mandy with the last comment, then promptly turned and walked smartly toward the vehicles.

The constant low rumbling of Vesper's growl hadn't ebbed. Kate could feel the vibration under the callouses of her fingers, the scent of eager dog breath gamely assaulting her nose. Her grip on his collar loosened, and for a split second, Kate thought considered letting go. "Not this time," she whispered, closing her hand.

It had taken nearly an hour to get the girls to settle into something resembling relative calm. Mika was still glued to Kate, with little fits of tears as she kept trying to burrow closer. Birdie was as stoic as an eight-year-old could be, sitting near enough to stay touching, one small hand holding her mother's arm and the other resting on Mika's foot to reassure them both she was there. Kate read them stories like when they were babies, in hopes of distracting them. Jenna set about brewing tea, making casserole, and baking cookies in an attempt to feed them into secure comfort. Kate took note of the fact that Jenna had closed all the windows, in case the men smelled the cooking and thought to come back.

Mandy pattered off after Lucy, the two of them intent on turning the house into a defensible fortress with door and window locks and a cache of armaments meant to dissuade the casual invader: a cheese grater affixed to a wood pole like a medieval mace, and sewing shears whose blades had been separated, the two spikes nailed to the end of the mop. Mandy went outside and started the process of leaching wood ash, proving she had indeed been paying attention during chemistry. Kate suppressed an uneasy pride, resolute she would be a bit more measured with her daughter's curriculum in the future.

The media wall finally flickered on just after supper, breaking the peculiar silence that had grown in the gap of time between. Kate felt disembodied, as though her skin were stretched over a remnant carcass. She hadn't spoken to Lucy beyond what was necessary: where the nails were, the scissors, the drill, spare wood. But now Lucy sat beside her, close, with an arm around her shoulder as though it were just another day that meant nothing at all, when it meant everything all at once. Kate wanted to crawl out of her skin and set it aside for someone else's body to wear.

The voice of the first minister of the CRZ filled the room in soothing tones, gentle and singsong, her image subdued by soft lighting and a benevolent expression. She spoke of a miraculous discovery. An enclave of the Last Men had been discovered, hidden all these years like some lost tribe of Guinea. An unfortunate disruption had caused them to leave their refuge, and declared they were *"unfamiliar with social norms, and citizens of the Central Rural Zone should be cautious and report any sightings, so they may be properly looked after."*

The minister paused, her hands neatly folded in front of her. A soft smile, a look of earnest. *"They are our last hope. They are humanity's saviors."*

15

IRREPARABLE

DUST MOTES FLOATED DOWN from the ceiling, catching the sunlight in unseen whispers of air. Noemi pursed her lips, blowing as though to whistle, the lint dancing and spiraling upward only to begin its slow descent again. There was something peaceful about living in a quiet world. Her remaining senses had become keen to all the little things, the distractions and nuances previously overlooked. She could see depths of colors more acutely. She could feel the energy of things beneath her fingertips. Her nose had become sharp to the acrid scents of clinical care, smelling the festering sickness biding its time in some of the women around her. She wondered if, after the surgeons had their way with her, the little things would still be there.

The irony Noemi was being treated and cared for in a Governing Council penitentiary wasn't lost on her. She'd been wary in the beginning of the caregivers assigned to her, waiting for unkindness to be offered, or neglect. But none came. Everyone had been efficient, thorough—sympathetic, even. No matter her pleading, or her desperate cries for alcohol, please, just a little. Or diazepam—anything to make the incessant convulsive shaking stop.

The first days had been a blur, and since then, Noemi had suffered a steady regimen of nightmare-ridden sleep to remind her of the events. It was strange, the notion she could hear them in her dreams, the endless screaming of every woman burned, fallen, or crushed. In these nightmares, each woman wore the face of her daughter; all of them were Rosena. Her nightmares were little different than what had occurred, and there were times when Noemi questioned what had really happened and what hadn't.

She remembered the men lying on the ground, unmoving as the wounded below. Dark figures had appeared from the heavy woods, as though they emerged from the trees themselves. Garda, dressed all in black, faces covered, coming towards them with pump guns at their sides. Undeterred, Noemi ran forward. Her boots slid to the precipice as the concrete crumbled beneath her feet, blocks shifting dangerously as she made her way down, aided at times by terrifying slides of debris, crouching down as though skiing a slope of scree strewn snow. The people above kept waving at her wildly, but she paid them no heed.

There had been a girl in the rubble, not much older than Rosena, staring at her with slow-blinking eyes. Both of her legs were gone just below the knees.

"Hello there, love," Noemi said, kneeling and taking the girl's hand, cradling it in her own. "Your family will be so proud. You're a hero. I don't know if you got a chance to see them, but I did—the men you freed. My gosh, it was such a wonder to see them all."

The girl's lips pressed into a tiny smile, a last breath escaping her before the light disappeared from her eyes. Noemi held her hand a little while longer, brushing aside the hair from the girl's face.

There had been so many others, too late for comfort, but Noemi touched the body of each woman she found anyway, offering a quick benediction before moving on to the next, desperate to find one she could save, hoping one of them would be her sister, Jayne. She made her way down into the cavern of wreckage, scanning for any signs of survivors. Noemi had found one, a curiously muscled leg protruding, still attached to its body, and she recoiled when she realized it didn't belong to a woman. She gawked at him, hairy chest laid bare with a gaping wound down its center, marked by shallow breaths, and a look of pleading in his old eyes when she passed him by.

The dome had fallen inward from the edges, leaving a catastrophic heap in the center none could have survived. Noemi focused her attentions on the outer ring, tripping over twisted rebar and skinning her knees on the rough edges of broken pebbled walls. She spied a pair of limbs, attracted by a bright orange sleeve, torn and bloodstained, some twenty meters distant. Noemi was halfway to them when a rope dropped down in front of her. She gasped, not hearing her own curses, before falling over backward.

The women in black were rappelling down into the pit in droves. Noemi rolled to her knees, then onto her hands and feet, scrambling as fast as she could towards the exposed arms. There was something familiar about the wild hair shooting out like a halo around the woman's head. She drew closer. Two bodies, one atop the other, holding tight. Noemi fought the garda when they grabbed her shoulder, twisting to get away, shrieking at them with a voice she couldn't hear, pleading with them to leave her be, to let her help them. She was a nurse, Noemi yelled. She'd found one she could save.

"Can you open your eyes for me?" A strong hand rubbed her arm. "Noemi, if you can hear my voice, I want you to say so."

Noemi groaned. Her eyelids were heavy, opening just enough to let a crack of light in before shutting tight again. Realization dawned that she could hear a familiar racket nearby: the steady beep of monitors in the background, the hum of machines, the chatter of nurses at the station deciding on whether to risk the curry in the cafeteria or resign themselves to the monotony of their bagged lunches.

"Noemi, I need you to open your eyes now. We're going to sit you up, okay?"

The whir of the bed motor vibrated, the sound buzzing in her ears. Noemi fought to open her eyes even though all she really wanted was to sleep, if not for the cold and the thirst and the incessant noise. Her mouth opened to speak, the dull ache of her raspy throat making the words hard to form. "Cold," she whispered.

The bed clicked into place halfway between flat and raised. Blankets were laid over her, heavy and warm, the shivers coursing through her body slowing. She opened her eyes a little more, the organized chaos of the blue and pale-green room a mix of fuzzy shapes in a hurry, crisscrossing her field of vision.

"Here's some apple juice. Take a sip, and then we'll see how you're doing, okay?"

Noemi nodded, the paper straw clenched between her teeth. She was fairly certain apple juice had never tasted so good.

The PACU nurse taking care of her was a tiny thing, barely five feet tall, darting around with measured efficiency and a no-nonsense demeanor contrary to her size. The nurse performed the usual routine post-care, asking a litany of questions about Noemi's comfort and pain level, the scanner tracing the air around her body for rates and rhythms and temperatures.

"Your surgeon will come and explain the procedure performed, then we'll transfer you to aftercare," the nurse said in a lilting voice. "You've got your pain meds on board, and an auto-pump will continue maintenance based on the response levels in your neuron receptors, tapering over the course of the next twenty-four hours."

Noemi pulled the blankets to her chin, mouthing the words *"Thank you"* before remembering her voice had found its purpose again. But it was too late; the nurse had already gone.

There were clear tubes running from the IV panel into Noemi's arm. The intermittent drip of saline and medication would have been hypnotic, if not for the fact she knew how to bypass the controls for narcotics. The thought of thick oblivion was luring in its promise of comfort and respite from the nightmares soon to revisit her. Noemi did not mind pain of the body, so much as she did pain of the mind.

She was half gone when the surgeon finally arrived. They shook her, and Noemi smiled in a contented stupor. Their complaints of what she had done did not register, their fuss no more worth hearing than before, when she had been deaf by injury instead of by chemically induced indifference. But it was the small voice of Stella and the snide statement of disgust from Rosena that marshalled her focus.

"Mommy, are you okay? Mommy?" Stella's voice fell to a whimper. "What's wrong with her?"

"Same thing as always," said Rosena. "Never mind, Stell. We don't need her anymore. We can live with Auntie Jayne now."

It was the sound of her daughter's voice uttering Jayne's name that catapulted Noemi through the fog. She tried to sit up, tried to see her daughters. She needed to touch them, to know they were real. She needed to know what had happened to Jayne. But the nurses were already strapping Noemi's limbs into restraints, while another was ushering her daughters out of the recovery area with murmured words of reassurance.

"Where's she? Jayne?" Noemi knew she didn't have much time, words slurring into a jumble. "Stella, baby, lets your Mama see you."

Stella paused, twisting around to see her, Rosena's tight grasp of her sister's hand demanding she leave instead.

Noemi's body was becoming heavy, unwilling to heed her mind's commands to kick, to fight, to do anything more than beg. She would do anything they wanted her to, anything at all, if only they would just let her hold her daughters. The sedation was cold as it coiled through her veins in a slow, dark creep, into her arm, through her head, down into her toes. She could still hear them, Stella crying in soft sobs, the shuffle of her feet on the floor as they pulled her away, calling for her mother.

The oblivion Noemi had so desperately wanted washed over her with dark edges and soft centers. Consciousness was elusive, untenable, but she could not close her eyes. It was as though they had been pricked open with tiny claws, body anesthetized while her mind remained alive and aware, but unable to process cohesive thought, only flashes of ideas, memories racing by just long enough to frighten her, never long enough to settle into a thing she could contemplate. Everything in her heart was firing at the same time. And she could not bear any of it. She could not bear any of it at all.

The woman leaned forward, hovering over the notepad with a stylus tucked between her fingers, absently tapping her teeth. Noemi wondered about this sort of woman, with a sharp-cut suit and hair pulled back so tightly it made her eyes appear as though she were in a constant state of amazement. This was the third one they'd brought in. The first one had failed to elicit a single word from Noemi. The next one had left nearly in tears after Noemi began flinging a litany of insults, the likes of which had not been heard since before the Fall of Men.

It was good sport, really, as far as Noemi was concerned. And she had nothing left to lose. She wondered, sitting there watching this new woman fiddle with a sheaf of notes, what there was left for her to do. Most condemned women ended up assigned to labor, tasked with jobs not fit for the decent among them, work relegated to those women whom society deemed irreparable.

And she was. Irreparable.

The woman sighed, closing the folder over her notes. She kept her stylus though, tapping it now on the table like a small furious baton. It was times like this when Noemi wished the damage to her ears had remained. The little habits of others drove a person to irritation: the tapping, the sighing, the shuffling, the shifting in her seat, the zipping sound of the hemp trousers when the woman uncrossed her legs. All were inconsequential in isolation, but maddening when bombarding a silent room.

The woman began puffing up, shoulders tightening and body animating into a posture of authority. It was like a neon sign flashing to indicate the interrogation was set to begin. Noemi's gaze drifted out the window, indifferent.

"I'm Overseer Evelyn Emmett of the CRZ," the woman said. "You will tell me what occurred at the Battle of Abscond—"

"The battle of what?" Noemi's head spun around to stare. She hadn't meant to say a word, the question falling out of her mouth against her better judgment.

"The Battle of Abscond. That's what they've come to call it—that little brouhaha you all boiled up last month," Evelyn said. The stylus had momentarily stalled, the indentations of teeth marks apparent, before it started to flitter again. "You will tell me what occurred, and I will tell you what happens to you next."

Outside, there was a gathering of birds strung like notes on an old telecom line. It was an odd sight, as most relics from that time had been torn down, long since replaced by underground ethernet. The flock took off, one by one, then in droves, their radiant underbellies glinting as they turned in synchronized flight.

"Endangered," the woman said, briefly distracted. "It's why they kept those lines. Apparently, they come every year on migration." She crossed and uncrossed her legs again, pulling the chair closer to the table, its feet scraping across the floor, then leaned back as though settling in for the duration. "You're going to tell me how many women were in your camp, before you marched on the bunker you discovered, and who was leading these…" She opened the folder, glancing at the papers as if she didn't recall. "… these Freedom Women. Were you the leader's companion? Is that how you got wrapped up in all this?"

"I'm an uninclined. Never been partnered," Noemi said.

She was among the sect of women without preference, those that had eschewed social norms for a life apart. In her adolescent years, she'd been presented with the traditional array of sexual identification. There was the norm of women companions, those who held the feminine aspect to the highest order, women and women's sexuality the rightful evolution of humankind. Then there was the fringe of contrived biologicals, those who had assumed the masculine in homage to times before. And there had been the free love and the prim girls, and the commitment-only girls. Noemi had been inclined to none.

"So, you thought it would be a bit of fun," Evelyn said, scribbling on her notepad, "to rampage across the valley and destroy things, destroy people?"

Noemi inwardly rolled her eyes. At times, she found it useful to dig her thumbnail into her skin to distract her from the nonsense of inquisition, as a reminder there was nothing left for them to take from her. She had caused enough of her own pain already.

"It's documented here," Evelyn continued, tapping the table with a long, thin finger. "You were a nurse at a moderate-risk facility before. You were reassigned there. Why?" She stood up, walking around the table, coming to a stop squarely in front of Noemi. "The thing I don't understand in any of this is why on earth you would bring your daughter."

Blood began pooling into the palm of Noemi's hand, thumbnail cutting the skin, pressing in harder and harder. But she couldn't make it hurt enough. She slammed her hand down on the table as hard as she could. The crisp outline of her hand left a red stain, like the mark of an old cave painting. She stared at the woman, unwavering, silent.

"Are we done with the theatrical standoff now, Noemi?"

"Let me see my daughters."

"Tell me what happened at the Battle of Abscond. Tell me," she said, pausing as she returned to her seat, "and I will tell you what happens to you next. And your daughters, too."

Noemi's hand dragged across the table in a long red smear as she sat back, crossing her arms, hands in fists. The pain had come now, pulsing in time with her heart, unable to be remedied, only endured. This was a barter she was willing to make. Anything to know what happened to Jayne. And whatever she would have to say to see her daughters, even if for only five minutes, long enough to tell them she'd love them forever.

The woman scrawled notes in longhand while the recorder absorbed Noemi's words, halting at first, then flowing as though she needed to get them out of her body, to be free of them. She talked about Odelia, about Jayne taking the letter and embracing the banner of rebellion, of Rosena wanting to be a part of it and running off in the night without a word. She talked about the girls in the camp, swept up by the fantasy of men. Of the leader of them all, Carol, feeding the frenzy.

"I tried to leave so many times," Noemi said, resigned to surrender. "But I couldn't. It was my fault. I couldn't stop it. It was too big."

"And when you saw the bunker fall, what did you see?"

"I saw them," she said. "Crawling out of the ground like cockroaches. Some of them ran straight into the woods, never even looked back. The rest—"

"How many? How many went into the woods?"

"Maybe a dozen, maybe two. I wasn't counting, wasn't really paying attention to the ones who had run off. They weren't an immediate threat, you know? The rest, well, I saw their collars. Saw they were confused. I wanted them to stay away, to be afraid of us."

"You were seen pointing a device at them?"

Noemi couldn't help but grin. "A vitals scanner. I thought it had worked, made them believe it was something that could hurt them. But then I realized, it was your people coming out of the woods."

"They retrieved you from the bottom of the wreckage," Evelyn said, manicured eyebrow arched in question.

"I'm a nurse. I had to go in there." Noemi ran her hands down her thighs, the sting of sweat mixing with the cut on her hand. Being powerless against her own fate was something she had come to terms with, to a degree. Her daughters were another matter. She'd known Stella was safe, home with an ornery yet doting grandmother. And Rosena had been next to her on the edge of the field, so she knew her elder daughter was at least whole and unharmed. Noemi had only worried for them to the usual extent—which is to say, with every fiber of her being. But she didn't know what had happened in between then and now, didn't know what had been said, if they'd been frightened, or if they'd needed her.

"Now, tell me what happens next, to me and my daughters," Noemi said.

The woman looked up from the paper, slowly placing the stylus down exactly perpendicular to the page, before sitting back in her chair. "To face the consequences proactively, you have been assigned to care, convalescence, and rehabilitation of those affected by the battle you were a part of. You will see firsthand the damage done by your actions. Your sentence is fulfilled when they no longer require care."

Noemi's momentary relief was replaced by a quick realization, her memory etched with a scene of burned and broken women. "What if they don't recover?"

Evelyn's mouth twitched, the corners upturned with an air of suppressed smugness. "Like I said, you are sentenced for the duration of their care. You will be transferred tomorrow." Standing, she tucked the notepad under her elbow, turning to go.

"And my girls?"

"Care goes to next of kin by election. They've chosen your sister, Jayne."

A rush of questions stampeded through Noemi's mind: How had her sister escaped capture, much less sentencing? Where had she been? Had she gotten hurt? But none of that mattered so much as what she really needed to know. "When will I see them? When will I see my daughters?"

"We are a free society, Noemi. You will see them whenever they choose to see you," Evelyn said. "That is, if they ever choose to see you again."

16

IF I COULD KILL A THING

IT WAS THE THIRD time that morning Lucy was cursing under her breath, thumb shoved in her mouth like a toddler while the girls giggled at the sight. Lucy hadn't been in the habit of doing handiwork in a while, and it seemed like the hammer had a mind of its own. Her thumb was beginning to take on a deep shade of violet, blood pulsing just below the surface in angry complaint.

"Trade ya?" she asked, grinning at Mandy, her new constant companion. The girl was wielding a small handsaw as if she'd been born for carpentry.

"No, ma'am," Mandy said. "Surely I'd smash my fingers, same as you, and mine are littler, so 'stead of them getting purple, they'd be squashed flat. I'd just as soon keep them round. I'm betting if you hit your thumb one more time, it'll go splat, and then you'll only be able to count to nine and a half."

"Nine and three-quarters, probably," Birdie said with a shy smile, face blushing pink. It was uncommon for her to pipe up with humor. "Here, Miss Lucy, I can trade for a while if you want," she continued, holding out a screwdriver. "I haven't slipped even once. I'm sure I can spare a few tries."

"Kind of you, Birdie, but it's alright," Lucy said. "It's rare I got to count to ten anyhow. How's about you fill up the basket with more hardware, and see if you and Jenna can grab a few more boards, too? I'm betting we can get the rest of the floor done before the day's out."

Set to her task, Birdie started the long climb out of their perch, down the tall ladder they'd leaned against the trunk. The platform was well above the main branches, tucked into the crux and hidden deep inside the canopy. It could only be seen from directly below, and that was if you knew it was there in the first place. The raw boards had been painted mouse gray, with remnant bark affixed for better camouflage. All that was left was to add the floorboards and railing, and soon the girls would have their new hiding place.

Lucy had even managed to secure a rifle and a few dozen rounds of buckshot for Kate's shotgun from an old woman, Donna, who had an underground trade up in the hills. No one asked the woman where she'd gotten the munitions from, and no explanation was ever offered. Lucy speculated Donna had been military long ago during The Waning, judging by her short-cropped hair, brusque demeanor, and habit of standing at ease, despite the fact she had to be at least eighty years old. Usually, the old ones were brimming with bygone stories of a world with men, back in the time when they'd had husbands of their own, not shared or loaned with express intent. But not this one. At the first mention of why Lucy had sought her out, Donna had barely said a word.

"I see," Donna said, her voice hoarse with age. She nodded once, face like stone, but her lively eyes revealed a mind running a silent inventory of what might be on offer. "Wait here," she finally said, walking into the next room with slow but deliberate purpose.

Lucy wandered around the front room, observing the spare decoration and utilitarian ease with which the woman lived. The cabin walls were made of stripped whole log timber pine, with windows carved out for light, but no frills or fancy drapery to cover them, only solid shutters adorned with small decorative stars cut clean through. She probed one with her finger, noting the opening was perfectly eye level.

"Some for the barrel, some for the eye," Donna said.

Lucy shuddered, turning around. The woman had returned without a sound. Donna was standing a foot away, holding a metal ammunition box and a rifle. The rifle had a wooden stock, its old nicks and scrapes smoothed to a soft luster, with a rose-gray steel barrel nearly two feet long. Donna thrust out the box, shoving it into Lucy's hands. It was heavier than she'd expected, belying the old woman's wiry frame. Lucy set it on the table, popping the brackets off the lid to reveal an army of bullets, the brass tucked in layer upon layer of tight, shiny rows.

"That'll do ya," Donna said, then gestured with the rifle, cradling it in her arms. "Remington. Thirty-aught-six. Bolt action. Good for when your target is a ways out. Better for when you want to keep it that way. But mind you now," she said with a warning glare, "it'll kick some." She proceeded to show Lucy how to load it, the sharp sound of the mechanism locking in place. "If they're close enough to hear that, often enough, they'll scamper away, and you won't have to bother with them at all. But if it's already started, don't hesitate. Aim for the meat of them and pull the trigger."

The rifle had the weight of a half sack of potatoes, heavy, but not so much it was hard to hold. Lucy put the stock up to her shoulder, lining her eye up with the sight at the end of the barrel, wondering what it would take to be willing to shoot it. But the memory of that day was vivid, of the filthy creatures stalking the farm, and of Kate huddled naked in a corner. Maybe it wouldn't take much at all.

"We've got a shotgun, too," Lucy said, looking out the window and shifting her target from tree to fence post to chattering squirrel, wondering if she would be able to hit any of them. Dropping the rifle to her side, she turned back toward Donna. "But we only have bird shot. It's barely enough to scare off the foxes. Would you happen to have anything better?"

Donna's hands planted on her straight hips, expression unchanging.

"We've four girls to look after," Lucy added.

"What I've got of that is mine." Donna brusquely clamped the cover down on the ammunition box, her bony hands still deft and strong. "Daylight's running faster than you are. Best you pay your trade and get on with your business, and leave me to mine."

They went outside, pausing for a moment on the porch next to an old blue rocking chair. The sun was trailing low on the horizon. Part of the journey off the hill would be in twilight if she didn't hurry. Shoving the ammunition box in her pack, Lucy hefted it onto her back and stepped down into the yard.

"They said you don't take credits, being all the way up here and all, so I've brought you trade I thought could help tide you over for the winter. There are three laying Orpington hens, three sacks of ground grain, a dozen or so jars of tomatoes, plums, and rhubarb, a quart of clover honey, and six yards of mixed wool bolt for clothes or quilting. And I'll leave our cart here for now, if you don't mind. I might be able to make it down by nightfall without it."

"It's a fair trade," Donna said. "Cart'll keep."

"The girls sent bread and oatmeal scotch cookies." These last items Lucy pulled out of her waist satchel, handing them to Donna as though making a peace offering. It had been Birdie's insistence to give Donna an extra kindness. "Oh, almost forgot." Lucy reached inside the outer pocket of the backpack, withdrawing a small frame. "The little one's got something for you, too. When I told her you lived all the way up here by yourself, she wanted to make you a picture to keep you company. Not sure why she picked the goat though. It's meant to be our Agatha." At five, Mika wasn't much of an artist. But Lucy thought she'd captured the ornery old goat's essence entirely, with a long, skinny neck holding up floppy ears and mismatched, square buggy eyes, with a tongue stuck straight out to the side. One could almost hear the *'baaa'*.

Donna held the picture with both hands, studying it silently, her mouth twisting slightly at the corners. "Four of them, you said?"

Lucy began nodding in affirmation, but it went unnoticed, as the old woman had already turned on her heel and gone back inside. She returned almost immediately, carrying a burlap pouch. "It's buckshot. Best you go now, afore I change my mind."

The red plastic cartridges were lined up on the linen placemat in five-by-five rows. Kate's chin rested on her hands, elbows on the kitchen table, as though she were studying each and every one. She picked one up, letting it roll back and forth in her hand over and over and over again, not saying a word.

Kate had become utterly withdrawn, and Lucy hated how it made her feel. It was like the woman she'd loved had crumbled, and a statue had been rebuilt in her place, cold and hollow and not the same. She was sure Kate hadn't told the truth of that day—and Lucy knew she hadn't yet told the truth of her part in it either. But she was damned well certain she wasn't going to ever let it happen again.

"Don't hesitate. Aim for the meat of them. That's what the old woman said," Lucy advised, desperate to break the unbearable silence. Careful not to move too quick, she took a cartridge out of Kate's hands, trying to feel the warmth of her fingers without it being obvious, hoping for the spark that used to ignite them when they touched.

Kate sat back, retreating, arms folding across her chest. "I won't tell you I don't wish them all dead, because I do. But what if it's me who kills the last one?"

"It's not as if there wasn't plenty of pater-seed harvested before. Can't see as how one of that scurvy-ridden lot is going to make any difference now," Lucy said.

"I don't know if I could kill a thing," Kate murmured. "Even if I wanted to."

"You would if you had to," Lucy said. "You would for the girls."

"I would never let anything happen to them..." Kate's voice trailed off into a whisper. Her fingers were pressing deep indentations into her arms, likely to bruise come morning, as though she were hoping to stifle the tremors coursing under her skin and obvious to anyone with eyes. "But they have to have caught them all by now, don't you think?"

"If they had, they wouldn't have broadcast a message requiring us to report sightings. No, Kate, they're still out there, and we need to be ready. The tree house is done, and the girls have their hiding place. The house is secure, and I'm adding portholes to all the sides tomorrow. Then we practice. We shoot targets. We run drills. We show the girls what to do. Where things are. When to hide. How to stay safe." Vesper came into the kitchen, walking right up to Kate and resting his blocky head on her thigh. "And you work on making that dog of yours useful."

Where Kate would put on a façade of ease with the girls—a veneer so thin even Mika could see past it—the dog appeared to calm her when no one else could. Vesper seemed to know exactly when Kate needed him, too, always showing up when she was on the verge of true despair, which lately had been whenever Lucy was talking to her.

"Useful how?" Kate ran a thumb between the dog's eyes up and over his head. His coat was smoothed flat nearest his face, but grew thick and rough around his neck, like a wolf's, the fur black-tipped at the ends, yet blond underneath. He was a mutt of unknown variety, but looked as though he ought to be a breed of his own.

"'Heel'?" Lucy suggested. "'Come'? 'Sit, stay, leave it'? 'Attack,' maybe?"

"Oh, I think he knows how to do that already," Kate said confidently. She ran her hand down his head in gentle strokes, the dog looking at her reverently.

Vesper was the one who'd run them off. He was the one that saved her. He was the one Kate loved. Lucy hadn't thought she could be jealous of a dog, but maybe she was. "Nonetheless, it'd be helpful if he, you know, responded to basic commands."

"Maybe," Kate said, retreating from the table and busying herself with making yet another pot of tea, even though the last one still sat full, cold as the air between them.

Lucy walked up behind her, resisting the desire to take Kate in her arms and hold her tight. She wanted to. And she almost did, taking a step closer, until all she had to do was reach out and caress her neck, run her hands down Kate's arms, then fold her into a reassuring embrace and tell her it was all going to be okay, that she would protect her this time. Lucy took another step, near enough for Lucy to smell the scent of bergamot cascading into the pot. Close enough to change her mind.

Lucy traced a strand of Kate's hair, letting it run through her fingers and across her palm.

The pot dropped, the dry tea spilling over the counter when it fell out of Kate's hands, tumbling across the floor, miraculously staying in one piece. Kate slid out of Lucy's grasp like an eel, slinking away and down to the ground, picking up the pot as though plucking it off hot coals. She clutched it to her stomach and backed up against the corner of the cabinet, shaking her head, eyes shut in a silent, pleading *No.*

"Tell me what happened, Kate. Just tell me?" Lucy would have held her breath had she not stopped breathing already, for fear anything but silence would be too loud.

"Nothing," Kate whispered.

"Goddammit! If truly nothing happened, why on earth won't you come near me? Why can't I be with you? Why won't you let me touch you or hold you?" Lucy slammed her hands down flat on the counter, letting the sound cut through the room and bounce around its edges in hopes it would shock Kate back to life again. To make her angry, to make her speak. To make her anything but silent.

"I know I'm a coward. And maybe you judge me for it. For being fragile," Kate said. "But where were you when I needed you?"

17

WOUND IF NECESSARY

THE NOTION OF WHAT she was doing whispered like a ghost in Kate's ears. Words of blame and feelings of distrust would be given as a gift of discontent to a woman she loved—the woman she'd waited her whole life for. There were times when it was simplest to take the worst of the thing that couldn't be reconciled or overcome or forgiven of oneself, and make another carry it for you. Kate had already performed the exercise of her own self-loathing, and there was no space left for more. She hoped Lucy would bear it, because Kate knew she could not.

"But where were you when I needed you?" Those words were uttered to draw up resentment, to sharpen the wedge. Kate didn't need to hear Lucy's reply. The sound of blame was always deafening. But the feeling of it was like spending every day and every night in an ocean, head beneath the waves, with only enough energy to kick to the surface and breathe for a moment before slipping down into the black depths and starting to drown again.

"I said I'm sorry!" Lucy grabbed Kate's arms and shook her, eyes wide and searching. "I didn't know what to do. Okay? I saw them, and I just … froze. All I could think about was you, and the girls, and how was I supposed to protect everyone in two different places, and I didn't have anything, not even a damn knife—noth-

143

ing. Kate, I would do anything to take it back, to change it. Do you even hear me?"

It didn't matter to Kate where Lucy had been. Lucy had kept her daughters safe; nothing mattered more. But she just wanted to be left alone. She wanted it to be another time, far ahead when it was no longer a fresh wound, when she didn't have to live with it crawling across her skin, in her every thought, wondering if every shadow at night or every breeze through the tree was *Them*, returned for more. She could not tolerate the sympathetic glances, the worry, or Lucy's desire to smother her with care, when it felt as though her skin, her body, her thoughts had been caked with filth that could not be scrubbed clean.

"The girls like having you around," Kate said. "I won't take you away from them. Not now. But what's between us is ... is done." Kate slid past her, out of the kitchen, the scent of tea still lingering in the air. She was running down the hall filled with photos of her girls—first birthdays, cake-smeared faces, flowers clutched in tiny hands—her hurrying feet taking her out into the yard, beyond the barn and it's bleating occupants protesting her passing, down into the meadow by the old Chestnut tree with its deep shade and low, sweeping branches. She collapsed into the grass, knees drawn up to her chest. Her hand covered her mouth, stifling the sound of love being dashed out of her soul.

The next days were a fog of muddled activity, numbness, and distraction combined. The girls' tree house was finished, a feat of engineering and stealth. The house had become a fortress, with defensible positions from both floors and every side. A closet was turned into a hiding place by moving an old wardrobe in front of its door, affixed with a sliding back panel. The attic access was in the closet's ceiling, and Kate was delighted as much as she was horrified that the girls had thought it great fun to have so many places to secret themselves away.

And Lucy persisted. When she showed Kate how to sight the shotgun, she stood close, arms around hers to steady the barrel. When she painted the inside of the girls' hideaway closet like an enchanted garden, she invited Kate inside, taking her hand as she stepped through the wardrobe and holding on longer than necessary. She showed her the girls' tree house, bringing Kate up to the platform, sitting next to her amongst the branches, near, silent, and still enough for the birdsong to resume. It was as though Lucy were trying to gentle a wild doe. She was constant, never asking for more or saying a word about what had happened.

But kindness was not what Kate wanted. All she could think about were her daughters, huddled in an attic, terrified. Or worse, motherless. To be treated as though she were broken only served to make her angry, and that rage began consuming her fear. She daydreamed about taking the shotgun and seeking out the thing that had frightened her most—to make it as afraid as she was. Kate imagined seeing *Them* at the end of the barrel, speechless and scared as she had been, wondering what a woman's next move might be. It became a daydream, creeping into her everyday chores, until she found herself staring out the window washing a dish for so long, she was surprised the pattern hadn't worn off.

There were new broadcasts on the intermodal in the ensuing weeks that only fueled her desire. More sightings. More encounters. More instances of "unfortunate outcomes" that no one bothered to explain or expand on, only to say there were new rules:

Warn first.

Wound if necessary.

Kill as a last resort.

18

Number 792

Fifty-seven years after The Waning: Three years after Liberation

It was three years since the first time the men came. Their return didn't surprise Lucy. She'd known the men would come back eventually, if they'd survived the time between then and now. She was only surprised it hadn't been sooner.

There had been seventeen fugitives accounted for since the Battle of Abscond. A few had been found dead in the woods after the first winter thaw. More had been caught, lured into a house with the sweet scent of baking bread, only to find the keepers of their collars inside, waiting. A few had been killed by women defending their homes and children, who were set to live with the terrors of an experience beyond any nightmares previously conjured.

For Lucy, there was satisfaction in knowing a few more could be added to the inventory of the dead, and she would take no small amount of pride in her contribution to the roster. She marched over to the man on the ground, tearing the tape off his mouth. "How many more of you are there?"

"I don't know," he croaked.

"You have a camp somewhere? More men in your crew? How's it work?" He didn't answer. Lucy wasn't one to abide silence, and

146

she kicked him without hesitating. "Damn the lot of you, just going around taking whatever you please!"

He winced only a little, as though he was used to it and had come to expect violence for the little things. "These guys are the only ones I know," he muttered, looking sideways at Lucy, his head half-cocked. "I only come across them maybe a week ago. I haven't seen any others—haven't for near three years now. Been on my own."

Lucy gestured with her chin towards the dead ones just beyond. "Then why'd you come here with them?"

"Long time to be with just yourself," he mumbled.

If he had no information to offer on the whereabouts of any others, then as far as Lucy was concerned, the man held no use at all. She picked up the roll of duct tape, intent on shutting his mouth for a good long while. Maybe then he'd changed his mind on what he knew.

"I haven't seen one of you," he said, staring at her with wide eyes.

"What do you mean, you haven't seen me?" Lucy wondered if he'd been a watcher in the woods, an unease starting to creep up her spine while a barely quelled fury started to reignite. She reached for the buck knife at her hip, hand resting on the smooth burl of the handle, thumb flicking off the holster snap.

"Never seen ... never seen a woman before."

"Until a few years ago, I ain't seen one of you neither. Now I've seen your sort twice, and that's more than plenty, and I'd just as soon not see your lot ever again." Lucy cut off a length of tape and moved towards him, intentions plain. "Now, unless you got something useful to say..."

"I'd have told you if there's any to tell, I swear it," the man said. "They're no friends of mine. But they're the only ones I know—and they're dead. So, it doesn't matter now, does it?" He tried to shimmy away, but a man who'd been shot in the foot doesn't' run, and he fell over onto his back. "Please. Don't!" His large hands rose in surrender. "I won't say anything you don't want me to, and I'm not going to do anything troublesome for you folks to fuss on."

"Where else have you been? Who else have you stolen from?"

"Been eating rabbits and dandelions, mostly. Those boys, well, they try and bother some old woman up them hills. But she wasn't having none of that. Run us off, yelling some about she shoot us ones just like the last, no bother at all. That old woman the only one they bother, when I was with them, before coming down here. We come here because them boys say they been here before. Thought maybe you'd have gone city way, scared like some others been. But you're still here, and they needn't have bothered. I told them so, but they don't listen to me."

Kate stood by, eyebrows knitted in vexation, fingernails between her teeth, the other arm wrapped securely around her waist. She was swaying ever so slightly, as though rocking herself for comfort. "Changed my mind," she said, eyes never leaving the man on the ground. "Just call that government woman, the overseer. They'll take the dead ones, too. We'll be done with it. I need to be done with it."

"Never mind that, Kate. I got this," Lucy said. She wanted to say she'd take care of her this time, to finally make good on the promise she'd made—to protect Kate—when she hadn't before. But it was as though Kate had gone someplace else in her mind entirely, oblivious to what was unfolding before her.

"The girls can go to your house, stay with you, until it's sorted," Kate said.

Lucy patted down the tape on the man's face with a few sharp smacks, trying to ignore the damp springing into his eyes. She turned away, unwilling to dwell on it.

"You're going inside now, Kate. You're going to mind your girls, see to it they're alright." Lucy put an arm around Kate, hand pressing lightly against her back to start Kate's feet moving towards the house, as though it was a notion of her own making. Vesper trailed behind. They made it all the way to the door before Kate hesitated. She twisted out of Lucy's hold, turning around to look at him, eyes pooling with tears.

"I killed one of them," Kate whispered. "But how many more will there have to be?"

Lucy pulled her close, arms wrapping around Kate so tight she felt the tremors coursing through her body. Kate's hair smelled of elderflower and honey, soft against her face, and Lucy's heart ached for every lost thing. She could have told Kate she loved her, because she did—more than she ever had before. Lucy could have promised to protect her, because the years between then and now had only served to make her resolute. She could have held Kate for hours or days or years, and it would never have been enough. So, she told Kate the only thing she could.

"I'll take care of it. You don't have to worry about a thing."

Sweat was pouring off his face in rivulets, quiet grunts emphasizing his every move as he dumped the last of his friends into the bed of the truck with a resonant thud. The delicate scab on his foot had reopened and was bleeding profusely. He'd turned alarmingly pale, sitting down abruptly with his back against the truck tire.

Lucy had set the vehicle downhill, tailgate opening to an almost level ramp, so all he had to do was drag his buddies in. It was no matter to her whether he keeled over right then and there, except she'd be the only one left to drag a dead man into a truck.

"Get in," she said, pointing at the truck bed with her buck knife. She'd left his arms tied at the elbows and the tape across his face. Meek as he seemed to be, he'd been strong enough to live rough for all these years. No good would come from underestimating him.

"Sooner you get in, sooner you're out of here. Might even let you wash up a bit in the creek. You've got a fair stink about you."

The man's head hung like a rag doll, eyes vacant, staring off into the distance. His hands lay palms up atop his sinewy thighs, legs splayed out before him. Lucy began to wonder if he'd died right there on the spot without a note of warning. A fly landed on his arm, evidently of the same notion. His eyes slowly trailed down towards it, watching lazily as it made a quick flight and landed on his shin.

"You sit there any longer, that thing'll make a home of you. Get up. It's time to go."

He shook his head, 'no,' just once.

"Get up!" Lucy shouted, holding out her knife and pointing it towards the vehicle. There was a part of her that wanted to prick him, make him see she wasn't one to be trifled with. But that was the problem with knives: proximity. Lucy wasn't willing to get close enough to use it. She'd left the rifle on the front stoop, all the way across the yard, and she admonished herself for the rookie move. She should have known better.

"Get up, goddammit, or so help me..."

His head turned toward her, slowly. Then his expression changed to that of surprise, looking past her.

All Lucy's mistakes flashed through her mind: more men, it had been a ruse, Kate and the girls were already dead, she hadn't protected them, and now they'd come for her... She spun around, knife at the ready, heart pounding. She dropped it almost straight into her toes.

"Sorry, Miss Lucy! Didn't mean to frighten," Birdie said softly. She cast a glance at the man on the ground. "I mean for him to have my supper."

"You're not supposed to be out here, Bird. Your mama know where you are?"

"Maybe not," Birdie said. She held up a small linen-wrapped bundle, mustering her resolve. "It's just a cheese-and-tomato sandwich. Mama didn't feel like cookin'. It's for him, Miss Lucy. I got plenty, and he don't." Her long, thin arms held out the small parcel, but she wouldn't look at him, eyes dancing around from the ground to the truck and back again, eventually settling on Lucy's chin. "You'll let him have it, won't you?"

Lucy was suddenly able to see him as Birdie did. He looked as near to death as a person could while still among the living, so pale and painfully thin and bleeding. It was a wonder how he'd managed to spend the last hour dragging bodies, himself still bound, still muted, barely able to breathe.

And in that moment, it dawned on Lucy how Birdie must have seen her, too. She took Birdie's meager offering, guilt washing over her in waves. "Of course. I'll make sure. As soon as I've taken him to my place. Promise."

The man got up without a sound, pausing long enough to steady himself, and long enough to take in the sight of Birdie skipping back to the house, pleased with her errand. His expression wholly changed, from dogged resistance to grateful submission, and he set himself down in the truck bed alongside his dead companions with no more than a wary glance and a sigh.

Lucy got in the truck, situating herself in the bucket seat, running her hands over the steering controls, the old plastic covering the wheel torn in some places and exposing the glint of aluminum beneath. The stir of excitement buzzing under her skin was mixed with a dose of trepidation. She'd seen vehicles of this sort as a kid, but had no recall of ever being in one. There was a dashboard of instrumentation, offering temperature levels and driving ranges based on current light conditions—the sort of autonomous vehicle of yesteryear, abandoned for the sake of collective progress.

The truck rattled to life, its solar engine vibrating to a low hum. Lucy pressed the truck forward, slow at first, oscillating down the driveway until she got her bearings, steadying into a straight path off Kate's property and onto the common throughway. The CRZ maintained some of the old primary roads for inventory trucks to make collections from the production farms, but Lucy hadn't driven on one before. She'd never had the need to own a one-car. Most folks biked the roads if they wanted to get somewhere fast, instead of the usual walking trails connecting the countryside to the monorail hubs.

It was a new vantage point, sitting up in a truck with the windows down and the air in her face. The paved thoroughfare bisected meadows of tall grass rippling in the wind, birds soaring upward on swells. Despite everything that had happened, and everything she knew was to come because of what was in the back of the truck, Lucy couldn't help the fact she was grinning ear to ear—so much so that when she arrived at her property, there was reluctance to turn down the lane toward her house. Lucy wanted to keep going, to gather up Kate and take her away and drive somewhere neither of them had ever been. Resolute in this plan, Lucy arrived home, determined to rid herself of the men with haste.

Lucy had been granted a two-hectare rural residence for apiculture management and research. At one time in its history, it had been a working farm with a large barn and outbuildings dotting the property. She'd left them standing, some in better repair than others, letting nature reclaim the landscape as it may. Other areas had been cultivated for her bees, alfalfa and clover for the spring, aster and goldenrod for autumn, with meadow rue and liatris winding through as it may.

The truck came to a rolling stop, the hum of its motor going quiet. Despite her determination to get on with things, Lucy was also filled with dread. The CRZ would arrive, relentless in their questions, demanding information Lucy was reluctant to give. It was tantamount Kate and the girls be protected from another inquisition. She would be damned if she'd let Evelyn Emmett get a hold of the girls. Lucy glanced at the man in the bed of the truck, wondering for the briefest of moments what would come of him in the overseer's hands, and just as quickly, she dashed the thought out of her mind.

With a long sigh, she got out, placing her rifle on top of the cab before walking to the back of the truck, hand skating across her hip to make sure the buck knife was still there. His knees were drawn up to his chest, arms listless. He'd ripped a portion of fabric off one of his dead friend's shirts and had wrapped it up tightly around his foot, hands bloodied with the effort.

"Hold out your arms." Lucy unclasped the knife, holding it at the ready. He watched with half-lidded eyes, hands outstretched and wobbling with effort. She nicked the binding enough to tear it open, freeing him.

"Take the tape off your face, and then you can have this," she said, tossing Birdie's sandwich into the man's lap. He was so eager, he didn't even wince when the tape was pulled off, shoving the bread into his mouth as quickly as he could, groaning when the taste of tomato reached his tongue.

It did not seem to matter to him that he was eating lunch among the dead. His desperation was plain as day, and Lucy reckoned he hadn't eaten much beyond weeds and rodents for some time. The last corner of the sandwich was held contemplatively between his fingertips, as if he were savoring it as much fearing it would be a long while before he ate again.

"If you swear you'll stay put, I'll get you water."

He nodded, just barely, not bothering to look at her.

Lucy grabbed her rifle, hurrying into her house and back again, cup and pitcher in hand. He hadn't moved. She set both atop the old stone wall abutting the barn ramp, motioning for him to get out when she backed away.

Watching her warily, he moved slowly over the side of the truck, sliding down to the ground and hobbling over to the wall. With restraint—for surely, he'd rather have upended the whole pitcher into his mouth—he poured the water into the cup, drinking in great gulps. The skin of his exposed neck revealed a line of scars, worn smooth.

"How'd you get it off?" Lucy gestured with her hands toward her own neck.

He tugged at his shirt collar, shoulders drawing up toward his ears as though he were a turtle trying to shrink into a shell. "Hacksaw," he said. "Just come off. Day before yesterday. Those boys had one. I been at it the whole time I know them." Then he froze, catching his breath, eyes straight down on the ground. "You got a collar for me now?"

"Of course not," Lucy blurted out. "Why on earth would I?"

"Then what you want me for?"

She tipped the barrel of the rifle towards the dead men. "You're lining your friends up on the ground, then I'm stashing the truck. I'm calling you in just as soon as that's sorted. You'll have time to wash up in the creek before they come for you, 'cause I said you could. I don't go back on my word."

"Please don't give me over to them," he said softly, stroking his neck, almost meditative. "I won't be no trouble."

"What was it for? That thing that was around your necks," Lucy asked.

"Why you think anything wears a collar? To keep us in line, so we do as we bid. Move when it say. Sit when it say. Get away from the wall when it say. Go to the wall and do what it make us have to do when it say." His voice shook as he spoke, hands gripping the capstone wall as if it were all he could do to hold onto the edge above an abyss. "I say I won't be no trouble to you, and I don't go back on my word neither."

"I have to call you in. Too much trouble if I don't. Go on, now, lay your friends out on the dirt." Lucy eyed the sun's descent towards the horizon; twilight was coming fast. "If you think I'm not a good shot in the dark, go on and test me. Do like I told you and unload them."

He stood up abruptly, fists clenched at his sides, eyes intent on the barrel of Lucy's rifle pointed at his chest. "Do it. 'Cause I'm not going back. What's the point of being alive if all I'm ever going to do is rot in a hole?" He puffed out his chest, eyes closed so tight there were deep furrows down his face. "And I already forgiven you for it, so you don't have to go worrying on that. Honest. I said do it."

Lucy wanted to. She would never forget the first time the men came, what they'd done. How Kate wasn't the same and seemed like she never would be. Everything they'd taken from them, all the worrying about the next time, wondering if they'd hurt the girls... She was tired of it—tired of all of it. And she could end this one just like the others in the truck. What difference would one more make?

His cheeks were streaked dark with the tears running through the dirt stains on his face, chin trembling, eyes still shut tight. Waiting. He was barely standing, balanced on his good foot, legs beginning to fail, and he sank down to the ground.

"I'm no murderer," Lucy finally said. "But I can't let you go, and you're not staying here. I have to call them."

"Let me stay, just a while. Just long enough I'm not broken no more," he said. "Please. I'll do anything you want. I'm not like the others. I told you, I been on my own, not bothering no one. I won't be no trouble."

Lucy looked skyward, sighing and shaking her head. A little part of her felt sorry for him. She didn't like the sensation. "A week. Better hope you heal fast."

His shoulders slumped, and his head hung—in relief or despair, Lucy couldn't tell, but it was of no concern to her. What was of concern was the pile of dead men. The weather was turning, but it was still warm enough they'd be problematic, and she certainly didn't want bodies stashed under a tarp for any length of time. If the girls didn't stumble across the grisly scene, the damn dog certainly would. If she called in to report just the dead men, the CRZ would search her property and find the stowaway and her truck.

"I'll bury them," the man said, as though reading her thoughts.

She eyed him up, rags and bone, shattered. Seemed likely she'd be burying him, too, when it was all said and done, but at least he'd get the digging started.

"Figure if you're stayin', I ought to be calling you something," Lucy said. "You got a name?"

He climbed into the bed of the truck, arm resting on the side. "I was number 792. But my mother called me Abe."

19

GAVE FAIR WARNING

BRANCHES WHIPPED SIDEWAYS, CRACKING and shattering, the tumble of leaves parting as Vesper hurtled up the trail. Birds and squirrels angrily chattered at him from above, and one jaybird was bold enough to swoop down and admonish him for the intrusion. Kate followed, shotgun in hand.

It was an old forest of oak and basswood, with fingers of tamarack and spruce winding into the soft gullies. Whereas the hint of autumn had just begun down valley, it had arrived in the upper hills in earnest, with the sweet scent of leaves beginning to molder and a tinge of crispness in the air.

Kate called Vesper to heel. The dog ran a wide loop through the undergrowth, sending a rabbit to ground as he did, coming back and sliding to a stop at her feet, eager and panting wildly, looking as though his eyes were fit to pop right out of his head.

"Settle down, buddy, 'cause I ain't carrying you." She sat down on a nearby snack log, her legs straddling an old maple that had fallen some years ago, circles of mint-green lichen ornamenting the length of it. It offered a fine vantage point, looking down the mountain toward home. The first hint of fog had crawled into the lowlands just as Kate had climbed above the river that morning. It was one of her favorite things, being able to look at the soft clouds glowing pink with sunrise below, like she was a bird flying above.

Kate shimmied out of her backpack, retrieving water and lunch for them both. Vesper seemed to appreciate the reprieve, lying on the ground beside the tree, eager to see what was on offer. They ate in companionable silence, the dog intent on the biscuits the girls had made for him, and Kate glad of the sandwich and chips and pickle and pasta salad and cookies and pumpkin bread they'd made for her. She speculated her daughters were trying to force-feed love into her with an excess of culinary offerings. Kate had half a mind to be gloomy more often, if for no other reason than to appease her fondness for pudding.

It was the girls' first full day back for a week of away school. Kate usually enjoyed the initial few days of a quiet house. But this time was different. Part of her was glad they were gone; it meant they were safely inside the walled campus. Security measures had been heightened after the Liberation, and in that time, there hadn't been any men sighted anywhere near a hub, much less in a village center. The girls would be safe there. At least, that was what Kate had been telling herself. Part of her heart had gone missing when she waved goodbye to them at the station the day prior, waiting until the train vanished down the tracks before she began the walk home with the other mothers, all of them a bit quieter than they had been on the walk there.

Kate was the only one who'd had a run-in with men. She hadn't told her neighbors yet about the men coming back. What would they think, knowing men had returned to Kate's house? What had Kate done the first time, they might wonder, to cause them to seek her out again? The rumors that would come from it. The things that would be said about her. The way the girls would be torment-ed and subjected to the same rumor, having to defend themselves and their mother against the gossip. Kate wouldn't have it. And so, she'd held her tongue.

Vesper got up and rested his chin on her knee.

"Last one," she said sternly, then passed him a corner of pumpkin bread, before dusting off her hands and holding them up, empty. Content there were no more scraps fit for him, the dog walked a few feet up the path, looking back expectantly. Kate paused, listening for the warning sounds of alarmed birds or panicked squirrels, but there was nothing more than the flitters of chickadees and the usual birdsong. She twisted her arms through the shoulder straps of the pack and resumed walking up the trail in earnest, knowing she would be there within the hour.

The cabin was tucked into a knoll heavily wooded with enormous fir trees, offering an expansive view downslope. The porch was empty but for a solitary blue rocking chair, and the yard was quiet when she approached. Kate briefly wondered if the old woman had gone, but everything was too tidy to have been abandoned. There were fresh crosshatched rake marks in the dirt, and a full stock of winter wood was piled neatly to the side. She stood thirty feet off, bellowing, "Hello the house!"

The familiar click of a firearm sounded behind her.

"Thought it might be one of you," Donna said, walking past Kate and toward the cabin, casually slinging the rifle over a shoulder. "Come inside. I'll put the kettle on."

Kate let out her breath, shaking her head in dismay, looking accusatorially at the dog. He regarded her with an expression of equal disdain. She stroked behind his perked ears, offering an apology under her breath. "Didn't see her, did ya? Well me neither." She stepped onto the porch, setting her gun beside the door and commanding Vesper to stay before going inside.

The old cast iron kettle was already beginning to hiss. Donna had two hand-tossed mugs on the table beside a ceramic teapot, it's fine mesh steeper filled with turmeric and ginger.

"Aye, it's a bit frilly," Donna said, nodding towards the tea. "Helps the old bones though. You won't mind it." Her eyes casually landed on Kate's pack, a thin arched brow asking the question without a word.

"Shortbread with candied cherries and pecans, from my eldest, Jenna. She said the shortbread will keep longer, but I'd be surprised if you don't eat the whole lot of them before I'm halfway home." Kate set the cookies on the table beside the tea, then continued rummaging through her bag. She set down a pewter flask, the old etching of Celtic knots on the sides dulled smooth, but still visible. "And mulled cider from Mandy. She suggested it'd be better with whiskey, but declined to offer how she knows that for certain."

Donna opened the tiny screw cap, sniffing the contents. "I'd say she's right." Then she set it down, gnarled hands clasped neatly in her lap, expectant.

"Mitten gloves from Birdie. She's been knitting like a fiend afore winter comes, and she wanted you to have them before the snow arrives. Not too flashy, 'cause she didn't think you were the sort to go in for loud hues." They were a soft gray-and-oatmeal color, with fleece lining the inside, and a carved button adorning the back to hold the mitten top out of the way.

These Donna put on, flipping the top over the fingers and back again, shaking her head with a wry grin. "If I was a betting woman, I'd speculate you come today with a big ask. No reason I can ponder why your girls be buttering me up so."

"And this," Kate continued, circumventing the remark, "is from Mika. She was quite specific about you placing this latest one in the front room, where all your visitors will see it. I'll warn you though, it seems she's of a different opinion on colors than her sister." She placed the thick envelope in Donna's outstretched hands.

There was a glimmer in the old woman's eye and the hint of a smile barely contained. Donna withdrew the picture, eyes growing wide, and then she threw back her head and laughed, a bellowing whole-body delight. It was a rendition of every animal that had ever set foot on the farm, wild and domesticated beast alike, painted in a palette that tested the limits of the spectrum: each and every creature was wearing plaid pajamas.

"Tell your daughters I thank them kindly. They please me beyond any expectation," Donna said, the smile still present. "You tell Miss Mika her latest painting is my favorite." She shook her head, looking at the picture, laughter bubbling up again. Donna got up and put Mika's picture on the wall in place of an old map, standing back to admire it before turning back around and looking Kate square in the eye.

"I saw you brought the shotgun," Donna said without preamble. "I gather you're looking for ammunition. What else?"

"If you have any to spare, I'd be glad to take it," Kate said. "Otherwise, I'm asking for naught else but information."

Donna sat down, arms across her chest, still wearing the mittens. "I'll tell you if I know of it."

"How many men did you shoot?"

A flicker of impatience ran across Donna's face, quickly subdued with a heavy sigh and a rap of her knuckles on the table. "Pair of them came through not long after your Lucy come calling the first time, some years back. Didn't mind 'em then, but told 'em not to bother again. When they came back next day with three more, I shot the lot of 'them. Gave fair warning. T'was their own doing." Her bony hands wrapped around the tea mug, but she didn't drink, leveling a steady gaze at Kate.

"We've got three dead of our own doing," Kate said. "Showed up a few days back. One more wounded." She took a sip of the tea, resisting the urge to scrunch up her face or ask for honey. It was bitter, and the insides of her lips tingled between heat and numbness. "What did they tell you when you called yours in?"

Donna hesitated, thumb methodically caressing the smooth part of the ceramic mug. "Didn't bother callin'. Set 'em out in the forest to rot. Council found what was left of them come spring," she finally said. "Why you asking?"

"The man I shot. He was ... he was in my house, the first time they come, four years past. I'll remember his face until the day I die. And I thought..." Kate's voice trailed off, throat choking back tears as she shook her head to be rid of the damp in her eyes. It seemed to Kate she was never quite as strong as she thought she'd be.

"You thought making a man dead would settle your mind," Donna said.

Kate shrugged, before leaning over her elbows and pressing her forehead against her hands, mumbling, "Yes, as a matter of fact, I did." She took a deep breath, trying to control her quivering chin when she sat back up, staring at a fixed point on the wall. "I'd spent all those years waiting, wanting them to come just so I could finish what I'd meant to do—what I wished I'd done—the first time. And the whole time I was waiting for that day to come, I was afraid they *would* come back. Now it's done—and I'm the same. Not a damn thing has changed. I'm still too goddamn scared to do anything. And I wonder every day if it's going to happen again."

"You still ain't saying why you come," Donna said. "Less you been shootin' rocks, you ought to have enough ammunition to bide. When you called your dead men in, what'd they tell ya?"

"I didn't," Kate said. "Call them in, I mean. Lucy managed it. Hasn't been anything new broadcast. The CRZ is quiet about it, so us in the valley don't ask questions. That's why I came."

Donna took off the mittens, as though surprised to still be wearing them, and laid them flat on the table. She got up, withdrawing into a back room without a word and returning just as quickly, placing an old paper photo on the table. It was a picture of a wide swath of open land, edged by a conifer forest and rocky outcroppings. An enormous concrete dome was in the center, and a solar light cube protruded alongside. Women in uniform stood around the periphery. Then Donna pulled an image card out of her pocket, pushing it across the table next to the old photograph. It was unmistakably the same place.

Kate leaned over, looking at them both, drawing the paper closer. "What is this?"

Pointing to the new image, Donna said, "The site of the Battle of Abscond. Where the men were found four years ago." Then she pointed to the other photo, at a woman wearing combat utilities. "My post for twenty years."

20

They Don't Take

Dawn had barely come when Lucy heard him scream. A heavy fog lay across the fields as though asking the night to stay a while longer—the sort of mist that consumes the light and creeps into a person's bones like a ghost's cold fingers running down their spine. Lucy slid out of the house with her rifle as escort, stepping silently through the dew-laden grass towards the barn.

The outer door was still barred, and there were no footprints in the soft mud anywhere nearby. Abe should still be inside. Unwilling to trust the notion, Lucy slipped around the corner, looking for signs of escape or intrusion, but finding none. She unbarred the door, cringing at the sound of metal grating in the tracks. With the element of surprise lost, she swiftly went inside, eyes trained through the sight at the end of the barrel, holding her breath, keen to any sign of trouble. The mustiness of straw and damp ground assaulted her senses, but there was nothing amiss.

His stall was closed, the chain through the bars still weighted by the padlock, exactly as she'd left it. Lucy approached from around the side, peeking in. Abe was huddled in the corner, knees to his chin, eyes wide as saucers. Opposite him was Mooey Gorda, with a dead mouse dropped at the cat's feet.

Lucy stared at him, then at the cat. "Goddammit... Really?" she muttered, setting the rifle against the wall. As had become her habit, her hand skimmed across the buck knife at her hip in reassurance.

"You can't go hollering like that," Lucy said. "Anyone within earshot would come looking." With a wary eye towards Abe, who was still cowering and not looking at all sheepish about it, she unlocked the chain and slid open the stall door just enough to coerce the cat out. Mooey was kind enough to leave her gift for Abe right where she'd dropped it and was surprised when the mouse popped right up and scurried off into the straw.

"Only seen one of them once," Abe said, gesturing toward the cat. "When I was living out, year or so past, up in them hills. It was following me. Whole lot bigger than this one. Haven't seen a young one before."

The cat was twining around Lucy's legs, tail up and back arched. She scooped down and picked up the feline huntress, holding the cat close enough, Mooey's whiskers tickled her face. "You must have seen a catamount. But this ain't one of them. Moo is just a plain ol' house cat."

"You sure?"

"Maybe, maybe not. We'll just have to wait and see how big this one gets. Best you be nice to her, so as she don't try and eat you when you're sleeping." Lucy turned around to hide a thinly concealed grin. She kissed the cat's face, putting her down to resume the hunt, hopefully with a bit more success. Grabbing the rifle, Lucy turned back, taking in the disheveled man on the ground. "May as well come on outside. Good day for it."

Abe stretched out his bony limbs, bandaged foot showing faint pink stains when he got up. He folded the blankets Lucy had given him, piling them neatly in a corner. All the straw had been pushed to the side as bedding next to a makeshift table set with containers of food and water. Lucy had been supplying foodstuffs for the three days he'd been here, but he only ever ate half. She knew he was hungry; all one had to do was look at him to know he'd be fit to eat a banquet if given the chance.

"Don't like my cooking?"

"Best I've eaten since I can remember," he said. Abe followed her gaze to the small pile of apples and cheese, bread and honey. "When they took me, back when I was a kid, I didn't get to eat for a week. I'm saving up this time."

"You remember how old you were, when you went ... wherever it is you were?"

"My mama was having a party for me," Abe said. "Just turned eleven. I remember the candles on the cake. I'd just made my wish and blown them out when they come."

Lucy walked behind him, ushering Abe outside. He hobbled, flat-footed on one side, using his big toe for balance on the other. She'd seen the wound—it'd been shot clean through—and speculated it hurt worse than he was letting on. The likelihood of him taking off was doubtful, but Lucy wasn't going to take her eye off him either. The fog hadn't lifted a wisp, and almost seemed as if it were settling in for the duration. If he decided to run, she'd never find him.

"These are my favorite sorts of mornings," Abe said. "When the sky falls down and the whole world's been washed out, and you can't even see the knobs on your own knees." He wore a faraway smile, sitting down on the stone wall, his big hands coming to rest over his knees as if to check for them. The man spoke as though living in a barn—after having been shot by the woman standing in front of him and who'd forced him to be an ad hoc undertaker—was somehow the highlight of his meager life.

"Spent most my life inside. Then I got free and spent most my time outside. I like going inside and coming outside at this place. Reminds me of living at home when I was little."

"Where's your mother now? You try and find her?"

"Don't remember what she looks like," he said, shaking his head slowly. "Don't remember where I come from neither." Abe's voice trailed off, dull eyes looking down at the ground. "It's alright. Man as grown as me shouldn't be going on about his mama anyhow."

Lucy tamped down the pang of sympathy bubbling up and threatening to overwhelm reason. She would not relax her guard just because he was wistful. "Well, maybe the CRZ will help you find your mother if you give them information about the others. You've got a few more days before your week's up and I call you in. Maybe you'll be walking better by then." She paused a moment to take in the form of the pitiful man slumped on the wall. The least she could do was feed him first, she thought.

"I've got an egg pie. If you say you're true to your word, I'll bring it on out to you, so long as you eat all of it. Cooked eggs won't keep."

"I know what I said before, about giving my word," Abe said, looking at her with mournful eyes the color of autumn oak leaves. "Truth is, I'd be lying if I said I wouldn't be gone if I could. What they did to us, it's a life no one ought to have." He held his foot out in front of him as though to check it was still as useless as it had been the minute prior. "And even if maybe I got lucky enough to slip by you, I won't get far. I know it. Maybe I try anyway. But I know you don't want to go shooting me, and I wouldn't be wanting you feeling bad if you had to. So, I'll stay here and wait for some egg pie, and thank you for the offering."

The sun had risen enough to make an effort, but the fog was stubborn, unwilling to let go of its claim on the day. Lucy could just see the creek bridge and could almost make out the girls' tree beyond. She wasn't partial to shooting a man in the back. But she was a good shot, and her rifle was true, and she could maim a man just as easily. Lucy held up the rifle, checking the chamber even though she knew damn well it was loaded and ready, casting a quick glimpse at Abe to be sure he was watching. He was.

When she returned with breakfast, Mooey's black-and-white form was solidly embedded in Abe's lap, curled up tight and intending to stay a while. Abe sat with his back ramrod straight, both hands up as though in surrender, despite the fact his knees were stuck like they'd been glued together to keep the cat from falling through.

"The cat's not partial to strangers," Lucy said, putting the plate down beside him. "She's there just 'cause you're warm."

"It's alright. I don't mind the warm myself," Abe said, picking up the plate and holding it awkwardly to avoid disrupting the furry creature underneath. His eyes fluttered shut with the first mouthful of food, and he emitted quiet grunts of satisfaction with each subsequent bite. He cast a shy glance towards Lucy. "Sorry, miss. Been a while since my food come hot. Had myself an old can of beans once, cooked up in the tin over a fire. Thought I could die happy that day."

"It's quiche," Lucy said. "Just a fancy name for egg pie." She plucked a piece of shell out of the egg and spinach and Gruyere, setting it to the side of the plate. It had been some time since she'd put forth the effort of cooking, having been in the habit of finding herself dawdling at Kate's place until an invitation to stay for a meal was extended, or otherwise being left to forage for whatever was in her own pantry. But with the girls gone away to school for the week, and Kate curiously absent this morning, she'd found herself cooking despite herself.

"I like the crunchy parts," he continued, eyes trailing after another shell she'd pushed aside. She was primed to snatch his plate away for the insult, before he added, "Honest, it may be the best thing I've ever eaten in my whole life."

Lucy hesitated, scanning his face for mockery, yet found none. There was a flush of appreciation for the compliment, which she quickly tamped down in disgust at herself for being so easy to placate. "Finish up. Fog's lifting. You gotta go back inside, keep out of sight, and I got things to do. Can't be watching after you all damn day."

"Well, it's nice of you having me out here and giving me a fine breakfast," Abe said. He ran a tentative hand down Mooey's head, still snugly atop his thighs. A hesitant smile grew across his face as the cat hummed, stretching out a paw and curling it over her nose as she nestled closer. "You both been nice company."

Lucy grabbed the plate from him, scooping up the cat in her other hand. "Moo, you're a damn traitor," she whispered, putting the disgruntled cat down on the ground. "Inside," she commanded Abe. "Let's go."

They were quiet as he stood up obligingly, his stooped body limping back to his makeshift quarters in the barn and into the stall she'd converted to a holding cell. The stall door slid shut, and Lucy latched it into place, resetting the lock and chain. Her hands wrapped around the bars as though she needed something to steady her.

There was a pang of remorse in Lucy's gut, seeing him housed like an animal and knowing it was her who was responsible for it. She simply didn't know what else to do with him besides keep him confined until the time came for the CRZ to take him. She wanted to call him in—she almost had twice—but the guilt she felt for keeping a veritable hostage was overcome by his begging to stay. It was obvious he was barely fit to stand. She had no idea what an interrogation would do to him, no idea what would be done after she turned him over, and no notion as to what had happened before he'd shown up at Kate's.

"Don't mind it, miss," Abe said. He was sitting on the ground, looking up at her, palms open like a supplicant. "I'm alright here. Got food. Got water. Got a roof over my head. No one's bothering me. Don't seem like you mean to hurt me neither. I'm only asking to stay here long enough so I don't break when the breaking time comes."

Lucy stared up at the rafters, shaking her head. Cracks of light ran in long lines where the roofing had fallen to disrepair. The crossbeams were painted with remnants of excrement from pigeons and their avian brethren that had taken up residence, and a very industrious spider had spun a web spanning at least three feet. She felt regret for keeping Abe in a box, even though she wished he and his kind didn't exist. She hated them all for what they'd done to Kate. But whoever had kept them like animals in a cage had done so for a reason.

"You know why they keep you? Why they snatched a kid up from his own birthday party and took him away?"

"I wondered why my whole life. Still got no answer for it. What'd a boy do to get locked up with those men? What'd I do that my mama never come and fetch her boy back?" Abe laughed a little, shaking his head and staring at the rafters, too. "No, miss. I don't know. They put us in there, and they never come back."

The cat slipped through the bars and down into the straw and stalked across the floor right back into Abe's lap. Mooey didn't even pause, simply stepped across his leg and curled up against his stomach, as if he'd been put there for the sole purpose of providing feline accompaniment. Abe circled his arms around the cat, and they both sighed.

"I was just a kid. Maybe one or two of the others were close to thirty or so years old, but most of them were twice older than that. Whole lot a fussing in the beginning, all o' them banging and hollering... When that don't work, they turn on each other. Ain't nothing in there to fight with but our fists, and mine were too small to matter, so they never bothered with me," Abe said, his voice growing quiet. "At least, not that way." He shook his head, mouth pressed together as though his memories might escape. "Never understood how womenfolk could let us rot in there, doing what they did to us all those years."

"We didn't know," Lucy said, her voice rising with frustration. "We grow up learning what they tell us. You hear a thing said enough times for long enough by everyone saying it, then you get to being grown, and it just ... is. After a while, it's not a thing you think on anymore. Men were gone, the same as dinosaurs and dodos. When's the last time you thought about a dodo?"

She told Abe what she'd always been told, what they had all grown up believing: men had stopped being born. It was simple as that, the lot of them waning over the course of time until none were left. Before men's extinction, their seed was frozen and stored, meant to tide womankind over until some new biological invention, or until a woman bore a viable son.

"What's it been like, what with all the men gone?"

"Can't say I'd know the difference one way or the other." She sat for a moment, trying to form a summation of her history lessons from grade school. "There was a disarmament between countries, gosh, maybe fifty or sixty years ago, after The Waning Wars—oh, those were conflicts from when hardly any men were left, and everyone was trying to take the last of them. Now everything's sorted out through each nation's councils.

"The way it's been for us around here, gosh... As far back as I can remember, it's all about eco-rehabilitation and living within our bioregion's capacity. It's everything we do now; the whole industry shifted to it. 'Science is our economy. Education is our success.' That's what they always say. Everyone has a job, so's they can contribute something and be useful. The ones livin' in cities and hubs, they work six hours, morning or evenin' shift, four days a week. No one really lives better than anyone else. It's like, we all have what we need, and no one's tryin' to get more than they ought. Hell, we didn't even have locks on our doors until your lot showed up.

Abe said nothing, looking at her expectedly.

"Every woman is given the chance to have at least three children," Lucy continued with a sigh. "First boy who comes will be called Savior. But there haven't ever been any."

"Them ones yours? The girls over there?" Abe gestured vaguely in the direction of Kate's farm.

"I wish they were," Lucy said. "But no."

Abe's eyes traveled around as though a daughter of Lucy's would suddenly appear from under the hay bales or from behind the agricultural miscellany left to rust in the corners. His wandering gaze landed on her, his question plain as day.

"I'm not fit for it," Lucy said too loudly, voice cutting through the quiet. "They don't take."

"I haven't any notion of the workings of a woman," Abe said. "But I see it troubles you, and I'm sorry for it."

"Don't be. It's no matter anymore," Lucy said sharply. "Now, I've got chores to do. Looks like you're settled, and it seems the cat ain't bothering you over much, so I'll leave you to it." She didn't wait for a reply, spinning on her heel and retreating toward the door, hearing a faint "Thanks, miss" as she stepped outside and shut him in.

She leaned against the barn siding, tears welling up so high in her throat, Lucy thought she might choke. She was halfway down the path to the creek before her mind even registered it, her feet moving of their own accord, bounding across the bridge so loud it made ducks burst out of the water with a startling slap of wings. She was running by the time she reached the meadow. Out of breath by the time she got to the yard. Face wet from crying by the time she was pounding on the door of Kate's house.

But there was no Kate. There was no thundering of the girls' feet. No smiles or giggles of glee. No open arms of welcome or excited chatter. There was nothing but emptiness, locked out of the house Lucy had once hoped would be her home.

21

AROUND TO WATCH

MORE THAN FORTY YEARS had passed since Donna was as-signed to a pop-up station three klicks north of the dome. Marines had been embedded at the site under the jurisdiction of the highest levels of the Governing Council. Those working there were under the impression they were maintaining a secret prison for violent women who had committed high crimes and were an ongoing threat to society, their identities cloaked for their families' privacy.

The prisoners were managed by an artificial intelligence inter-mediary providing data feedback to the handlers, a role Donna had assumed for more years than she was inclined to admit. All of their actions were scheduled. When a prisoner was noncom-pliant, the staff engaged the collars worn around their necks.

"In the early days, I'd engage a dozen times or more in an hour. They were always warned first: comply, or receive pun-ishment," Donna said. "We couldn't see them. Couldn't even hear them. Only knew them by number, 'cause it'd flash up on the screen and get logged."

"The people that delivered supply though, surely they knew when they went inside and saw them?" Kate asked. "Or when they removed the ones who died?"

"It never had doors. Place was a concrete bunker, built like it was for the end times. Once the last one was deposited inside, it was sealed off for good. Supplies—foodstuffs and the like—were tubed in. Deceased were tubed out, incinerated on the way," Donna said. "Never thought it was anything but what they said it was. There were so few men left by that time, there was no reason to think we were watching over the last of them."

"When did you find out it was men in there?"

"Same time as you," Donna said, nodding toward the image card. "When Abscond happened, some photos got into the ether before the Council found out and quashed them."

"How many were in there?"

"Been retired some years, so who's to say?" Donna said, her bony shoulders hinting at a shrug. "I suppose near on eight hundred when I started. Maybe a few hundred gone in my time. Can't say how many'd gone dead and been barbecued since I left."

The notion there could be so many still unaccounted for made Kate shudder, a sudden nauseousness making her skin go clammy and the room sway, heart thrumming in a quick patter inside her chest. It was never going to end.

"Afore you trouble yourself over much," Donna said, pushing the tea towards Kate more as a command than a suggestion, "no others ever went in. The place was sealed up tighter than a gnat's ass. Whoever was left livin' by the time Abscond happened, well, they was just plain old. More than most of them probably died without ever feeling the sun on their face."

"I know it ain't kind to say so, but I'd rather they never did—see sunshine, that is," Kate said. The tea was strong, the scent of ginger tickling her nose. "Should have just let them die off natural. Can't see as how locking them up made any difference."

"It was because of The Waning," Donna said. "That was before your time, of course, and it ain't part of most schooling history.

Before the Fall of Men, everyone was fighting over the last of 'them. They were a commodity, same as oil and water was in old times."

"So, take them all, lock them up without telling no one. No more wars," Kate said.

"That's the sum of it, yes." Donna ran her hands across the bridge of her nose, rubbing wearied eyes that held memories few others living still possessed.

"Why's the Council acting like they're some lost tribe, then?" Kate put her mug down too hard, tiny waves of tea sloshing over the sides and spilling onto the table. "Are we supposed to believe they were hiding in the woods of their own accord, and after fifty-some-odd years, they just all of a sudden decided to come down out of the hills and start assaulting us in their old age?"

"If you keep folk ignorant, you keep folk scared. It'll be a rare day when what the top says happened is the whole and true account," Donna said. "If I wanted to be kind about it, I'd say the Council of these days has no notion of what was done before. But people were still stationed there, zapping those collars. Someone always knows."

Kate sat back in her chair with a long, heavy sigh. She wanted to know everything, as much as she didn't want to know anything at all, to close her eyes and wake up from a years-long nightmare. She wanted her old life back, to look out the kitchen window and see her girls playing in the meadow, afraid of nothing. No locked doors. No hiding places. No guns. No worry for the unknown, when night was as safe as day. "I'm sitting here listening to you, and all I can think of is how much I hate everything about it. What on earth was it all for?"

Donna took the old photo, staring at it for a long while before putting it neatly back into her pocket. "Same as anything else that's almost gone. You hoard it, then you squeeze out every last ounce. Whether you keep it for yourself, so it's you that lasts longest, or you sell the rarest thing to whoever has the most to offer. Oil wars lasted until everyone took the sun and the wind and the waves. Can't see how taking those men would be any different."

"I don't take your meaning," Kate said. "Bunch of old beasts like that, what could they possibly be good for?"

"What do you think?" Donna leveled a gaze at Kate, quizzical brow arched as though waiting for Kate to say more, then let out a raspy laugh, shaking her head in mock dismay. "Seed."

Kate and Donna parted ways with the promise of another visit, maybe with the girls coming along next time to offer their trade in person. The morning's conversation ricocheted through Kate's thoughts, but her effort to keep pace to get home quelled them for a time. Vesper trotted along happily beside her, finally having settled after the day's excitement off property. She neared the bottom of the mountain and was just shy of the river lands, only an hour or so before the plot of new woods and then her farm. Kate slowed her step, thoughts beginning to sort themselves into some form of lucidity.

The notion the men had been kept for fifty some odd years to be used like stallions to stud repulsed her. But Kate's mind wavered on which aspect her disgust should land on: that the Council would reserve such decrepit old men for such a thing, or that the Council had kept this secret in the first place.

She needed to direct her anger towards something: the Council for the lie, the Freedom Women for finding the men, or the men for what they'd done. "Fair to hold them all to account," she muttered. Vesper cocked an ear at the sound of her voice, then kept going, nose to the air. Kate would never have made the journey without Vesper, but she regretted having left the farm without his watch. She should have asked Lucy to keep half an eye on the place, but things between them had become so cold, Kate couldn't bring herself to ask any favors.

Lucy hadn't said anything at all about what had happened when the CRZ came, only that Kate oughtn't to worry about it, she'd handled it. Part of her wanted to know every gory detail, just as much as she wanted to set it aside as though it had happened to someone else. Because she'd killed someone, a person, even if it was a man. And she should feel horrid for it. But those feelings hadn't come. Maybe they would. Maybe eventually she'd break down with remorse and cry herself dry. But what if she didn't?

There were days when she'd just as soon stay in bed. Sometimes she even tried to, but there was always something or someone demanding she get up, bandage a wound, make lunch, fix a coop. And so she did, but her insides didn't twist at the sight of Mandy's cuts, and there was no guilt when Mika said she was hungry, and she didn't really care if there were less chickens than there were the day before. It was tiring to be so tired.

She was down off the mountain, close enough to home that things were becoming familiar. The trail through the new woods shot straight as an arrow among the lines of pitch pines, affording her quick and easy progress. Vesper had found a proper stick and was carrying it like a trophy, tail wagging methodically with glee as he pirouetted down the path, stopping and looking back occasionally to make certain she was keeping up. *To find joy in a stick,* Kate thought. If only it were that easy.

It was not long until they were on the lane toward the house, Agatha's bloaty tail swishing furiously as she bleated in happy greeting, with Fred whinnying his bass chorus. The chickens erupted, clucking percussively, their caramel-colored feathers aloft on the soft breeze of the day. Despite their greeting, it was not the same coming home to an empty house, devoid of the girls. Even though Kate was relieved by the peace and relief of their absence even more so than usual, the sense of the maternal tie—like ribbons connecting her heart to her daughters'—could not be denied.

Kate walked her usual perimeter of the barn and courtyard, shotgun in hand, looking for any signs of disruption, but finding none. The kink in her gut relaxed just a little, a long, low sigh whistling between her teeth.

"Vesper! Come to heel," Kate called. The dog dropped his stick instantly, running a loop around her and sliding to a hasty stop at her side. His haunches were firmly planted on the ground, eyes steady on hers, awaiting her command. "Around to watch," Kate said, her arm sweeping out as though throwing a fishing line. He bolted, running in an arc—around the courtyard, around the barn, around the house, in ever-widening circles, nose to the ground, searching for traces of one scent or another that would make a dog signal something was not as it ought to be. It was quite possibly the best thing she'd ever taught him.

While Vesper ran his circuit, Kate turned to her own tasks. With the girls gone, chores had become Kate's sole retreat from the wanderings of an idle mind, and she'd found some comfort in the monotony of it: collecting eggs, cutting and stacking hay, raking and mowing and harvesting the garden's late offerings. She'd grained the chickens in the morning when the stars were still out, before she'd gone up the hill to Donna, but she knew the hens would still be keen to roam. They expressed delight at her return, guttural clucks and squawks, tumbling atop each other in their hurry to race through the opening gate and scatter into the courtyard in their hunt for crawly things. Agatha ambled along behind, making a beeline for the weeds Kate had neglected to pull.

Kate's afternoon was set out for her, the last hay of the season already cut and dried in the fields, ready for baling and stacking. Haulers would be picking up most of it in the coming weeks to bring it to the central distribution site to allocate to livestock owners. With the girls still at school until the weekend, it would take a while to bale it all, and the rest of the week to get it ready to go. *Should have planned that better,* Kate thought, a sense of urgency flooding her and quickening her step.

She was halfway to the tractor when the sound of Vesper's short yip stopped her cold.

The dog was on the front stoop when Kate found him. She was out of breath from dread and running alike, head on a swivel, looking for what had prompted Vesper's alarm. The front door was still locked, but the small piece of tape she'd put on the bottom of the screen door was broken. Someone had tried to get in. "Show me," she said to Vesper.

He spun around like a top, then sprinted toward the field, nose to the ground, raised tail like a flag for her to follow. Kate sighted on the tree house, keen to any movement or color that did not belong, but finding none, she kept following the dog toward the creek. It was then that it struck her: something had happened to Lucy. She didn't wait, running down and across the bridge and up the other side, through the standing dead flowers of the meadow on Lucy's property. Vesper was beside her, keeping in lockstep, bounding along silently with his ears pricked forward.

They both stopped at the edge of the clearing, Kate crouching down alongside the dog, putting an arm over his shoulders to settle him. She was breathing hard, a stitch in her side forcing her to wait. Lucy's place was eerily still, and a slow, dark creep started worming its way under Kate's skin. Visions of a dead Lucy permeated her brain.

She got up slowly, unable to wait any longer, body bent low, shotgun raised. "Around to watch," Kate whispered.

As though mimicking her, Vesper lowered his head in a pad-footed stalk, nose and ears and eyes working on overdrive. Kate tried to follow, unwilling to leave the dog to fend off whatever he might find, as much as she was afraid to be without him by her side.

She peered through the front window, beyond the drawn sheers. There was a light somewhere in the back, but no movement inside. Kate turned the handle of the front door, surprised to find it unlocked, and hesitated, unsure if she should go in or keep with Vesper, who'd started moving toward the barn.

Kate retreated, cautiously backing out of the house. The dog had started to go around the barn, then abruptly turned back, intent on the base of the old stone wall. He let out a sharp yip, different than before, the hair along the ridge of his back standing straight up. With the shotgun at her shoulder, Kate slowly began to open the huge sliding door to the barn, the metal grating on its track.

The cat ran out of the narrow opening as though shot out of a cannon, and Kate's insides instantly turned to liquid. "Goddamn fucking cat," she muttered, heart going like a jackhammer run amok. She ran her sweating palms down her thighs, trying to peer into the recesses of the barn, reluctant to step inside. Vesper barked once, twice, and tried to shove his head through.

"What are you doing?!"

Lucy's high-pitched voice cut Kate's nerves to the quick, and both she and Vesper spun around at the shout that had come so close behind them. Kate may have flung her arms around Lucy in relief at seeing her whole, if not for her rifle, which had barely been lowered.

"Vesper... He... There was... He came over here... I thought... I was worried. My god, Lucy, are you alright?"

"What are you doing?!" Lucy repeated.

It looked as though all the blood had drained out of Lucy's face. She'd turned worryingly pale, and Kate reached a hand out as though to steady her, retracting it when it was greeted with a dagger-eyed stare.

"I was worried, dammit! I thought something had happened to you, and I came..." Kate flailed a hand in Vesper's general direction.

"We ... we came to check, to see that you were alright, and not being molested by some goddamn rag-abouts. What the fuck is wrong with *you*?!"

"Why would you think anything's wrong? We've barely spoken since... I can't even remember the last time you've been here. What would possess you to come over here and go poking around now?"

"Did you come to my house this morning?" Kate shot back.

"What? This morning? No. Well..." Lucy shifted from foot to foot, glancing from Kate to Vesper to the barn and back again. "Oh, yeah, maybe just for a second. But ... but you weren't home. Never mind it. You should go. And tie your damn dog up, too. He can't be coming over here, going around scaring my cat and all."

"Go to hell, Lucy. I was worried about you, but if you don't want me coming over here, fine. I don't care. And the dog ain't chasing the damn cat, and you know it." Kate slung the shotgun over her shoulder. Her eyes drifted toward the barn. There was something unsettling about it, but she couldn't put her finger on why. Vesper looked at her, emitting a soft, low whine.

"It's new kittens," Lucy blurted out. "That's why he's come to bother and ... and that's why I'm tellin' you to go and keep him gone."

With the variety of farmyard creatures in residence—the chickens, goat, pony, rabbit, and occasional window-downed sparrow—Vesper had a fair tolerance for just about any little beastlings skittering about, cat and kittens not excluded. But she wasn't going to argue. If Lucy wanted to use her cat as an excuse, far be it from Kate to stop her. Lifting her face toward the sky, Kate wore a tired grin that was nothing more than an ornament of frustration.

"Fine. Don't matter that I can plainly see you're lying, Lucy. If that's where we are now, so be it. Suit yourself," Kate said, setting off with Vesper out of the courtyard as though her boots were on fire. "And don't come calling for the girls neither," she called back over her shoulder. "They ain't yours to be bothering with anymore."

22

THE PRAYING MANTIS

THERE WAS A TIME when Lucy could stand the notion of a life alone, just her and her bees and the damnable cat. Her first pregnancy had been lost within weeks. Lucy thought she would never breathe again. The second stayed long enough she could feel the initial flutters of life, like butterflies darting about inside. Afterward, she thought the crying would never end. Her third daughter she could have held like a tiny porcelain doll, with skin like a pearl. It had been six years since, and the mourning had yet to end.

After completing her three chances for pregnancy, after she'd mourned the loss of each tiny soul that couldn't bear to survive her womb, after she'd left behind the sorrow-filled stares of her friends and coworkers in the hub city to find solace in the quiet of a country life where no one would ever know her, Lucy had come to welcome solitude like a protective shroud. Most days, Lucy set the pain aside, to be dwelled upon later when night came. She preferred the crying to come in the dark. Tears in the daytime could be seen.

Kate had not been part of the plan. But she and the girls had become everything Lucy wanted—everything she'd lost. They'd filled her days and her heart almost enough that the times before had dimmed to a tolerable flicker, not the glaring spotlight it had been.

Lucy watched Kate's retreating form as though burning it into her memory. The flush of Kate's cheeks as she tried so hard to quell the anger, her face alight, eyes piercing and beautiful. The way Kate's hips swayed and her shiny hair bounced when she was walking home fast. It didn't matter to Lucy if Kate wanted to be mad at her. Anything was better than silence.

And the reason Lucy had lost it all was sitting in the barn.

It didn't matter when Abe backed into the corner at the sight of her approach. It didn't matter when he protested, "No," over and over and over again, even though he wouldn't have known what he was saying it for. What mattered was she wanted to hurt him. She wanted him to feel physical pain—the same pain her heart felt, the same pain her mind told her life would become without Kate, without the girls, without any love for her at all.

Lucy's hands shook so badly, she kept dropping the padlock key that held the chains around the stall door. She grabbed the bars, shaking them, screaming at Abe for what he had done, for what the men had done. It was as though she'd been possessed, a demon come to claim its due. The key jammed into the lock, and Lucy flung the sliding stall door open so hard it ran off the tracks, canting dangerously at the end of the rail. She shoved Abe hard against the wall, once, twice, and again.

The man's hands had been up in surrender from the very first moment he saw her coming, but as soon as Lucy was in front of him, Abe's arms dropped to his sides, and he stood stock-still, waiting for it to happen. Watching with sorrowful eyes, body taut, he braced for assault, waiting for the end to come, accepting whichever fate was on offer without a word of protest.

"What the hell is wrong with you?!" Lucy screamed, fists clenched, daring him to do something, anything, to invite the violence she wanted so desperately to commit.

His head bobbled side to side, a hand reflexively touching his throat, an expression of quiet bewilderment across his face when his fingers touched the scarred skin.

Lucy lunged forward at the movement, expecting Abe to come at her, nearly striking him and only withdrawing at the last moment when he didn't. "Goddamn you to hell!"

"Ain't I been already?"

She stopped cold, struck by his voice as though cut. "Who the hell are you to pass judgment on me?"

"No judgment, miss. It's how it's always been. You're the same as they were, same as all of them. Never should have held the notion you weren't," Abe said. He deliberately clasped his hands behind his back, eyes going vacant as they drifted to a spot on the straw-strewn floor as though trying to burrow under it. Ready.

Same as who? Every ounce of fight deflated from Lucy in an instant. How could you fight someone when they'd already curled into themselves, silent, defenseless?

"I don't even know what you're talking about," she finally said, rushing to fill the void between them. "I don't even know who 'they' are. Goddammit, Abe, I don't know what happened to you. I don't know where you've been. I don't know anything. All I know is you showed up with those men that come here before. And before it happened, you all had been gone and didn't even exist, and now you're here, and everything's gone to shit. I wish I never come here. I wish it was just fucking over, and goddammit if I don't hate you all for what you've done. You ruined everything that ever fucking mattered to me, and I don't know how to get any of it back." Lucy leaned against the wall, bent over, hands on her knees, trying to breathe.

Abe didn't move. He didn't speak. No comfort was offered. He simply looked at the floor. Mute. Waiting.

Lucy thought to join him there, under the straw, burrowed into the ground, cozied up in the dirt where no one could find her.

Abe was so solemn, so still, it was as though he had become a fixture, invisible, not there at all. Realization flooded her senses: he was right; she was the same as they were. Good god, what was she doing?

"I can't do this," she whispered, running her hands through her hair in agitation before crossing her arms protectively in front of her. "I'm sorry for it, truly. Can't say what's in my head. It's all just … just too much. I'm not them. Abe? Do you hear me? I won't be like them."

"Heard you and your woman," he said, voice low, cautious. "I know you said what you did for me, and it pained you to say it."

"Didn't say it for you," Lucy said with a long sigh. It felt as though her soul had been ripped out from its place inside her body and strung up to fend for itself, unsheltered, vulnerable to the bombardment of chaos." But no one can know you're here. Especially not Kate. I've got to get rid of you in case she comes back." There was an audible hitch in his breathing, and she noted Abe's eyes were fixed on the buck knife at her hip.

"Much as I don't like to admit it, I know all this ain't your doing. I can see plain you been through things. I don't mean to be one of the ones who keep doing it to you." Lucy stepped through the threshold of the stall opening, the door hanging on its hinge, the key broken inside the lock. She turned around, looking at Abe, then his feet. She took off her boots and tossed them on the ground. "Put those on as far as you can get them."

He didn't hesitate, sitting down in the straw and peeling off his blood-spattered canvas slippers, held together by baling twine and tape. Abe slid his long, wide feet into Lucy's boots, only able to get them in far enough to put the ball of his big toes on the bottom. He looked at her with an arched brow of skepticism, but didn't say a word.

Lucy peered out the barn door, the cover of fog gone just when she needed it most. The yard was quiet, no chattering finches or whisper of wind. The abundance of serenity was almost loud, as though the heated scene earlier had been imagined. She turned around. Abe was still at the threshold of the stall, gripping the iron bars, watching her. Lucy turned back, scanning the surroundings one more time.

"Let's go," she said over her shoulder, and stepped out into the sun.

The old canvas shoes Abe had worn burned to ash in her fireplace, crumbling into the embers, bits of white fluff lofting into the updraft before being consumed by glowing sparks. It had taken her nearly an hour to clear the stall of all trace of its former tenant. She'd had to cut the lock through with a hacksaw, blistering the meat of her hand raw in the process. Lucy hoped the vinegar she'd poured around the wall where Abe had been, and in the stall, too, would be enough to throw Vesper off the scent. She'd even gone so far as to bury the straw in the compost, hoping the heat and bacteria would do their job.

"Ever been drunk before?" Lucy poured another shot of mezcal into a short glass and pushed it towards Abe, sitting across the kitchen table from her.

"No, miss. Can't say as I have." He warily lifted the glass, running it under his nose with a sniff, face wrinkling in revulsion. He put it down and gave it a little push back towards Lucy. "What's it do, being drunk?"

"Makes hard things easy," she said, holding up the glass. "Here, drink it like this." Lucy threw it back, shuddering as the earthy liquid hit her tongue, closing her eyes and sinking into the warmth of it sliding down her throat.

She had followed Abe's steps into the house, him in her shoes, herself barefoot. She had no idea if it would muddle scent, but she convinced herself Vesper wasn't really trained to track, so much as he was simply overenthusiastic to please Kate. With a bit of luck, dry weather, and wind, maybe enough time would pass it would not matter she was harboring Abe in her own safe room.

Just a little while longer, and she'd get what she needed. Then it would all be over with.

"Go on," she urged, pushing the glass back towards him. "It'll only hurt for a second."

"Hurt?" Abe picked up the glass again, holding it like it might explode, raising it to his lips as though to sip it to be sure.

"Drink it all down at once," Lucy encouraged, mimicking the motion.

He did, and nearly spluttered it all over the table, gasping and hacking, eyes watering. "Why?" he croaked. "Why would you drink that?"

"Give it a minute. You'll see," she said. "Suppose I should have been nicer about it and given you something easier your first time—wine or beer, maybe. Just don't have any, and honestly, it's been a mezcal kind of day." She poured herself another full shot, and a half for Abe. "One more ought to do ya."

It didn't take long. They hadn't eaten anything since morning, and it was already past midday. After Lucy's third, her lips were numb. She touched her forehead, leaving indentations but feeling nothing but the press of finger to skull. "That'll do it," she said with a lazy smile. "Better now?"

Abe was sweating, squinting as though his eyes couldn't decide if there were two Lucy's or three. His face split into a wide grin of fine straight teeth. "Don't mind it. Don't mind it a'tall."

"You'll know what I'm asking of you, then," Lucy said.

"No, miss, I surely don't." Abe chortled in reply, shaking his head side to side so slowly and for so long, it was as if he'd forgotten why he was doing so.

"What I want from you," she continued, tapping the table in front of her with the tip of her finger. "What I want you to do... What I want you to give me..."

"Man like me's got nothing to give, miss. But you can tell me anyways."

The kitchen chair slid across the tile floor when Lucy got up, going around to sit down next to Abe. She hesitated, wondering for a moment whether she should touch him, put her hand on his. Lucy's guts were roiling, and it wasn't from the mezcal. It was rare for her to imbibe, but liquor offered boldness when she needed it. Lucy thrust out a hand, wavering only just a moment, before letting it rest atop Abe's knuckles.

"Do you know how it's done, Abe? The making of a child. In the old way."

His jaw gaped open for a second, before shutting so hard his teeth clacked. Abe withdrew his hand like she'd touched him with a hot fire poker, shoving both fists between his knees. Where he'd been swaying and shifting and bobbly before, Abe became still, scouring Lucy's face with serious intensity. "Don't think I heard right. What it is you just say?"

"You heard me plain. I'm asking what sort of thing a man knows, when they been ... been as far from that sort of thing as a man can be."

"Heard some talk on it. The others, they all had their times, but I was just a kid, and I didn't have those times before going in there. So, honest, can't say as I know much. Don't even know how it's done now."

"How it is now, well, they have it—the pater-seed—froze up from a long time ago and saved at the fertility clinics. Then, they ... they, well, they put it in, when the time's right," Lucy said. Her face was flushing hot, and she'd become fidgety, thumb rubbing back and forth along the edge of the table as a distraction.

"Well, I'll be," he said, voice trailing off. Abe ran a sleeve across his brow and down his face before casting a sideways glance at Lucy and shoving the errant hand back between his knees. "Always wondered where it all went."

"Where what all went?"

Abe shifted in his seat, shoulders hunched, new beads of sweat forming along his hairline like he'd just stepped into a sauna. The man appeared ready to crawl under the table, only fixed in place by some unseen anchor of obligation or compliance.

"What they make us do," he finally said, voice quiet. "When they make us go to the wall. To earn our keep. But I'm telling you miss, I ain't for that no more."

Lucy looked at the kitchen walls, freshly painted last spring, beadboard running top to bottom in a pleasing sage green. Her eyes returned to Abe, wondering if he wasn't just a bit mad, with all those years spent locked away; now he was scared of walls and confined spaces with no doors. She began to worry the hideaway spot she'd intended for him would be problematic. She had a cubby under the eaves, tall enough to sit up in, long enough to lie down, but with little more space than that, and no windows at all.

"Walls ain't got a thing to do with it. And there's none but me here. So long as we keep you a secret, there's nothing to worry about," she said in a reassuringly gentle tone. "All I'm asking for, Abe, is for you to give what a man has—his part in the making of a child. 'Cause I need a daughter of my own—one that's mine to love. I won't make you do it, but I'm asking if you will."

The house's inner workings hummed, accompanied by the soft *tick-tick-tick* of an antique clock keeping poor time, the icebox chipping away as though invisible gnomes were hard at work inside, and the soft whistle of Abe breathing in tiny huffs of subdued despair.

"The places you say—the ones that put in the pater-seed. You can go there again and—"

"They won't take me. Pater-seed is regulated because it's finite," Lucy interrupted. "Three tries, no child, no more. I'm classified as a 4W: 'woman with wasted womb.'"

The sadness in his eyes that he'd worn from the start shifted to sadness for her. "You want me to do this thing... Are you asking ... are you asking me to do this right now?"

"Oh, god, no! Best I be sober for it, and I sure ain't that," Lucy said. She'd shot up out of the chair and began pacing along the length of the table, hands on her hips and chewing her bottom lip. She tipped her head towards the half bottle of alcohol and two empty glasses. "I get daft sometimes, drinking. Maybe I sleep on it, and come morning, I find I'd lost my mind."

She sat down next to him, just a little closer, hand firmly on his arm and leaning close. "You can stay here, long as it takes to know it's done. No more sleeping rough; you'll be stayin' in a proper home. Get hot food every day, as much as you want. Will you do it, Abe?"

Lucy hadn't made him sleep in the cubby after all. Whether it was the wooziness from too much drinking, or the guilt that would come from stuffing him into a space so tight it would drive a mouse to claustrophobia, she didn't have the stamina to ponder it. Abe could stay in a proper room, bed and all, so long as he promised to hide in the eaves should the need arise. But Lucy barred the door anyway, hanging a strap of Christmas reindeer bells on the doorknob as fair warning should he try to leave.

Despite the mezcal head start, sleep was elusive, and Lucy was up at dawn, same as any other day. She crept on tiptoes through the hall to find Abe's door still securely shut. She wondered if he'd slept—or had his mind been wired to spark a barrage of imaginings caught up in sweat-inducing dreams, as hers had? She leaned towards the door, quietly removing the doorstop wedged in the bottom while listening for any indication the man was up to no good. But there was only the light rumble of sleep, steady and constant.

The promise of what Abe could give her hadn't waned in the night. Instead, it was heightened by a growing sense of urgency. Lucy flitted around the kitchen, preparing tea and coffee, juice and eggs, and honey blueberry pancakes. She would feed him into a lulled stupor, leave him comfortable and content and unafraid, compliant. And then what?

Pater-seed implantation had always been a clinical process, with a host of staff to manage the timing, medications, and insertion. All the while, the woman lay flat on her back with an eye to counting ceiling tiles and little recall of what precisely had just happened. Everything Lucy knew about the workings of the old ways of reproduction had come from watching animals, and it always seemed on the border of violent when they did it: the howl of dogs linked together; the stallion biting the neck of the mare, eyes wild with lust; the praying mantis killing and eating its mate.

The shuffle of bells made Lucy jump, and she dropped a stack of pancakes on the floor. Abe was up and out of his room. She dumped the pancakes back on the plate, scuffing the surface free of remnant lint and telling herself that a man who'd been living rough wouldn't know the difference. He appeared in the doorway just as she added another hotcake to the stack.

"Sleep okay?"

"Best I slept since I can remember." His eyes held a glint of curiosity, surveying the array of foodstuffs on offer. "More folks coming to eat all this?"

"Oh, well, no, of course not. I didn't ... didn't know what you'd like."

"Man like me, well, I ain't fussy," he said, quickly adding, "not to say your cooking isn't the finest I ever did have, 'cause it is."

They both fell silent, Abe holding onto the back of the chair, gaze fixed on Lucy, while Lucy clutched the carafe of coffee, staring at Abe. Mooey Gorda stalked into the room, tail held high, tip twitching, and stopped dead. All three of them nearly jumped to the ceiling when the toast popped.

"Dammit!" Lucy grabbed the bread, a gradient of brown to black, edges smoking as she flung it onto a plate, and it skittered off and onto the floor. The cat bolted, racing between Lucy's legs, the carafe of coffee she was still holding going straight up and straight back down again, raining a caffeinated flood over the entire plate of eggs and across the counter, dripping down the cabinets. She threw the carafe into the sink, the clamor echoing around the room as Lucy took off after the cat, screaming a string of obscenities fit to make her mother rise from the dead and rinse her mouth out with soap.

The feline queen of mayhem had vanished, likely to be scarce for days. "And bloody stay out!" Lucy screamed to the empty room, fists clenched at her sides. She stomped over to the front door and latched the cat door, content to leave Moo outside in punishment and let the wretched creature remember who fed her. After taking a few—or several—meditative breaths, she returned to the kitchen, shamefaced and resigned.

Abe was on his knees, a corner of burnt toast hanging from his mouth, mopping the remnants of coffee off the floor with a kitchen rag. "Not all gone to waste," he said upon seeing her in the doorway. "There's at least a half cup for you." He pushed the mug across the table, along with two plates of soggy eggs and pancakes, pushing one towards her before sitting down to eat his, entirely content.

She sat down across from him and shoved a forkful of coffee-infused pancake into her mouth. "Sorry," Lucy muttered. "I get mad sometimes."

"No need for sorry. Been around mad plenty, and yours is an easy enough kind." Putting the coffee cup down, he leaned back in the chair, arms folded tightly across his chest. "Been thinking on what you're asking, and just so's you don't have to wonder on it, I'll tell you straight. I will, if you're still wanting it. But I'm asking that you let me leave when the time comes to go."

Lucy's eyes welled up with unexpected tears, her hand clasped tight over her mouth, nodding furiously. She let out a gasping reply, "Yes, yes, I do."

"Well, alright. It's settled then," he said softly.

The fertility clinic pamphlets from the last time she'd been in clinic lay strewn across the desk. Lucy looked at the calendar, counting the days forwards and backwards on her fingers. If her cycle was typical, today was her last day of ovulation.

"Best to get it over with," she said under her breath. The tremors of nervousness started in her stomach, spreading through her body and down into her legs, heels tapping in time to an unseen drum.

"In the clinic, everything is sterile," Lucy said. "So, we'll wash up first, and then ... then we'll do the other bit."

Abe buried his eyes in the floor, shoving his hands protectively into his elbows. "This has me feeling all sorts of odd."

"Just ... just the one time today. Then if it doesn't work, we do it again next month, if you don't mind staying long enough to find out."

"Got a warm bed and a roof and more than plenty to eat. I don't mind staying, long as you let me, and long as trouble don't find us.

As to the other part..." He paused, swallowing hard and shifting from his bad foot to the other. "I know the workings of it—for a man, anyhow. Suppose we'll sort out the rest when it comes to it."

They walked down the hall to the bath as if on their way to the gallows. Lucy set out towels and soap and a scrubbing mitt, placing witch hazel, peroxide, and alcohol alongside sterile gauze on the counter, unsure of what was best. She felt queasy, stomach in knots, unable to stop the constant tremors coursing under her skin. The shower was set to blasting hot, on the edge of intolerable. They would wash, then finish the task.

Lucy turned her back to Abe, discarding her clothes in a heap on the floor and stepping into the steaming shower, sucking air between her teeth. The water was skin-meltingly hot. She scrubbed her body raw before washing between her legs. She left the water running, stepping out from behind the glass partition and sliding into a white terry cloth robe.

"You're up," she said.

His was a fixed gaze, curious as much as shy, and wearing a peculiar expression. Lucy paid Abe no mind, toweling her long hair, separating the strands with her fingers methodically. She heard him step into the shower behind her, and the yelp that followed when the heat touched his skin. His back was turned, and she dared a look. Lucy was surprised to see a man appeared much as a woman did from the back, if a bit hairier. Abe had wide shoulders narrowing to an overly trim waist, each rib still very much defined, sitting above round, tight haunches and sinewy legs.

Of course, Lucy had seen male animals, knew their anatomy well enough. But she'd never seen what made a man, a man. Her eyes went round as an owl's when Abe turned. She couldn't contain her surprise as she looked at him, wondering what on earth she was supposed to do with *that*. Implantations at the clinic were done with a long, narrow pipette, and those were intrusive enough as it was. Lucy didn't know what she'd expected, but she wanted no part of it.

She was still staring when the water turned off. Still staring when he stepped out of the shower and she handed him a towel. Still staring even when the towel wrapped around his waist and covered the offending thing.

"I don't think so," Lucy blurted out.

"You changed your mind?"

"No, I didn't, but... I don't know... I just wasn't expecting..." She gestured in his general direction. "I don't know what to do with it."

He returned the stare, fixed on her breasts peeking through the gap of the robe, and her body lower still, gesturing back at her in much the same way. "Don't quite know what to make of you either."

"I want a child. I need it more than I can say."

"Well, I suppose we just figure out how it's done, then. It's got to work somehow. Like I say, I know how men go, what ... what things happen." He scanned the perimeter of the room, drifting past her. "There's space in there." He tipped his chin towards the bedroom.

She went in, moving towards the bed, Abe following.

"No, miss, here—" He pulled her towards the wall, putting her back flat against it. He began to hum a familiar tune under his breath, hand drifting down to touch himself. Abe's eyes fixed on Lucy's navel, widening his stance until the offending part of him was level with it.

"What?" Lucy cried out. "No, not there."

He looked at her, surprised, hand and humming ceasing. "You sure? That's where babies grow, don't they?"

"Quite sure." She took his hand by the wrist, putting it between her legs. "Up there."

The humming resumed in earnest, his hands holding on to her hips as though they were handles, fumbling at first, then finding his way and pressing into her with a long, low sigh.

Lucy closed her eyes and tried to think of Kate.

23

CRACKS YEARS IN THE MAKING

KATE LAY ON THE ground, staring at the sky, trying to catch her breath. She was covered in chaff, tiny pieces of hay working their way into her sweat-soaked clothes and pricking into her skin. She just needed a minute. But Vesper had a different opinion on the matter. His wet nose snuffled across her face, finding her ear and skimming it with his drool-laden tongue.

"Don't even think about it," Kate growled.

Vesper dropped to his forelegs in an invitation to play, his entire body wagging in anticipation. The dog had been without the girls all week, and he had resorted to Kate for entertainment, having already depleted Agatha's tolerance and been summarily chased out of the pasture with an emphatic nip on the butt by the pony. Despite his advanced years, Fred was not the trifling sort.

"Last day. They'll be home tomorrow," Kate promised, ruffling the thick scruff around Vesper's neck. Rolling over, she pushed up to all fours and sat back on her heels with a grunt, every part of her body registering a complaint. Looking across the barren meadow always made her miserable, the soft seed heads gone, no grasses swaying in the breeze, only the scoured remnants to offer any memory of the season past. It was a harbinger of winter, the last cut for the season before the gales blew and darkness crept into the days, the sun tucking in to hibernate, too.

The hay had been baled, loaded on the tractor, and unloaded into the shipping shed. And she'd done it all herself. It had taken all week, with no girls to offer reprieve and no offer of assistance from Lucy.

"My timing is impeccable on both counts, I'll say that much," she said to the dog, awkwardly getting to her feet. They walked towards the house, Kate's legs dragging behind her. Tea and stale cake were her reward, and maybe a hot bath and curling up with a book on the couch under a blanket for an afternoon nap could be on the docket as well.

The couch called her name louder than anything else, and Kate curled up on it despite herself. The risk of getting dust and grass and seed heads on the furniture was no match for exhaustion. A throw pillow crinkled beneath her head, while visions of Lucy instantly played across the back of her eyelids. Thoughts that had long been intentionally suppressed came alight to offer an editorial: *You hate her for what she's done. You need her. Life was better without her. Life is unbearable unless she's near. You want her. You're damaged goods; she'd never want you back anyhow. You've hurt her too much. She doesn't care about you. You'll never be happy without her.*

"Get out of my head," Kate pleaded, sitting up and pressing her fingertips against her temples, to no avail. She shot up off the couch, despite the creak of her bones and the protest from the rest of her. "And you," she said accusingly to Vesper. "I can't believe you let me sit my filthy ass down." She hauled her tired body upstairs, past the girls' empty rooms, down the hall to the bedroom still strewn with dirty laundry. Kate rolled her eyes, adding that to the pile of shame she'd been building for herself. It would have to wait; the stench of the day hung in the air, demanding she bathe first.

The water steamed in a rising mist of citrus and bergamot, bubbles skimming the surface. Kate slid in, arms draping over the sides, head back against the edge. She'd worked from dawn to dusk all week, desperate to get the hay in as much as she was desperate to silence the plaguing memories. But now the task was done, and her avoidant efforts were used up. In the dead quiet of the house, in the absence of her daughters, in the waters meant to soothe and offer escape, she found no respite.

The visit to Donna's had only served to amplify the very thing Kate was hoping to let go of, solidifying a hatred toward the men who had come to harm and left more questions than answers. But the encounters with Lucy were where her thoughts dwelled. Their rapport had been on a path of measured decomposition, as though little pieces of Kate were sloughing off by the day, too slow to feel immediate pain, but instead gradually turning her into a desiccated husk with no feelings at all. At least, that was the lie she'd been telling herself. Kate slid under the water, so she wouldn't have to feel the tears fall.

The impact of the hammer against the tree trunk reverberated up Kate's arm, her muscles like jelly, barely able to hold the handle. She was checking the railings, making certain the floorboards were intact, and checking the knots on the rope ladder. She'd rationalized it would be the first place the girls would go upon their return, continuing to tell herself it was the only reason to be up there. Kate paused, looking out across the cropped meadow, down towards the creek bridge, and up the slope to Lucy's house.

She'd seen Lucy in and out of the barn and back and forth to the shed, pulling weeds that hadn't the benefit of a hungry goat to devour them. She watched Lucy scrubbing the frames from the bee houses, wrapping the extractor in canvas for the season, pulling the batting out to snug the hives for winter. She should talk to her, Kate justified, since the girls would be home tomorrow, wanting to see Lucy, and they needed to decide what to do about it. And maybe tell her what Donna had said. And to find out what was in the barn.

Maybe it was just an excuse to offer conversation. But Kate needed to tell Lucy she missed her, and that she was sorry. For all of it.

Kate found herself walking across the field, across the bridge, and down the path to the hives before she'd let her thoughts catch up and advise against it. She stopped twenty paces away, Lucy's hair shining in the last rays of sunlight. The soft scent of honey permeated the air.

"I'm sorry," Kate cried out, voice raspy, barely above a whisper.

Lucy spun around, the shock across her face morphing from anger to wonder to concern.

"I'm sorry," Kate said again, feet frozen in place, arms fixed at her sides. All the things she wanted to say were trying to come out at once—how for the last four years, she'd consumed the shame; how she was so angry at her helplessness, sickened by what she'd allowed to happen, despairing over ever having to confess it to anyone. But the words couldn't find their way out, instead drowning in a river of tears erupting like a broken dam, its cracks years in the making. Kate doubled over, crouching down on the ground with her face in her hands.

"It's okay. I've got you. You're okay," Lucy said, arms holding her tight as Kate collapsed against her chest.

The sun dipped behind the hills, columns of lights touching the clouds in rays of ephemeral color, from gold to orange to fiery crimson. Geese flew high overhead, their calls a distant clamor. Long after Kate's sobbing subsided, she stayed, listening to the thump of Lucy's heart, which provided a strange comfort, steady and sure.

"I've been hiding from you for so long," Kate murmured. "You have no idea—the shame of it. I felt like I was so ... so vile. Like I could never wash it off. And if I couldn't—if I couldn't get rid of that feeling, if I couldn't stop being so weak—then I had to be alone, so no one else would become tainted by it." She sat up suddenly, clutching onto Lucy's plaid overshirt with both hands. "I know it wasn't your fault. And I blamed you anyway. Because ... because I thought that would be easier, and oh god, Lucy, it's not. I have been so, so alone without you."

Lucy's hair smelled of chamomile and honey. Kate ran her fingers through the smooth strands, thumb tracing the blue moons inked into her neck. Lucy's hand covered hers, folding it into her own, eyes closed tight.

"You don't need to say you're sorry, Kate. But there's things—"

"I know, and it's alright, I understand. You did what you had to," Kate said. Lucy's lips were as soft as she remembered, and the sensation of touching her, being so close after so long, ignited every inch of her desire. Kate kissed her, inquiring, curious, hopeful, her urgency growing as she pulled Lucy close. She needed her.

"Kate, I... We..."

Kate pressed against her, needing to feel the warmth of Lucy's body, back arching, her wanting plain. Kate's mouth trailed down her neck, tongue exploring. "Let me touch you," she whispered.

Lucy's protests grew silent, turning to soft pants of pleasure. Kate drew off her shirt, breasts bared to the cooling night sky. Lucy grew bold, the caresses warming her despite her body's trembling, and she swayed until they both found themselves on the ground, entwined. Kate moved methodically along Lucy's body, familiar, the years lost between them vanishing in an instant. She knew Lucy, and she knew how to satisfy her. Kate's hands trailed along the smooth, plump thighs, her mouth soon to follow.

"Please," Lucy gasped, hips rising, hands reaching for Kate, stroking her hair.

The sound of the rushes crunching beneath them was rhythmic, the scent of wild bergamot, moldered and autumnal, filling the air around them. They held onto each other, Kate desperate to reclaim Lucy as her own. The gasps of Lucy's desire only served to drive Kate harder, until Lucy shuddered and bucked, her cries of release breaking the clear, cool night.

Kate shifted to lie beside her, head resting on Lucy's shoulder. She could hear Lucy's heart still pounding. The first twilight star appeared high up in the sky, next to a sliver of a waxing crescent moon.

"Venus," Kate said lazily, unsure where her own limbs ended and Lucy's began, and unwilling to move to find out.

"I see it," Lucy said.

They would have stayed there for the rest of their lives, Kate thought, if not for the pervading chill of the night creeping across their skin, causing patterns of gooseflesh to rise across their naked bodies. "Come stay with me tonight," Kate whispered.

There was a sharp hitch in Lucy's breathing, her muscles tensing a moment, then she held Kate tight. "I can. For a little while."

Kate propped herself up on her elbows, shuddering when the cool air touched her love-warmed skin. "You got better plans?"

A frown flashed across Lucy's face, quickly transforming into a smile of reassurance. "Have to ... to be up early. Got a, um ... a pickup of a batch of manuka honey to be tested at central labs. Phytochemicals and selective toxicity and whatnot."

"Well, come on, then. Come to the house a while and maybe I can convince you to stay." Kate leaned over and kissed Lucy, long and slow, dizzied by the mixture of love and lust coursing through her as though everything were being set alight.

"Wish this could have happened days ago," Lucy said, almost wistfully, but her voice held an edge of something more.

"I know. The girls have been gone all week, and we would have finally had the house to ourselves," Kate said with a laugh. They got up, shimmying back into their discarded clothes. Kate took Lucy's hand, pulling her down the path. "I have so much to tell you, too."

They got to the house, Vesper sitting like a sentinel on the front porch. "Release," Kate said, giving him a quick pet and a treat for his diligence. The dog bounded off his perch, racing in circles around them in quick bursts of speed, spinning on his heels, then racing off in the other direction and starting the pattern again.

"Never thought that dog would have turned out so well," Lucy said.

"He really did turn out to be a great watchdog, didn't he? I'm thinking about getting another one, so it'd have Vesper to learn from. The girls would love a puppy, and—oh! How're the kittens? I'm sure that'll be the first place Mika goes when she comes home tomorrow." Kate busied herself with putting the kettle on and laying out a plate of cheddar, apple slices, stuffed olives, and almonds, famished after their rendezvous. She kept a keen eye toward Lucy, curious about any confession or excuse offered. Or would she commit to whatever secret—for surely there was one—she'd been keeping in that barn of hers?

"Oh, well, I, uh, haven't see Mooey in a few days, and I haven't found where's she's got them hid." Lucy was studying the wood grain of the kitchen table with undue intensity, unwilling to meet Kate's eye, adding, "Not altogether sure she actually had any." She stuffed an apple slice in her mouth before Kate had even put the plate down, waving a hand to indicate there was more to say, if not for the chewing.

"It'd be a help if you sent the girls into the barn to find them," Lucy finally said, looking Kate dead in the eye. "I really needed you the other day. I was pretty upset about some things, and I came to find you, but the place was all locked up and empty as a ghost town. Where were you?"

"I'd wanted to tell you," Kate began, absently folding her napkin into a fan, then a swan, then back again. She'd learned to fold napkins at the university, working a catering gig, and had never shaken herself of the habit. "When I came by..." She waved a hand in the air, indicating the unspoken words hanging between them. "I went to Donna's."

"I'd have gone with you," Lucy said. "She's an interesting old bat."

"Donna told me she'd been in the military," Kate said.

Lucy nodded in agreement, plucking up almonds and tossing them into her mouth one by one, licking the salt from her fingertips. "Figured as much. She's got that way about her."

"But here's the part I wanted to tell you," Kate continued. "Donna used to be stationed at the bunker where the men were found. Said she was stationed there for twenty years, and never knew what was inside."

This statement stopped Lucy cold, chewing suspended, mouth only shut because she had a sense of decorum. She swallowed hard, leaning on the table with both arms, shaking her head. "What?"

Kate proceeded to tell her the whole of it. How Donna had been a handler, and had been told it was a prison for women who'd committed violent crimes, their identities masked for privacy, no way in or out. How the highest levels of government had been involved. And how many had been housed there.

"Apparently, there were nearly eight hundred of them. She did say quite a few died, and any remaining would have to be real old by now. But that one we saw... Well, he couldn't have been much more than fifty or so, right?" Kate had gotten up from the table, distractedly cleaning up the plates and wrapping the cheese, not paying any attention to whether Lucy was done eating or not. "I thought after killing the one—the one from before—that it would settle me, give me closure," she said, waving around the cheese knife she meant to be drying with the dish towel. "But I realize now, it wasn't enough. I'll never rest until every damn one of them is found."

Lucy hadn't stayed the night, offering the excuse she had too much to think on, what with Kate's news from Donna, and the chores needing doing by morning. Kate had tried enticing her to stay to no avail, the evening tinged with regret for having let conversation about the men consume the moment, instead of them becoming reacquainted like she'd hoped. But there would be time again for that, Kate was sure of it.

The girls would be arriving on the midafternoon train, and Kate spent the better part of the morning putting the house back together. She'd let things slide, what with the girls gone and Lucy estranged, having no one to hold her to account for leaving laundry on the floor and dishes in the sink. She was like a whirling dervish, flinging items into their respective washers, clearing things from where they lay to allow the vacuum a clear path to scavenge for all the dust and leafy particulates that had gathered during the week and been deposited in her wake.

Dinner for the evening would be the girls' favorites: lentil sweet potato curry, followed by fried peaches and honey cream. It was a decidedly orange-hued dinner, and Kate determined she could do even better. "Carrots, peppers, hummus, and sun-gold tomatoes to snack on before," she said aloud, inventorying her options. She prepped all she could, chopping the sweet potatoes and soaking the lentils, slicing peaches and carrots and tomatoes, so she wouldn't have to spend time away from her daughters, sure to be bubbling with excited stories of their week away at school.

Kate pulled the heavy cream from the refrigerator, trying to recall what she'd gotten it for and when. She shook it, feeling chunks of entirely-too-old dairy bumping against the sides. She put a hand over her mouth to suppress the gagging—a response born more from the idea of lumpy cream than anything. She wasn't partial to milk to begin with, and she hated old food to an irrational extent.

"Dammit, I don't have time for this," Kate cursed under her breath, gladly flinging the carton into the incinerator as she bolted out the door towards Lucy's. Hopefully she'd have some to lend, or maybe be willing to go to the dairy down the road and get some. Kate speculated that Lucy had probably been eating saltines and butter all week. She looked forward to inviting Lucy to dinner again. The girls would be ecstatic to see her, too.

It was only eleven o'clock; Kate still had a few hours before going to the hub. There weren't any one-cars out front of Lucy's place, so it seemed likely the scheduled pickup by central labs had already occurred. The barn was still shut up tight. Kate suppressed the curiosity to peek inside, quickening her pace towards the house. Maybe they'd have a little time together after all.

Movement inside the house caught her eye as she raised a finger to tap on the kitchen window. Kate's hand hung in midair, body motionless, breathing stopped, the edges of her vision growing dark, heart pounding adrenaline through her veins in ready violence.

He was in her house. Sitting at her table, relaxed, drinking coffee. And Lucy was standing in front of him, as if she hadn't a care in the world.

24

A Barren Field

THEY SAW THE DUST rising in the distance first. A line of one-cars raced along the perimeter road, at least a dozen, moving fast and heading their way. Lucy didn't move, watching as they briefly slowed, then turned down the long lane toward her house.

The crash of Abe's chair startled her out of somnolence. She spun around, catching a glimpse of the pained reproach broadcast across his face before he bolted out the back door. He was going to run. Lucy didn't hesitate, dumping all the dishes in the washer to hide the luncheon spread for two, then ran for the room Abe had been staying in. She ripped the linens off the bed, dumping them into the washing machine just as the first shouts reached her ears.

Lucy was trying to catch her breath and calm herself, wiping the sweat of fear off her forehead. They were pounding on the front door, not waiting for an invitation. There were three garda, walking fast, spreading out inside her home, one with a body heat scanner pointed at the walls while the others checked behind doors and inside closets. She was standing still, hands up, when one approached.

"The CRZ has received notification of men sighted in the area. Are you aware of or have you been abetting any of unknown acquaintance?"

Lucy shook her head, unwilling to trust her voice.

"We have oversight to search the premises of this house, the outbuildings, and your land," the garda said. "For your own safety, please step outside."

Lucy was escorted out and made to stand in the center of the courtyard. She had no idea where Abe had gone. There was little vegetative cover, the nearest tree line being at least a quarter mile away, and the flower meadow was nothing but remnants of the season gone by, leaves wilted and brown. He couldn't have gone far; his foot had barely healed, his limp was still pronounced whenever he moved. If he'd truly run, she wondered how far he could possibly get. He didn't even have shoes.

A familiar figure walked toward her in a crisp pin-striped suit. The woman hadn't aged a day in the years since Lucy had seen her last, adding that to the tally of her detestable features.

"There have been reports of men in the area," Overseer Evelyn Emmett said.

"So I gathered," Lucy replied.

"Harboring a man is a criminal offense, warranting loss of regency of all properties in your possession and punishment in servitude for up to twenty years," the woman continued. "Have you any information to offer?"

Lucy had practiced her speech, expecting this day to come. But the sentencing of anyone guilty wasn't something she'd paid heed to—until now.

"Heard nothing but rumors, same as anyone," Lucy began, shoving her fidgeting hands into her pockets. She put on a wry smile, hoping for folksy affect. "Ladies in these parts sure do like to chatter though. Some said they were in the uplands, others said they were in the lowlands, some swore to God herself they'd shoot a man dead on sight, and another said she'd be pleased enough to see for herself if they were saviors, if she ever got her hands on one. So, no, ma'am. Been nothing but gossip. None to warrant a call,

I assure you that, and suspect you're wasting your time comin' all this way. Ain't been men 'round here, not so far as I know."

"With all the gossip you say you hear, I admit to some surprise you haven't heard we've found a few," Overseer Emmett said.

"Can't say I have, but I been busy, what with end of season and all. But since you've mentioned it, how is it after all these years, you're still looking for 'em?" Lucy risked riling the woman up, but also figured it would be the only time she had the opportunity to ask the question. It was all she could think to do for Kate, to finally set her mind at ease, or at least give her a concrete notion of what it was they were in for, if more remained to be found.

"Suffice it to say, I would not normally be at liberty to tell you," Overseer Emmett said with a bright smile and glint in her eye. "But today, I will make an exception. If we find these rumored escapees, it may be the last of them. Four remain unaccounted for. If they're alive, I'm confident they will be found."

As if on cue, shouts erupted from the edge of the property, about two hundred meters upstream of the creek. Evelyn began running. Lucy was in close pursuit. They went down the trail near the beehives, where she'd been with Kate just the evening before. Past the bees and beyond the field, down the old dirt path toward the abandoned shed. It was where she'd hidden the truck. They'd found it, stowed under an old green canvas tarp. Abe was hiding underneath. He was screaming, begging, his hands outstretched in surrender.

"Please! Don't take me ... Don't take me! I never done anything wrong!"

His pleadings fell on deaf ears, the garda pulling him out from his hiding place by the ankles and across the graveled ground, depositing him in a heap. They snapped a collar around his neck. Abe went still as a statue, mute, his gaze landing on Lucy and staying there.

"You know this man?" Overseer Emmett asked.

Lucy stared at him, eyes growing wide. "No," she whispered.

With a sharp nod, Overseer Emmett gave the order to the garda to take him.

Good god, what had she done? Abe's eyes never strayed, watching Lucy the entire time he was being dragged away. She should have told them he was harmless. She should have told them he was kind and wouldn't hurt a fly. She should have told them a lot of things. But she'd told them nothing at all.

"What will they do to him?"

"After he's processed, he'll probably be housed with the other remaining men," Overseer Emmett said, before launching into a walking public relations campaign for how to manage government cover-ups. "The Reserve is state of the art, built for the care and keep of our Lost Saviors. The men will be cared for as they should be, living out their days in peace and tranquility after all their years of hardship. There are even plans for interactive educational displays and exhibits, so our girls and residents can remember our history and—"

"A man zoo," Lucy interjected.

Overseer Emmett cast her a sideways look, a derisive grin flashing across her perfectly maintained face—manicured brows, waxed upper lip, flawless skin, a hard woman well kept. "Some may see it that way," she stated, uncharacteristically contrite. "But I prefer to think of it as a kindness. They've never known the outside world. Besides, from the behavior we've seen, their reintroduction to society would be catastrophic."

Lucy did not bother to ask whose behaviors she was referring to—the men's or the women who'd tried to free them. She could only imagine the chaos. Men running amok. Women trying to claim them. Foreign entities trying to take them for whatever little the men had left to offer, if anything at all. She ran a hand distractedly across her stomach, wondering about the viability of decrepit seed on a barren field. The desire she'd had to have a child of her own was fleeting madness—a madness so easily born, she could see it spreading like wildfire if given the chance.

The garda brought Abe back to the courtyard, setting him down on the wall where they'd shared breakfast not long ago. Her gut wrenched at the sight of him, collared and bound, the wound on his foot oozing, shoulders hunched, his overly large head hanging so low, it was as if it were barely attached to the rest of him. At her approach, his eyes lifted. Lucy thought they'd be filled with unbridled contempt. But instead, he regarded her with such longing it startled her. But it wasn't her face he was looking at; it was the hand that rested instinctively across her womb.

Abe whispered so quietly it was only his mouth forming the shape of her name: *"Lucy."*

Overseer Emmett shifted into Lucy's gaze, obscuring Abe behind her as the garda pulled him to his feet and toward an awaiting carrier car. "If I didn't know better," the woman said, "I'd think you had never seen a man before."

"It's ... it's still quite a shock to see one," Lucy stuttered. Her eyes shifted, trailing him as he was shoved into the waiting vehicle, body bent double as he ducked into the seat, the outer door coming down to seal him inside. She gestured with her chin, eyes returning to the woman in front of her. "Who called him in?"

"No call," Overseer Emmett said. "Just an anonymous tele-text from one of the kiosks at the transportation hub early this afternoon."

Lucy sat across the table from Kate, her hands wrapped around a mug of tea, the familiar comfort of the room offering a creeping unease. Kate had barely said a word when Lucy knocked on the front door, as though she wasn't going to let Lucy in, only succumbing after Mika's ear-splitting screech of excitement upon seeing Lucy on the stoop.

Part of her wanted to settle in for the evening and listen to the detailed accounts of all their stories: Mika talking about the inner workings of nano biosensors, or how Birdie had been chosen as an academic youth leader, the youngest one in the history of the conservatory. Or how Mandy had been caught not once, but three times sitting for other's exams in exchange for sugar pops, lighters, and other contraband, much to the chagrin of her mother. Then came the long-awaited telling by Jenna, acting as the epitome of the eldest in her patience in waiting for her turn and her measured demeanor alone. She told of her decision to commit to an advanced course of study, genomic forestry, and prospective acceptance at the university.

Kate beamed at her daughters as they returned one by one, arms hanging loosely around their mother, with kisses on cheeks and hands clutched in brief returns, all of them so happy, she was brimming with love and joy and pride.

Lucy's fingertips trailed across the emptiness of her middle, images flashing through her mind of Abe in his collar. She pushed back from the table, quietly slipping out of the room, and was halfway down the hall when Jenna called out to her.

"Stay, Miss Lucy! Mama said we're having an all orange supper!"

The other girls squealed with delight, erupting in a fit of laughter at the prospect of only orange foods for dinner, each of them speculating with a bevy of guesses as to what they would be having. "Pumpkin pie! Cantaloupe! Papaya!" And Kate would gleefully declare "Nope!" at each guess, before finally telling them the menu for the evening. "And fried peaches for dessert, too" she added. "No cream though. I hadn't time to go to the dairy, and Lucy didn't have any to borrow."

This statement stopped Lucy dead in her tracks. She spun on her heel, marching straight back into the kitchen. The thrumming in her ears was like waves so loud, Lucy couldn't focus.

How could she?

"It was you," Lucy said. She was standing in the doorway, forefinger pointed accusingly at Kate, voice growing louder. "You called them. *You* reported me! Do you have any idea what you've done, what could have happened to me?"

Everyone stopped what they were doing and turned to stare.

"Mama, what's Miss Lucy talking about?" Mika asked.

Kate paused, looking lovingly at her youngest, hand stroking back Mika's unruly hair to make space for a kiss. "Haven't a clue," she said, with a twist of her mouth and a smile that didn't reach her eyes. "Never mind that now. Who's hungry?"

The sounds of family faded behind her when Lucy walked out of the house, swearing to herself it would be the last time she set foot in it ever again.

25

WHAT'S DONE IS DONE

THE HEAVY FOOTFALLS OF a horde of girls came bounding into the house. Kate looked up from her book, wondering with eye-rolling skepticism what all the fuss would be about this time. The storm door slamming and the thump of shoes being flung off onto the mud tray was followed by the rushed footsteps of her daughters rapidly approaching the reading nook Kate had declared was decidedly off-limits for any interruptions.

"This better be good," she said to the first face peering out from behind the door.

"Mama, you'd better come," Jenna said.

It was rare to see her eldest so serious, and Kate laid the book down, peering over her newly acquired reading glasses. "You know this is my time."

"It's important, Mama," Birdie emphasized, offering sisterly moral support. "Miss Lucy is real sick."

Kate had not seen or spoken to Lucy in two months and had no intention of changing that now. Lucy had simply gone silent. There was a time when Kate had been anxious for the moment of confrontation where all could be laid bare, accusations and insults flung about in rapid exchange. But it never came. And now she was almost glad of it.

"I'm sure she's fine," Kate offered in the most sympathetic tone she could muster. "Lucy can always call in for care or go to clinic if she's truly unwell. It's sweet of you girls to worry, but I'm sure there's no need for it."

"She won't though. Says she can't," Mika said. "Honest, Mama, we tried to convince her."

"She's green as a pickle," Mandy added.

"Miss Lucy isn't one for the finer art of cooking, girls. Probably just ate something old. It'll pass. Now shoo." She waved her hand at them, accompanied by a stern glare warning that she was not to be trifled with. "I've still got twenty-one more minutes of me time."

"Mama, I really think you ought to come," Jenna said. "She told us she hasn't been able to eat anything for three days."

The window rattled as the bare-branched fruit trees bent and swayed in the winds coming down from the northwest, sweeping winter across the plains in a wretched deep freeze. The idea of abandoning her cozy retreat and forfeiting the one hour a week she'd demanded to have to herself was wholly unenticing. Besides, Kate really didn't know what on earth they expected her to do, but she also knew the girls were ever fond of Lucy. And staying put, even when she so desperately dreaded the idea of bundling up and going out, much less over *there*... Well, neglect wasn't the look Kate was going for.

"Alright. I'll go," she sighed. "Does she know I'm coming?"

"Miss Lucy specifically told us not to tell you," Mandy said, eyeing up the sugared butter crisps set neatly on the tea plate, a hand hovering towards them. She retreated when her mother's scowl implied imminent dismemberment should Mandy venture to take one.

"She's sick enough, Mama, we thought better to tell you anyway," Birdie said.

"Fine, but afterwards, I'm coming back here and reclaiming my time," Kate said, "And you all will cook dinner, set the table, *and* clean up. Got it? You're plenty old enough now. I'm not at your beck and call. And not Lucy's either."

Each of them nodded, Mika mumbling a quiet, "Yes, Mama," under her breath.

Kate set the book aside and thrust off the chunky knit blanket, shoving her feet into her fuzzy slippers with a perverse amount of aggression. The girls trailed behind, following to the front door as though to be certain she was actually going, and not about to dash upstairs in an evasive maneuver. She pulled on knee-high insulated muck boots, a hoodie, a fleece, and a knee-length overcoat, a fleece-lined headband, gloves, and over-mittens. She hated winter with a deep-seated passion.

"Suit up, girls. If I'm going, you're going," Kate said, turning to look resentfully at her brood. They were all already bedecked in cold-weather wear, patiently waiting. A butter crisp was hanging off Mandy's lips while she was tying her bootlaces. Kate plucked it away from her daughter and shoved it in her own mouth, whole. Not to be outdone, Mandy pulled another out of her pocket and ate it, complete with a defiant head waggle.

"You're lucky I don't reach down there and take it back, Amanda Jean MacKatherine!"

"I'd like to see you tr—mmphh!"

Jenna's gloved hand clamped down securely over Mandy's mouth. "We should hurry, Mama, afore it gets dark," she said in a rush, knowing full well the promise of plummeting temperatures with the onset of night was sure to get her mother moving.

They all tumbled outside, bracing against the bitter cold accosting them. The farmyard was quiet, the animals tucked inside the barn, with a deep bedding of straw and some solar lamps to keep them warm. Fred had grown a proper coat, with hair long enough to grab by the handful, looking the part of an equine yeti. Agatha's hair was now so long that it nearly trailed the ground. From the looks of them both, Kate expected a wicked winter to come.

They silently walked over to Lucy's, stomping across the bridge, the creek still trickling, but ice was already forming at the edges. Vesper had appeared at Kate's side, ears folded back against the wind. He was never one to miss a romp with his pack, no matter the inhospitable weather. Lucy's place felt far more desolate, the absence of animals making it seem nearly derelict.

Kate rapped the front door knocker hard, not waiting for a response, rushing inside to escape the cold. The girls and Vesper filed in after her, Mandy shouting, "Miss Lucy! We're back!"

The smell of sick assaulted Kate's nose as she peeled off her outerwear, dropping everything on the kitchen table. There were dishes in the sink, crusted with days-old food. It wasn't like Lucy to be slovenly, Kate thought, and a tinge of unease crept under her skin.

"Amanda, go on and wash those up. And I don't want to hear a word about it," Kate warned, but needn't have. Her daughter went straight to it without a word of protest, as though to wash dishes at home were a punishment, but to wash them at Lucy's was a reward. Kate held her tongue, ever tired of the constant battle with a fourteen-year-old amid her defiance years.

"Bird, check and see she's got groceries. Compost anything that looks old," she directed, relieved at least that Birdie had always been sweet and was likely to remain so. "Jenna, see about cooking up some rice. That's always easy to get down if you've been sick a while."

"And what do I do, Mama?" Mika tugged at her mother's shirt, not wanting to be forgotten.

"You're backup, sweetheart. Help your sisters if they need it, or me if I call for you, okay? Otherwise, keep Vesper from poking around. That cat's likely to be around here somewhere, and the last thing we need is a ruckus, alright?"

Kate ventured down the hall toward the back of the house. There were no lights on, only the dim cast of the waning day coming in through the curtains. She really didn't want to be here, but her concern for Lucy had ticked up a notch, despite what had transpired between them and the silent void that had ensued these past months.

She found Lucy curled up on the floor of the bathroom, arm wrapped around the base of the toilet, face pressed against the tile floor. She had the pallor of a fish belly, and the sheen of one, too. Lucy cracked a reluctant eye open, then promptly closed it. "Go away," she moaned, with a voice like she'd swallowed nails.

Lucy flinched when Kate held a hand to her forehead. She was warm, but not burning, which surprised Kate a little. "Come on now. Can you sit up? Do you feel cold? Or hot?"

Lucy pushed her away with a flailing arm. "Leave me be."

"I'm calling services if you don't sit up and tell me what's going on," Kate said.

Lucy groaned as though unable not to, pulling herself up and leaning her back against the wall, arms limp. "Fuck you, Kate," she whispered. "I didn't ask you to come here."

"Tell me what's going on, Lucy, or I'm calling. And fuck you, too," Kate said. "I'm only here because my girls are worried about you."

"Your girls..." Lucy scoffed, looking towards the ceiling as if seeking divine insight. Her head lolled to the side, looking at Kate over the end of her shoulder. "You have no idea what you have. What I'd do—what I've done—to have what you have..." Her gaze drifted back to the ceiling, breath escaping in a long, low sigh. "Now get out of my house."

"I'm calling," Kate said with finality, standing up to leave.

"Don't—"

"Then tell me what's going on!" Kate hissed, coming back so fast she nearly toppled over, kneeling in front of Lucy, close enough, their noses almost touched.

Lucy's whole body was trembling, eyes brimming with tears. "Morning sickness."

"What?" Kate gasped, sitting back on her heels and staring, shaking her head as though she could rattle the words into something coherent. "I thought they wouldn't give you another..."

Realization struck like a zephyr on a tumbleweed, every speculation clamoring for attention, rolling and spinning out of control until the next shoved it aside and shrieked to be heard. He'd done to Lucy what she had most feared for herself. Lucy couldn't stop him. When had it happened? Where had Kate been? Why didn't Lucy tell her?

Then into thoughts drifted a vision of Lucy with him, together, companionably drinking coffee at the kitchen table.

"You have no idea what I've done to have what you have."

All Kate had wanted was someone to love, and someone to love her. But after what the men had done to Kate, Lucy had invited one into her home. Sought it out. Chosen ... him.

Kate got up, desperate to leave. It was Lucy's mess. She'd made it; let her deal with it.

The sound of Lucy's pained voice rose up behind her as Kate walked out. "It won't matter. I always lose them."

"Hyper... Hyper... Jenna, what's it say?" Mika thrust the reading tablet under her sister's nose.

"'Hyper-emesis-gravid-arum.' It means a pregnant woman who throws up a lot." Jenna put down her own reading, getting up to peer over Mika's shoulder. "Mama, it says here she needs hydration, and would benefit from specialized treatment. Shouldn't we have taken Miss Lucy into care?"

Kate looked up from the agriculture catalog, jotting down the seed order for next season's planting. She'd planned on overseeding the rotation plot with vetch in the fall, but hadn't gotten around to it yet, and she needed something early for spring. "Mika, why are you reading that? It doesn't concern you. Don't you have schoolwork to finish?"

"It ... it ... it is my homework," her daughter said with shifty eyes and fidgety feet.

"Don't fib. I said never mind it. It's not for you to worry on. Miss Lucy is a grown-up. If she says she doesn't want help, then she doesn't. Now, it's late, go get ready for bed."

Mika sulked away from the table, literally dragging her feet all the way to the stairs and walking like a drunk hippopotamus, the *thump-thump-thump* down the hall making her displeasure known. Jenna remained, quietly taking up her sister's reading with obvious intent.

"Don't you start, too," Kate said.

Jenna shut her eyes a moment, closing the reader and placing it carefully down on the table as though it were made of fine China.

"You look just like your grandmother just now," Kate said. "Jenna, I know that look. I grew up with it. Don't bother. My mind is made up."

"I'm just ... very ... disappointed in you, Mama," Jenna began.

"Oh my god, Jenna, really?"

"You loved Miss Lucy. We could all see it," Jenna said quietly.

"Well, she didn't love me back."

"Yes, she does," Jenna persisted, her clenched jaw evidence that she wasn't about to let the topic go easily. "It's obvious."

"You don't get to have an opinion on the topic of my love life," Kate said, pointing a warning finger at her daughter. "And even though you think you know it all, just like every other damn sixteen-year-old does, you don't. There's more going on here. It's not as easy as whatever it is you think. I'd say one day, when you're old enough, you'll understand, but I hope to god you never have to. But I'm not asking. Leave it alone. What's done is done."

Kate slammed the seed catalog down harder than intended, then got up and began clearing the table loudly, dishes clanking together as they tumbled across the counter.

"Why does that have to be the answer, Mama? How can you just stop … stop *caring* for someone like that?"

Kate held onto the edge of the counter to keep from throwing things. "You'd best be on your way, young lady."

"I'm going over there to stay with her, Mama. With Lucy," Jenna said, voice wavering only a little. "She's alone. And she shouldn't be."

Kate spun around in ready retort, but Jenna was already bounding up the stairs in retreat. It felt as if she'd just had all of the life sucked right out of her. There was a small inkling of pride, inexorably tangled with the desire to punish Jenna for such insolence. Kate wondered if there was, perhaps, an ounce of relief, too.

Lucy had looked dreadful, and in the time since seeing her, sickly and limp on the floor like a wilted flower, Kate had had time to consider the reality of the situation. A child conceived outside of the clinic couldn't be hidden. Everything was managed, tracked, regulated, down to the last detail.

Lucy would eventually have to tell them what she'd done.

26

Sorry Isn't Enough

Lucy was sure there was nothing left in her but bile. Her whole body ached, as though it had been stretched on a medieval stock, each limb tied and pulled until the bones popped out of their joints and the ligaments extended to threads. She cracked opened her heavy eyelids, trying to muster the stamina to sit up, wash her face, rinse her mouth of the taste of metal, and wait for the cycle to repeat.

The sound of the front door opening again made Lucy groan with trepidation. She'd been glad when Kate left; she didn't have it in her to fight anymore.

But the figure in the doorway wasn't Kate. It was her eldest, Jenna. The girl knelt beside her, gently brushing the hair off Lucy's face.

"It's just me," Jenna said. "Don't worry, Mama's not coming."

It was such a simple statement, but the desolation of it ravaged Lucy, followed by a torrent of gut-wrenching sobs that would have stunned anyone, especially a girl who'd only just arrived to offer kindness. In between gasps, Lucy tried to offer apology, but to no effect, the words vanishing along with any sense of reason.

Jenna offered a tentative arm around her shoulders and let out a little yelp when Lucy clung on like a drowning person being pulled from the sea.

"Mama always puts a washcloth on my neck when I been sick," Jenna said, peeling away just enough to look at her ward. "Can't remember if it should be hot or cold though." She turned the water on while casting a wary sideways glance at Lucy. "I think warm ought to feel nice." Jenna rung the cloth out and slowly ran it across Lucy's tear-stained face before rinsing it and warming it up, then placing it around the back of her neck. "I can warm up a barley-and-bran pack, too. That's good for when you got cramps from monthlies. I suspect maybe it feels somewhat the same?"

"Honestly, Jenna, I don't even know what it feels like. This time ain't like the last times."

"Tea, then. Tea's good for everything," Jenna suggested, poised with uncertain eagerness. Bracing an arm under Lucy, she helped her up off the floor and held on until the wobbling stopped.

Lucy closed her eyes, hoping the queasiness would pass. She was not altogether sure it would. "Best find a bucket, just in case. There's one under the kitchen sink." Lucy was deposited on the couch, carefully tucked in under an old blanket, bucket surreptitiously placed nearby. It was not long before she was presented with ginger tea and salted crackers.

"Best to eat a little bit and never let yourself feel empty," Jenna said. "At least, that's what the book said."

"What book?" Lucy nibbled the corner of a cracker and chased it with a sip of tea, testing for comfort or menace.

"Mika was reading up on it, after Mama said you were pregnant. It said to keep you hydrated and have you eat small meals often." Jenna fished around in her pocket, presenting what looked like wide hair bands with a single bead. "Give me your wrists. These are supposed to help. It's acupressure." She bent over, face furrowed in concentration, poking and prodding and squeezing various points on Lucy's wrist before setting the bead at a specific spot and tying it tight enough to stay put. "If you think you're startin' to feel queasy and stuff, press the spot with the bead, and it might help."

"You're good to come here. But I'm sure your mama would want you home." Even though Lucy knew all her crying was just hormones running amok, she still couldn't seem to help it once it started. She ran the heel of her hand across her face, trying to smile at Jenna, who was watching with increasing concern. "It's alright. Never mind it, Jenna. It's just how it is, bein' pregnant."

"Already told Mama I'm stayin'," Jenna said matter-of-factly. "I won't be a bother. I'll make sure you're eating and drinking, and if you get too sick, I'll know when it's time to get you help. But don't you worry," she said in a rush, seeing Lucy's apprehension, "I know you want to be home, and you have to be, and going into care ain't something you want. I promise, I won't call unless I really have to, and I'll make sure I tell you first."

Lucy stared at the girl, dumbfounded, while trying to keep the absurd tears at bay. She could see how much it meant to Jenna, taking these first steps towards maturity, and choosing an impossible circumstance in which to begin. But nonetheless, Lucy couldn't bring herself to protest—not one jot. The notion of being alone throughout it all... Well, it terrified her.

"It means the world to me that you're here, Jenna. And even little Mika, readin' up about how to make me feel better. You girls... I hope mine's..." Lucy's voice trailed off, the words caught, clutched by the fear of speaking what she wanted out loud, as though if she said it, it would be stolen.

"You been pregnant afore," Jenna said softly. "And it ... it was hard for you."

What a diplomatic way to say it. "I lost all three, yes. And I'm scared I'll lose this one, too. It's the last chance I'll ever have."

"What's it like, bein' pregnant? I was only seven when Mika was born, so Mama didn't talk about that sort of thing," Jenna said, tugging at a thread in her pants where a bare spot showed through. "I mean, we've done the module in school and all, but that's not the same. It's just history and the science of how it is now."

"Suppose I'm rather unique, come to think of it." It abruptly dawned on Lucy she was likely the first woman in decades to become pregnant the old way, for surely Abe's mother had been one of the last. "Bein' pregnant is like having a parasite, makin' you tired all the time and sick all the time and cranky all the time."

"Our teachers told us male zygotes are rejected by our bodies, how we can't host them anymore, and they're just being—what'd they call it—exuviated."

"Well, seems my body likes to exuviate them no matter what they are. I never got to hold any of my daughters. Suppose I should just talk to this little one for as long as I've got her." Lucy's eyes rested on her stomach, hand slowly stroking the new softness at her middle. "You love them more than makes sense, afore they're even here." She looked at Jenna, eyes bright and curious. "You four girls... Your Mama is so lucky."

There were days when it was all she could do to hover over the toilet, Jenna stroking her back, always with the ever-present cloth on her neck, hot or cold depending on the passing need of the moment. Lucy quickly concluded she would not have survived without Jenna. An exaggeration born of gratitude maybe, but she felt adamant about it and would have fought anyone who said otherwise.

Despite Jenna's attentions, the sense of impending loss never waned. And contrary to that, Lucy wanted to prepare, to have tiny clothes and a clean house and things for a child she was sure to never hold. She needed the comfort of another; the vulnerability of the circumstances was overwhelming. At times, Lucy wanted to stay cocooned in bed, only getting up at the insistence of Jenna, coming in each morning with ice-cold root beer—the only thing she could tolerate some days—and opening the shades to let in the pale winter sun. She would sit on the edge of the bed, listening to Jenna make recommendations of yoga or reading or walks, as though she were a host at a luxury retreat, ending with, "And your dinner choices tonight are..."

The day Lucy felt the first flutter was the day she begged Jenna to go home.

"No, Miss Lucy, I don't want to," Jenna pleaded. "I know you're starting to feel better and all, and you ain't been as sick as you were, but it's no bother, I swear it. Even my teachers say I'm doing so well I can go straight to applied theory at the end of the quarter and start writing my capstone. It's quiet here, without my sisters and all, and Mama asking me to do this and that..."

"It's been more than seven weeks you been here, Jenna. I can't keep you, much as I wish I could. Your mama's mad enough at me already. No need to add to it by keeping you to myself, now, is there?"

"Why is she so mad, Miss Lucy? I see how you both been, before."

"You ever ask her about it?"

"She won't say. Just that it ain't my place to know her business."

Lucy sighed, wiping the damp palms of her hands along her thermals. The one thing she'd always offered the girls was implacable honesty.

"Took a long while for your mama to love me again. It broke her, when the men came the first time. It broke her again when they come back. Then I took a man into my house, despite all that. Hurt her whole heart even more when I took what I needed from him."

"Can't you say you're sorry?"

"Sometimes sorry isn't enough," Lucy said. "And your Mama has some sorry to give, too. So, I suppose, since I ain't said sorry and she ain't sayin' sorry neither, we're both just gonna stay mad and miserable about it. And either we'll find our way back to each other, or we'll find our way without."

"What'd Mama do that she's got to be sorry for?"

Lucy couldn't admit Kate had stopped loving her, how she'd shut Lucy out, or how Jenna's mother had nearly cost her everything. She shook her head with a wry grin. "It's not for me to say what your mama did. Best she tells you herself what she wants you to know."

They parted, Lucy watching the girl bracing against a stiff winter wind coming in from the artic north, hunching into her long quilted coat, hair lashing around her face like Medusa's snakes. The snow whipped up a white haze along the ground, sparkling like glitter in the sun. When Jenna disappeared across the bridge, Lucy pulled on her down jacket and boots and headed out into the cold.

The old truck sat dormant in the shed, under the cast-aside tarp where Abe had been hidden months ago. Lucy pushed aside any thoughts of wondering what had happened to him, knowing those thoughts would return in the evening just before the solitude of sleep teased—the thoughts that had tormented her with sleeplessness every night since he'd been taken.

The vehicle rattled to life, despite the cold. Lucy breathed a sigh of relief.

It took nearly an hour to find the place by road, and all the while, she questioned what she was doing. There was a sense deep inside that making plans for this child was as sure as anything a promise of ill tidings to come. Her hand rested on her middle, a habit of late she could not break.

"It's alright, little one. This is just in case." Lucy turned the truck off, sitting in the cab long enough to be seen. The old woman had surely heard her coming.

Donna appeared in the rearview mirror, approaching from behind with a rifle held casually in her hands, and walked up to the passenger side. She leaned in, elbow resting on the window. "Been wondering where this old truck of mine went off to," Donna said. "Surprised you brought it back."

"Hadn't planned to. Didn't know it was yours," Lucy said, voice tinged with regret. She got out of the truck and followed Donna up to the cabin. It was warm inside, the pellet stove glowing in hues of amber and gold.

"I've come to ask a favor. I'll be needing a midwife." Lucy unzipped her coat, the evidence of her need plain. "And no one else can know about it."

27

SOMETHING FAMILIAR

THE MONITOR DISPLAYED A steady rhythm, the heartbeat reassuringly, constantly, infuriatingly strong. Noemi rolled Etta onto her back, supine, returning the posey foot tent to an upright position. Etta's toenails had been painted a garish blue—a poor choice, given the circumstances.

"Doesn't suit you, now does it, Etta love? I think you're more of a coral sort, no?"

Etta offered the usual silent response, eyes fixed somewhere between the clock and the door.

"One of these days, Etta... One of these days," Noemi murmured. She ran the hammer along Etta's foot, her big blue toe extending as it always did. Noemi dictated into the patient record, "Babinski, dorsiflexion observed, no change."

In the early days on the long-term care unit—a place that'd come to be known as the Waiting Room—Noemi had had seven full-time patients in care. But in the years since Abscond, as the patients dwindled due to recovery or death's invitation, eventually only Etta remained, resistant to the lure of either. Noemi had been imprisoned in the care system for four years, bound to a woman who seemed more immortal by the day. Now Noemi could see the decades laid out before her, Evelyn Emmett's words still echoing

230

in her ears: *"for the duration of their care."* She might as well have etched the damnable woman's words into her own skin.

Sitting in the chair, Noemi curled her foot under her thigh. Her tracking bracelet had recently been replaced, the new one made of elasticized metal mesh and not nearly as heavy or irritating as the old one. It still itched though, and she ran a finger between metal and skin to ease the pressure, if for just a moment. She leaned back, looking out the window at the bright blue sky, horsetail clouds whipping across the upper atmosphere like brushstrokes. It was the first sunshine she'd seen in weeks, midwinter finally relinquishing its hold. It seemed to Noemi that the clouds rolled in on the first of November and didn't leave again until April, constant dreary companions throughout the long dark days of the season.

"What do you think, Etta? Maybe we go outside, get a little sun on that face of yours." She gave Etta's hand a soft pat, holding it for a moment, uncertain of whether she hoped for a response or not—maybe some tiny flicker. But there'd never been any sign, and this day was no different than all the rest. Noemi picked up her reading tablet, skimming to where they'd left off.

"I believe we're in the midst of a few *Wayward Girls & Wicked Women*," Noemi said.

"Which wicked women would that be?" Kieva appeared in the doorway, leaning against the doorjamb with a host of canvas bags slung over an elbow.

Noemi got up, leaving the tablet on the sill, and hurried over, taking the bags from Kieva and setting them on the side table. "Wasn't expecting you 'til later. How are you?"

"Same as always," Kieva said, shuffling over to the bed with a hitch in her step, left leg stiff. She leaned over, kissing Etta and whispering, "Hey, old thing," taking her wife's hand. Kieva sat, face twisting with discomfort.

"Might be able to find some meds, if you need," Noemi offered.

"Naw, that's alright. Just needed to sit a minute. Been filling in for custodial. I was mopping floors for six straight hours." Kieva tipped her head towards the bags. "Brought clean linens. There're some starched nighties in there, too, though I still can't figure why anyone would want stiff knickers."

Kieva had been a patient in the Waiting Room for six months before her sentence began. She'd fractured a hip and compressed her spine, as well as broken a host of ribs, the tibia in one leg, and the femur in the other. It was a wonder she had survived, let alone be able to walk. She wouldn't have lived had it not been for Etta, who'd wrapped herself around Kieva when the roof collapsed and never let go.

Noemi's nightmares from that day had not ceased, and more times than she cared to remember, she'd woken up soaked in sweat, crying out into an empty room. She suffered endless visions of Kieva, always wearing that orange hoodie, more rubble falling atop her for each chunk Noemi threw aside, or the ground caving in just as she was about to free them, falling and falling again. The dreams and endless days wore on Noemi. Kieva's regular visits were a welcome distraction, desperately needed and possibly the one thing keeping sanity within her tenuous grasp.

The soft tones of Kieva's voice filled the room while she took up reading to Etta. There was something unsettling about it as much as it was comforting—someone as young as Kieva being so committed to a woman who would never again be conscious of her presence. Noemi quietly slid outside, thankful for the reprieve, unwilling to bear witness to such devotion.

The Waiting Room was housed in an old wing of the hub hospital. Her quarters were adjacent to Etta's, a converted patient room outfitted with a lone steel-coil twin bed and one sad cactus set on the cinder block windowsill The walls were adorned with the discarded remnants of former inpatients, their visitors keen to cheer up their loved ones with scenes of the outside world. Noemi had never had a visitor, making do with the images from the lives of others simply for the distraction.

Noemi wandered down the empty corridor towards the cafeteria in the main building. She was at liberty to wander her own unit and the interior courtyard, but the bracelet adorning her ankle stopped her from going anywhere else. She'd only tried once, and now she couldn't go within five meters of a prohibited exit without flinching.

The security guard, Jasmine, was doing rounds and offered a grunt of greeting as Noemi ambled by. They were a stout, disagreeable woman whose flowery name did not match their appearance. Despite this, Jasmine had come to be an unfailing gossip, and a reliable source for smuggled cigarettes, homegrown and hand-rolled by someone outside the purview of enforcement.

Noemi had been given a weekly allowance of seventy credits, good for the cafeteria and commissary. But it wasn't long before she'd realized it wasn't enough to cover all her food, much less anything extra. Had it not been for her middle-aged metabolism and skimming off Etta's liquid nutrition, she speculated they would have starved her out long since.

The cafeteria offerings had remained constant, never deviating in what culinary delights were available. It ran the gamut from runny scrambled eggs and runnier porridge in the mornings to dry beans and dry rice in the evenings, with little variation on the theme in between. Of course, there was made-to-order food for the real visitors, complete with an on-site chef and daily specials delivered to the patient suites overlooking the forests and lakes.

Noemi sidled up to her usual spot, tucked away in a corner in front of the media wall, and propped her feet up on the chair opposite. Most days, if she timed it right, there would be a serenade of symphonic music from the capital orchestra, complete with ethereal landscape scenes fading in and out across the screen in high-definition dimension. It was the closest she could get to being somewhere else. She'd long since given up on caring about what was happening "out there," once the realization came, she would likely never get to go "out there" until she was of an age where it no longer mattered. Media reports came and went, and they had no bearing on her personal experience, so she paid them no heed.

The sounds of chamber music ebbed and flowed, a mournful bassoon carrying the melody while woodlands bedecked with ferns and evergreens appeared before her. When the music soon faded and no more commenced, Noemi sighed, expecting the day's reports she had no interest in knowing. She began folding the remnants of her butter-and-ketchup sandwich into a napkin, to tide her over during the afternoon doldrums. She was halfway out of the seating area when the voice of none other than Evelyn Emmett stopped her cold.

The media wall lit up, the woman's severe figure appearing from floor to ceiling, larger than life. Evelyn was walking slowly with her hands clasped together in a practiced manner. The grounds of a sprawling campus of low buildings fanned out behind her, the unmistakable physique of elder men in blurry repose not far distant.

"Greetings and good tidings from the Central Rural Zone. It is with authorization from the Governing Council, I offer the following special announcement. Savior number 792 was returned to us by his own will in good health and free from harm. All may offer their welcome to number 792 in due time. Three still remain at large. Anyone with information leading to the location and recovery of our last saviors will receive just acknowledgment and reward."

The image of a man was presented on the screen, with *792* shown on a banner below his face. He was a far better specimen than any Noemi had ever seen, and she couldn't help but wonder what his life had been like since he crawled out of that hole at Abscond. There was something familiar about him, and she wondered if he was one she'd seen, ever so briefly, standing at the rim before he escaped into the woods.

Kieva had quietly appeared beside Noemi. "You think it could be him?"

"You think we'll ever know?" Noemi said dryly, casting a sidelong glance at Kieva, standing there with a look of earnest on her sweet face. "What, you really think so? Hell, Kieva, no one will ever tell us if he is or isn't. Does it matter?"

"Can't all have been for nothing," Kieva whispered, still staring. "He's got the look of her, if Etta were older and nicer. For a man, he ain't even all that ugly."

Noemi looked at him, just before the image faded to nothing and the sounds of orchestral music returned. *Maybe...* she thought, but stuffed the idea back in her box of useless notions where it belonged. It *had* all been for nothing—that much was certain—and Noemi would go to her grave unwavering in that belief. But Kieva needed something to hold onto, and Noemi was the last person to keep that from her.

"You go on and tell Etta, then," Noemi said softly.

"What if it ain't him?"

The sound of woodwinds offered Noemi a moment's distraction she wished would last forever. But she looked at Kieva, face bearing an expression of sincere gravity, and elbowed her with an accompanying smile. "If Etta sees fit to wake up and scold you for lyin' about it, go on and let her."

Kieva brightened in an instant. "You think she will? Wake up?"

Noemi regretted it instantly, willing to swallow barbed wire if she could have shoved the words back in her mouth. She knew better than to give hope in a hopeless situation.

If Noemi could have had a day of penance removed for every time she'd had to shatter someone's hope for good news, she would have been out a long time ago. Etta would remain inert and unmoving as a fallen tree, unaware that life had ended.

Noemi put an arm around Kieva. "No, love. She won't. Not ever."

28

LIKE IT OUGHT TO HAVE BEEN

THE OFFICE DÉCOR WAS as cold as the woman in front of her. Overseer Evelyn Emmett sat across from Kieva with the indifference of a woman who had heard every excuse and story conjurable and had stopped believing in the possibility anything came unexpectedly.

"I'm submitting my request to offset the remainder of my sentence in exchange for the implantation study, and I am requesting to be matched with number 792," Kieva said. She'd never been one to dither. It had to be him. And she was going to do something about it.

"And why would we do that?" Overseer Emmett rolled a stylus back and forth across the top of the table with the tip of a manicured finger, voice flat with menacing disinterest.

"I've served all but the last five months of my sentence," Kieva said, trying hard to keep her composure when she said the next part. "And I'm married to 792's sister."

The stylus stopped rolling, and Evelyn's eyes shot up, but she wouldn't concede the notion of surprise so easily. "And which one is that again? Oh, that's right—the comatose one who won't die."

"Oh, and she ain't likely to," Kieva said with a rejoining smile. "Etta's no quitter. She'll just keep on goin' out of spite. Probably outlast us both, livin' like a dandelion in a hothouse the way she's been doin'."

Evelyn's mouth twitched, and she stuck the end of the stylus between her teeth. She gave Kieva a steady appraisal, eyes lingering longer than would be considered well-mannered.

"Says here you were in reforestation," Evelyn said, scanning through the documentation on the screen. "Advanced specialization in sustainable forestry and bio-habitat regeneration. High performer, well liked. Dozens of petitions by your former supervisor to have you released early." She dropped the reading pane and looked at Kieva. "Remind me, how'd someone like you end up cavorting with some incompetent bunch and blowing up government property at Abscond?"

"Same way someone like you keeps old men in a cage, letting them rot to death instead of saving womankind," Kieva replied. Her steady gaze never left Evelyn, the challenge for the woman to deny it plain. "Shit happens. You go along with it 'cause you're hoping you can keep it from getting worse. And by the time it's too late for that, you're just trying to do the best you can. And I can't figure out why you're saying they was incompetent, seein' as they did what they meant to."

"Social commentary notwithstanding, you've failed to make your case," Evelyn said, standing up and tucking the file under her arm, turning to leave. "Request denied."

"Ain't you related to Carol?" Kieva blurted out the last card she had to play. "Sister or aunt or companion... Something like that? Always thought it was awful peculiar that woman seemed to slip through every crack, you being so thorough and all. Surely there's folks 'round here might be interested in knowing just how you two are acquainted. How after all this time, someone like you might have overlooked the one woman responsible for the whole damn thing."

Evelyn stopped dead, shoulders stiff and knuckles gone white, still clutching the file. She slowly turned around, leveling a glare at Kieva intended to make a woman go mute. "I'm sure I have no idea what you mean," Evelyn said, each syllable clipped to the quick.

"And I'm sure I won't either," Kieva said, "as soon as you let me go and do what I asked."

Kieva hadn't any expectations of what a man would be. Noemi had tried to prepare her, said they were foul and beastly things. Abe was nothing of the sort. His smile was the same as Etta's, lopsided and toothy, and his head tilted to the left like hers, too. Kieva wondered now, with Abe standing in front of her, how there had ever been any doubt he was Etta's brother. While the likeness flashed on the cafeteria screen had offered more than suspicion, Abe in real life was a carbon copy, albeit of a masculine variety.

"Is this written in my mother's hand?" The paper quivered in Abe's grasp, face bright with unspoken joy.

"Oh, sorry, no," Kieva said distractedly. He had Etta's eyes, too. "The original letter was lost. But it's written to the best of our recollection, as true as the real deal."

Kieva had decided the man ought to know his mother's dying words, and Noemi had written out Odelia's letter from memory. It had been filled with a mother's love and regret and promise, telling him she'd loved him every day of her life—had fought for him and spent her life in penance for it, and would do it again—and may he know it now and never forget.

Abe's eyes drifted down to his mother's letter time and time again, a look of gratification congealing with mournful relief and a mountain of regret. "It ain't worth it, what my mama did, when all she got was nothing but life in a box. Same as me."

"I don't imagine she was thinking about the future when it all went down," Kieva replied. "I doubt she was thinking at all, so much as she was a mama fierce lovin' her son and tryin' to keep him safe. Sometimes that's all you get, even if what you were tryin' for don't happen. It's having a thing matter so much more than yourself that you'll do anything for it. That's what I think love is, anyhow."

Kieva told him the rest, about the letter to Etta and their mother's dying wish, the things Noemi had told her of Odelia, and what had happened to Etta at Abscond.

Abe shuddered with the mention, shaking his head, face paling with the memory. "Seemed like the sky opened up and the whole world collapsed. Don't remember nothing but scrambling towards the sun. And when I found it, I just started runnin', and I kept on runnin' and didn't stop until I was nowhere," he said, voice trailing off. "Got a bit strange after that."

"Afraid it's about to get a bit stranger," Kieva said. "Did they tell you why I'm here?

"They said there was someone to meet and brought me in here. Told me I'm real important." Abe sat down on the narrow metal bench, casually leaning against the cinder block wall of the visiting room as though wary of the prospect of further revelations.

"There's research the council wants to do," Kieva said, then stopped short. Somehow, she'd thought it would be easy to proposition a man, but the words got caught in the maze between her mind and her mouth. "Research with women, and um ... you and your friends here, to see if maybe, that somehow if ... if maybe men and women might... 'Cause, see, there's no boys, and there's all kinds of theories on what to do about it. And they been trying in the lab and all, but now that your lot is here, we can try things different. So, they're wanting some of us to come in here and see if, well ... maybe if some of us are willing to try different sorts of things, then maybe we could fix all that, and then it won't be a problem anymore."

Abe's body slumped into a soft curve, narrow shoulders curling inward and arms tucked tight across his body. His voice belied a suspicion born of a man long used. "And what different sorts of things are they askin' to do with me?"

"The research study I'm in, well, it's to spend time with you, just us talkin' and being around each other. See if being sociable and whatnot makes a woman's body have to be less ... defensive ... and maybe less likely to reject male seed."

"I ain't never been the sort to hurt no one, not ever," Abe said definitively. He sighed as if resigned. "After we've been sociable, they'll take what they always been taking from me, and give it to you?"

Kieva nodded, unable to meet his eye. "Yeah, I suppose that's the way of it."

"And you don't mind bein' used like that?"

"I want to be used like that," Kieva said in a rush. "It's as close as it comes to having a baby with my Etta. Something of her—sort of, anyways—to keep going in the world. Like it ought to have been, had Etta not saved us both."

Abe looked around the concrete cell, a beam of sunlight coming from a high barred window and glinting off the tips of the long lashes that curtained his dark eyes. He slid to the end of the bench, a tentative hand gesturing toward the space beside him in invitation.

"Wouldn't mind knowing about my sister, if you'd be willing to tell a story or two, and you think that's a sociable sort of thing to do."

"The first time I met Etta," Kieva began with a smile, sitting down beside Abe, "I spent the night holding her head out of the toilet..."

There were times when Kieva wondered why she'd had to go and fall in love with this woman. But she never wished she hadn't. Even if it meant only having had Etta for a little while, she was glad to have loved her at all, no matter the hurt that came as a consequence.

"Can't say why though, ol' thing. You about the crankiest woman I ever known," Kieva said, leaning over and pressing her lips to the smooth spot between Etta's temple and forehead. Before, Etta used to squirm away whenever she tried to kiss her there. Since Abscond, Kieva had kissed Etta there every day, probably a thousand times. It was an act of defiance, mixed with the bleak hope it would rile up her wife enough to wake her up.

"You always been stubborn, Etta, but I ain't givin' up, no ma'am." Kieva smiled and closed her eyes, mustering a ball of light and love and energy from deep inside her soul, imagining it floating from herself, through the air, and into Etta's body, as if it were the last spark needed to make her live again. Even if it was just long enough for the light to flicker in Etta's eyes in recognition, just long enough to see Kieva was still here, still loved her, still wouldn't let go. Just like Etta hadn't let go when the whole world fell out from beneath them.

"There are women of many descriptions in this queer world..." Kieva sang the old folk tune louder than was natural, carrying the water basin and washcloth to the bedside. She hummed the middle part while folding back the thin blue cotton gown wrinkled against Etta's body, then belted out the refrain: *"Who have charms made of diamonds and pearls. But the only thoroughbred lady is the rebel girl."* She could picture Etta smiling inside right now, despite herself. Kieva would never stop wondering if Etta was still in there—if she could hear things, see things feel things, think

things—but had forgotten how to do whatever was necessary to make the right synapses fire and become extant again.

"Kieva, you don't have to do that, I'll get to it," Noemi said, coming into the room at an easy amble, setting down a coffee cup and picking up a towel. She took the wilted arm Kieva had just washed and began patting it dry.

"I don't mind. It means I can tell her about all the things been goin' on, and she just has to sit quiet and listen." Kieva turned back to Etta, expression fading like a cloud crossing over the sun. "You can chime in anytime, now, Etta love."

Noemi laid Etta's arm down gently. "You tell her about you and Abe yet?"

"No, I ain't told her. But I suppose it's time I ought to." Kieva resituated Etta's blanket, tucking it tight under her atrophied legs before sitting down beside her.

Noemi drifted toward the door, looking immediately uncomfortable. "Want me to go?"

Kieva shook her head, swallowing hard to try and keep her voice from breaking. "Please stay." She rested a hand over Etta's, which was always curled like a bird's foot, and tucked her own index finger in between the stiff knuckles.

"Etta, love." Kieva waggled her finger inside Etta's hand and leaned close. "I've something important to tell you, so I want you to listen up and pay attention, okay? You saved him, Etta my darling. We found your brother. Abe made it out. You did what your mama asked, and I know she be real proud of you. I told him he ain't never been forgot."

The reassuring weight of Noemi's hand on her back helped to ease the violent shudders of every emotion coursing through Kieva's body. It was relief and hope and fear all clamoring for attention, when all that mattered was the promise—a promise Kieva made sure she kept.

"We're makin' a baby, Etta love." Kieva gazed at her wife and squeezed her hand tight. "There'll be a little part of you in this child of mine. And I'll love her just as fierce as you and your mama."

Etta's body remained forever still with this news, face expressionless, but for the soft mist gathering in the corners of her eyes.

29

Simple Gifts

False spring returned—the first unseasonably warm, sunny day before the inevitable return of snow—enticing people to venture outdoors. Noemi's blood was viscous after a bitter winter, and she wore nothing more than a T-shirt and scrub pants, despite the glint of frost still in the deep recesses of the north-facing parts of the building. In her state, Etta was susceptible to changes in temperature, and needed to be bundled with warm blankets and a hat for their foray outside.

Noemi slung the wide strap around Etta's upper body, heaving the woman up with a grunt and transferring her to the wheelchair. "If I didn't know better, I'd think Kieva's been feeding you chocolate cake," she huffed, angling one of Etta's arms out of the way and sliding her into position. Noemi left her to stabilize, checking to verify that the sudden change in altitude hadn't sent Etta to the precipice of crashing.

"You're a sturdy old thing, not to worry," Noemi said, stripping the linens from the bed and shoving them down the laundry chute. She pulled blankets out of the warmer, tucking them around Etta's legs and torso until she was snug as a swaddled infant, no limbs left to dangle about.

The courtyard was filled with staff on break, their faces turned reverently towards the sun. Families were picnicking, their loved ones bedecked in thick quilted gowns. Noemi took her place among them, wheeling Etta to a tidy spot with dappled shade, the light filtering through leafless branches. Sometimes Noemi thought she could see the same spark of something more behind Etta's dour expression as when Kieva had told her about Abe, and this day was no exception. It hadn't ever amounted to anything more, always the same quiet immobility, but it made Noemi feel as though there was still something of left Etta inside, and made the labors in the name of comfort and variety worthy of the task. She ran her fingers along Etta's wrist, verifying the thrum of life persisted. It did, steady and constant.

Leaning back in her chair, Noemi closed her eyes to the sun, too. Her awareness traveled between hazy and none, the low hum of conversations rising and falling around her. When a shadow fell across her face, she waited, expecting it to pass, only opening her eyes when it didn't. The woman standing before her was silhouetted by the sun, almost glowing.

"Get out of my light," Noemi snapped, squinting with a hand across her brow and trying to see. The woman didn't move. Noemi sat up, practically growling at the inquisitor. "What's your problem?"

"Mom?"

Noemi shot out of her chair like a rocket, looking at her only long enough to check—yes, it really was her—before throwing her arms around Rosena and hugging her daughter so tightly that the girl couldn't help but to squeak. But Noemi wasn't about to let go. It didn't matter if they were a spectacle. She would stay there for hours or days or years, wanting with every fiber of her being to consume the moment, to be indelible in Rosena's mind. She could not take in enough of her daughter, stroking her tear-dampened hair, kissing her forehead, pulling Rosena back into an embrace and swaying, rocking, holding her, whispering repeatedly, "Oh my god, Rosena. Oh my god."

Suddenly, she pushed Rosena to arm's length, still clutching her daughter's arms to be certain it was real, unwilling to let go. Noemi scanned the courtyard, eyes coming to rest again on her daughter, questioning.

"She's with Jayne," Rosena said, almost apologetically.

Noemi shook her head, lips pressed tight together. It was alright. She had Rosena. "Let me look at you," she said, still holding her daughter's hands tight.

Rosena had bloomed, growing into a woman's body, all curves, and taller, too. Her face had lost the final softness of childhood, but her cheeks were pleasingly round, the first creases of humor decorating the corners of her eyes. Rosena suffered her mother's maternal fussing with measured reserve, the quiet, easy demeanor a trait Noemi had never known in her daughter.

"Will you sit with me a while?" Noemi asked.

Rosena agreed, sitting down next to her mother. "I remember her," she said, gesturing toward Etta. "She was at the camp. She was always feeding everyone."

"Turns out, I took care of her mother, too. Odelia. Ain't that a hell of a thing? I'll be taking care of this one for a long while, I suspect," Noemi said. She was still holding her daughter's hand and couldn't bear to let go. "Rosena, I think of you and Stella every single day. I love you both. I need you to hear that. You know I do, right?"

"I know, Mom. Stella knows too, although she's turned into a proper little monster these days." Rosena smiled briefly, casting a glance at her mother, but unable to hold her gaze.

"Whatever you've come to tell me, whyever the reason you're here ... it's alright, Ro." Noemi squeezed her daughter's hands gently in encouragement, at the same time trying to quell the stampede of explanations for her daughter's sudden visit after so many years. "Whatever it is you've come for, it's alright."

"There's something I want to tell you." Rosena withdrew her hands, rifling around in her satchel until she produced an image card with a picture of Stella, handing it to her mother. "But I'll tell you about Jayne and Stella first, okay?"

Noemi held the card with both hands, trying to remember what Stella sounded like, or the scent of her childhood, a mix of apple juice and paint and dirt. She hadn't heard what Rosena was saying. "What? I'm sorry, I..."

"I said Stella is the newest member of the capital orchestra. Started three months ago." Rosena was leaning forward, trying to lure her mother's focus away from the image of Stella and back to her. "Second-youngest member they have right now. It's a really big deal, Mom."

Noemi was nodding in agreement, hand firmly clasped over her mouth, tears of pride threatening to overflow. She listened intently then, hanging onto her daughter's every word. Stella had taken up the bassoon, of all things, at the urging of her school counselor, who'd identified Stella as having keen musical interest and an affinity for peculiarity. Stella thrived with all the attention for being unique, and she was soon invited to youth symphonies and began winning competitions. Before long, she had been invited to sit in with the capital group.

"Grandma said anyone that could pick a bassoon out of a pile of objects could get a chair playing with the orchestra. But actually, Mom, she's really good" Rosena grinned, face lighting up with sisterly pride. "Jayne went with Stella. The CRZ hired them to record an anthem. It's called *Copeland's Appalachian Spring*, I think—some ancient Shaker song called 'Simple Gifts.' Supposed to be a pretty big deal."

"Your Auntie Jayne always did like to be involved in big deals," Noemi said, trying to suppress her sarcasm and envy and resulting inclination for sisterly violence. While she was fit to burst with happiness for her daughters, Jayne's assumption of a mother's role to her children—and her escape from retribution for her role at Abscond—made Noemi's heart race and her vision blur.

"Mom, are you alright? I'm sure it's upsetting, you being here and Jayne not."

"I'm alright, Ro. Go on and tell me. I've always wondered. I need to hear it."

Jayne had been one of the first bombers out on the dome—and it turned out, one of the first ones off. She'd carried nearly ten kilos of explosives, lit a long fuse right in the center, and started running. When everything collapsed, both literally and figuratively, she grabbed Rosena and kept going. They never went back to the camp. They had walked seventeen kilometers through the forest, up the mountain, and down the other side, unwilling to go anywhere near the monorail hub closest to the camp for fear of being caught.

"We called for you, Mom. Auntie Jayne was screaming for you to come with us. But you couldn't hear us, and then it was too late. You'd already gone to help. I tried, I really did, but she wouldn't let me. And then when I saw you at the hospital, same as you'd always been ... I just ... I was just so angry. I told myself I never wanted to see you again. I told Stella if I ever found out she'd been to see you, if she ever talked to you, I'd smash her fingers with a sledgehammer. I'm sorry, Mom. It's all my fault."

Noemi opened her arms toward her daughter, and Rosena curled up inside them like she was a little girl again, letting her mother rock her and hold her. "Not your fault for not wanting to be around a mother like me. Not Stella's fault either for having to choose between busted-up hands or a mother beyond care. It's alright, honey. It's not your fault, and I don't blame you for any of it, I swear."

"And Auntie Jayne? Do you blame her?"

"Of course I do. She's my sister and it is her fault. I blame her for everything," Noemi quipped, only half joking.

The visitor bell rang its warning overhead: fifteen minutes to close. Noemi's heart fell, the time having gone by in a flash. There was so much more she wanted to talk about, so many years between then and now. So much time had gone by, and her daughters had changed so much. Without her.

She propped Rosena back up, running a hand down her daughter's face, brushing the hair behind an ear, holding her arms as though to remember Rosena in that moment forever. Just in case.

"Will you visit me again?"

"Yes. And I promise to bring Stella, too."

Rosena stood up, casting a long glance at Etta, silent witness to the reunion. "It's good that you take care of her... Oh my gosh, Mom, I almost forgot what I came to tell you! I finished nursing school and did my last round of clinicals a month ago." She stepped closer, voice dropping to a whisper. "And I just got my first gig, but..."

"I am so, so proud of you, Ro. Where are they sending you first, and..." She leaned in conspiratorially. "Why are we whispering?"

"It's off the books," Rosena said. "Grandma got me a job as a midwife down in the rural zone. I start next week."

30

EXCEPT IN CASE OF EMERGENCY

IT HAD BEEN UNSEASONABLY warm, and Lucy suspected the old queen would be inclined to restlessness. She silently admonished herself for leaving the brood-super in place the past autumn, but quickly remembered what had distracted her that evening: Kate. She wrapped an arm around the empty metal bucket, resting it on the protruding shelf of her pregnant belly, and began banging the side of the bucket with a hammer.

The swarm of bees was flying above in a tight crowd of frenzied little bodies, a few stragglers trying to catch up, while some others began to peel off one by one, reconsidering. Lucy kept up the timpani, ready to add her voice to the clamor.

"Get back here, you little bastards!"

A few accepted the rude invitation, erratic and confused as one and then another and then dozens began streaming back into the hive, until eventually every bee returned.

"Mandy, grab the empty frame and stack it on top. We'll have to split them once they've settled," Lucy said.

"Got it, Miss Lucy. I'll pull another frame and get it ready," Mandy said, carefully fitting the square on top of the others before replacing the lid and dashing back to the barn.

Lucy waddled after her in slow pursuit, a hand beneath her belly to ease the weight of it. She hadn't meant to be up, but the warmth of the day and a sudden unease had bid her to check the hives in spite of herself.

Her pregnancy had advanced to the final weeks, much to Lucy's disbelief. She'd never carried a child so long, nor come so close to the reality of having a baby survive beyond her womb. There were still days when she couldn't believe it, expecting to wake up from a dream to find herself reinhabiting her proper body: soft stomach, wide hips, feet that hadn't swollen to resemble ticks on parade. But it hadn't happened. Each morning following another restless night of peeing every godforsaken twenty minutes and perpetually trying to get comfortable, Lucy woke in a daze, still huge, still very much pregnant.

She hadn't been alone in it as the girls slowly crept back into daily life, appearing as if by magic every time there was something to lift, something to fetch, something to do. Lucy hadn't meant for them to be here. She didn't want them involved, didn't want them to get attached, for when the loss came—as it surely would, as it always had before—it would devastate them. Lucy wouldn't be able to bear their pain along with her own. And yet here they all were.

Lucy went inside, putting the kettle on for tea and plating treats for the girls. Birdie was preparing the room for the midwife, while Jenna and Mika had taken on finishing painting the baby's room in sunset hues of lavender and orange and rose. At times, it was overwhelming to have so much love in the house. It made Kate's absence all the more acute.

The couch beckoned her, and Lucy sat, eager to be off her feet. Mooey immediately hopped up, paws atop Lucy's stomach, kneading and staring and purring with abandon. She pressed a cheek against the cat's, settling Mooey atop her thighs where she could just barely see feline ears sticking up above the roundness of her belly. The cat had been stuck to Lucy like glue for the better part of the last month.

All at once, the girls came careening into the room from bedrooms and barn alike, faces eager yet wary. "Someone's comin', Miss Lucy," Birdie said.

Jenna retrieved the cat, depositing Mooey into Mika's arms, then stuck out a hand and pulled Lucy to her feet. They all looked out the front window like a gang of meerkats, watching the lone figure make their way down the drive.

Lucy did not wait for the knock, opening the front door wide, to the surprise of the woman approaching. She was tall, her long, dark hair pulled back into a neat ponytail with a utilitarian band at the nape of her neck. She carried one small suitcase and a large medical bag.

"You must be Rosena," Lucy said.

"Yes, ma'am. Pleased to be here."

She was younger than expected. A qualm of unease coursed through Lucy, but she quickly pushed the feeling aside, knowing this wasn't the time to be particular. Inviting the girl in—she looked no more than twenty—Lucy guided her past Mika's and Birdie's wide-eyed curiosity, Mandy's cross-armed territorial skepticism, and a look of absolute esteem from Jenna, only a few years Rosena's junior.

After a short introduction, a barrage of questions ensued, the poor young woman defending herself with no more than a mug of tea and her wit.

"Do you have a pony named Fred, 'cause we have a pony named Fred?"

"Got any sisters?"

"Where'd you go to school?"

"If you're a real midwife, what are the four types and risk factors of placenta previa, and what supportive care is recommended?"

"I haven't got a pony named Fred, but I've always wanted a pony, and I surely do hope you'll make our introductions," Rosena said to Mika, who eagerly agreed.

She turned to Birdie, withdrawing an image card and handing it to her. "I've got a sister named Stella. I expect she's near your age, but not half as kind as you are, I'm sure of it."

Rosena leveled an equitable gaze at Jenna. "I went to day school in the hub, studying physiology in mid-levels, and I earned advanced bio-anatomy placement in uppers, before studying innovative care and processes for the maternal mother at the university. Then I completed my clinicals at the city center hospital. I can tell you anything you want to know about exams and all that, if you like."

Rosena paused, taking a thoughtful sip of tea, steadying a long gaze at Mandy, who was returning the look in kind, sans tea, but with a gingersnap firmly in her grasp. "I am indeed a real midwife. The answer to your questions are: Partial, low-lying, marginal, and complete. Para gravida, age, race, illicit substances, and scarring. Bed rest, medication, and birth intervention," she said, rattling off each answer with measured authority. "Have I passed your test?"

"We'll see," Mandy said in a huff.

"Alright girls, off you go. No doubt your mother will rent out your rooms to a less inquisitive bunch if you don't go on home soon," Lucy said.

The girls left with a degree of reluctance, each with promises to return to finish one task or another soon enough. Jenna was the last to go, slyly fixing her hair before passing Rosena by. Visitors were a rarity, less so those as young and interesting as Rosena.

"I'm starting at the university next fall, and anything you can tell me about it would surely help, if your offer stands," Jenna said, eyes wide and face pink.

"I surely will," Rosena said, a mirror to her admirer.

Lucy sighed inwardly, amused, but in no mood for the dramatics of prospective young love, and she ushered Jenna out, shutting the door at last with a resounding thud. She proceeded to show Rosena around—in part to distract the young woman, whose gaze was lingering on the door.

"The girls have been helping with chores and whatnot, and they've got things ready for this one," Lucy said, patting the top of her stomach. "So, there's not much to do but wait, I suppose. You've a room of your own. There's not a book or a bite off limits. It's not fancy, but it'll do."

"I've spent most my life living in the hub city, ma'am. It's nice to be where it's quiet. If you'll forgive my boldness, I've seen the state of your poor feet, and I'd like you to sit awhile. It'll give me a chance to ask some questions, too, if you don't mind."

"Have at it," Lucy said, sitting down heavily on the couch, and a bit shocked when Rosena set her feet up atop a pillow.

"My grandmother told me this was some sort of unauthorized implantation, though she didn't offer particulars. So, I understand there'll be no cause to call for care, except in case of emergency. And we surely do hope there's none of that," Rosena said, voice lilting and comforting. "Have you a place in mind for where you'd like to deliver? Some women prefer to be abed, and others like to kneel. If you've a bedroom with space to move around, and a bath adjacent, that'd be best."

"The bedroom will do," Lucy said, her insides tightening at the thought.

"You'll show me, and allow an exam?" Rosena asked, and upon seeing Lucy's reaction, quickly added, "Nothing intrusive. Just to give a listen and to see how she's positioned."

"Oh, right, of course." Lucy began laughing nervously while trying to suppress a rising tide of trepidation. "She's never stopped moving since the first moment she started. See? There's an elbow." Lucy pushed back at the bumps and ripples running across her skin. It was a wondrous sensation—despite the pokes in her ribs and stomps on her bladder—and Lucy almost dared to believe she might finally be a mother. She lay on the bed as Rosena pressed and prodded before wrapping a fetal band around her midsection.

"As you haven't any prenatal care, it's important to have a listen," Rosena said as she positioned the monitor. "Do you have a name for her?"

"Didn't want to jinx it. Won't even think about a name 'til I see her, live and whole. Only just got the baby's room done this past week," Lucy said. Swishing sounds were followed by the solid *thump-thump-thump* of the baby's heartbeat, reassuring and strong. Lucy fixed a hand over her mouth, tears springing to her eyes at the sound—a sound she'd never heard, not from this child, or from any of her others.

"Well, she sounds strong as a bear and is in a good position. Head's down already."

"Will she come soon, then?"

"Everyone's different, so there's no telling," Rosena said, removing the monitor.

Lucy wished she'd left it on; the sound of the little life inside her filled her heart. "How many deliveries have you done?"

Rosena turned away, folding up the band into a neat circle and tucking it back in her medical bag before making notes on a makeshift chart. "I've been present at six," she said, back still turned, adding, "and provided supportive care for two."

The answer was obvious before the question had been asked, but Lucy had to ask anyway. "And how many deliveries have you, specifically, been in complete charge of?"

The girl's shoulders stiffened, head down as she tidied up the supplies. She turned around abruptly, chin raised just a little. "You're my first."

Lucy's sharp intake of breath was sufficient to cause Rosena to launch into a flurry of assurances. "I aced my clinicals, ma'am, and was top of my class, and I've studied every conceivable presentation and all the methods to remedy, and the signs and symptoms of every sort of birth—"

"I'm not a textbook, Rosena," Lucy interrupted. "But I've no choice in the matter. It's not that I don't appreciate your being here, 'cause I do. But I lost three, and I won't lose this one, you hear me? I won't."

"No, ma'am. I'll make sure of it."

Lucy hung up the last picture above the baby's crib. She'd photographed an array of meadow flowers and butterflies and bees from around the farm.

"Are they level, Mandy?"

"Looks fine to me." Mandy was sitting in the corner chair, rocking away as though set to take flight. "Got's to go, Miss Lucy. Mama said I already been here too much lately, and I'm likely fit to drive you crazy."

"Well, you've been a great help, Manda. Couldn't have done—" Lucy's breath hitched as she felt a sudden sharp cramp. "...couldn't have done a lick of this without you," she said, her smile fading.

"You alright, Miss Lucy? Should I fetch that woman?"

Lucy shook her head, though not sure it was the right answer. She stood still, eyes closed, hand flat against the wall while trying to concentrate on what she was really feeling. The baby hadn't been moving much lately. The time was coming soon.

"It's alright. Go on home," Lucy said, trying to sound reassuring—though to herself or Mandy, she wasn't sure.

"Don't think so. I'm getting her." Mandy bolted out of the room, footsteps thudding down the hall as she yelled, "Hey, lady!"

"Please be alright. Please be alright," Lucy whispered, walking slowly towards the rocking chair, hips feeling as though they were greased, and eased herself down. It was all she could do to hope she'd be able to get through it.

Hurried sounds came from the hallway. Rosena appeared at the threshold, Mandy beside her, both looking expectant.

"Not yet," Lucy said, breathing out in a measured exhale.

"All the same, I'd like to do a tiny check," Rosena said. "Let's have you in your room, where it's comfortable." She helped Lucy to her feet, supportively stretching an arm around her waist and guiding her across the hall before setting her down on the bed.

"Let's have a listen, shall we?" Rosena didn't wait for a response, unrolling the fetal monitor. The band was fitted around Lucy's middle and the monitor turned on. The steady sound of the baby's heart echoed through the room. Rosena had brought the medical bag—Lucy had begun thinking she slept with the thing beside her—withdrawing gloves and snapping them on without hesitation. "Just a quick peek, now," Rosena said, parting Lucy's thighs and ducking out of sight. Lucy held her breath.

"You're completely effaced and three centimeters dilated," she said in a rush, then popped back up again, smiling wide. "What do you think about having a baby?"

"You think it's today?" Lucy asked, eyes wide.

"Well, more likely tomorrow, but yes, labor appears to have started," Rosena said. "But that doesn't mean you need to lay abed like a hen with an egg. Better to be up and about. Walk some, do anything else that needs doing before it really gets going in earnest. I've got some prune tea for you to drink, to clear your innards. Better to do it of your own accord now than have it be a surprise later."

"That's so gross," Mandy said, face scrunching up with distaste.

"And you, my meddlesome little friend, had best to go home and mind your mother," Rosena said, adding surreptitiously, "But send Jenna back, if I should need help."

Mandy ignored her entirely, going in and sitting down beside Lucy on the bed. "Better I stay."

Lucy squeezed the girl's hand tight before letting go. Hers had been a reassuring presence, despite her age, and Lucy would just as soon have Mandy here. "Best to placate your mother for a time, afore you come back. Tell Jenna to come for a while though. If anything starts to happen, she'll fetch you."

"Alright, Miss Lucy. I'll help Mama, so she don't bother fussing when I come back neither," Mandy said matter-of-factly, getting up from her post and walking out of the room, not even acknowledging Rosena when she passed by.

"That one reminds me of my little sister," Rosena said, watching Mandy go as if to assure herself the girl had left. "Now then," she said, turning back to Lucy. "Upsy-daisy. Let's get you up and about."

They made their way to the kitchen, Lucy moving at a slow waddle. "Feels like my bones are going to pop out of their sockets, and everything's stretched fit to burst." The cramping radiated around to her back, and she stopped at the table, hands flat on top, trying to wait out the pain with a loud puff of breath. She wondered if she would be able to endure it, how long it would last, how bad would it be, who would hold her hand to comfort her, or remind her to keep breathing. Would her daughter be healthy, or was Lucy too old, and the child would be deformed? Or was Abe's part in it damaging somehow, and what parts of him would the baby inherit? She hoped it wasn't his ears. Lucy took another sip of the prune tea, choking the horrid concoction down with a long gulp and a puckered face, the better to get it over with.

It wasn't long before Jenna arrived and set to work preparing for delivery with towels and blankets layered over oiled tarpaulins.

"Keeps the floors and bedding clean," Jenna said. "That much I remember from when Mika was born. It's a messy business."

"Suppose takin' a thing that's been living inside you and forcibly evicting it would be cause for mess," Lucy said. She paused as the pains came, this time stronger than the last, blowing air out of her mouth and looking like a puffer fish.

The day passed in a hazy blur of pain and apprehension. Lucy had begun walking circuits through the house, living room to bedroom to baby's room to kitchen, then around the table and back again, until she'd seen every corner a hundred times and again. It was sprinkled with intermittent bouts of her insides seemingly trying to twist themselves inside out, and Lucy realized that description was not far from truth.

The waiting had left Rosena and Jenna without distraction, their preparations long since completed hours prior. Jenna made soups and casseroles, stocking the freezer with an abundance of meals for after. Rosena huddled in a corner, poring over literature about various presentations and complications, which did little to settle Lucy's imagination.

When finally the time came to get down to the business of it, they ushered Lucy into her bedroom, Jenna supporting one side of her, Rosena the other. She could not bear to lie down, instead kneeling on the padded floor, leaning against the bed as if praying, hands clasped in appeal. Mandy had appeared without beckoning, at first disgruntled at no one remembering to get her, but quickly becoming consumed by the evolving spectacle.

"You'll hold her hand, Amanda, if she's wanting it, and you're to help her breathe proper, like this," Rosena said, demonstrating with a few short huffs of *hoo-hoo-hoo* and *hee-hee-hee*. Then she turned to Jenna, voice dropping low. "And you'll be ready to pass me things if I need them." She'd laid out a variety of instruments in sterile packets, neatly labeled on the packaging so Jenna would know what she was asking for.

The sight of them made Lucy shudder, remembering the times before, when her daughters were taken away from her, so tiny and lifeless, an array of cautery and specula gleaming under surgical lights. She could smell them, her nose keen with the advent of motherhood, the scent of antiseptic and metal mixed with the memory of blood.

"Here we go, Lucy. A few big pushes, and then it'll all be over with."

31

None of You Matter as Much

"Mama, Mama! Help!"

Mandy's voice shattered the house, the screams unlike any Kate had ever heard from her before. She was running without a second thought, fixated on the sound of her daughter's voice. Kate found her at the front door, face streaming with tears, eyes wild with despair. She grabbed her daughter, enveloping Mandy in reassuring arms, making certain she was whole before pushing her daughter to arm's length and searching for clues as to whatever had set her running like prey pursued.

"There's something wrong with Miss Lucy's baby, and she called... Mama, that woman called them, and they're coming to take it, and Miss Lucy is wailing and thrashing, and Mama, you have to make her stop!" Mandy tugged at her mother's arm, pulling her outside onto the stoop. "Mama! Come *on*!"

Kate looked across the fields towards Lucy's place, expecting to see evidence of turmoil, and was surprised to see nothing at all. The day was still, no clouds, no sounds, not even birds calling. If something was wrong with Lucy's baby, she was sorry for it. But she wasn't going over there. Lucy would have to account for herself eventually, and it might as well be now.

"It's not for me to do, Amanda. I'm sorry for Miss Lucy, but it's something for her to reconcile, and I can't stop it from happening." Kate turned to go back inside, but her daughter grabbed hold of her arm with a fierce grip.

"Mama. You have to. She's our friend!"

"Sweetheart, she's not my friend anymore. You know that. I'm sorry for what's happened to Miss Lucy. But I mean it. I'm not going. I can't stop what has to happen."

"Jenna said she's not going to let them—not over her dead body. Mama, she's serious."

"Oh for the love all things and damn it to hell anyway," Kate muttered. She stepped down and began marching out of the courtyard, intent on reaching Lucy's place. "Tell your sisters to stay here. And you stay put, too," she warned.

She hastily walked the path through the field, the first green sprouts of alfalfa pushing up through the dirt, buds on the old tree fat and ready to open. Lucy's fields were further along, meadow plants inches above the soil in a lush green carpet.

She could hear the raised voice of Jenna as she approached, and the sound of a very new baby crying. "Can't be too bad. She's got a set of lungs on her for sure," Kate muttered.

"Oh, that baby was crying afore it even came out, and it hasn't stopped since," Mandy said.

Kate turned, seeing her daughter trailing behind her. "Goddammit, Amanda! I told you to stay home."

"Best you get in there, Mama. I'm sure you'll deal with me later," Mandy said rationally, undeterred in the least by her mother's scolding.

A loud crash from inside followed, and Kate decided her daughter was right. She didn't knock or announce herself, half wondering whether she should be armed and what the nature of the complaint was with the midwife. She rounded the corner of Lucy's bedroom, the scent of blood and fecundity assaulting her nose.

The baby's cries had diminished to a soft mewling, but Lucy's hadn't.

Kate found them in various states of disarray. Lucy sat in the corner, fiercely holding a bundle of blankets. Jenna stood in front of her, looking intent on dismembering the woman before them—presumably the midwife— who was red-faced and about as distraught as everyone else. Kate ventured in, wary.

"What's going on?"

At the sight of her, Lucy gripped the bundle in her arms. A tiny fist thrust up from the white cotton folds of the blanket, rebellious. Lucy's face was swollen and puffy, and there were dark shadows under her eyes. The joy of finally having a living child seemed curiously lost on her.

"That woman reported us," Jenna said, pointing a finger at the midwife. "She had no right. And now they're coming." She looked imploringly at her mother. "Mama, do something!"

"Mandy said there's something wrong with the baby, Jenna. If she needs care, it was right to call," Kate said, all the while looking at Lucy, desperate to know what had happened, and yet unable to divine the cause for so much anguish.

Lucy stared at them for a long moment, then slowly stood up, edging toward the bed, wincing as she moved. She laid the baby down, unfolding the swaddle down to bare skin.

A tuft of dark hair like a mohawk. Tiny hands curled up tight. Legs bowed and bent from nine months in the womb, squirming a little, just enough to see that damning little appendage.

A boy.

"Good god, Lucy! What have you done?" Kate whispered.

"I can't let them take him," Lucy pleaded. "He's mine."

"He's the savior, ma'am. You have to," the midwife said.

Kate had half a mind to lock the woman in a closet and scuttle Lucy and the baby—the boy—off to her house, but it was no use.

She turned on the midwife, taking three big steps right up to her, toe to toe.

"Get out of my sight. Get out of this house. And get off this property, or so help me, I will rip out your hair and feed you to my dog and bury what's left under the shit pile."

The woman didn't move, didn't even bat an eye. Kate grabbed a fistful of the midwife's hair, pulling hard enough to make her yelp. Kate was left with more than a lot of hair in her hand when she let go. "I ain't playing! Get out of this fucking house, and don't you even look back!" she shouted.

The midwife reached for her medical bag, muttering, "You people think you can just—"

Kate grabbed her arm, twisting it behind her back and pushing the woman out of the room, down the hall, and out the front door, slamming it behind her.

Jenna followed, watching it all unfold with an expression of absolute bewilderment. "Mama, what on earth has gotten into you? I've never seen you this way before!"

"Never mind that now, Jenna," Kate said. "Doubt we got much time. Got to get our stories straight. How soon before they get here?"

"Rosena called them maybe fifteen minutes ago. It'll take them a half hour, driving fast," she said.

They returned to the bedroom, finding Lucy right where they'd left her, the baby on the bed still naked as a jaybird with his mother hovering over him and looking as though she were lost inside a dream. Kate had a mind to hold Lucy, but quelled the urge. Lucy had always been the strong one, and now it seemed as though she was the one who'd shattered into pieces, needing someone to gather them up and glue them back together.

"You've got a child. 'Twasn't what any of us was expecting, but he's healthy, and he's plenty whole. And he's yours," Kate said. "Tell me what you want to do."

"What they'll do to him, what his life will be... I can't let them. I can't let that happen." Lucy carefully folded the blanket around the baby and picked him up, rocking gently. "Should I drown him, Kate?" she asked, voice airy as a wisp. Her gaze drifted toward the window, outside and down toward the creek, as though in solemn contemplation. "Don't worry, I'll go, too. I ain't letting' him go without me."

"You're not going to do that," Kate said softly.

Mandy had tears pouring down her face, her whole body shaking. Jenna went to her, wrapping an arm around her sister, before both girls took Lucy into their fold. "You're staying here, and you're not going anywhere," Jenna said, voice breaking. "You belong to us."

"Lucy, sweetheart, listen to me." Kate glanced at the time, heart pulsing as though it were about to break in two and readying to fight a lion at the same time. "There's got to be a way out of this. I'll talk to them, okay?"

"They'll take him, Kate. You know they will. That overseer said it'd be twenty years of service. They'll punish me for having him, at the same time as they make him an idol. Only child I'll ever have, taken—and he's no more than an hour old. Spending his whole life never knowing why it happened, thinking he wasn't worth looking for," Lucy said. "Same as his father."

"Is that what happened to the man, Miss Lucy?"

"We haven't time for a history lesson, Amanda," Kate interrupted sharply. "Give me a minute to think."

The CRZ would protect the boy as if he were the rarest gem on Earth—for he was. Humanity would continue because of him. But his life would be little more than a stud to an eventual sisterhood of women. Or should he have sons, too, his dynasty of offspring would be relegated to an unknown fate. Kate swiftly realized the weight of Lucy's fears and why she might want to save him from it in such an unimaginable way. And from the looks of Lucy, huddled in the corner and holding her newborn son, protected by Kate's own daughters, she could see no other solution.

Should the promise of a decent life be forfeited for the sake of everyone else's?

"Let me hold him," Kate said. It was partly curiosity, the notion of holding a boy such an oddity, and for a fleeting moment, she wondered if it would matter someday, to be able to say she held the first one. The savior. But while his mother's face showed a measure of adoration, it held a shadow, too, and Kate wanted to take him to remove the temptation of Lucy's paradox.

He was relinquished from his protective embrace and passed over to awaiting hands. Kate took him with a well-practiced arm, snugging him into the crook of her elbow. He was so small, eyes shut tight to the tedious world that had so ungraciously welcomed him, the trials of delivery a grueling affair. He was no different, as babies went, barring the one exception hidden under the folds of his blanket. Lucy had made a miracle. Kate doubted anyone yet realized how much more of a miracle he was than if he had been a girl, presenting only the usual marvel of birth.

"He should have a name, Miss Lucy. A name befitting what he is," Jenna suggested.

"Haven't thought of one," Lucy said, voice vacant. She'd sat down on the bed and was leaning against the headboard, listless and wan with a waxy sheen to her skin. "He was to be Sophie, or Beatrice. I'd not decided. Thought to get to know her a while afore settlin' on a name."

Mandy's shoulders stiffened all of a sudden, and she rushed toward the window. "There's dust on the border road. They're coming!"

Kate put the child back into Lucy's arms, seeing her face alight at his touch. She didn't like the look of Lucy though. It was as though her body had determined it had served its corporeal purpose and decided it was done.

"Best you put the little guy to your breast while you've a speck of time, see if he's willing." The suggestion was not solely for the baby's benefit. Kate remembered the rush of euphoria she'd felt when her daughters were born and put to breast and hoped the same would be true for Lucy. Maybe the more strongly they bonded, the less likely Lucy might choose to harm him. At least, that's what she hoped.

"Jenna, you'll stay here with Lucy while I head off the CRZ," Kate said, then turned toward Mandy. "Sweetheart, I won't have you in the middle of this. I need you to go home and look after your sisters, okay? Can you do that for me?"

"Yes, Mama," she said. Mandy rushed to the door, pausing at the door before looking back. "I love you, Mama. And you, Jenna. And Miss Lucy. And the baby." Then she was gone in a flash.

Kate was overcome with relief, the desire to protect her daughter as fierce as it was the day Mandy had been born. With her resolve reaffirmed, she went to the kitchen, watching out the back as Mandy ran across the fields, down the bridge and past the tree, safely home. Kate exhaled, not realizing she'd been holding her breath.

Returning to the front room, Kate went out to meet what was coming, only to find the midwife, Rosena, looking expectantly down the drive. The woman turned when she heard Kate swear under her breath, the crunch of gravel under her feet offering fair warning of ensuing assault.

"What the hell do you think you're still doing—"

"Making sure what's supposed to happen actually does," Rosena interrupted, trying to look defiant.

"You bring a rain of heartache down on us, and you still think you're fit to stand here and give a lecture? If I wasn't acquainted with your grandma Donna, if I didn't hold the respect I do for her, you'd not be leaving this property. Know that."

The midwife tipped her head at the approaching one-cars, arms crossed. "Brave words for a woman who can't do nothing 'bout it now. None of you matter as much as that baby does, and I'm fit to see the boy go with them," Rosena said with a winning smirk.

Kate had her on the ground before the expression could fade, the loud *thwack* onto the crushed gravel expunging any remaining air from Rosena's lungs. Kate pressed a knee into her chest, leaving the girl wide-eyed and gasping like a fish.

"I've yet to find a woman can back up such attitude with any muster. Your grandmother would be ashamed on both counts, and you can be sure I'll tell her so." Kate watched the midwife turn a fair shade of blue, only withdrawing at the sound of running footsteps.

The garda and Evelyn Emmett were hurrying towards her down the drive, and there were approaching shouts as Jenna came from the house.

"Mama, we need her! Mama, there's blood everywhere!"

32

LIE WITH A NOD AND A SMILE

THE CEILING WAS MADE of clouds. Smudged edges and soft colors were accompanied by music meant for meditation, with the sounds of water and waves and harp strings. It was as if Lucy's limbs were filled with sand, boneless and heavy, unwilling to heed her mind's commands. The rest of her felt hollow. No familiar presence keeping her company, no somersaults or poking feet.

What have they done to him?

Do they know he's hungry?

Does he know he belongs to me?

There were people coming in and out of the room, the lot of them mute. No one would answer her. No one would say where her baby was, or even what was happening. Lucy was sure she was asking, sure her mouth was putting sound to her voice, even if it was only a whisper.

Someone was beside her, saying her name. It took every effort to turn her head to see. Was it Jenna? Was it Kate?

"You hemorrhaged," Rosena said when Lucy's eyes came around and tried to focus on the woman's face. "You're in the hospital."

Lucy tried to curse, but the sound wouldn't come.

"You are the mother of the first one. And I am the one who delivered him," Rosena said. "We're important, Lucy. Both of us are part of something bigger now. Always remember that." She smoothed her pale blue scrubs and affected a beaming smile. "You get better quick. You've more important business to do. I'm sure we'll see each other again." Then Rosena slipped out of the room without a backward glance.

A red fury was rising inside Lucy with such swift intensity, she could scarcely breathe. She needed to get out of here. She needed her baby. Lucy waggled her fingers, trying to wake them and remind them of their duty to obey, hoping the rest of her would soon follow, if only a finger, then a hand, and then an arm would lead the way.

"I see you're well enough awake, my dear? Good."

Lucy knew that voice. She turned her head slowly toward it.

"You're a teensy bit sedated, for your own safety. And maybe ours. Though I rather doubt a woman who left that much blood on the floor will be a threat. It's better this way, don't you agree? Leaves out the question of will you or won't you." Evelyn Emmett took up Rosena's brief throne, sitting down beside Lucy, audacious enough to take her hand, but quick enough to let go when Lucy dug her fingernails down into the meat of the woman's palm.

"I do admire your spirit," she continued. "On to business then? Good." Evelyn shifted in her seat, crossing her long legs, pressed pants and navy cardigan neat as a pin, not a hair out of place.

There would come a time, Lucy thought, when she would relish ruining every speck of the woman, from her tightly bound hair to the tips of her patent leather toes.

"We've managed to tidy you up, after your rather dramatic parturition. Good as new. In a short time, I'm sure you'll be ready to give it another go with number 792." Evelyn paused, brows raised in evident amusement at Lucy's silent protestation. "Your successful coupling is a remarkable achievement. We intend to duplicate it. Now, I understand from your friend, you may have some reservations."

Kate had offered an entreaty on Lucy's behalf on many counts, not the least of which was convincing the CRZ that Lucy's pregnancy resulted from an encounter not of her own choosing, the man in question having successfully forced himself upon her. Kate had gone on to inform that Lucy's shame was so great, she'd lied to Evelyn during their prior encounter when they'd retrieved the man hiding in the shed. A lie, Kate had said, was assuredly understandable, given the humiliation a woman must feel when so affronted. And after the threats the CRZ had made, it was no wonder that a woman would remain silent in the face of such evidence as pregnancy. Evelyn had listened to this story with a measure of incredulity, but seemed inclined to disregard any suggestion of lies or impropriety on their part.

She stood up, peering down her long, straight nose at Lucy, elegant fingers clasped in front of her as if to cradle an envious womb. Her parting words cut Lucy to the quick.

"It's your obligation to society and womankind to endure this, my dear. I'm sure you understand what we ask of you and why. Should you be successful at providing another boy, an eventual new contributor to our stores, you will want for nothing in your lifetime. When these days are written and recorded, you will be revered as a goddess of humanity for a millennia. You will be our new Eve."

They named him 793. But among Kate and the girls, he was called Ben. Lucy had been granted six weeks to have her son in her care for breastfeeding, "for the benefit of mother and child," they'd said. Lucy didn't care why; she only knew she needed Ben near, to hold him and touch his hair and the softness of his plump, round cheeks. He smelled heavenly, and at times Lucy pressed her face against his head and simply breathed in deeply, eyes closed so she would remember.

Kate visited most days with a or two daughter in tow, the girls giddy to hold Ben and beaming with near sisterly pride each time he offered a new sound or expression since their prior visit.

The CRZ had given Lucy everything she'd asked for—everything but to go home and live her life with her son. "Too dangerous," they'd said. Kate wouldn't speak of it, but the girls had confessed to her that groups of women were now at Lucy's farm. There were those calling her a whore—or worse—for taking something that didn't belong to her, but they were largely outnumbered by the ones offering their adoration, as though on pilgrimage to an ancient holy site. While others went so far as to bathe naked in the cold creek, filled with snow melt from the mountains, a few daring souls ventured to stick a finger in the beehives and suck the honey off of their stung fingers, believing it was the source of Lucy's good fortune, though this endeavor swiftly became less popular.

And she was anointed with a new name, too: Lucy Milagros, Woman of Miracles.

"They've posted garda at your house and ordered them to disperse," Jenna told her. "Those who don't are taken into custody, and their offences are published each evening as a warning to anyone else with the same notion. Been less fuss now. The numbers have been dwindling by the day." She'd been sheepish, visiting with her mother but unusually quiet, offering only glimpses toward Ben or Lucy.

Enough silence passed between them to become awkward, Jenna casually glancing at the time or intently watching the ceiling change from blue to amber to pink and back again. Where Lucy's attentions were ever entertained by her son, it seemed Jenna had enough weighing on her that the baby merely warranted a glance and a pat. Jenna shoved her hands under her thighs to keep from fidgeting, and now her knees were shaking with the incessant tapping of her feet.

"I thought you tried to die," Jenna finally blurted out one day. "That you'd done it on purpose, and there was naught to do to stop it. There was just so much … so much blood … everywhere, and I couldn't understand where it'd all come from, if not by your own hand. Because you'd said so—that you wanted to—and it were all my fault that you had."

If Lucy could have leapt out of her chair and held the girl, she'd have done so. But as it was, Ben was in her arms, latched on and very intent on his task.

"Jenna, I'm sorry for it, what it must have been like for you. I'd never have wanted you to witness such a thing, no matter the cause." She ran a thumb over her son's cheek, wishing to shield him from every measure of pain in life, and knowing just as sure as the sun rises, she never could. "I won't let you see such a thing ever again, not if I have any say in the matter."

"It's not that I can't handle it, Miss Lucy. It's that you matter to me, and I couldn't bear it if you died. You won't, will you? Do the things you said?"

Lucy didn't answer. She rocked her son slowly, consuming every little detail—his stern expression of concentration, the flex of his small fingers pressed against her, the wave of his dark hair, the small dimples in his cheeks, the tiny sounds he made when content. Would she smother the life out of him when he was six weeks old to keep him from a life of torment? Was it love to let him have a life, no matter how wretched, or was it love to spare him from it?

Lucy offered a reassuring smile. "It's not something to think on now," she said quickly when Kate came into the room, returning with tea and sandwiches and pastries.

"What's not something to think on?"

"Mortality," Lucy said.

Kate glanced at the baby, then back at her, plainly comprehending everything with one look. "Yours, or his?" Her voice was quiet and level, with no tone of accusation or worry. She was spreading strawberry jam and cream on a scone, breaking it into bite-size chunks and aiming it towards Lucy's mouth, as though it were better not to hear the answer.

"You'll not leave me again," Kate said quietly. She brushed her hands free of the crumbs, a sideways look all that was needed to send Jenna scampering from the room with a mumbled excuse.

"We've tried, Kate. But it's been one thing after another. Maybe we aren't—"

"I've spent my whole life waiting to love someone the way I love you," Kate interrupted. She was intently pleating the end of Ben's blanket when her eyes shot up to Lucy's, lashes clumped with tears. "What happened between us... The way I feel with you... How much you mean to the girls..." She threw up her hands in frustration. "It's no easy thing to navigate, but we have, haven't we?" Kate's eyes shifted back to Ben, lingering on the boy a moment. "With some bumps along the way, surely, and more to come."

"They've been more than bumps, Kate. After those men came the first time, whatever it is that happened—it changed you. It changed us." Lucy shook her head, searching for the right words. There was a soft *pop*, her nipple flung loose. Ben had fallen asleep, milk drool trickling down out of the corner of his mouth. She looked at her son, and her heart filled with love and dread alike. Her eyes drifted to Kate. "It changed everything."

Kate touched her face and leaned toward her, their foreheads touching. "I love you, Lucy. I'll love you both," she said softly. "Tell me you'll come back to me."

Lucy wouldn't—couldn't—say it, knowing it was likely she would never leave this place. She pulled away, eyes downcast, unwilling to look at Kate for the guilt of what she knew would soon be the end of everything. But in that moment, Lucy couldn't bear giving so much pain to the woman she knew in her soul was hers to love. And so, she offered her a lie with a nod and a smile, unwilling to say the words.

They took him on the Monday of the fifth week. It was first thing in the morning, and Lucy was still groggy from sleep, bleary-eyed and hoarse.

"Good morning, ma'am. We're just going to take him down the hall and do his monthly screening and immunizations. Back in a jiffy," the nurse said brightly, whisking Ben out of the room without a backward glance.

But they never returned. After thirty minutes had passed, Lucy was pacing the room, her arms useless without a child to hold. After forty-five minutes, she was walking the halls, looking into each room, asking everyone if they'd seen her baby. Each shook their head. "No."

After an hour, she was screaming.

And then they came for her.

Evelyn Emmett stood behind the nurses, observing as they secured Lucy's arms, then her legs, then her mouth when she would not stop thrashing. The woman waited patiently after they'd left, watching without a word, until finally, Lucy submitted to stillness.

"Our 793 is quite a stout little thing. The physicians are quite pleased with his progress," Evelyn said, coming to stand beside Lucy. Her hands rested on the bed rail, manicured fingernails tracing the line of padding meant to keep Lucy from bodily harm. "He'll thrive under the care of our volunteer wet nurses, all of childbearing age and fertile. We are researching whether exposure to such an innocent male will incline a woman's body towards them, to keep them from rejecting implantation as they always have. Some have been implanted with 792's pater-seed the clinical way. And the others... Well, we'll see what happens with you first."

Evelyn leaned over, glaring at Lucy as if to remit her to silence twice over. She cautiously removed the linen strap covering Lucy's mouth, pausing to see if there would be protest, but none was offered.

"You're something of a curiosity," Evelyn continued. "The first woman to offer a boy. Yet, after all we've promised, and with everything you know to be true, did you really think you could take him away from us?"

If Lucy could have wrapped her hands around Evelyn's long, thin neck, she would have, but her wrists were restrained. And good thing, too; she would not have had an ounce of self-control had they not been. "Who told you?"

"You think we don't listen? Maybe we would have let you keep him as we'd offered, had you not been so inclined. He's not yours, Lucy; 793 belongs to all of us. And so will the next one. And the next."

"And if I don't? Is it not rape by proxy?" Lucy glared at the woman, trawling for some shred of fear, if not decency. "Have a care, Evelyn. There are masses of women at my house. My name has been broadcast into every godforsaken home as your 'Eve.' What happens to you, do you think, if your name is affixed as Eve's oppressor?"

"And what happens to you if your name is affixed not as our redeemer, but the source of our demise?" Evelyn said, mouth twisted with conceit. "Give us another boy, Lucy, and you'll want for nothing. Give us nothing, and I will be certain you will wish you had chosen differently."

33

A God Caged

This confinement was at least nicer than the one he'd had with Kieva. The walls changed colors, and music came from everywhere whenever he wanted. He had food aplenty. There was a whole wall for story pictures, and he didn't have to share even that, or worry on fightin' with anyone about what he be seeing. There was a door to the walled garden outside with a hammock that was his, grass that was his, flowers and trees and birds that were his any time he was wanting to look. No one to bother him. He'd seen the others, walking the yard across the way. Not even wearing their collars. Abe supposed there were none left inclined to run. He wasn't so sure he would either; living came easy now. Besides, there was nowhere left to go.

But sometimes he wished he could anyway. Of course, he knew they always be watching.

The day they gave Lucy to him, he felt like he wanted to burst; he was that glad to see her. Abe was drawn to the woman—couldn't help it, despite her betrayin' him. But she was none too pleased to see Abe, and she went into a crying fit for near an hour afore he could get a word in edgewise, no matter how hard he tried.

"Just leave me be." Lucy was lying on the floor with her knees drawn up to her chin, persistent sobs no match for her quick rage when he tried to touch her. Her hand flew out so fast that Abe fell onto his backside in a tumble, knocking his head on the nice chair they'd given him to sit on. He could see she felt sorry for it, hearing his head *thunk* and his sharp complaint. She didn't say so though.

Abe left her there, retreating outside to a deep blue sky with wispy clouds and warm sun on his skin. He rubbed the back of his head, checking for damage, a little surprised to find none. He sat on the garden wall, staring back at the little house and the woman now occupying it. She looked different than before, nicely soft around the middle, and tired and worn like someone weary of living. He knew that look well.

The peonies in the garden were blooming a pale blush, the petals accented by streaks of magenta, their heady aroma lifting on a quiet breeze. It was morning still, the ants not yet come for nectar. After so many years in an environment of nothing but concrete and aging male bodies, he couldn't get enough of flowers. He plucked one off its thick green stem, closing his eyes and breathing in deep, letting the smooth silk of the petals brush against his nose. He'd never known such fine and lovely things. Abe brought it inside, putting it in a glass of water, and set it on the table. He couldn't resist inhaling the perfume of it again, his easy smile growing wide.

Lucy had picked herself up off the floor. She was studying his quarters, checking the doors and windows, then the garden, scoping the height of the fence and walls before coming back inside and sitting sullenly on the couch. The tears were held at bay, but her face was red and swollen, and she looked intent on impaling anyone she encountered. Abe paid her no mind, even though he had a thousand and one questions. They'd bide.

He set water to boil, setting his cup on the counter. Thinking better of it, he grabbed another, putting sweets alongside on a small plate. Abe said nothing when he walked by, leaving the bergamot to steep in the mug and deftly placing it beside the peony, pushing both in front of Lucy without a word before taking his own outside. Maybe Lucy was meant to be his new companion. He was glad of her company, regardless.

"It wasn't me that told them about you. I want you to know that."

Abe set his reading aside. Lucy was standing on the patio, hair shining in the sun, arms crossed tight in front of her body, weight shifting between her feet as though uncertain whether should she sit or run. He looked at the chair beside him, then at her in invitation. Lucy hesitated, leaning back on her heels before coming over and sitting down all in a rush.

"I didn't. I swear it," she said.

The honesty in her eyes was plain, along with the urgent need to be believed. Abe leaned forward, arms resting on his knees, hands clasped as if in prayer. "Been thinking all this time it was unkindly you got rid of me that way. I'll believe you though, what you're telling me now. And I'm hoping you can tell me your part in whatever all this is."

"Fucking hell." Lucy sprung out of the chair and began walking in circles around the garden, hands on her hips, shaking her head and looking at the sky. She returned just as quick, angrily dragging the heel of her hand over tear-dampened cheeks.

"We made a boy, Abe." She hesitated, as if expecting some response. "... You and me."

Abe knew it was likely his progeny numbered in the hundreds, now that it'd been made plain what they'd been using the men for all those years. But he'd yet to know one of his own making, and he half wondered why it was she hadn't brought it with her.

"If'n you got what you wanted, why you here?"

"They took him," she choked, "and now they…" She gestured over her shoulder towards distant outbuildings. "Now they want us to make another."

Abe ran his sweating palms down the length of his thighs. He'd thought of her that way often. Thought of the moment he'd had her, a woman, for the first time. Not a hole in the wall to spill himself into, whether he was inclined or no. The honeyed scent of her hair, the musk of her body, the way her skin felt smooth like the petals of the flowers in the garden… The warmth and softness of her joined with him, his hands holding onto her round bottom. And the want to do it again consumed him. To press himself into her and—

"Are you even listening?"

He offered an agreeable nod, with no notion at all of what she'd been saying, but appreciating the way her lips moved when she spoke, the creases between her brows when she was frustrated, her dark eyes lively with agitation.

"The one we made, the boy—they call him number 793," she said, silent a moment, as though waiting for her words to fly from her mind to her mouth to his ears to his brain, its synapses firing with recognition of the import of her words. "I call him Ben."

It was like a brand being seared into his skin. Flashes of all those years living confined sparked in his memory. The voice overhead, everywhere and yet nowhere, reprimanding them by their assigned numbers. That voice haunted his daydreams as well as his nightmares. A warning would come before the shock coursed through their bodies, some so afflicted, they would writhe on the floor until they lost their bowels. Them that were fighters learned to be quick about it—quick to assault, and quick to move on as though nothing had occurred.

And now they'd numbered one of his.

"There been any others, aside from this boy you say we made?" Abe's voice shook, a spike of anger and fear roiling in his guts. "They take him from you, to make him be what I been?"

"Ain't been a boy born since you, Abe. Not 'til we made Ben. They'll call you Savior, if'n you put another one in me. Life be whatever you want it to be, so long as there's a few more who'll live your burden."

Lucy's eyes flittered across him with shy glances. She was more inclined, it seemed, to count every blade of grass than to linger on him long enough to hold a thought and risk having it seen.

"They're wondering if Ben came 'cause with us, it was done the old way. And they figure we should do it again, see if the same thing don't happen twice."

They'd told him he was special when they'd moved him to his own place—only, they hadn't said why. Abe's heart skittered and jumped, absorbing the notion of a boy living his life, no more than a thing used to provide offspring, little more than property for gain at the bidding of any who decided it, with no choice in the outcome.

"And if we don't? If we won't follow their bid, if we don't do what we did, if there ain't a boy made in the end? What comes of us then?"

"I think the boy we already made will suffer for it. We'll all suffer for it. If Ben was the last—if no more pater-seed is sourced, and if science can't replicate it—then when the stores run out, so do we." Lucy drew her knees up to her chin, wrapping her arms around her legs and resting a cheek on her knee. "Sometimes I wonder if it would be better to die than bear either."

It was a sentiment he could plainly understand and felt sympathy for. He wanted to be with Lucy. He had a desire to hold her, to tell her it would be all right, when he knew it never could. No matter what they did, it would be self-serving. Make another, so they could live. Decline, and push the burden onto another. Or end themselves because the choice was too hard to make. It was an impossible thing.

"We can't be the only ones," he said suddenly. "The other men are still being used. I hear the music every three days. I know they still harvest them. They even take some of mine for a woman some weeks ago. This obligation they've given us isn't ours alone."

"Harvest? They ... they ... harvest you, how?" Lucy shot up from her personal embrace, feet flung out and back onto the ground. She was alight with a mixture of irritation and interest.

Abe liked the way she looked when she was agitated. Her cheeks flushed, and her whole body came to life as though readying for battle. Her motherly figure was belied by strong, defined arms and the tattoo adorning her willowy neck. He wanted to feel that way with her again, keep her for himself and take her body with his. He'd not mind running his hands up into her hair and pulling her close, remembering the welcome softness of her body.

"Abe! Pay attention," she reprimanded. "What are you talking about?"

A creep of heat ran through him, betraying his thoughts. It was his turn to count blades of grass and think of things to distract. "They've not made me do it but one time, in the place I was afore I was put here. Haven't been the tones in here. But there's a place for it. Behind the front door."

He could see she had no idea what he was talking about. He dared to reach out a hand to hers in invitation. Abe was shocked when she took it. They went inside, to the front of the place that had come to be his home. He closed the door, revealing behind it the hole in the wall meant for donation.

"All the cells had them at the bunker. Every three days. Music comes, and we do our business to it. Can't even help it now, when I hear it played," he said, studying the curve of her breasts with interest, the faint strains of "Simple Gifts" echoing in the recesses of his brain.

"Pavlovian," Lucy said simply. He arched a brow in question. "A stimulus used to prompt a conditioned response They play music, and you ... you're primed to contribute whenever you hear it. I won't ask you to, erm ... whistle it," she said, glancing down and quickly away. "Those must be connected to the cryo-labs," she said under her breath, looking at the spot behind the door thoughtfully. "My god, it makes so much sense now. You lot do what you do, then it's sent out via those tubes to the fertility centers."

"Where you think it come from all this time?"

"Saved up. From before you lot were gone. We'd always been told not to worry, that we had stores to last five hundred years," Lucy said. She eyed the door again suspiciously, edging away from it and back toward the sitting room. She took a sip of cold tea, staring out the window a long while before she spoke again. "Been wanting a child my whole life, and they took Ben as though he ain't mine to have, as though he don't belong to me. How can I do it, Abe? Be a broodmare for the CRZ and just hand my babies over, as if they don't mean anything at all?"

"Seems to me, that boy means everything to everyone," he said.

Abe scouted the garden walls for the possibility of escape, much as Lucy had, wondering if it'd be better to take his chances free. But what of her then? And the boy?

"They'll never let you go, Abe," she said, her eyes following his and knowing what he was considering as though it were plainly written on his face. "They'll ply you with other women who are keen to be acquainted, to see if it's only us or if it's anyone. They'll treat you like a god, a Zeus to my Hera. But you will be a god caged."

When Abe had been given a place of his own, he'd felt like a god of sorts, offered every comfort he had never known. He had thought it recompense for an unfair life hard-lived. It had taken him unexpectedly; he'd been prepared for a collar and concrete, not freedom and flowers. Abe looked at Lucy speculatively, the only woman he'd ever wanted to know. The one he'd come to want. He'd not mind setting aside his morals to have her and worry on the consequences later, except for the sadness of her expression and the burden of guilt he'd carry for it. He wondered if it was so bad, really, living this easy, wanting for nothing, a woman that was his to have, and maybe others too, more willing. Would any offspring of his suffer so for it? Or would it not know the difference? Or would any boy pine for freedom as a man would?

Abe's life had been too long before. He didn't want it to be too short now.

"I'll do whatever you have me do," Abe said. "Put you over the top of the wall, or leave you be 'til they fetch you back one way or another. But I'll not die for trying, and I won't take this misery away from you that way either. Don't ask it of me. I won't. I can't."

"And so, we're back at square one," she said with a heavy sigh. "I confess, I don't want to concede to them. But why must I sacrifice my own child, his life, his experience, every burden that I can't bear myself, to force it on a child barely parted from my womb? You're a savior. I'm their Eve. Grand things for history to say of us."

"Can't see as how it's to matter. We'll be dead before history gets written," Abe said. "I expect I've progeny in the hundreds, and more when they grown and have a child, too. Never will bother me a split second of a day what come of them. Ought maybe we don't worry on it overmuch. Maybe worry instead on what comes of those already living if'n the world goes on ending 'cause we ain't do our part."

Lucy went to the window overlooking the garden. "I've already lost everything," she whispered. "I suppose there's nothing left for them to take."

They'd given Lucy to him for one purpose. And Abe was eager for that purpose to be realized. It was an awareness unfamiliar compared to anything he'd ever felt, the desire to touch and possess, the willingness to do anything for her, the need to see her happy and be the cause of her joy. But she'd dismissed him at every turn, no matter his kindness or his desire or his expressions of love. For he did love her.

But she loved another. It was her reluctant confession, her pining for the woman Kate, which instructed Abe on the notion of what it was to love. He was sure he'd felt some such thing for his mother, but he had no memory of the feeling, and this was a different sort of feeling anyhow. He needed Lucy. He wanted to protect her. He began to better understand the desire to defend a child of their making, an expression of themselves, made of parts of them both.

They'd become familiar in their weeks together, comfortable in each other's company without any shyness, for there was no escape from it, their defenses diminished to little more than a wall of rubble. Abe ran a finger down the lines of her abdomen, the skin in pleats, still warm and damp from the shower. Lucy smelled of citrus and roses.

"When a body grows too fast, the skin breaks," she said, wide-stretched palm self-consciously covering her stomach before tucking the robe around her body. "Then there's the quick vacancy, and all that's left is a baby pouch. For the next time, I suppose." Lucy went to the door, looking at him from behind half-lidded eyes. "Not yet, Abe. Just a little while longer." She pulled the courtesy curtain of the washroom closed behind her with a knowing glance.

It felt a sacrilege to spill his seed in the shower. It was a quick exercise, the need to quiet his lust all he could think about at times. Lucy had said she wouldn't with him, not yet, for near on three weeks now since she'd arrived. And he couldn't make use of the wall, for then it would be known they were not attending to their task. She was afraid of what the CRZ—especially that woman, Evelyn—would do if they knew. Lucy's vulnerability made him willing to do anything.

He'd begun to be driven mad with it, the need for her, when finally, she consented. It had only taken one visit from the woman from the CRZ to change her mind.

They arrived in the morning. The garda held him at bay, his ears straining to listen, his fists clenched, craving action. Abe had never been inclined to violence and was surprised at his new hunger for it. Evelyn appeared, sequestering Lucy in the back room, deaf to her pleas for information on her son's well-being. The woman ignored the petitions for information entirely, instead purchasing Lucy's compliance: Give them what they wanted, and they would reciprocate, letting her see her son again. Don't, and the experience of his survival would be her burden, him suffering because of his mother's selfishness.

"If he's the only one, do you not see the way we will use him?"

Abe could feel Lucy's pain in his heart, hearing the tremor in her voice. "Okay," she said, followed by a long silence.

A woman skirted past Abe, dressed in paper blue, pulling on exam gloves and disappearing into Lucy's room. He knew the kind, the sort that probed and prodded and asked questions about the body: a physician. He'd seen them aplenty when he'd first arrived and would just as soon never see one again.

When Lucy cried out, Abe's fists realized their purpose, garda shoved aside as he ran towards the sound of her voice. They had her on the bed, legs spread wide.

"She's fertile."

They grabbed him. There was a quick buzz and zap of a shock gun, accompanying shouts from Evelyn to stop. "Don't! You'll damage him!"

The sight of Lucy's open-mouthed terror was emblazoned on the backs of his eyelids as he fell, arms and legs thrashing. He shuddered with a start, the sharp scent of ammonia in his nose, writhing and twisting to get away from it.

"None the worse for wear," the physician said, voice echoing in his ears. She was little more than a shadowed outline, collapsing in on itself as it retreated from his view. "Best we leave them to it."

Evelyn's face suddenly appeared in front of him, taking up the entirety of his focus, face questioning and furrowed with worry. "You alright, old boy? Sorry about that. It was an accident, you see? You'll not tell anyone, will you?" She gave him a pat on the arm, lithe form standing upright and regarding him with lingering concern before withdrawing through the front door after the others.

Everything became quiet. Lucy was kneeling beside him, face filled with the same mixture of worry as Evelyn's, only different, soft and kind, not afflicted with guilt and dread. Abe leaned against the side of the couch, pulling Lucy down to him, holding her tight in his arms, holding her long enough, her shaking could cease, and they could both breathe again.

The light had waned, and yet they stayed as they were, each entwined and consoled by the other, until eventually Lucy spoke. "We'll do the same as last time." She got up, her departure causing a sudden chill in his body where she'd been a moment before.

They ate a little. Drank more. Showered in blazing-hot water. None of it mattered. Abe couldn't feel any of it, moving by rote in a dusty fog. Waiting. Needing her desperately. He wanted to go slow, to make it last. To linger on her neck, to travel down her collarbone, the graceful dip of her shoulder, the pleasing curve of her breasts, the marks of where their child had dwelled, the softness between her legs. His hands followed her hips, thumbs pressed against the bones as he found purchase, her back against the wall. No need to ready himself; he would not hum the tune. This time was his for the taking. All he need do was see her bare body, take her in. Long, deep groans unrestrained as he found her again, slipping into her with long strokes, wishing it would last forever.

34

I Hope You Remember Me

SHE KNEW EVEN BEFORE the morning sickness started. She knew before she felt the tenderness in her breasts. She knew before Abe commented on her mood and her radiance and the softness of her body. Lucy knew, because fate was cruel.

Where the first sensations of life had been thrilling last time, now they brought only dread—for the sickness she knew would come, and for the pain of a child born, a child lost, a child stolen. Lucy's body had reliably failed her in the past, never giving her the child she so desperately wanted. It had become traitorous, offering a child only when it couldn't be hers to keep. Now, Lucy made deals with whatever invisible goddesses or spirits would listen: Ravage this womb and make it useless like it always was. Release her from the obligations she'd been shackled to. Don't let another child come, or at the very least, don't let her live through its delivery. Don't make her bear another to be used, to be caged, to live a life without ever knowing his mother, without ever knowing love.

The pregnancy had not happened on the first try. Or the fifth—much to Abe's initial delight, and much to Evelyn Emmett's increasing dismay. Lucy was confined to a state of incessant mating, alone in her thoughts, her legs ever open for Abe. They gave her monthly exams for viability and fertility checks. They poked and prodded and admonished. Chatter had begun: should they use another man for Lucy, another woman for Abe? Her recalcitrance was blamed. Was she too old, her womb too hostile? Was she causing her own miscarriage in defiance? Eventually they simply reprimanded her, calling her a detriment to the future of womankind, the burden of humanity to be carried on her shoulders.

Lucy had become dull to all of it.

But Abe had not. Worry was on his face and in his every gentle word of kindness. He would make her breakfast and present it with a flower. Take her outside to listen to the birds. Sit beside her at night, each day becoming physically closer to Lucy, each day Lucy withdrawing further into her mind.

Lucy didn't know men could cry, but there was a day Abe wept when she did. And it was the thing that broke her heart into even smaller pieces, since it had been broken already when they'd taken Ben away. The garda had left with Evelyn and the physicians in tow, their threats increasing. She didn't cry because of that. She didn't even cry for herself. She hadn't meant to think of him. Ben was six months old, and Lucy couldn't remember what he looked like, or felt like, or sounded like. Abe held her in his arms. He whispered kindnesses in her ear. He told Lucy he loved her.

It was then that the next one was made.

"We'd begun to think you didn't have it in you," Evelyn gasped, holding the test with the pink plus sign—the one Lucy had just peed on fifteen minutes prior—like it was a handful of precious jewels. The woman's wide eyes traveled between the stick and Lucy and back again, bewitched, her mouth hanging open. "We'll move you to your own quarters at once. You'll have twenty-four-hour care and keeping and—"

"No," Lucy said, snatching the pregnancy test out of the woman's hands and throwing it in the trash. "You'll leave me be. I'm fine where I am, and I ain't goin' nowhere else."

Evelyn picked up the waste bin, upending it onto the floor, all the while holding Lucy's eye with a menacing glare as she fished the revered object out of the litter. "All items are to be retained for proof and eventual exhibit," she said, any evidence of awe quickly diminished. "You say you want to stay here? Don't I recall a little story spun by your friend—what was it...? Rape, did she say? Hmph, I think maybe not," she simpered, arms crossed in front of her body. "Have a care, Lucy. That..." She tipped her head towards Lucy's middle. "That belongs to us. Besides, we've a new lot of volunteers for number 792, now that his work with you is done."

"If I'm to be your Eve, and he is to be your savior," Lucy said, pressing her hand against her womb, "then you'd best treat me as such."

"You're a vessel," Evelyn shot back, taking a step forward, close enough that Lucy's hair fluttered in the passing of the woman's breath as she spoke. "We will use you. We will use him. We will use the one you gave and the one that comes next. And we won't give it a second thought. Because we're meaningless if we cannot perpetuate ourselves. Your comfort is meaningless in the face of extinction. You can cooperate, or you can be forced. We are, after all, a free society, Lucy. It is your choice."

Evelyn left her there like a scolded child sent to her room. The last time Lucy had felt such a desire to harm the way she wanted to hurt Evelyn, to claw out her eyes and watch death take her slowly, was when the men had returned to Kate's farm—with Abe. She'd wanted to harm him, too, to throttle the life out of him. And now he was her sole comfort.

Garda lined the halls of the tiny dwelling. Their furtive glances made Lucy wonder if they would mind their master still, in the presence of the first Eve, should she resist. But what woman murdered all of humanity? She passed by them, head down, subservient and weary and disgusted.

"I need time," Lucy said bluntly.

"You have twenty minutes," Evelyn said just as quick. "And you will be supervised." She didn't wait for acknowledgment. She checked the timepiece in her pocket against the one on the media wall. Then without another word, she departed, leaving one garda and the physician to remain.

There was nowhere to hide. Abe pulled her outside to the garden, where there was space and air and room to breathe and feel as though there was naught to worry on, so long as one knew where to look. The maple tree with its multiple trunks and fan-shaped viridian leaves. The creeping flowers beneath it. The rocky stream running a path. The bright blue sky with its swept clouds like a painter's brushstrokes.

"Only look at the pretty things," Abe said as he took her in his arms and held her tight.

Lucy knew he loved her, just as sure as she knew she could not love him—not that way. But he eased the pain of living, and for that she would be grateful always.

"There will be more like me, Abe. Maybe they'll be a tad less disagreeable," Lucy said, her hand closing around his as he rocked her slowly.

"Ain't none like you," he said. Then he kissed her for the first time, knowing it would be the last.

They'd allocated Lucy a dwelling, much like they had for Abe, only this one with a chef's kitchen and a spare bedroom besides. Meals were prepared by a rotation of chefs engaged to formulate meals for "enhanced maternal nutrition," whatever that meant. The in-home chef and nutritionists were a dream she would have enjoyed under any other circumstance. As it was, she resented them for their complicity, just more cogs in Evelyn's machine.

Lucy took no small amount of pleasure when the morning sickness finally started with the same gusto. She'd vomited the entirety of some culinary masterpiece across the kitchen floor, leaving the chef disgusted and Rosena dismayed.

Rosena was always there. And while Lucy harbored fathomless resentment toward her, the girl knew how to manage the morning sickness. "Sit still and let me put these needles in you," or "Scratch the lemon and inhale if you feel queasy," and finally, "Here's some drugs," for relief from seemingly unending bouts of violent retching.

Their original promise to let Lucy see her son was hollow, no more than an image of Ben flashed on the wall. But she stared at it anyway, incessantly, wishing she could feel the smoothness of his cheeks, wanting to hear his little baby sounds. It pained her that he smiled. It wasn't his mother he smiled for. He didn't know yet what his life would be. His innocence was devastating.

"If you'll not come away, ma'am, it will be removed," Rosena said.

Lucy glowered silently but turned away even so. She'd barely said two words to the girl. Rosena had incited the turn of events that had made Lucy lose her child and be kept as a broodmare for the CRZ. The girl was lucky Lucy didn't kill her while she slept.

Rosena made up for Lucy's quiet with never-ending chatter, seemingly impervious to Lucy's disinterest and giving voice to both sides of every exchange. "Should we have sweet potatoes or broccoli?" Rosena held up an enormous rough orange tuber and a broccoli bunch. "Ooh, that's a grand idea, we'll have both!"

This child was quieter than Ben had been, only ever moving in small flutters, never kicking or pushing. She ran a hand across her rounding middle, skin stretched tight, now some six months gone.

"You're at twenty-six weeks, but fundal height is thirty centimeters—a bit more than I would have expected, based on the known date of confinement," Rosena said. She was trying to hide the insecurity brewing beneath the surface, but her face offered no quarter to secrets. "I'm sure you're just loose from your last pregnancy. Not like it's been that long." She'd begun tucking the measure back into her bag with more enthusiasm than the effort required, a quick forced smile in Lucy's general direction all that was offered in parting as she vanished out the bedroom door.

Lucy pulled her shirt down to cover herself, rolling out of bed with some effort. Too small for twins, too big for its age; it was going to be another boy. She sighed heavily, staring at the ceiling with a silent string of profanities. She paused at the threshold, Rosena's hushed voice reaching her ears in interrupted snippets.

"Weekly check-in ... concerned ... going to be big ... hemorrhage ... old resonance machines been repaired so we can take a look? If not a boy ... then she doesn't matter..."

Worry was a communicable affliction, and Lucy caught it like an airborne flu. Childbirth was a hazy recollection of pain and fever and blood. Lucy's mettle to escape by any means was immediately subdued by the possibility of what that might feel like. She slipped into the room as stealthily as her stature would allow. The call concluded, but Rosena hadn't moved.

"What did you say to them, and why are you worried?"

The girl jumped, spinning around, hand clutched over her heart. Rosena's mouth was working like a goldfish, and her eyes looked fit to pop out of her skull.

"Nothing... I... It's just..."

"They'll bring me into care when the time comes, won't they? And not leave me here to bleed out like last time, when you were responsible? And why is it they've decided to let some girl with no experience be midwife to a woman they've declared to be their Eve?" Lucy advanced on the girl, seeing a crack in Rosena's thin veneer of bravado.

"I'm not your midwife," she uttered, face gone red as a beet. "I'm your, uh, care technician. I'm assigned to manage your day-to-day, check your food intake, do ... do your laundry. But not to midwife."

"So, you're a maid, then? Well, I'm relieved to hear it," Lucy shot back. "But why you?"

Rosena crossed her arms protectively around her waist. "I... I ... volunteered," she stuttered, looking at Lucy with such earnestness, it was disconcerting. "They wouldn't have let me be your midwife, after what happened last time. But I wanted to be here, to be part of it, to do something that matters, to know I have a place in history. Because I deserve it. Because I was there when the first one was born. I was part of it, and I should be part of this one, too. I need ... need to be someone who does something significant, someone who's remembered."

"You think cleaning up after me will secure you a place in history?"

Rosena's face fell, the pride she'd armored herself with succumbing with the first cut.

Lucy seized on this, thrusting in the figurative knife and twisting it deep. "You don't matter, and you never will. Best you get that notion square in your pretty little head before it gets the better of you. They will use you and throw you away, same as me. And there won't be anything left of you to show for it. Get out now, Rosena, before everything you ever wanted, everything you ever loved is taken from you."

"No one tells me what to do," Rosena said, jutting her chin out defiantly. "And maybe you're cowardly or egotistical enough, or whatever the hell is wrong with you, that you can't see what's happening here. But I can. There has never been a more important moment in time than this one. And I'm part of it. Like it or not, believe or not, I don't care. If that means I have to listen to you complain and whimper and bitch day in and day out, if I have to pick up your giant pregnancy underwear off the floor and mop up your sick, so be it. If you can't understand how significant this is, that's your problem, not mine."

"I never thought I would wish this on anyone," Lucy shot back, "but I hope the day comes when they tear your baby out of your arms and tell you it isn't yours anymore. And when it happens, I hope you remember me."

Lucy was doubled over, gripping the back of the chair with one hand, the other pressed against her belly. The tight cramping had been going on all day, but she'd set it aside as nothing more than Braxton-Hicks contractions, though the same hadn't happened with Ben. She reminded herself this child was different. Besides, she was at thirty-four weeks. It was too soon for it to be the real thing. Rosena had checked her just a few days prior and stated she was still closed up "tighter than a duck's butt" and there was naught to worry about.

The animosity between her and Rosena hadn't changed, but a cease-fire of sorts had allowed them to settle into a fair routine of daily tedium. Meals, exercise, reading, walks, health checks, and as much time in the garden as she could finagle.

Sometimes Lucy wondered how Abe was doing. She didn't exactly miss him, but his companionship had been tolerable—nice, even—and an easier rapport than the one she was afflicted with now. Other moments she thought of Ben, trying to conjure what he would be like, whether he would favor the quiet temperament of his father, or the sharp edges of his mother. And when her imagination became too still, Lucy wondered if Kate thought of her and if she would ever see her again.

But she avoided the idleness of an unoccupied mind by keeping up the conversation with the child inside, running her hand across the roundness protruding so far out, she hadn't seen her feet in ages. "You'll have a brother. I hope you get to know him."

Lucy walked outside to the garden, her hips swaying loosely. She had to stop, hand on the masonry wall, breathing slow and waiting for the aching tightness to pass.

Rosena appeared in front of her without a word, her concern plain.

"Braxton-Hicks," Lucy pronounced.

Rosena took hold of Lucy's arms, gripping tighter than was comfortable. "When did they start?"

"A few hours ago," Lucy said. "It's no big deal."

"Braxton-Hicks isn't in your evaluation history for any prior pregnancies," Rosena replied.

"Didn't have any. But this one's been different." Lucy stood up, the moment passing, and continued on her path to the chair. She was enormous, angling herself sideways to find the seat and sitting down with a heavy sigh.

"All the same, I'd like to check you anyhow." Rosena was nearly vibrating with the need to take action.

"All the same, I'd rather you not," Lucy said. "I'm fine. It ain't time yet."

Rosena didn't budge, fixing her hands firmly on her hips, elbows stuck out so far, she looked like a cormorant drying its wings. "Either you come inside, like I asked you nicely, or you come inside because I've called the physicians, and they drag you kicking and screaming. What'll it be?"

The thought of clawing her way back out of the chair Lucy had just gotten herself into made the temptation to test the girl's fortitude more appealing than it ought to be. She wondered if Rosena had always been so stubborn, or if it was a trait Lucy brought out in her. And yet there was still a small part of her that appreciated the girl's diligence. With a heavy sigh for the drama and effort combined, Lucy heaved herself up.

The rush of wet down her legs and pooling at her feet was a shock to them both.

"Your ... your water's broke."

"It's too soon," Lucy said, voice edged with quick despair, fingers clutching her belly. "You know I lost one late before, don't you? It's too soon!"

Rosena paid her no mind, spinning on her heel and going straight to the communications link. "Urgent to care. Obstetrical. Domicile seven," she said succinctly, nodded once, then hung up. She returned just as quick, putting both hands on Lucy's arms and squeezing.

"They'll be here in three minutes. You will be taken into care in the obstetrical unit, and seasoned midwives and physicians will be there waiting for you. I'll obtain comfort items to bring with you for your experience."

Lucy could only bob her head in gaping agreement. The girl sounded like she'd rehearsed those lines, robotic in their delivery, despite being laced with unsuppressed worry. She followed Rosena, slow and deliberate, wondering if she was careful, could she not get the baby to stay in a while longer? Lucy stood in the open doorway, waiting, time seeming to stand still and speed up into a discombobulating blur like skipping ahead in an old movie.

There was a flurry of bodies rushing towards her, gently, urgently, guiding her forward. She was in the medical car, bands strapped to her belly and limbs, port placed into her arm, defrocked and re-robed in medical gray. The sterile scent of the ward affronted her when the sliding doors opened, the flash of the overhead lights piercing her eyes when she floated past.

There was a host of women at the ready, gloved hands held before them, hair netted and capped, gowns looking as if they'd been starched, masked faces revealing an array of eyes, blue and brown, excited, but without apprehension. Lucy found herself searching for Rosena, for anything familiar, no matter that the young woman had been nothing but a thorn in her side.

Would they let her hold him before they took him away?

And then time slowed, for pain begged its due. It required the attention of the afflicted. Every deep ache of her body was demanding, contractions coming in ever increasing waves, sucking out her life bit by bit, taxing her heart, her lungs, her will.

Lucy had wanted death to spare her this duty, this ancestral torment to be lived out, one life after another. She ignored their pleas to push, her body wasted, her desire to do their bidding long since gone.

Time stopped altogether.

Darkness was followed by light—such bright light.

Her body did its own carnal bidding. Torn. Shredded. Bleeding.

Rosena was yelling at them to push Pitocin, her hands kneading Lucy's body. Clutching Lucy's hand, begging her to stay.

The cries of her baby.

The weight of a tiny body on Lucy's chest as Rosena's voice filled her ear.

"Lucy, you've a daughter to live for. Don't die on me now."

35

EVES

TWO YEARS AFTER THE SOWING

THE SPRING STORMS CAME with a startling vengeance, the creek overtopping its banks and flooding the lower field. The wash of debris carried down from the mountains lay strewn about the meadow's edges, and the girls had gone scavenging for anything of interest. The waters had been fierce enough to form a new path, cutting off the small oxbow and leaving a new section of swamped shoe-sucking mud, to which Mandy had already made offerings of clog and boot and socks alike. Kate had lost count of how many times her daughter had come into the house barefoot and covered in mud, and she'd simply made habit of putting the hose to her without so much as a fair warning.

"Mama! Come on! Stop, it's cold!" Mandy's hair was plastered flat and dripping against her face, hands thrust out in front of her body in useless self-defense.

"You're too old and too human to be wallowing, Amanda. I'd have thought you'd sense enough to know better by now, this being, what, your umpteenth hosing? Well water ain't gettin' any warmer this time of year." Kate stood with one hand on her hip, the other gripped on the hose, nozzle on full blast. Chunks of dirt molted off with the rest, leaving a mud stew at Mandy's feet and turning her daughter from filthy to something approaching ... well, less filthy.

"A geologist has to dig, Mama," Mandy said with a patronizing tone. "What on earth do you think we're supposed to do?"

Jenna had come up beside her mother, watching with glee while her younger sister got soaked. "Least you could do is wear overalls, Mandy. Your clothes have all turned the same shade of beige."

She hadn't come for entertainment alone though. "New broadcast, mandatory viewing. Coming on in fifteen minutes," Jenna volunteered without prompting. "Birdie is over checking on Miss Lucy's bees. I think one hive swarmed—no idea where they've gone to. Mika's in the fort."

It had been nearly two years since they'd seen Lucy. There'd been no calls, no letters, nothing. All they knew was, one day, they'd been able to visit her, and the next, she'd been removed from the care unit. They'd been told she was transferred to the capital. Kate had tried to find her, ask after her, and written letters to the CRZ demanding information, but she got none.

There'd even been some semblance of a protest at the hub when word got out "Eve" was missing. This was immediately quashed, of course; there was no tolerance for uprisings of any variety since Abscond.

After all this time, there was still no word. Maybe Lucy didn't want to come back. Kate knew Lucy had stopped loving her, after everything Kate had done. She tried to push the notions aside, but sometimes they would bubble up anyway, usually at night when the house was quiet, leaving her wanting, needing to say anew that she was sorry for what she'd done. Desperate to tell Lucy she loved her no matter what and always would. But it was hard to tell someone anything if you had no idea where they were.

"Should I fetch them, Mama?"

Kate refocused her attention on her daughter. Jenna had recently grown tall and trim with the benefits of youth, her face starting to lose the softness of adolescence. Kate absently smoothed Jenna's hair, pushing it back over her shoulder. "Go on and wrangle your sisters. I'll put a kettle on. Tell them there's blueberry cake; that'll get them home quicker than asking." She turned toward Mandy, who'd sat down in the dirt so Vesper could rub his shedding face against her before plunking down, equally muddied, atop her legs.

"And you, Little Miss Piglet, go on and take a shower and scrub that dirt off of yourself before I set up a spot for you in the barn."

"I'd rather live with Fred and Agatha and the chickens anyhow," Mandy said with a grin.

Kate glared down at her daughter, sticking one arm straight out, finger pointing to the house. "I mean it. Now."

Vesper had the good sense to immediately slink off with a backward glance, ears flattened. Mandy got up slowly, as though testing her mother's resolve, before starting a slow, foot-dragging walk to the house.

There hadn't been much news from the CRZ—not since the call for volunteers for a centralized pregnancy research study, asking for women of prime fertile age who were willing to accept "any form of implantation." The response, evidently, had been overwhelming. Kate wondered if this would be another recruitment and was loath to subject herself—and particularly her daughters—to another shiny ad campaign for procreation.

"Found the bees, Mama. In the barn eaves," Birdie said, bursting into the kitchen and giving her mother a quick hug. "Can't see as how to get them down from there though."

"Best to leave them, sweetheart. They ain't been collected for a while now, and anyone that comes to take over Miss Lucy's place will manage it," Kate said.

Birdie's face fell, and she stopped cold. "You really think she ain't comin' back, Mama?"

"Can't see as how they'll let the place go fallow, and it's been two years. Suspect they got better plans for Miss Lucy now, and she decided this ain't her home anymore. Sorry, Bird, I know how much you like her."

"But you loved her, too, Mama. Ain't you sad?"

If she were honest, Kate would have told her daughter that Lucy's absence broke her heart. How she regretted every day the time wasted being angry, for blaming Lucy for a thing that wasn't her doing, and how she'd come to reckon herself a coward for all of it. And if she had been as strong as Lucy, maybe none of it would have ever happened to begin with.

Kate kissed Birdie's cheek, her one daughter who still relished expressions of affection. "I did love her, Bird. Always will. But she's moved on from us now. What's done can't be undone." She turned away, pulling the kettle off the stove and filling it with a rush of cold spring water, taking long draws of air to stifle the threat of tears that never seemed to want to stop whenever thoughts of Lucy surfaced. What did it mean to mourn a person still living?

Jenna and Mika filed into the kitchen, the warm aroma of blueberry cake an unfailingly reliable temptation. Mandy came careening down the stairs, skating across the tile floor in her socks and skidding into the wall. Kate shook her head with an eye-rolling sigh, wondering if that girl would ever settle.

"Come on, get your plates. It's on in a minute, girls. Guess we'll see what it's all about this time, eh? Mandy, take a napkin!"

They sat in their usual places on the couch, chair, and floor, Mika cozied up to her mother, always keeping a toe or an arm in contact, as though the ties from the womb had yet to be cut. Mooey sidled up to Jenna, standing with her paws on the young woman's chest, kneading and purring until Jenna conceded and obligingly began petting her. The media wall came to life, the black screen fading into a forest scene, then mountains, then prairies, the melody of "Simple Gifts" growing and swelling, the new anthem of the CRZ. The girls chattered between them, questions and wonder and speculation, between bites of lemon blueberry poppy seed cake drizzled with a sweet glaze.

The full orchestra reached its crescendo, the big brass blaring with gusto in Copeland's finale before Evelyn Emmett's face came to life before them.

"Greetings from the Central Rural Zone. On behalf of the Governing Council, we broadcast this message. May we never forget, science is our economy. Education is our success. And this has never been truer in all history than it is now. Our research has proved fruitful. We are delighted to announce that we have produced perpetuating specimens from several of our saviors. This would not have been possible without the brave Eves who volunteered for this journey, who have given themselves, body and soul, to the most significant cause of our time. Be proud. Be strong. Be grateful. The path of womankind will endure."

The screen went dark, and the room went silent.

"'Perpetuating specimens'..." Mika echoed, voice trailing off, yet overflowing with curiosity. "Mama, what does that even mean?"

"They created men. New ones we can use for later," Birdie said. Her face scrunched up into a fit of worry as she turned to look at her mother. "Mama, what if they make more men than we need?"

Kate shook her head, unable to focus, so many things stampeding around in her mind, she couldn't catch a single thought and wrangle it into sense. "Society will have to decide what rights they have and who gets to keep them," she said absently. "Now go on and wash up for dinner."

The girls stared at her, their blue-stained fingers holding crumb-strewn plates.

"Mama, we just had cake," Birdie said. "And it's only two o'clock."

"Go do your chores, then. Or your studying. Or whatever you were doing before. Except you, Mandy. You clean up the dishes."

"But why do I have to..."

"Do what I told you," Kate said sharply, letting any further chatter fade behind her as she walked out the door. She needed to move, to feel something else to distract her.

She went to the pasture, Fred whinnying to her in a low-throated greeting before pinning his ears with menace towards Vesper, who'd followed. The dog taunted the pony from safely outside the fence, bouncing and spinning on his heels just out of reach, yelping when the pony stretched out his neck and nipped Vesper's backside.

Kate walked the fence line aimlessly, no sense of purpose to her path, just moving.

They would have exalted Lucy for the making of a boy. And then they would make her make another, and another, and another, until her womb or wits were exhausted of it and rejected the notion. Lucy could not be the only one though. There had to be others, capable of breaking the curse of the feminine that had rejected the aspect of men for so long.

But none of that mattered to Kate—though she knew it ought to matter more than anything else, the prospect of whatever future society her daughters would be subject to. Lucy was gone, her life given over to the greater good. Kate would never get the chance to tell her she was sorry, to tell her she loved her, to hold her one more time, to feel her or experience life with the woman she loved by her side.

Kate found herself standing next to the old chestnut tree, beneath the fort Lucy had made to keep her daughters safe. She pressed her hand against the gnarled trunk, tracing the crisscrossed furrows of bark. She sat down, leaning her back against it, Vesper coming to sit beside her, resting his chin on her shoulder.

"Who's the best dog?"

Vesper's tail fluttered three times, and he scooched closer before plunking down with a heavy sigh, front legs across her lap, nose tucked between his paws.

"Don't you ever go running off on me, okay?" Kate stroked his velveteen ears, trying without success to keep her emotions securely tamped down and buried. She tipped her head back against the tree, eyes raised to the indigo-backed sky with its clouds billowing and spiking out across the prairie, crepuscular rays breaking through in beams. She closed her eyes to the beauty of it, hoping to capture it in her mind and send it to Lucy, so Lucy would know she was still loved.

She'd set herself to work like a demon possessed, cooking, scrubbing, rearranging, until the girls knew better than to let their mother set eyes on them, lest they be conscripted, too. All except Mika, who was attuned to her mother's temperament and stayed by her side no matter the consequence.

"Vinegar on all the countertops. Make sure you scrub the back of the faucet and the drain. They ought to be shiny enough to see yourself in." Kate had donned yellow rubber gloves, a kerchief around her head to keep the sweat from stinging her eyes. She was on the floor with a stiff brush and a bucket, hoping to see white grout again for the first time in ages. She'd been scrubbing for minutes before she realized Mika had frozen, back straight as an arrow, eyes fixed outside.

"Storm coming?"

"No Mama, not that," Mika said, voice tremulous.

Curious, Kate picked herself up off the floor, moving to stand beside her. She followed Mika's gaze out the kitchen window past the courtyard, across the meadow of new spring shoots of wild grasses and flowers, and beyond the grand old tree, to the new swing hanging from the branches.

It was a woman, walking across the creek bridge, carrying a baby in a lavender dress.

"Mama, is that—"

"It is," Kate whispered, her words disappearing in the breeze as she raced out the door.

ACKNOWLEDGEMENTS

I first started writing this book in 2019 after reading a New York Times article about a village in Poland with no male births for nine years (NYT: 8/6/2019) and began speculating what would cause nature to behave this way. I'd also been revisiting *The Handmaid's Tale*, by Margaret Atwood, and wondered what kind of story it would be if the premise was "flipped" to a matriarchy instead. Little did any of us know at the time, the world was on the brink of a pandemic, an addition to new and ongoing wars and political upheaval, significant climate events, deterioration of women's rights, and a host of change that continues to up-end all manner of things in so many ways for so many. I began questioning what would have to happen in order for things to be different than they are, and so began writing this story.

Writing a novel may seem like a lonely endeavor, and while it can be, in reality there is an entire supporting cast behind the scenes. There are many who deserve all of my gratitude in helping me get through this thing – and likely more still who will help me after these words are long since written. I want to express my sincere appreciation to all of you, including you, the reader, willing to take the chance on an new author.

My gratitude extends to numerous kind souls—

To the most generous beta readers a writer could ask for, being willing to wade through early drafts and provide thoughtful feedback - Emma Smith and Amy Eaton.

To Dina Nelson, Irene Evans, and Anne Schwabik for being willing to read it before it was ready, and your confidence boosting encouragement.

To S.B., of the United States Marine Corp, retired, for answering the things one should not look up on the internet, regarding guidance on munitions and firearms and how things blow up.

To Mo Fleisig for insight into women's prison systems and procedures.

To the LitForum members at large for all of their advice and encouragement along the way. And specifically:

To Brendalynn, who ought to win an award for this gem: Early in the writing of the first chapter, I posted an excerpt in the LitForum critique group and there was some dispute regarding how many shotgun shells one could stuff in one's bra—at which point Brendalynn proceeded to test the theory with ammunition from her husband's hunting rifle. In the midst of said exercise, her husband walked in and asked what on God's green earth she was doing, to which she yelled, "Research!" and told him to get out and leave her to it. She returned to the forum thread to inform everyone that yes, one could in fact stuff a dozen in there, if one was so endowed.

To J.N. Winkler and Betty, for sharing the experience of hearing loss.

To the mothers and nurses of the forum, Liz, Elle Druskin, Beth, Jen, Laura W., Katie, Susan, Diana, Corrie, Rebecca, and Rita, for insight and experiences related to pregnancy, morning sickness, and delivering babies.

To Diana Gabaldon for inspiring me to write a novel of my own. I'd first read the entirety of the available *Outlander* offerings, and I was so consumed by the writing and the story, I had to know more. Diana had said she, "wrote a novel to see if she could," and it was that simple statement which prompted me to do the same. Diana continued to offer guidance and encouragement to me along the way. I don't know if I'd have taken this giant leap, without her suggestion to give it a go.

To the clinical folks, Tiffany Ferguson, FNP-BC; Kenny Schwabik, RN CEN CFRN MICN CCT, for keeping things accurate and answering my litany of, "how much blood would there be if..." type of questions.

For their thoughtful editorial insight and feedback, Rowan Baiocchi, Mary Borgerding, Shannon Roberts, and Robin Fuller. You all got under the hood, asked all the questions, and made this book more than it ever would have been.

To Professor Tiffany Aldrich MacBain, PhD, University of Puget Sound, for her generosity of spirit and facilitating access to editorial input.

To my favorite literary shark, Janet Reid, for kindly enduring a multitude of questions over the years and providing feedback on all manner of things. I promised her an 'Ode'. Here it goes (and my most sincere apologies):

A Special Ode to Janet Reid
The kindest of sharks in all the reef.
Reading pages, synopses, query letters (oh my!)
She is the New York helpful to my Midwest persistence.
She is my Yoda.
My Mr. Miyagi.
My Minerva McGonagall.
If fuchsia were a person, it is she.

To Laura Duffy, for creating such a beautiful cover, and providing publishing guidance along the way.

To the Svalbard or Bust Braintrust, Amy, Emma, Tiffany, and Hannah, for patiently answering my multitude of, "Which one do you like...this one? That one? The other one?"

To Mary Ellen Aishton, for an abundance of support, encouragement, feedback, guidance, being both an alpha and a beta reader for all of the bits and pieces of my writing, and for being the unfailing cheerleader for all of these many years. I would never have been able to do this without you.

And for my husband, for being the most kind, tolerant, and supportive person anyone could ever wish to have in their life. I love you.

QUESTIONS FOR DISCUSSION

1. What do you think society would be like in the absence of men? As it relates to home life? As it relates to infrastructure? As it relates to how society is governed?

2. If you were like Etta and discovered a previously unknown family member after your parent(s) passed, would you choose to contact them? Why or why not?

3. Kate killed a man. Odelia went to prison. Noemi left one child to keep her other child safe. Etta sacrificed herself for Kieva. Lucy considered death for herself and child to spare them from a questionable fate. Would you be willing to do these things for someone you loved?

4. In the story, men had become myths, akin to unicorns or dodos. Imagine if there was a sudden discovery of—for example—unicorns. How would you feel about the discovery? How do you think society would react? What would be your reaction if you saw one outside your window like when Kate saw a man for the first time?

5. Noemi felt responsible for inciting a societal rebellion; was she? If not Noemi, then who?

6. In terms of choices made or reactions to events - which character do you relate to most? Which character was most difficult for you to empathize with? Why?

7. Considering Abe's experience of going from an 11-year-old birthday party into permanent confinement with adult men, what do you think Abe's point of view and experience was like?

8. The first time the men come, Lucy calls the overseer against Kate's wishes. What would you have done if you were Kate—or Lucy—and why?

9. What do you think the overseer—Evelyn Emmett's—involvement and responsibilities may have been regarding the discovery and acquisition of the men?

10. When Lucy's child is born, Rosena contacts the authorities. What would you have done in Lucy's position—or Rosena's—and why?

11. Who do you think was the hero of the story? Why?

12. Who do you think was the villain of the story? Why?

13. Of the point of view the primary characters—Kate, Lucy, Etta, Noemi (and secondarily Rosina), did they find redemption or resolution in their story? If so, how? If not, do you think they ever would?

14. What was Lucy's motivation behind building the treehouse and acquiring firearms—was it solely for the purpose of defense? A desire to protect Kate's children in absence of her own children? A demonstration of atone-

ment for Kate?

15. Why do you think Lucy took Abe after he first arrived? What would you have done in that situation—leave him at Kate's? Offer shelter? Turn him in? Let him go?

16. What are some of the "near future" innovations you noted in the story? Are there any you want / don't want to see in the present day?

17. What do you think caused the decline in the male population, and what factor may have caused them to start being born again?

18. In Kate and Lucy's situation, would you have forgiven the other person after years of distance within their relationship? Do you agree/disagree that saying sorry is enough?

19. Lucy is given an impossible choice when her first child is born; what would you have done? Give the baby over for the sake of humanity? End the child's life so it wouldn't have to suffer a fate like Abe's?

20. Do you think Abe was content with his life after Lucy, having his own (albeit restricted) place, wanting for nothing? Was he a "god"-caged like Lucy stated?

21. Evelyn states Lucy is a "vessel". The fate of humanity seemingly rested on Abe and Lucy. What do you think about what was asked of them? Was it fair? Should it have been done even if it wasn't fair?

ABOUT THE AUTHOR

After living near both coasts, the mid-Atlantic, and the mountains, K.A. Claytor now resides in the United States Midwest. Her novel writing began in earnest after coaxing her family to compose short stories during summer breaks and realizing she was the only one who actually enjoyed that. Her short fiction has appeared in *The Metaworker Literary Magazine*. *All the Men Are Gone* is her debut novel.